REIGN
OF TERROR

THE APOCALYPSE : EPISODE FOUR

DAVID O. BULLOCK

Black Rose Writing | Texas

ISBN: 978-1-68433-901-3
PUBLISHED BY BLACK ROSE WRITING
www.blackrosewriting.com

Printed in the United States of America
Suggested Retail Price (SRP) $20.95

Reign of Terror is printed in Calluna

*As a planet-friendly publisher, Black Rose Writing does its best to eliminate unnecessary waste to reduce paper usage and energy costs, while never compromising the reading experience. As a result, the final word count vs. page count may not meet common expectations.

To my dad, Denton Bullock
You are the most godly man I know
Your example inspires me to follow Jesus
and to be a true man of God
I aspire to be like you
David

ACKNOWLEDGEMENTS

Thechurch@cedarcreek: Thank you for your love and support. I love you and count it a privilege to serve as your pastor. Here's to great days ahead!

"Woe to the earth and the sea, because the devil has gone down to you!
He is filled with fury, because he knows that his time is short."
–**Revelation 12:12 NIV**

"The whole world was filled with wonder and followed the beast.
People worshiped the dragon because he had given authority to the beast,
and they also worshiped the beast and asked,
'Who is like the beast? Who can wage war against it?'"
–**Revelation 13:3-4 NIV**

REIGN
OF TERROR

Anders heard voices. Where was he? And what about Ally? He recalled grabbing her and throwing himself on top of her to shield her from the explosion debris as she stood grieving for Evan. The thoughts left his mind as quickly as they came, replaced by brilliant light. It should have blinded him, but it heightened his senses and brought remarkable clarity of vision and keenness of hearing. Things were more vivid, more vibrant than he ever remembered. He felt so alive!

What is this place? Am I dreaming?

Drawn to the voices, he ran, heart pounding, mind racing. Who is that? *Angie!* It was the sweetest sound he had ever heard, causing his heart to explode with love. He saw her now, more beautiful than ever. Three figures stood with her, and their words floated into his ears.

"Baby..."

"Dad!"

"Angie! Kids!" He sprinted now, moving faster than he thought possible. She stopped him, her eyes twinkling, her face betraying a secret she could not tell.

Others stepped out from behind her one at a time, as if she was introducing them. She smiled as each came, watching for his reaction when they spoke.

"Hey, buddy! I just got here, and the food smells amazing! I cannot wait to eat!"

Evan! He would recognize that voice anywhere. Evan died in the explosion just minutes ago, but he was alive! *Now* Anders understood where he was. He did not survive the first half of the Tribulation either! But none of that mattered. He was home, reunited with Angie and his kids, and Evan! Another man came, as Anders stood listening for the voice. His words were brief, but clear.

"Just call me, Source," the next said, grinning.

Malachi! What...? He had died too! How...? A brief tinge of sadness entered his mind, but overwhelming joy replaced it in an instant. Those details mattered not. They were all here together! *Who was that?* Two people... a man and a woman.

"We wouldn't be here if you had not told us about Jesus that day outside our shop. Thank you!"

John and Mary! He wanted to call out their names, but he could not speak. He was there when both died that night at Steve and Linda's house; now here they were, also *alive*. Happiness flooded his soul! The parade of greeters did not stop.

"Anders, did you know God created the universe in just six 24-hour days? Of course, you did!"

There was no doubting the voice and the intent behind the question. *Johnathan Baldwin!* Anders and the others watched him die at the hands of Messai's firing squad. But they knew where he went when the bullets riddled his body. And now here Johnathan stood before him, living and talking, and they were together again! This was awesome!

"Hello, cameraman; we meet again. You and Blake sure pulled the wool over my eyes, but I'm glad those bunkers worked out for you. Bet you never thought you'd find me here!"

Doc Sanderson! Wow! The look on his face was as rapturous as John and Kathie described it the night AMPP murdered him. *Incredible*, he thought.

All of them waited for him and came to welcome him home. He ran again, but gained no ground. Why couldn't he reach them? Another man. *Who was that?*

His face glowed. Anders saw his form, but could not make out his appearance because of the radiant glory surrounding him. Still, there was no doubt who he was. *Jesus!* The others would have to wait a little longer. He had to get to Jesus! His spirit cried out to fall at Jesus' feet and thank him for the gift of a second chance to believe in him. A nail-scarred hand extended toward him, stopping him in his tracks. Words would not come from his mouth, but they came from Jesus.

"Welcome, Anders. It is good to see you!"

Such love and grace he had never known. He collapsed to his knees and bowed his head to the ground in worship and awe. This was *home*. He longed to stay in this position forever, but his heart also screamed out for Angie and the kids and his friends and fellow Smyrnians. Weakened knees refused to push him to his feet. The hand reached down and lifted his face. Gazing into the brilliant light, he extended his hand and felt himself being pulled up.

"We have been waiting for you, Anders," the Savior said, waving his hand toward the others. "You fought a good fight and kept the faith. My Word became your guide, hidden in your heart. You told others about me and helped them believe in me."

A glow surrounded John and Mary at that moment.

"Well done, good and faithful servant!"

Tears of joy streamed down Anders' face. It was impossible to describe the happiness and peace he felt at this moment. There was only one explanation: he was *home*...

CHAPTER 1

The group in Missouri dashed to the barn and dove behind large round bales of hay, as debris from the explosion that destroyed their safe place flew around them. A narrow opening offered a refuge from the outside chaos. They grieved the loss of Evan, fighting to save their own lives as they did.

"*Ally!*" screamed Mila. "Where is Ally?"

Blake leapt to his feet. "I'm going to find her. Anders didn't make it, either!"

"I'm going with you," said John as he jumped up behind him.

Before they took a step, another massive explosion rocked the ground, hurling wood and tin toward them, as the side of the barn blew in and the roof collapsed. All of them lunged face-first, covering the backs of their heads with their hands. When the noise subsided, they found themselves cramped in a tiny crevice between the hay and the remaining outside wall that fell inward, covering them.

"A second bomb!"

"Let's go, Blake... *now!*"

The two men crawled out and stood to their feet. Both recoiled at the sight that greeted them. Only a cavernous hole remained where the bunkers had been. Any seed of hope that Evan had survived vanished. They dashed forward, searching for their comrades and almost passed them before seeing shoes sticking out from underneath a pile of rubble. Blake and John fell to their knees and started dragging off debris, yelling for the others to come and help.

Mila screamed and cried as she frantically dug through the heap of rocks, concrete and steel. When they uncovered the two bodies, Anders lay on top of Ally, arms outstretched. He had protected her and taken the brunt of the punishment. His body lay on hers, battered and bruised, clothes ripped, with a large opening in the back of his head. Steve rushed to his side as Blake and John pulled him off Ally and turned him over. He was not breathing, and his face was ashen.

"He has no pulse!" Steve said as he jumped into action, trying to resuscitate him.

"Help me with CPR!" he yelled again, louder this time, as he began chest compressions.

Blake dove beside him, breathing twice into Anders' mouth after every thirty compressions. Nothing. Both worked until they collapsed from exhaustion, but their comrade still lay lifeless on the ground. They knew he was gone. Blake rolled to one side sobbing, his body convulsing with grief, as Beth fell beside him, holding him in her arms.

Ally was unconscious, but breathing. Steve moved to her, Linda rushing to join him. Anders had shielded her from the deadly debris, putting his life on the line to save hers.

"Get them both to the van and let's load up and go! We have to get them to our house."

Blake and John lifted Anders' lifeless body, tears still pouring from Blake's eyes as he helped carry his partner and friend. Steve and Linda carried Ally with Mila walking by their side, praying out loud, begging for her daughter's life. They were all weeping as the vehicles pulled away, bound for the Phillips' house. Ally needed urgent medical attention, so there was no time to worry about how fast they drove. Minutes may determine whether she lived or died. They had lost Evan and Anders on the same day. The thought of losing Ally too was almost unbearable.

$$\cdot \quad \cdot \quad \cdot \quad \cdot \quad \cdot$$

Anders stood before his Savior, still unable to speak. He longed to tell Jesus how much he loved him and say *thank you* a million times, but the words failed to come. Why? It made no sense. His family and friends stood with the same look he saw on Angie's face earlier. It said, *we have a secret!* What were they keeping from him? That would come, but a few surprises awaited him first.

"Follow me, Anders," Jesus said, then turned to walk away. The others followed, motioning for Anders to join them.

They entered a massive circular hall, too enormous to comprehend. It appeared to be miles in size, rather than feet, yet he found himself in the center at once. A colossal throne sat in the exact midpoint of the hall. He realized someone sat on the throne, but he could not make out his form or face. Vivid colors emanated from the figure, and a stunning emerald rainbow circled him. A translucent floor in front of the throne prevented him and the others from going near it.

A gust of wind accompanied by a powerful storm caused him to pull back as lightning flashed and thunder rocked the floor beneath him. The others smiled and stood with hands raised in worship. Seven fiery torches blazed before the throne. He now realized where he stood and who sat on the throne. This was the throne room of *God* he had read about in Revelation Chapter Four in the Bible. The heat of the Holy Spirit reached him from the torches and ignited him with love and passion for his creator.

He counted twenty-four additional thrones surrounding the main throne. Someone sat on each of them too, but their faces were also obscured. Four grotesque, yet magnificent beasts stood nearby, crying out praise to the occupant of the throne.

"Holy, holy, holy, is the Lord God Almighty, who was, and is, and is to come." (Revelation 4:8 NIV)

He prepared for what was coming next. Those seated on the surrounding thrones fell on their faces, removed their crowns, lay them before God's throne, then broke out in a chorus of praise.

"You are worthy, our Lord and God, to receive glory and honor and power, for you created all things, and by your will they were created and have their being." (Revelation 4:11)

Anders fell with them. He lay flat on his face, crying out praise. Nothing could have prepared him for this welcome to heaven. He understood this would be a part of his eternal experience in this place. It was good to be *home*.

The one on the throne extended his right hand, which held a sealed scroll. He watched as Jesus morphed into a bloody lamb and walked toward the throne. Anders may not have seen Jesus, but he saw the lamb! He understood that Jesus was the lamb of God, slain on the cross. And he had forgiven him for failing to believe in him before the Rapture. Gratitude and thanksgiving overcame him, causing tears to flow once more. He longed to rush to the lamb and embrace its blood-stained body, but realized he could not interrupt this moment.

The lamb took the scroll from the hand of God, causing the four beasts and twenty-four occupants of the other thrones to fall before *Jesus* in worship. They held something in their hands. He had read this in the Bible, but in this rapturous moment, he did not recall what it was. He strained to look, and it came back to him. Bowls of pure gold with the smoke of incense rising from them.

He understood what they signified. The prayers of God's people! *His* prayers! Every prayer he and the Smyrnians had prayed came to the throne of God! His mind drifted back to the flight from the farm to New York with Trey three years earlier. The horrific storm. Trey preparing for a crash landing as he, Blake, and Beth prayed. The immediate transformation from life-threatening turbulence to smooth air when their prayer ended!

Prayer after prayer flooded his mind. Ally's escape from Messai; Ollie and Amelia evading AMPP in London; Beth's rescue from Messai's mansion; Rickie stabilizing on the flight from Germany; Kathie's family spared from certain death. Each happened because God answered their prayers!

A song of praise to Jesus now erupted from everyone in the room.

"You are worthy to take the scroll and to open its seals, because you were slain, and with your blood you purchased for God persons from every tribe and language and people and nation.

You have made them to be a kingdom and priests to serve our God, and they will reign on the earth." (Revelation 5:9-10)

Anders had memorized the song as he studied this chapter and sang it with them. It was a glorious moment, and he knew it was not over. Millions of angels appeared and burst out in praise!

"Worthy is the Lamb, who was slain, to receive power and wealth and wisdom and strength and honor and glory and praise!" (Revelation 5:12)

Then all of creation broke forth in magnificent celebration.

"To him who sits on the throne and to the Lamb be praise and honor and glory and power, for ever and ever!" (Revelation 5:13)

The four beasts spoke. Anders said it with them: "Amen."

Jesus, now wrapped again in brilliant light, motioned to Anders and the others, and the same nail-scarred hand pointed toward the outside. They followed. Their first step transported them to another location and a future time. Anders knew they had arrived back in the present. He had just gotten there and yet he had experienced the awe of glory! What awaited him next? It must be glorious again. This had only just begun!

At once, a mighty angel stood before him, holding a scroll in his hand. The angel let out a fierce roar. Anders wanted to run, but his legs refused to move. A voice commanded him to take the scroll from the angel's hand. *No! I am not worthy*, his mind cried. Yet, he had no choice but to obey. As he walked toward the mighty angel, the realization hit him like a ton of bricks.

"No, Jesus, please," he said in a whisper. He looked at Angie. She smiled and spoke.

"It's okay, baby; we all knew. Just trust him and do what he says."

Her voice sounded so sweet. The thought of what was about to happen broke his heart. His mind screamed to run to her and the kids, hold them, and never let go. But he obeyed, took the scroll, and followed the angel's instructions.

"Eat it," he commanded. "It will taste sweet in your mouth, but will turn your stomach sour."

The first bite was delicious! He watched Evan smiling. That boy loved good food. The scroll was so delectable that Anders consumed it much faster than he should. After taking the first bite, there was no stopping. But when he swallowed the last bite, his stomach turned sour, and he thought he would throw up. Once again, he knew what he was about to hear. There was no way to stop the words from coming.

"You must prophecy again about many peoples, nations, languages, and kings."

Angie smiled again. *"I love you, baby."* Their kids echoed her words. She said something else. He couldn't understand it, but knew Jesus would make it clear when the time came.

•　　•　　•　　•　　•

Blake sat beside the bed where Rickie had once lain after Steve's operation to save his life. Before him lay his best friend and long-time partner in the television news industry. They had arrived only a few minutes earlier, and he begged them to allow him to sit alone with his friend for a while. The others worried about him. He had grieved until it seemed no more tears would come. Now, he asked to sit alone, with Anders' dead body lying on the bed and the door closed. Beth begged him to let her sit with him, but he refused.

"I love you more than anything, Beth, but please let me do this, for my sake. Give me one last hour with him."

She granted his wish, as did the group. They would pray for him, and for Ally, but they knew it was useless to pray for Anders' lifeless body lying on the bed. Beth prayed that Anders' death would not drive her husband insane. He had been through so much in recent weeks and months. Now he had lost Evan, the one who told him about Jesus, followed right after that by his partner of several years; and Ally may be next. Blake entered the room, shut the door, and pulled up a chair beside the bed.

In another bedroom, Steve and Linda were taking care of Ally. He bandaged her head wound and kept a close eye on her. Mila sat, holding her daughter's hand and talking to her. Steve assured her all of Ally's vital signs were good, and he expected her to regain consciousness, but there was no guarantee that would happen. The wait was on as the others sat praying in the large open area comprising the living room, dining room, and kitchen. It was all they could do at this point.

Blake prayed, thanking God for the years he was blessed to work with Anders. He recalled their first meeting, and his mind raced through the important events of those years. The tears would not stop. His mind drifted to the flight from Germany and Rickie's grave condition. What was that verse Anders prayed? It came to him just as Anders avowed God gave it to him. Blake did not remember it, so he retrieved a Bible that Steve now kept lying on the dresser and opened it to Jeremiah 17:14.

"Lord, please help me. You understand how much this man means to me. You brought us together, and we formed the perfect team. I could not have done my job without him. He helped make me the successful reporter I became. This breaks my heart. I need you now more than I have ever needed you in my life. Forgive me if it is wrong to pray these words after Anders has died. They are your words, and I believe them on behalf of my friend, your child, Anders Norstrom." He placed the open Bible on Anders' body and read the words.

"Heal him, Lord, and he will be healed. Save him and he will be saved, for you are the one I praise."

Steve maintained his vigil, checking Ally every few minutes for signs of consciousness. Small signs had occurred, as Mila talked to her non-stop, hoping she would respond. She held her daughter's hand and continued praying and talking.

"Steve!" Blake's scream reverberated throughout the house. Beth raced toward the bedroom, with the doctor close behind her. Linda stayed with Ally and Mila.

Anders opened his eyes. *Where am I? Angie! Where are you? Kids! Jesus! The others! Don't leave me!* The words poured through his mind as he looked around, trying to determine where he was. Blake stood gazing at him, a look of amazement on his face. Anders listened to him reading his healing verse, then opened his eyes and saw him sitting beside the bed.

When Blake finished reading, he glanced at him, then leapt to his feet and screamed Steve's name. None of this made sense to Anders. He was in heaven with Jesus, Angie, the kids, and his fallen comrades. But things looked different. This did not look at all like that place. What happened to the joy, the peace, the happiness, the glorious feeling, the worship, the beauty, the splendor? The first words slipped from his lips.

"Angie. Don't leave me, baby. Please don't leave me."

Steve passed Beth on the way to the bedroom and almost ripped the door from its hinges as he burst into the room. What he saw defied medical knowledge. Reality fought against faith in those few seconds as he struggled to grasp what had just occurred.

"Blake? Steve? Beth? Where am I?"

He tried to sit up, but Steve put his hand on his chest and stopped him.

"Anders, can you hear me?"

"I hear you, Steve. Blake, tell me where I am."

"You are at Steve and Linda's house," Blake said, tears of joy streaming from his eyes.

"Let me get up, Steve. I'm okay, just confused. I don't understand what happened."

"I don't mean to scare you, Anders, but you died. The explosion killed you while you shielded Ally from the debris, and you've been dead for over an hour. I'll be honest, I don't understand any of this. We've seen a lot of miracles happen, but this one is impossible. Yet it just happened. You were dead, and now you're alive! There is no reasonable explanation for that."

"I need to tell you guys where I went and what I saw. Not just *what* I saw, but *who* I saw. And not just what I *saw*, but what I *heard*. Where's Ally? She must be alive because I didn't see her there."

"Where, Anders? What are you talking about?" Beth had a look of bewilderment on her face.

"Get everybody together, so I can tell all of you. Believe me, I'm okay. In fact, I am more alive than I have ever been in my entire life!"

•   •   •   •   •

Bradley Rodgers stared at Oliver and Amelia Barton standing in front of him inside the hangar.

"What are the two of you doing here? If they catch you..."

Ollie cut him off mid-sentence. "Look, Bradley, we need your help. You're our only hope for getting out of the UK and back to the States. Trey isn't with us this time, but since you're one of us now, I hope you will help us."

"I've put my career on the line helping you guys in the past, so what's one more time? But who cares about a career, anyway, when we only have four years left till the world ends?"

"How soon can we fly? We need to go now!"

"There are a couple of problems, but if you're willing to take the chance, so am I. We have no way of communicating with the bases in the U.S., so I can't tell them we're coming. Then I don't know what kind of shape the base is in, or if it is even there after the nuclear attacks."

"We have to get out of England so we're ready and willing to take the chance. I need to find out what is happening with the rest of the team. They're in a safe place, and I assume Messai doesn't know where that is. Missouri wouldn't be a nuclear target of the coalition either. I can't imagine they're not safe. We'll take you there and let you see it and meet the others! How about that?"

"That is an offer I can't refuse! I can get clearance to fly today, if you're ready."

"How soon? There is nothing stopping us, so whenever you can leave, we'll be on the plane!"

"Give me two hours to get everything in place. Stay in this hangar and don't leave. Hide behind this equipment, and no one will notice you. I'll be back as soon as I can."

Bruno and Magnus sat in the cave, trying to determine their next moves.

"Face it, Magnus, we're trapped here. We have no way of contacting anyone without phone service, so we're stuck in this godforsaken place with no way to escape."

"Then we need to make the most of it, because I refuse to let Malachi down. We're going back into Beijing and try to get information. Any intel we get will help the others, especially the group in Israel. We need to find out everything possible about what's coming next."

"But what if *he* shows up again?"

"You mean the *dragon*."

"Yes, the dragon! I don't want to face him again and end up like Malachi."

"We handled his fire once; we can do it again. He told us he knows where we are anyway, so it's impossible to hide from him, even in this cave. If he wants us, he can send a cave in and kill us on the spot. We have to be proactive and out think him *and* the entire Chinese Communist Party."

"You just assume we can out think *him*? I don't think so. He is Satan, remember?"

"Yes, and *he* is Jesus," Magnus said, pointing upward. "The last I heard, he is stronger than Satan. I don't know about you, but my faith is in Jesus. He can protect us. He spoke to me personally and called me to join him, and I'm in to stay. You can be in or out, but I am telling you I am all in, with or without you."

"You're right, Magnus, and I'm in with you all the way. We're in the middle of this war, so we may as well fight! Let's figure out where we go tomorrow and get on it. How do we do that?"

"What would Malachi do? That's the question. When we answer it, we'll learn our next moves."

In Israel, two of the men refused to stay hidden in the kibbutz any longer. Ben did his best to rein them in, but to no avail.

"Listen up, everybody," exclaimed Moshe as the leaders met. "The Bible says God did not give us a spirit of fear, but of power and love and a sound mind. Eliyahu and I are going out there, because our people still need Jesus!"

"Yes, Moshe," said Ben, his voice firm, "a sound mind! No one in their right mind would go out there now. Unless...," he whispered now, "Jesus told them to go. Did he?"

"That's what we're trying to tell you, Ben," said Eliyahu. "Jesus told us to jump on that stage in the valley, and you watched what he did. Now he called us to go out and proclaim his name to everyone who will listen. We sure can't do that in here, so we're going out there!"

"Then go and we'll ask Jesus to protect you."

The group prayed fervently as they commissioned the two men to leave the kibbutz and go to war.

$\bullet \quad \bullet \quad \bullet \quad \bullet \quad \bullet$

Anders stood in Steve and Linda's living room surrounded by wall-to-wall people, eyes glued to him, eager to hear what he would say. He convinced Steve he was strong enough to stand and speak. Nothing about him resembled a dead man who came back to life only minutes earlier. Ally was awake now. Mila led her in and seated her in front of him.

"I died and went to heaven!"

Those opening words left them speechless and caused them to tune in to his words even more.

"I saw Angie and my kids!"

He smiled, and his face beamed with a transcendent glory that almost blinded them. The room lit up as if illuminated by a thousand glowing lights, so bright the surrounding people shielded their eyes from its brilliance. The radiance reminded Blake of the night in Ben's house when his producer first put his faith in Jesus.

"But that's not all. Every member of our team who has died came to me and spoke to me. Only a couple sentences each, but they sounded amazing! Jesus wanted to tell us they're alive and with him, and we will join them one day!"

"Ally, I saw Evan."

She put her head in her hands and sobbed. But his next words brought a smile to her face and a tearful chuckle from the others.

"He said he arrived minutes earlier, and the food smelled so amazing he couldn't wait to eat!"

"I hate to tell you this, Blake, but Malachi is there. He stepped out and said, 'Just call me Source.'"

"Malachi? But how... what happened? He died in China?"

Mila started crying now. "Bruno...?" she asked through trembling lips.

"Not Bruno or Magnus, Mila, only Malachi. He didn't tell me how he died, but I promise you he is happier than any of us ever saw him!"

"John and Mary showed up after Malachi and thanked me for telling them about Jesus."

Now *he* shed tears of joy, remembering the day he helped them give their lives to Jesus. The others sat still, giving him time to start again, their eagerness making it hard to wait. This was more than Anders' experience; Jesus wanted him to inform them of some things. They understood this meant more than telling them about their teammates, but he would get around to that.

"John and Brita, Johnathan walked out next!"

She fell to her knees in tears, and both John and Kathie knelt and embraced her.

"He asked, 'Anders, did you know God created the universe in six 24-hour days?' I wanted to speak, but words would not come. So he answered his own question. 'Of course, you did!'"

The three of them stood, joined by their families, grief turned to joy and tears replaced with laughter and shouts of praise. They quieted as he spoke again.

"Kathie, Doc followed him! He called me *cameraman* and said Blake and I pulled the wool over his eyes that day at PSI. His face looked as rapturous as you described the day AMPP killed him!"

Tears rolled down her face and weeping filled the entire room now. But she shed tears of happiness, not sorrow. His next words dried their tears and overwhelmed them with glory.

"Then I saw *Jesus*! Dazzling light covered his face, but I recognized *him* right away and he spoke to me and touched me! I fell to my knees before him, but he reached down and lifted me to my feet. His hand is nail-scarred, and his glory... you cannot imagine his glory!"

Anders became so engulfed in the glory of God, the intensity of the light overpowered them.

"Yes, we can," Blake said, covering his eyes with his hands as he squinted, trying to gaze into the face of his friend.

Anders continued, as if not hearing what his partner said.

"He welcomed me *home*..."

He said that word with such wonder that his voice trailed off, making them feel that he would leave without another word and return to Jesus.

"This world isn't home; *that* is home. I have never been more at *home* in my life!"

They stood in awe, staring at him, though still unable to detect his face because of the brilliant light. He continued as they sat still and listened, none of them saying a word. He told about worship in the throne room of God, the twenty-four thrones, the four beasts, and the Holy Spirit. Jesus transforming into a bloody lamb who took the scroll from the hand of God, followed by the song of praise from the angelic choir, served as the transition to what came next.

The glow surrounding him increased so much as he shared those experiences they closed their eyes to avoid the intense light. Then, as he told of Jesus leading them away from the throne room, his face returned to normal, and the radiance faded from both him and the room.

"Jesus led us all outside, and transported us to another place instantly."

He went on, telling them about the mighty angel and the scroll, and how Jesus told him to take the scroll from the angel's hand and eat it. Like Jesus promised, the sweetness filled his mouth causing him to devour the whole thing without stopping, much like Evan, he reasoned, bringing smiles to every face. But when he swallowed, his stomach turned bitter, and he almost threw up.

"That leads me to the contents of the scroll and their implications for us now. The words and their meaning became clear as I digested them, and now I must tell you what they mean for our future during the next three-and-a-half years."

• • • • •

Early the next morning, Moshe and Eliyahu kissed and hugged their families and drove away from the kibbutz. None of them realized they would not return. Jesus' plans for them involved far more than even they understood. The world would hate them and view them as perpetrators of a sinister message of gloom and doom, but their words would come from Jesus himself. Their destination? Jerusalem. The location? The Temple Mount.

• • • • •

Bruno and Magnus parked the car and walked a quarter mile to the building outside Beijing where the Chinese Communist Party leaders held covert meetings. Trepidation filled their minds as they neared the place. They had not returned here since that fateful night the Red Dragon burned their partner and caused his death, but they refused to turn back. Regardless of what happened, they would fulfill the job he loved so much and performed so well.

The same space Malachi used to enter the building remained accessible, allowing the two men to crawl inside. They squeezed through, leaving scratches and cuts on their bodies, but achieved their purpose. Both shuddered as memories of that night rushed in on them, yet they pushed them out of their minds and kept going. This mission required an unwillingness to let anything stop them.

Where did they go now? Neither would fit into the heat and air duct Malachi pulled himself into and slithered all the way to the vent above the meeting room. There must be another way to get close enough to make out what the men said. They needed to hurry. The leaders would arrive soon.

"Focus, Magnus. What would Malachi do?"

"I don't have a clue, Bruno. If I did, we would be on our way right now!" His frustration showed as time to get where they needed to go faded fast.

"Your dreams, Magnus!" Bruno said quietly.

"What about my dreams?"

"Jesus took you to the place where Messai met the coalition, and you watched the meeting and got every word they said. If he put you in the right spot, he can lead us to the right place, too."

"Why didn't I think of that? Help me remember, Jesus," he breathed in a soft prayer.

A faint glow appeared and led toward a steel door. The same thing happened for Beth when she escaped from Messai's mansion! He grabbed Bruno and said, "Follow the light!"

They ran to the door, being as quiet as possible. Magnus seized the handle and pulled. Locked! What now? They watched the handle turn and the door start to move. Their minds screamed *run*, like they fled from the dragon before. Yet this came not from the dragon, but from one far greater than him.

When the door opened, the glow led down a corridor with three options from which to choose. It continued straight ahead, with hallways extending to the left and right. The glow moved down the corridor and turned right, as the men glanced at one another, understanding what was happening.

It led them through a maze of hallways and ended behind a huge, thick curtain, where they found themselves on a large stage. No sounds came from the other side. Magnus pulled the curtain open just enough, allowing them to peer through.

The meeting room! They stood hidden behind a curtain in the room where the group would meet on a stage that provided plenty of places to hide, if they needed them. From this vantage point, they could watch and listen to everything that took place. Before they had time to discuss what they might do, voices filled the room. Fear gnawed at them, but Jesus led them here to accomplish their mission, and they refused to leave.

Neither dared part the curtain even the tiniest bit. Hearing would allow them to gather all the information they needed. Magnus pulled his phone from his pocket and opened an app which would translate and record every word the men said. Malachi spoke several languages, so he understood Chinese well, but they did not. Magnus turned down the brightness on his phone.

That would not have entered Bruno's mind. Magnus did not need him; the man was a pro at this. *Almost as good as Malachi*, he thought to himself. He longed to talk to his partner, but they must remain silent and listen to the conversation coming from beyond the curtain. The president called the meeting to order and discussion started. Bruno fought the urge to run, standing in his place, the voices claiming his attention. Two words jumped out at him, both impossible to miss: *America* and *Israel*. Another word caught him by surprise and sent a shiver through his body: *Smyrnians.*

CHAPTER 2

"I did not want to come back," Anders said, his eyes wandering off for a moment as the group gave him time, feeling the power of this experience for him.

"It is the most amazing place you can imagine. I was there with Angie and my kids, our teammates, and most of all, Jesus. The others knew he planned to send me back. It was the secret they could not tell. I begged Jesus not to make me leave, but after eating the scroll, I understood why I had to. Now here I stand to tell you what I learned about the next three-and-a-half years."

Everyone sat entranced before him, eager to know what was coming. The surrounding glow had subsided, and he was Anders again, the man they knew and loved, here with an important message for them. Ally was more intent that any of them, her eyes glued to the man who saved her life.

"I thought to myself, who can eat a scroll? We chewed up paper and made *spit wads* in school growing up, and a lot of us got into plenty of trouble shooting those at other kids."

He grinned at them, a look of mischievousness showing on his face. The Anders they all loved had returned, causing them to breathe a collective sigh of relief.

"But now I had to eat this scroll, not just chew it up. When I got the scroll near my mouth, it smelled incredible, like the Norwegian food my mother used to cook. Jesus drew me in with that."

"I took the first bite, then scarfed the thing down so fast it disappeared in no time. With all due respect to my mom and some of you, that was the best thing I have ever eaten!"

"With all due respect to you, Anders," Blake said, "get on with the story. You're driving us crazy!" His impatience came out before he caught himself, and he apologized to his friend right after the words left his mouth, regretting that he interrupted him.

"I'm sorry, partner. This is your story and your experience, so take as much time as you need. But please don't wait too long to get to the good parts. We want to hear what this means for us."

"Okay, *partner*," he said with sarcasm and a hint of humor, "but the details are so fresh in my mind. Remember, all of this happened within the last couple of hours! Now, as I said before someone cut me off..." He frowned at Blake, then smiled.

"With every bite, sweetness exploded in my brain, bringing joy I cannot describe. I sensed so much happiness from being home with Jesus and others I love and care about. I relived the night Blake helped me put my faith in Jesus, as if it happened all over again. Wow! A journey down memory lane, recalling our experiences as a team made me so thankful, even for the hard times. I understood the end result and wanted to slow down but kept eating until I finished the entire scroll."

"When the last bite entered my stomach, everything changed..."

•   •   •   •   •

Now just over an hour into its flight, the military plane flew over the Atlantic Ocean, with Bradley Rodgers piloting, while Ollie and Amelia Barton sat in the cockpit.

"Assuming we can land at the base in Missouri, how long before we can go to the Shelter?"

"Paul Johnson will give us something to drive, so we'll leave straight away. I cannot wait for you to meet everyone. They're a jolly good group!"

"I bet you don't talk like that when you're in the U.S.," Bradley said with a chuckle.

"Oh, he does sometimes, Bloke, but only when he wants to show off," Amelia said, chuckling too.

They needed some stress relief, and this may be their only chance to get it for a long time.

"What the...?!" Bradley asked, looking at each side of the plane.

Ollie whirled around and saw them, too. Two Chinese bombers flying alongside them off each wing. They left no doubt they meant business.

"We're in our own airspace, and *they're* in ours too! How did they get here?"

"H-20s: China's newest bombers with a flying range of over five thousand miles, and maybe even more. So, they can reach us here, but my guess is, they flew from another base along the BRI."

"I never trusted the Belt and Road Initiative. The Chinese manufactured military domination under the guise of financial prosperity with the world watching, and nobody did a thing to stop them. Now they're attacking us in a plane flying over the Atlantic ocean. What are you going to do?"

"The only thing I can do... radio the base and ask for help. But we need them now, not later. Those guys won't leave enough time for our jets to get here. We sure can't out-maneuver them or out-fly them. They'll shoot us down before help gets here."

The H-20s went into their own maneuver, one dropping to their rear, the other staying on their left.

"Okay, here we go! They're getting into position to attack."

"Do you think they knew...?"

"Oh yeah, their intel told them the two of you are on this plane. I'm sure they have the scoop on me too. No one can hide anything from their boss."

"You mean Messai..."

"No, I mean *his* boss. We all recognize who that is, remember?"

"The dragon is more than his boss, he controls the man!"

"Would you two stop it and figure out a way to get us out of this mess?"

"Unfortunately, there is no way out of this one, Amelia."

When those words came out of Bradley's mouth, a missile fired from one H-20, grazing the nose of the plane, lurching it sideways. Ollie and Amelia grabbed each other in a tight embrace. Any minute, the bombers would shoot them out of the sky, and they would never see the Shelter or the team again. He saw her bravery turn to fear for the first time and held her close.

"They meant to do that," said Bradley. "They're playing with us for a little while before they take us down." He yelled into the radio as he finished.

"Mayday, Mayday. B-1 to base, B-1 to base. We are under attack; I repeat, we are under attack. Two H-20s, one on each side. They fired a warning shot and scraped our nose. The next one will split us wide open!"

"Base to B-1. You're breaking up, so they may have damaged your equipment. If you're picking me up, we'll get to you as fast as possible, but we'll never reach you in time. Go into maneuvers and try to avoid them. I'll dispatch fighter jets at once."

Another missile clipped the rear of the plane. It shook and reeled from side-to-side. Bradley worked hard to keep the vessel from nose-diving to the water.

"Hold on! We're dropping five thousand feet."

His passengers understood what that meant and clung to their seats, preparing for the plunge. The plane plummeted downward, leaving them no time to respond and almost causing them to throw up. The H-20 pilots remained undeterred and followed them, remaining in a direct line of fire. Bradley pulled up hard and climbed a thousand feet within seconds. The bombers rose with him.

"They're toying with us again and waiting for the right moment. I'm afraid that time has come."

Amelia threw off her seatbelt and headset and dove to the floor behind them.

"Amelia!" said Ollie. "What are you doing?"

She did not respond, but screamed at Bradley.

"I told Ollie this once as we fled from AMPP. You fly, and I'll pray!"

Ollie now followed her to the floor, and they both began calling out to Jesus.

Bradley caught nothing they said, as he sought a path to escape the missiles the bombers would soon fire. When one dropped from his view and the other moved farther away to the left, he understood what that meant. The bomber to their rear would fire the missile, which would come through the center of the plane, causing it to explode in mid-air. He knew what to expect, having shot down planes in combat himself and going through training that prepared him for this.

He, Ollie, and Amelia would experience a brief violent surge of suction as the missile ripped the plane in half, exposing them to the atmosphere at high altitude. A deafening sound would pierce their ears for only a second as the aircraft exploded in a massive fireball, killing them instantly. Bradley Rodgers, new Smyrnian and follower of Jesus, relaxed and prepared for impact. He only regretted having such little time to work for his Lord and fight Aissa Messai. He prayed along with his passengers from the Captain's seat. Ollie and Amelia held each other on the floor behind him. It would be over within seconds.

·   ·   ·   ·   ·

Bruno and Magnus stood still and quiet behind the curtain as voices came from the other side. The latest translation app Magnus purchased not only recorded the conversation but also allowed them to read it in real time on the screen. They listened and kept their eyes glued to the screen. The men spoke with clear voices, one at a time, making for easy translation.

"We are well on our way to achieving our greatest aim," the president said. "America lies in ruins, and we have Israel under siege. World domination is within our grasp. Messai guarantees that. Check out the results of our efforts and celebrate!"

He showed pictures of the devastation from the nuclear attacks on America and its allies. Bruno and Magnus did not see them with their eyes, but the images still filled their minds. Spontaneous applause broke out in the room as the men lauded their accomplishment.

"Mr. Zhao will now report on the happenings in Israel."

The man spoke lower, but the translation app still picked it up.

"Our nuclear attacks hit their targets and achieved our purpose. The assault killed over one hundred thousand Israelis throughout the country and devastated the nation beyond recovery. We followed that with Z-10s and J-10s, creating intense fear and imprisoning the people inside their homes. When they emerge, the pain ray does it job with exceptional results and forces them back in."

"The siege continues and works as we planned, with Messai's help. He convinced both the military and civilians to yield to our pressure and not retaliate. The famine grows worse by the day, and desperation has set in. People are taking extreme measures to survive and save their families. But we refuse to stop until the country falls apart."

"Thank you, Mr. Zhao. Our military performed well."

Bruno and Magnus could not see the evil grin covering the president's face, but they sensed it.

"Now, General Chen will report the latest news about the *Smyrnians*. Their foolish worship of some imaginary god *flew* in the face of everything we recognize as truth and threatened our entire future. We must continue hunting their followers down and extinguishing them until we abolish their ideology from the planet!"

Flew? The word hit the men behind the curtain like a punch to the gut. *Flew* speaks of past tense, as if they no longer exist! What did the man mean by that? Panic set in as they continued to listen.

"Thank you, sir. Ah, yes, the *Smyrnians*. It appears their *god* could not protect them after all. It makes me happy to announce that we accomplished what even Messai could not and destroyed their *safe place* and all of their *leaders*. That should bring their cause to an end. You defeat an enemy by taking out its leaders first. We did that with the Smyrnians two days ago, and I believe we will now watch their movement slowly collapse."

The two big men stood in stunned disbelief, tears welling up in their eyes, but they had to stay until the meeting ended. Magnus shook so much he almost dropped the phone, and Bruno's entire body trembled. They listened as Chen spoke again.

"Once the dragon revealed their location, we dispatched bombers to Missouri armed with bunker busters. We confirmed their presence prior to dropping the bombs and are certain they were all inside when the impact occurred. Now I will show our video of the release and impact."

Silence ensued as the video played. Raucous applause and shouts of celebration interrupted the quiet, signaling the end of the video.

"A second bomb followed the initial strike to ensure success. Both hit the target and destroyed everything underground, the bunkers, and the people inside. This day represents a giant step toward our goal of worldwide domination with the removal of a significant enemy to our cause."

The room erupted in celebration again, leaving the men behind the curtain shocked and alone. Were they the only ones left to fight the enemy? Where would they begin? The president spoke again, picking up where General Chen ended.

"Thank you, General. The removal of the Smyrnian leaders, along with the destruction of America and subjugation of Israel, further guarantees our ultimate victory. Now, we must discuss our next steps. The war is far from over, but we set the plan in motion with this chain of events. Nothing or no one can stop us now!"

Bruno and Magnus wanted to run as they burst with grief on the inside, but they needed to learn what the Chinese planned next. How would they stop them without their teammates? They could not afford so much as a whisper, but Bruno pulled out his phone and typed in his notes: *Ben, Ollie, and Amelia.* No one else remained except them. He added, *I wonder if they killed them too?* Then his mind went to Mila and the kids, and his face turned pale. His knees buckled, and Magnus caught his partner and held him, preventing him from collapsing to the floor.

•   •   •   •   •

Bradley raised his voice but remained calm as he called his two passengers to join him. They stood from kneeling and returned to their seats, looking at him, wondering if the emergency was over.

"I cannot avoid them any longer. One plane dropped back behind us and has us squarely in his sights. The other moved away from us, well off our left wing. I expect them to release the missile any second. We will be with Jesus soon. Trey told me about him, but all of you played a role in that. I wanted to say 'thank you.'"

"Look!" Amelia said, pointing out the window on their left.

The rear jet appeared, and both moved toward the other, as if pulled by an unseen magnetic force. The trio watched as the two got closer to one another, fighting to resist the pull. Bradley turned to the controls and climbed upward and to their right, maneuvering away from the Chinese bombers. What happened next shocked them.

The two jets zoomed toward each other, as if someone released giant rubber bands that held them back. The impact was swift, as the planes slammed together and blew apart, leaving the remains to plunge thousands of feet into the water below. Neither pilot had time to eject.

Bradley Rogers had heard stories of miracles from Trey, but now he witnessed one of his own. He once again set the plane on course for

Missouri, and they flew in silence, still shaken and in disbelief of what just happened. Several minutes would pass before either spoke.

•   •   •   •   •

"Now comes the bitter part," Anders said as his eager audience listened. "Everything changes at the midpoint of the Tribulation. Things have been easy for us to this point, but that ends soon."

"The last three-and-a-half years have been easy?" Ally asked a question that was on all their minds.

"Yes, Ally. Compared to what's coming, that's true. In Revelation Chapter 12, a giant red dragon appears. The chapter tells us the dragon is none other than Satan himself. Whenever he appears, he assumes the form of a dragon. In the Garden of Eden, he appeared to Eve as a serpent that walked around until God cursed it to crawl on its belly for the rest of time. I can't help but wonder if he appeared as a dragon there and still uses that form today, even though snakes on earth can no longer walk around."

"The dragon is evil and vicious. His greatest desire is to overthrow God and take his place as ruler of the universe. That's why throughout history he has attempted to destroy the nation of Israel and prevent Jesus from coming into the world. Consider this: he tried to destroy them in Egypt when God sent the plagues to save them. I've never read the whole history of Israel, but Jesus showed it to me when I ate the scroll."

"His next attempt came when Assyria defeated the Northern Kingdom of Israel in 722 B.C. They carried the people away into captivity, removing them from the historical record. People refer to them as the Ten Lost Tribes, but they're not lost because God knows where all of them live in the world today. They're scattered, but they are not lost!"

"Satan's plan failed because the Southern Kingdom, Judah, remained, and Jesus would come from the tribe of Judah. However, Satan refused to give up. Babylon destroyed Jerusalem in 587/586 B.C. and took the people away as prisoners. Persia conquered Babylon, and the Jews came close to extinction again when a man named Haman concocted a plan to murder them all. God used Queen Esther, a Jew, to save his people, and many of them returned to their homeland."

"Satan's plots continued with Greece and Rome to do his evil bidding. He even tried to kill Jesus in Bethlehem by ordering every boy two years old and under murdered. But all his attempts failed. Jesus still came, died on the cross, and rose from the grave. That should stop him, right?" They all nodded in agreement, entranced by his words.

"He will not give up, but will make one more diabolical effort during the Tribulation. Satan assumes he will win the last battle, and will spend the next forty-two months killing everyone who stands in his way. He will hunt down every follower of Jesus and seek to destroy us and our cause. His man is already doing that, but something will happen soon which will turn up the heat with such intensity that survival becomes almost impossible."

"Messai," Ally said softly.

"Right again, Ally. Satan will soon indwell Messai and turn him into the most cruel dictator the world has ever seen. He will force every person in the world to worship him or face a brutal death."

"I will never worship him," Ally said, her voice much louder, "nor will I ever deny Jesus!" Her determination sprang from hatred for the man responsible for Evan's death.

"We all agree, Ally, but our greater task is to warn and protect other believers. Yet regardless of how hard we try, thousands, maybe millions, will die at his hands. That is only the beginning of what I need to tell you, but we should take a break and eat before I share the rest. After all, I've died and been to heaven and back, and all I've eaten was a scroll! I'm pretty sure Evan would tell us it is time for some food and be the first in line! I'll play his part. Let's eat!"

The group laughed at that but wanted more than anything to get back and listen to all he would say, a good thing, because he was only getting started.

· · · · ·

The president continued. "The Red Dragon, who gives our country its power, will soon indwell and empower Aissa Messai, and he will become the dragon incarnate on the earth. Messai will then assume control as a worldwide despot, a role that will be ours when the dragon helps us rule the world forever!"

"When the indwelling occurs, we will pull back and allow him to take control and enforce the dragon's will on the entire planet. He will purge the world of those who refuse to worship him, meaning all Smyrnians and those Jews who joined them. That will clear the way for our eventual march on Israel and total elimination of the Little Satan!"

"Now we return and wait for the indwelling. It will happen soon. Then we shall remain at the dragon's disposal to help however he needs us."

The meeting ended, and the men exited the room, turning out the lights and leaving Bruno and Magnus in the dark. They dared not make a sound yet for fear of being heard until they confirmed everyone else had left the building. When they decided it was safe to leave, the faint glow returned, leading them from the stage. They followed, being sure to not make the slightest noise.

Once outside, they walked to the car and drove to the cave. Magnus turned off the lights a quarter mile away and continued into the woods in the dark. When they were far enough off the road, he turned them back on and eased to the grove of trees. Bruno parted them, allowing him to drive inside. They crawled through the cave entrance, walked to Malachi's grave, then fell to the ground and wept. Agony poured out of them like a spring gushing from a rock.

"We must find some way to get back, Magnus. I have to know about my family and the others. How can we bear it if they are all gone? What will we do?"

"Both of us are mentally and physically drained, but we will spend this night praying and asking Jesus what we should do. It may not hurt to include what we have asked before: what would Malachi do? He understood how to get out of almost any predicament. I only know that we must escape China, or die trying. We cannot wait another day."

·　　·　　·　　·　　·

The group finished a quick, light meal and reconvened in the living room. Anders found himself once again surrounded by watching eyes and listening ears, eager for him to talk again.

"The Red Dragon...," he said, then paused for effect, letting the words sink in for a few seconds.

"What about the Red Dragon? You already told us about him," Blake said. He tried to stay patient, but didn't want to hear any more about the dragon. "Get on with the next three-and-a-half years."

"I didn't tell you everything about him. Think for a moment. Does he remind you of anything?"

"You told us the dragon is Satan," said Steve. "What can be more important than that?"

"China..."

"Thank you for changing the subject. Now tell us what the Chinese have planned for the rest of the Tribulation." Blake felt a sense of accomplishment at moving his partner on with the story.

"The *Red* Dragon...," Anders said, drawing out the word *red*, wanting them to get it. He was neither giving in nor moving on until they understood.

John leapt to his feet, startling the others, and causing those near him to jump too.

"*China's* Red Dragon!"

Steve joined him, along with Blake and Beth. "Why didn't we think of that?!"

"Correct! The Chinese have long held the dragon as sacred. Tradition says their legendary first emperor became immortalized as a dragon living in heaven, so they often refer to themselves *descendants of the dragon*. Their leaders rule on the imperial *dragon throne*."

"Dragons symbolize good fortune, and the Chinese revere them. They portray them in various colors, each with a different meaning. But when communism assumed control, the nation became known as Red China, with the red dragon as its most prominent emblem."

"The Chinese people view the dragon as positive, but it now personifies an evil ruling party raised up at the end of the age to dominate the world. Satan himself controls it and will use them in one last-ditch effort to destroy Jesus, overthrow God, and rule the universe."

"Wow, I remember all that, but never put pieces of the puzzle together in my mind," said John.

"Well, now you realize the truth, and we must fight him for the next 42 months. It's easier for me to talk about the earth's last days in terms of months, not years. It just feels shorter."

"What else did you see?" Ally asked again, mesmerized by his words.

"One more opportunity exists for people to turn to Jesus, but it will not last long. We must reach as many people as we can because the door will close soon."

"How can we do that? We have zero connection with the outside world. Beth and I can't use the internet, and none of us can travel or communicate with the others."

"Believers around the world will reach people in their own communities. The Smyrnians will also come back together for one last mission before the door of opportunity slams. After that, we will have two purposes for the rest of the Tribulation: protect other believers and protect ourselves."

The mood turned ominous as the group realized the horror they would face for the next three-and-a-half years. "We need to pray right now for Jesus to protect our teammates," said Blake.

In China, Magnus dreamed again as he and Bruno slept deep inside the cave. He found himself in a meeting between the president and General Chen. They had not seen the man's face when they stood behind the curtain earlier, but he recognized the voice when he spoke. He could not figure out where he was, but noticed it was a smaller room, with no one except the three of them inside. He understood the reason for the meeting as soon as the two men's conversation began.

"Three men have infiltrated the country, and maybe our ranks also," said the president.

"Are you certain of this, sir? None of my men have picked up any intel indicating that."

"Yes, general, I am certain. Otherwise, I would not have called you to meet with me in the middle of the night. Please do not question me again. Do you understand?"

"Yes, sir. It is just that we almost always discover these things first. Please continue."

"A trusted informant approached me earlier this evening with the news. You realize I have sources other than the military, I assume?"

Chen was silent, but his look showed he may not have been privy to that information. *I should have known*, he reasoned to himself. *I thought I was aware of every spy in our network.* The president snapped him back to the moment, without mentioning his obvious shock.

"The informant came to my house earlier with this news because it is so important. He does not know where the men are, but he feels certain they are somewhere near Beijing. Three of them came, but only two remain. The dragon took care of one of them and will now enter the room any minute to tell us the whereabouts of the other two. Then you and the military will bear the responsibility for finding and eliminating them. I suggest you do not disappoint the fiery beast because he does not handle disappointment well. You should stay on his good side."

The dragon! Magnus longed to run again, to escape from the evil creature who took Malachi's life and threatened their own, but his legs refused to move. His presence here was not an accident, nor was it only a dream. Jesus brought him for a reason. He must control his fear and stay as he had so often done, and just as he and Bruno did earlier this very day. The door flew open, and he steeled himself, hoping neither the beast nor the two men saw him. This time he knew they could not. The dragon ambled in, sparks floating from his long mouth, fangs showing, tongue extended.

"President... General... thank you for joining me tonight."

His words hissed out, sounding every bit like the serpent he was.

"I came to talk to you about the two men *you* allowed to enter the country. I hope you realize they are members of the Smyrnians."

Both the president and General Chen looked shocked, and the dragon took pleasure in that.

"You thought your bombs killed *all* of them, didn't you, general? Well, they did not!" he shouted, flames shooting out and coming within inches of the men's faces. Neither flinched.

"Do you know their location, general?"

"No, I do not," the man said, bowing his head in submission before the beast.

"Raise your head and look at me!" the dragon roared. Both men complied.

"I know where they are holed up, trying to avoid our sight. The Smyrnians seem to prefer hiding underground, but no one can hide from me! I will take you to them day after tomorrow. Assemble a platoon of your men and meet me here at 8:00 p.m. We will travel under cover of darkness, drag them from their hole in the ground, then lead them before the assembly in the meeting hall."

"You, *Mr. President*, will pronounce them guilty of spying, and the assembly will sentence them to death by burning. You understand what that means, don't you?"

Both had witnessed it many times before. The dragon loved nothing more than breathing his hellish fire upon those who attempted to interfere with his agenda. Neither enjoyed it and rued the times the creature forced them to watch. However, these were Smyrnians, so they would relish this one. Destroying those hated enemies of the cause topped their list of priorities.

"My men and I will arrive in time to leave promptly at 8:00 p.m., your majesty."

Magnus watched as the beast departed the room, the door slamming behind him. The two men started talking again, but he heard nothing they said. He awoke with a start, lying in the cave, then sat up, sweating and shaking.

"Bruno, wake up!" he said, shaking his partner so hard he almost turned him over.

"What, Magnus?!" Bruno asked, leaping to his feet, ready to fight but saw no enemy.

"I dreamed, and..."

"Here we go again," Bruno said, interrupting his partner in mid-sentence as he rubbed his eyes.

"Listen, this is urgent!"

"I'm listening. Where did you go this time? Who did you see and what did you hear?"

"I was in a meeting in an office with the president and General Chen. The dragon was there."

"The dragon! He must know where we are. Let me guess... that's what this meeting was about."

"Yes, Bruno, he knows where we are and will lead the general and a platoon of men here to capture us day after tomorrow at 8:00 p.m. We must get out of this cave and find another place to hide."

"Magnus, don't you think if he knows we are here, he will find us wherever we go?"

"He said the assembly will sentence us to death by burning, and he will carry out the sentence right there in front of them." He shivered, and his arms broke out in goosebumps. "Remember what happened to Malachi and what he looked like when he crawled out of that duct."

Bruno shook now, goosebumps covering his arms too.

"Okay, let's leave first thing in the morning. I can't stand to think of dying that way!"

"We need to do more than leave *here*, we need to get out of *China*!"

"How do you propose we do that since we've already decided there is no way out?"

"Both of us committed to pray all night, but we fell sleep. I think Jesus put me to sleep so I would dream and go to that meeting. But now, we must stay awake and pray until daylight!"

They hit their knees in urgent prayer, calling out to Jesus to rescue them from an impossible situation. Neither saw any way they could escape the country, so they asked Jesus to protect them and guide them where they needed to go.

In the kibbutz, while Trey slept, something happened to him. He dreamed and found himself in a remote Chinese valley surrounded by mountains. The place was expansive, and the ground was hard and smooth like pavement. What was this about? A thought hit him out of nowhere: *Bruno, Magnus, and Malachi are in China! Are they hiding in this valley?*

Jesus brought him here, like he had done for Magnus many times and had a message for him. That much was clear, but he needed to discover what Jesus wanted to show him. What was it about this valley? It was beautiful and peaceful, but something drew his attention to the earth under his feet. He walked, counting the distance by his steps, as he often did. *Why am I doing that? This is crazy!* Another thought entered his mind: *this is a perfectly hidden place to land a plane.* Was he supposed to fly here? Why else would Jesus bring him here? A gentle breeze blew against his face, with something wafting on the breeze. A voice!

Get them out...

He spoke out loud. "Get them out?" Bruno, Magnus, and Malachi were in danger, and he had to get them out of the country! But how could he do that? *Nobody can fly into China without getting shot down.* The voice came again.

Get them out...

"Lord, I will do anything you tell me to do, but I don't understand what you mean. Show me!"

Tomorrow night...

"You want me to fly *here* tomorrow night? But the Chinese will never let me fly in here!"

I will be with you...

Rickie...

"Yes, Lord, Rickie will come too, but tell me more."

The breeze disappeared, and the voice went with it. Trey realized he was just given a mission, the most dangerous mission he had ever flown. He awoke and turned toward his partner.

"Rickie!"

"What?" Rickie leapt from his bed, grabbing his weapon from underneath it as he did.

"I need to tell you what just happened. We have a tough task ahead of us tomorrow night."

Rickie was wide awake now and listening. He wanted some action anyway, so bring it on. With China six hours ahead of them, tomorrow night didn't give them much time to plan for this surprise mission, but it didn't matter. Regardless of what, where, or how dangerous, he was ready. Trey told him everything.

CHAPTER 3

Bradley, Ollie, and Amelia completed their flight and landed at the base in Missouri. They took time to sit and eat with Commander Paul Johnson and a few of his men who now believed in Jesus. Each of them told about the miracle they experienced with the two H-20s. The group celebrated with them and longed for the day when they would live through miracles of their own. Their conversation then turned to transportation to the Shelter.

"We need to get to the Shelter, Paul," said Ollie. "I want to see the team and make sure everyone is safe. You can't imagine how good it is to be out of the UK and back on American soil. Things may be a mess after the attacks, but the bunkers are always the safe place we can come back to."

"They may be safe once you get there, but the trip is still a dangerous one. I've wanted to go too, but none of us can take a chance on leaving the base. The military needs all personnel on hand and ready to fight with what little resources remain. But I will provide a jeep for you to drive, since that is all we can spare."

"We'll take it, Paul. Thank you! All three of us have serious jet lag and should rest before we go, but I can't wait any longer. We can rest when we get there."

Paul had already ordered the jeep and included some supplies for the two-hour trip. The trio loaded up and left for the Shelter, eager to see their teammates and spend some time in their special safe place. It was Bradley Rodgers' first trip there, and his adrenaline was pumping despite the fatigue that fought against him. They had to take care as they drove, but the trip was smooth.

●　　●　　●　　●　　●

Morning dawned in China as Bruno and Magnus prepared to leave the cave. One more time they stood at the grave of their fallen comrade and honored him for his service to the cause of Christ. Then Magnus drove from the woods and took back roads into the countryside, clueless to where they were going. Their goal was to find a new hiding place where they would stay safe from the dragon and from General Chen and his troops.

"Do we just drive till we run out of gas, then pull into the woods and lay low again? How long can we stay on the lam before they find us? They have the dragon on their side. He will know where we are anyway," said Bruno. His realism kept overriding his faith in dire circumstances.

"Yes, and we have Jesus on our side, and he knows where we need to go to avoid him," Magnus replied. "Come on, partner, don't you quit on me. Summon that courage and the fighting spirit that lives in you, and let's fight the good fight, and fight to win!"

"I'm sorry, Magnus, I admit I'm struggling. My mind is on Mila and the kids, not knowing whether they are dead or alive after what we heard in that meeting. The one thing I know is, we can't find the answer to that question unless we get out of this godforsaken country. Pull this thing over and let me drive for a while. At least the scenery is beautiful. We're climbing higher into the mountains, so it feels like home to me."

They continued the trip, with a fuel gauge showing less than a quarter of a tank, and unable to take the chance of stopping to fill it. Civilization was now behind them, and with it any opportunity to purchase fuel. They would do as Bruno said and drive until the tank was empty, then leave the car, walk, and see where the journey took them from there. Could they evade the dragon's lair, as they now called China, and escape the country? Only time would tell.

• • • • •

Trey and Rickie awakened Ben and called Michael, Hadassah, and her Uncle Mordecai to a midnight meeting, an hour after Trey's dream. The latter three stayed in the kibbutz for a few days, so they came fast, as did Ben. Trey shared his dream, leaving all four both excited and concerned.

"Trey, are you sure Jesus spoke to you in this dream? Maybe it was just a dream. *Or* is Messai leading you into a trap? Besides, how do you plan to find this valley when you get there?"

"I love you, Ben, but we don't have time for questions. Rickie and I have to get Bruno, Magnus, and Malachi out tomorrow night. Remember, China is six hours ahead of us. We have a ten-hour flight, so we need to fly before noon and get there by at least 3:00 a.m. Now, if you'll excuse me, I need to take charge. And to answer your last question, I have the coordinates."

Ben had never heard Trey talk so boldly, so he stopped talking and let him go.

"Mordecai, Michael, and Hadassah, we need a plane that will get us to China and back, with at least one base somewhere between that will allow us to refuel."

"Trey, you must know the Chinese will not allow you to enter their airspace or land in the country. They'll shoot you out of the sky long before you reach the border." Mordecai Chaim was a veteran of the Israeli military and had achieved the rank of Major General, known as Aluf in the IDF.

"The voice told me to *get them out*, and when I told him what you just said to me, he said, *I will be with you*. I trust he will, and Rickie and I are flying in less than twelve hours. You can either help us, or we will find a way ourselves. If you can't help, tell us now so we can leave and do that. If Jesus told me that, he will provide a plane. We just have to find it and fly."

"Pardon me, Aluf, but I know what we must do. The PLAAF has us locked down and will never allow one of our planes to leave the country. Muwaffaq Salti Air Base is less than a hundred miles from here, and America stations troops there. Hadassah and I are familiar with three of the border guards. We need to leave within the hour and take Trey and Rickie there. I mean no disrespect, but the lives of three of our teammates depend on us taking immediate action."

"Wait," said Ben. "Isn't Muwaffaq across the border in Jordan? That sounds too dangerous. They will never allow Israeli soldiers and two Americans to cross the border."

"No, Benjamin, it isn't too dangerous. I agree with Michael. That is a brilliant idea and one he did not come up with on his own. I'm not trying to be funny or disrespect you, Michael, but I believe what you suggest came from Jesus himself. We know the exact place to cross. The guards there are our close friends and will take us to Muwaffaq. Uncle, we must leave at once."

"The two of you have amused yourselves with the Jordanian border patrol when you should have been guarding our own border? Hadassah, I taught you better than that!"

"But Uncle, Jesus may have had a purpose for our *amusement*," she said. Her smile always melted his heart. "He intended to use it this day to rescue three of his men from certain death in the country that now enslaves our own people under a vicious siege. His protection will allow us to avoid them and reach the border. We need to leave now!"

"We're ready," said Rickie. "Trey packed supplies while I researched our flight pattern, so we can go right now. Please do not hesitate. As Michael said, the lives of three of our own depend on our swift action. If we do not act, they will not survive. Let's move!" He glanced at Ben.

"Don't look at me," Ben said. "I trust all of you, so don't wait. Go, and I will pray for a safe trip and your safe return with our comrades."

The five of them took Ben at his word and sprinted to the Wolf armored vehicle Mordecai borrowed from an IDF base. It might make them more visible, but it could go off-road, haul up to twelve people, and provide protection. They left for the Jordanian border and Muwaffaq Salti Air Base, taking back roads trying to remain unseen. Ben was amazed again at his two young soldiers.

"Tell us more, Anders," Ally said, her inquisitive mind yearning to learn all she could about the final three-and-a-half years of Planet Earth.

"There is much more, but I cannot tell you now because Jesus forbade me. Just be aware that the next forty-two months will bring little good news, but lots of bad news. I will guide you every step of the way, as things develop. Not all of us will survive, but we must fight to the end and never give up. Let's make Messai's life miserable!"

What a way to leave them hanging. Each wondered whether they would live or die, but none dared ask Anders to divulge that information, if he even knew. All of them knew, live or die, they would never deny Jesus and worship the Antichrist.

•   •   •   •   •

Ollie drove as the trio neared the turnoff that would take them to the farm. Neither could wrap their mind around it, but something did not feel right. The jetlag must have taken over their bodies and minds. They were quiet as they turned off the main road, now only a couple of minutes away.

Ollie opted to not give Bradley the experience all the others had gone through when he reached the secluded lane leading back to the Shelter. All before him had faced the shock of a sudden right turn into what appeared to be a grove of trees rather than a beautiful lane. Instead, he turned and drove slowly into the canopy of trees covering it.

But things had changed. The lane was no longer the pristine tunnel they had marveled at before. Light seeped through gaps previously covered with leaves. Fallen limbs forced him to weave his way around most and drive over smaller ones. The tires bumped across rocks and pieces of steel and wood. Horror set in as he looked at his passengers. Amelia's fear-covered face said it all.

"Clever blocking the lane with limbs and debris," said Bradley. "Few people would go through the trouble of driving back here. It looks deserted."

"You don't understand," said Ollie. "This was the most beautiful and peaceful drive you can imagine. Something terrible has happened." He stopped as if dreading to go farther.

"Maybe a storm blew through and messed up the trees," Bradley said with a weak sense of hope.

"No storm would explain the other debris," said Amelia. "Bradley, the bunkers are steel, the cabin is wood." She broke down.

Ollie continued driving around and over debris until they exited the lane into the clearing and found it vacant. Amelia screamed.

"No! Dear Jesus, no!"

Only a cavernous hole remained where the bunkers once lay underground, with the cabin sitting over them. The clearing looked like a war zone. In the distance, the barn lay in a pile of wood and tin. They leapt from the car and ran toward their former safe place. Standing on the edge of the expansive crater, Ollie said, "They're all gone," breaking into tears with his wife. Bradley joined them. He had looked forward to seeing this place and meeting the team with such anticipation. Now, he would never see it or them.

•   •   •   •   •

"Partner, the gas has reached empty. This thing will stop running soon and leave us stranded out here in the middle of nowhere. What do we do now?

"We are deep in the mountains, so we should have plenty of hiding options. I guarantee you there are caves all over this place," Magnus said. His optimism did not waver.

The car sputtered and stopped. Bruno pulled to the edge of the dirt road that looked like no one had traveled it for years.

"We need to push this thing into the woods and get it out of sight," Magnus said.

"Let's do it, but what then? We're miles away from other human beings."

"We have two choices: stay in the car or get out and walk. I say we walk."

"Agreed."

They pushed the car far enough into the trees that no one could see it, removed their stuff, and stood staring at the mountainous terrain around them. "Jesus, direct our steps," Magnus said.

"Which way should we go?" asked Bruno.

"I always see God as *due north* now. We are the ones who go south, so when we want to find him, we must turn around and go north."

"Due north leads to the highest peaks. Do you remember the Bible verse we read together our first night in the cave?"

"I will never forget the last line. Psalm 61, verse 2: *'Lead me to the rock that is higher than I.'*"

"Do you know what, Magnus? I believe it was no accident we found that verse. Have you noticed what I see due north of us?"

Magnus looked and saw the highest peak around. Trees lined the mountain, but rising majestically above them, a huge rock protruded and pointed to the sky. Both knew from a few hours driving, to the car running out of fuel at this spot, they had come right where they needed to be. They ran toward the mountain, dodging trees slapping them along the way. Jesus had *led them to the rock.*

•　　　•　　　•　　　•　　　•

Mordecai stopped the Wolf a quarter mile from the border fence. They would never get across at a checkpoint, so they traveled near the place where Michael and Hadassah patrolled the border on the Israel side. The Aluf left them there, aware that he would blow up the entire mission if the Jordanian guards noticed him with the others. No IDF Major General could cross at any point without them taking him into custody. And sneaking across would leave them without a vehicle to drive. Success or failure, and their comrade's lives, depended on Michael and Hadassah's friends.

While Trey and Rickie hid nearby, the two young soldiers made their way to the fence, flashlights in hand. Not seeing anyone, they continued farther down the border.

"Ahmad, Omar, Hala," Hadassah called out softly in Arabic, but got no answer.

They turned off the lights and crept alongside the fence, keeping as quiet as possible.

A light exploded into their eyes, as a voice yelled and two rifles appeared through the wiring. Both dove backward and drew their weapons, aware of the danger they now faced.

"Ha, ha, ha! You should have seen the two of you acting like scared little kids."

"Omar, I swear, if we didn't need your help, I'd deck you right through this fence," said Michael.

"No, you wouldn't. Hadassah wouldn't let you!"

"Stop playing around, you two. We don't have time for this."

"Why are you so serious tonight?" asked Ahmad. "Afraid the Chinese are going to *get you*?"

"Hala, are you back there? I need another woman to help me with these two little boys."

The girl stepped out and smacked Ahmad on the back of his head.

"How do you two need our help?" she asked, giving her two companions a threatening look. They kept quiet and let the Israelis speak.

"We have friends with us from America. They have comrades in grave danger in China. If they don't get them out tomorrow night, they will die. We need to get to Muwaffaq and get a plane for them to fly there. Both are former U.S. military pilots."

Omar shouldered his rifle and spoke in broken English, "Americans, come out now!"

Trey and Rickie stood from their hiding places, put their hands in the air, and came to join them.

"Stop it, Omar," said Hala. "Any friends of Michael and Hadassah are friends of ours. So you need us to drive you to Muwaffaq and vouch for you, is that right?"

From their time spent serving in the Middle East, Trey and Rickie spoke Arabic well enough to communicate, and took the Jordanians by surprise when Trey spoke.

"The Americans stationed at Muwaffaq will help us, if we can get there. We must fly before noon, or our friends will die. Please, help us, if you can."

"Bring them to the opening and get them over here. We will drive you to the base, but we are laying everything on the line for you. If we get caught, it may cost us our lives. We must get back here before daylight, so no one discovers we left our post. It will take close to two hours each way, and it is almost 2:00 a.m. We can make it back by 6:00 a.m., if we do not run into any problems."

"Hala is right. Come now, and we will leave in five minutes."

Ahmad finally agreed. The Americans breathed a sigh of relief as they ran to the opening and crawled through. Michael and Hadassah wished them well, then stood and watched as they got into the jeep. Omar drove as they pulled away, keeping the lights off so no one would see them. When they reached the main road, he turned them on and sped away toward Muwaffaq. The two Israeli soldiers walked back to the armored vehicle where Mordecai waited, got in and gave him the thumbs-up. They prayed again for the men's mission and headed back to the kibbutz.

• • • • •

Bruno and Magnus reached the base of the mountain, panting and out of breath.

"We need to find a place where we can climb. There's no way we can climb right here. If we can't locate a good crossing point, we'll bunk down for the night and try again tomorrow," said Magnus.

He took the lead, and Bruno followed. After walking for hours, they decided the climb would not happen this day, so they opted to make camp by a river, a peaceful spot for the night.

"I'll gather some boughs we can use for shelter. It's going to be cold tonight, and we need something to keep the wind off us. Stay here and find a good place for us to sleep. Tomorrow will bring a full day to get across the mountain."

Bruno left, and Magnus searched for their campsite. The river sounded so peaceful he thought he could go to sleep right then. Bruno's yell interrupted him. He stopped and raced toward the voice, ready to fight for his partner, then met the other big man sprinting back in his direction.

"I found a pass!" Bruno said, gasping for breath. He pointed and grabbed his friend by the arm. "Let's go!"

"A pass? Are you telling me you found a pass through the mountain?"

"Yes! Just ahead. It looks like an opening between two ridges. We have to find out where it leads. If it doesn't go all the way through, at least it will provide great shelter for tonight."

"Help me grab our stuff and let's go!"

Belongings in hand, he followed Bruno, racing around the foot of the towering peak that stood between them and the place Jesus was leading them. He saw the opening before they reached it.

"Bruno, this is perfect! You didn't find this by accident any more than ending up at this place was a stroke of luck. Jesus brought us to *the rock that is higher than us* and showed us the way to the other side!"

The two men entered what appeared to be the only gap in the entire mountain range. It was wide enough for them to walk side-by-side, with a slight ascent that took them up close to a hundred feet. Once they reached the top, a beautiful valley spread out before them. Its size astounded them.

Bruno hit the rocky slope first on his backside and slid toward the valley floor below.

"Yahoo!" he yelled like a kid on a playground slide.

Magnus came behind him, and they slid to a stop on level ground that led into the valley. They ran the rest of the way and arrived in the massive open area.

"You could build an entire city in here!" Bruno said.

"If Chen doesn't find us, we can live in here. Although, we still need to find a way out of this country as fast as we can. But how...?"

"We will," his partner stated, his faith returning. "If Jesus led us here, he will make a way."

"The floor of this valley is as hard as concrete. We will have to sleep on the grass around the edge," Magnus said, falling to the ground. "Wow! This is like carpet!" He laughed from pure happiness, as he rolled around in the lush green area surrounding the valley.

Bruno joined him. Both were tired, but the rest of the day provided a great opportunity to explore their home for the night, and possibly longer.

"Made it in an hour and forty-five minutes!" Omar said to his passengers as they neared the gate at Muwaffaq Salti Air Base. He got out and greeted the soldiers standing guard.

"Private First Class Omar Saleh," he said, saluting the guards.

"State your purpose for being here, private."

"I need your help for an urgent mission. Is it okay for some American troops to join us?"

It surprised him to see the guard on his radio so fast, calling for American troops to come. Two men arrived in less than five minutes. Omar motioned for Trey and Rickie to get out of the jeep.

"Retired Majors Trey Butler and Rickie Cruz," said Trey, saluting the guards.

"Hey, I have heard about both of you guys," said one of the Americans. "Your combat skills are legendary. It is a pleasure to meet you." He stepped back and saluted them.

"I don't know about legendary," said Rickie, "but we gave our all for our country."

"Come in and tell us what you need," said one Jordanian guard.

"We must return, so we leave them in your care," Omar said. "I trust you will give them what they need, because their mission is urgent and requires immediate attention."

Ahmad was out of the jeep now, too. Both men saluted the guards, then turned to Trey and Rickie, saluting them also before getting back in and driving away.

Thirty minutes later, the two Smyrnians sat with the base commander and American officers explaining their situation. Trey got right down to business.

"We need to fly before noon, 11:00 or earlier would be better. Anything later than that will abort the entire mission, and our comrades will die on Chinese soil. We can't let that happen! Please give us a plane so we can *get them out*." He intentionally used the words of the voice in his dream.

"You have no chance of flying into China, you understand that, right? I would be a fool to let you use a plane knowing neither you nor it would make it back here."

"Sir, I give you my word that we will return with our comrades *and* your plane."

"Excuse me, commander," one of the American officers interrupted the conversation. "These men are two of the best fighter pilots who ever flew for the United States Military. If they give you their word, you can count on it. I understand the impossibility of their mission, but I promise you they have a plan and understand exactly how they will carry it out."

"Okay, assuming you make it past the border without getting blown out of the sky, where do you propose to land? No airport or military base in China is allowing you in."

"In a hidden valley deep in the mountains, sir."

"Do you realize how big a plane you need? And you want to land in a valley between mountains?"

"Yes, sir. A C-5M Super Galaxy can make it..." The commander interrupted him in mid-sentence.

"I will not allow this to happen, even if the Americans are our allies. If the higher ups knew we were even talking about this, I would lose my military career. I'm sorry, but I cannot put my career on the line for an impossible mission!" He got up and stormed toward the door.

"Sir, please contact Sergeant Major Clark and ask his opinion. Since the two of you so often rely on each other for important decisions, shouldn't you get his thoughts about this?"

Trey and Rickie glanced at each other. The commander wheeled around and glared at the man.

"I will do just that, and we will hear what he says. That should put an end to this foolishness."

Within minutes, he connected Clark on a FaceTime call.

"Sergeant Major, I apologize for waking you at such an early hour, but we have a situation here that requires your attention."

"You did not wake me, commander. I may be in Jordan, but I *am* still in the United States Military... and it *is* after 6:00 a.m. Now, what is this pressing matter that is so important?"

"Two retired American fighter pilots are here asking to use one of our planes to fly a ridiculous mission to China. I have already told them *no*, but one of your men here said I should call you about the matter. Now they can hear it from you too." He glared at the man again.

"Who are these men, and what makes them think you would just allow them to take a plane from the base? Let me get a look at them."

Trey and Rickie walked into view. "Hello, Robert. It's good to see you again."

"Trey Butler and Rickie Cruz! What are you doing in Jordan? And why in the world are you asking for a plane to fly to China?"

"Robert, there are three American citizens there who are in grave danger and will die tonight if we don't *get them out.*" He used the words again, knowing they came from Jesus, and prayed under his breath for Jesus to take control of this situation.

"Commander, if these men say they need a plane, give them a plane! I will vouch for them and guarantee their return with the American citizens and your plane. You are looking at two of the most decorated pilots of the United States Military!"

"But Sergeant Major, this is crazy! I cannot do this!"

"Look, Zaid, this decision belongs to you. I cannot, nor would I try to force you to grant their request. However, it would mean a lot to me if you would do it. I will come to the base and be there tomorrow to greet them when they return. You and I can share a meal, a glass of wine, and a good time as we wait together. Come on, Zaid. Three men will die if you turn them down."

Everyone in the room watched the commander struggle with the decision. Trey and Rickie prayed, aware that Ben, Mordecai, Michael, Hadassah, and the others at the kibbutz were praying too. It seemed like hours, but it was only two minutes until Commander Zaid Hassan spoke again.

"You may take a plane, but I swear..."

"You need not swear, Zaid, nor will you regret your decision. Thank you," Robert Clark added, as he smiled at the commander.

The two Americans tried to contain their excitement and conduct themselves like professionals. They stood and reached for the commander's hand.

"Thank you, sir. You just saved three American lives, and you will meet them tomorrow."

There was much to do, but it appeared they would fly earlier than expected. *Go where Jesus leads you, guys, and we will come to you*, Trey said in his mind, as if they could hear him. From four thousand miles away, he believed they did.

•　　•　　•　　•　　•

Ollie, Amelia, and Bradley stood stunned and heartbroken as they stared at the massive crater where the bunkers once housed the team. Nothing, or no one was left of their former home away from home or their teammates and friends.

"A bunker-busting bomb," Ollie said. "But how did they find them, and who did this? Messai? Or did he use China to do his evil work? I am so angry right now, I would take him out if I could!"

He climbed into the cavity, followed by Bradley, while Amelia walked around the outside. Bradley listened as Ollie explained everything on their way down.

"A beautiful little cabin sat here, with a trapdoor hidden in a tiny closet that led to steps down to the bunkers. Even the steel walls didn't survive. It's incomprehensible that any bomb could destroy steel."

"China did this, Ollie. They have the technology to blow up anything."

"But how did they fly all the way to the U.S.?"

"Remember the planes that tried to take us down today? I told you flying to the UK and farther was possible for them. They now have fighter jets that can fly to the U.S. It was them."

While they walked, Ollie told him about each bunker and the good times and hard times the Smyrnians experienced living in them for three years.

"Amelia and I married right here in Bunker One." He broke into tears again, as Bradley did what he could to comfort him.

"Ollie, I am so sorry. This must hurt you more than anything else ever has. It hurts our cause for the next three-and-a-half years even more. But it also makes me more ready to fight Aissa Messai than ever! We will make him pay for this!"

"*Ollie!*" They heard Amelia scream and clawed their way out of the crater faster than either thought they could scale the dirt wall. They reached the top and climbed out, hearing her scream again.

"*Over here!*"

They sprinted toward her, hearts racing.

"Look!" she said, pointing at the ground and piles of rubble surrounding an opening.

"Someone was out here," she said, pointing to rocks and rubble on the side. "Blood…"

"Whoever was here got badly injured. There's blood all over this debris."

"But Ollie, notice something!" Bradley said.

"What? I see blood, meaning someone probably died here, Bradley. What else do you want me to notice? Isn't that enough? I can only think about which one it was."

"Ollie, whoever it was isn't here! The bombers didn't land. No soldiers came. That means this person either walked away from this or others carried him away!"

"Ollie," Amelia said in a trembling voice. "Do you think some of them…"

"Survived? We know they weren't all inside. Is it possible some or all of them got away?!"

"Did you notice something else?"

"What, Bradley, what?" Ollie asked, as he grabbed the man by his arms and looked into his face.

"There are no vehicles! Did the group park them away from the property, or maybe hide them?"

"Amelia, he's right! The vehicles are all gone. Enough of them must have survived to drive every vehicle. We have to find them!"

"Let's check the barn," Bradley said, as he dashed toward the fallen structure. Ollie and Amelia followed in a sprint.

"Under here!" Amelia was the first to find evidence again as she crawled under the side of the barn that leaned on large, round bales of hay. The men crawled in behind her. A torn piece of clothing hung from a nail sticking out of the wood.

"I've seen Beth wear this shirt! They made it to the barn, Ollie, and they're not here now!"

"Several of them hid in here. You can tell where they were and follow their tracks where they pulled themselves out! See how the straw on the floor was all dragged in this direction?"

"And it keeps going outside the barn," said Bradley. "Their feet pulled it out as they slid, which means the barn came down after they got inside."

"They ran in, but crawled out," said Ollie. "That means they're alive!"

"Right!" said Bradley, feeling the excitement of their discovery.

"How did they know the bombs were coming?" asked Amelia, amazed at what they found.

"Jesus," Ollie said. "No one else would've known bombers were on the way. It had to be Jesus."

"Where do you think they went?"

It hit Ollie as soon as she asked. "Steve and Linda's house."

"You're right! But we've never been there, so how will we find it?"

"I'm not sure, but I'm certain we will."

CHAPTER 4

Anders called the others together again, and they came running, hoping he would tell them more about his experiences in heaven. They were disappointed when he said why he called them.

"We need to pray. Something is going on with members of our team somewhere."

"Bruno," Mila said.

"I can't tell whether it's happening in China, England, or Israel. For all I know, it may be all three. I have an awareness now that wasn't there before I ate that scroll. It's like I feel it inside."

"You *are* different, Anders," said Ally. "Something changed when you went to heaven. I'm not so sure it was eating the scroll. I think it may have been spending time with Jesus."

"Well, I believe we need to pray, if Anders feels that," Blake said.

They held hands as Anders prayed. Something was different about the way he prayed, too. The words came out as though he stood face-to-face with Jesus talking to him about something important. His glow returned and filled the room with glorious light. None of them doubted Jesus was present with the others, as he was present with them in this moment, wherever they were, and whatever they needed from him.

Muwaffaq was abuzz with activity as a crew prepared the plane that Trey and Rickie would fly to China on a daring rescue mission. Trey got more nervous as the morning passed. At last, the big aircraft was ready to go, and the time to board arrived.

"Commander, you do not know what this means to us," Trey said, shaking Zaid's hand.

"You would not have flown without Sergeant Major Clark's recommendation. I trust you will take care of our plane and save the lives of your comrades. Do not waste my decision by failing!"

"We will not fail, commander, because an unseen one flies with us. I'd love to tell you more about that when we return."

They climbed aboard without saying another word, leaving Commander Zaid Hassan wondering what Trey meant by his last statement. But none of that mattered as long as his plane returned.

•   •   •   •   •

Ollie found himself frustrated to no end trying to find Steve and Linda's address in Springfield. The nuclear war wiped out technology and communication. Something that should have been a simple task, now felt like an impossible quest.

But Bradley seemed to have insight into every part of their situation. First, he pointed out the wounded person no longer lay there, meaning he either walked away or someone carried him. That meant not everyone died in the explosion. Then he noticed the vehicles were not there, meaning *they* drove them away. Now, as Ollie fretted and fumed over this problem, he came through again.

"You said Steve is a well-known surgeon. I assume that means many people in Springfield are familiar with him and Linda. Doesn't it make sense to drive into town and ask around?"

Ollie's face turned red from embarrassment. "This whole thing has me so torn up I can't even think on my own. I'm glad you are with us, Bradley. I don't know what we would've done without you."

"Just glad I can help. Now, can we get on with finding this surgeon's house? I have waited forever to meet the rest of the team. Please don't make me wait any longer!"

"You're right, Bradley. Why are we standing around here grieving like everybody died when we're pretty sure most of them are still alive? We need to leave. I can't take this place anymore." Amelia grabbed her husband by the arm and pulled him along as they followed Bradley to the car.

Miriam heard a knock on the door of their home in the kibbutz. Ben sat at the kitchen table with Mordecai, Michael, and Hadassah drinking coffee and talking about Trey and Rickie. Miriam answered the door, expecting a neighbor from the kibbutz showing up with some goodies, never an unusual occurrence in a close-knit community. She jumped back, alarmed.

"Ben!"

Her husband ran into the living room, startled by his wife's scream, and discovered a man dressed in a military uniform standing at his door. His dress wasn't that of a typical IDF soldier.

"May I ask why you are knocking on our door at this time of the morning?" he asked, just as the other three walked into the room, joining him.

"Omar?" asked Hadassah, the surprise in her voice obvious.

"You know this man?" asked Mordecai.

"Uncle, this is Omar, one of the three soldiers who helped Trey and Rickie this morning."

"So, this is the *friend* you hang out with instead of fulfilling your duty at the border."

"You're the Aluf!" Omar said, both shocked and afraid.

"And Hadassah's uncle," Mordecai said with a stern glance.

"Sir, I wasn't aware of that, so I apologize if I have caused her to do anything wrong. We intended no harm. She is Israeli, and I am Jordanian, but we are friends despite our countries differences."

Another soldier appeared from behind Omar.

"Ahmad?" Hadassah asked in a surprised voice again.

"We came to give you a report on the two Americans," said Ahmad. "May we come in?"

"Of course, you may," said Ben, "but how did you find us, and how did you get in here? This place is secure."

"Please do not think I am bragging," said Omar, "but we can find anyone and get into just about any place. You should tell your security forces to stay more alert to intruders."

Now it was Ben's turn to look shocked. How had these two young soldiers pulled this off with no one stopping them? He would talk to the leaders of the kibbutz about this before the day ended.

Without thinking, Ahmad said with a wry smile, "Omar can always find Hadassah."

Mordecai took a step toward the man, but Hadassah stepped in front of him, a sheepish look on her face.

"Uncle, they came to give us news about Trey and Rickie. Should we not listen to what they have to tell us?"

Ahmad noticed the Aluf. *He's Hadassah's uncle?* He stepped backward toward the door.

"Come with us into the kitchen. We will drink coffee while you tell us about our comrades."

Ben diffused the situation for the moment. He just wanted to hear about Trey and Rickie. The six of them, plus Miriam, walked into the next room and sat down to talk.

"Okay, out with it!" demanded Mordecai.

"Uncle, please do not yell at my friends. Do you want to hear what they have to say or not?"

Once again, she melted his heart, and he calmed down to listen. Omar seemed unfazed by the outburst.

"We drove your friends to Muwaffaq and left them there. We had to get back to our posts before 6:00 a.m. or we would have stayed. I am sure you understand that, sir," he said to Mordecai.

"I do," came the reply. "Please continue."

"We contacted the base just before we came here and received word that they granted them a plane for their mission."

The others in the room celebrated those words before Omar could continue.

"Do you have any more information about them?" asked Ben.

"They will probably fly earlier than expected and hope to depart no later than 11:00 a.m."

As the celebration continued at Ben and Miriam's house, a plane lifted off from Muwaffaq Salti Air Base with only Trey Butler and Rickie Cruz aboard.

"Okay partner, we're on our way to China," Trey told Rickie as the big plane climbed into the air and he retracted the landing gear. The time was 10:00 a.m., an hour earlier than expected.

"Yes, we are," Rickie replied. "Only two crazy people would embark on a mission like this."

"Or two people who have followed Jesus and believe he has everything under control."

"Right you are again! Let's go over the details and make sure *we* have everything under control on our end, too. We should make the flight in nine to ten hours, and they're six hours ahead of us. That means you should set this thing down in the valley around 2:00 a.m. over there, assuming the Chinese don't shoot us down first."

"Don't even say that! You're my co-pilot in this cockpit, but we both have another co-pilot who will protect us while we do the flying."

"Jesus... Of course, I realize that, but it doesn't mean we shouldn't also prepare the best we can. You have the coordinates, so they should lead us right to the valley. Are you sure it has ample room to clear the peaks and land inside?"

"Yes, Rickie, I am sure. Listen, Jesus gave me the command to *get them out*, and I planned the *route*. And yes, I made that rhyme on purpose so you will *chill*." He grinned at his buddy.

"Okay, partner, you got it. Now, tell me about the route you planned. Are we flying straight in?"

"Yep, we have no other option, if we're going to get in and out on time. I wish we could take an around about route and fly down over India and back up over Beijing, but time won't permit that. We're going directly over Iran and Afghanistan and straight into China. That should get us there in ten hours, or less."

"Hey, I'm with you, so wherever you go, I'm going, too. Just remember, on the way back, you'll fly with me, so wherever I go, *you're* going too! What mountain range is this again?"

"The Yanshan Range, at least that's what they call it. Most just say Yan Mountains. It's not too far north of Beijing, maybe seventy or eighty miles. We'll be close to the Mongolian border and too close to North Korea for comfort, if we flew this mission alone. But we aren't on our own. The one who told us to go will take care of us. Now, just sit back and let me fly."

"I trust you, so I'd better get some sleep if I'm bringing this baby back. I can't wait to see Bruno, Magnus, and Malachi."

"Neither can I, partner, neither can I. Good night."

The flight continued to the most dangerous country in the world, where three of their comrades would die if they did not *get them out.* Neither realized one was already with Jesus.

•   •   •   •   •   •

Ollie, Amelia, and Bradley arrived in Springfield and began stopping to ask people if they knew where Steve and Linda Phillips lived. Almost everyone recognized Steve's name, but either no one knew the location of his home, or they refused to divulge that information. Several looked at them suspiciously, and some asked why they came searching for the surgeon and his wife.

Finally, they stopped at a small market that was still open and asked the owner.

"Are you three friends of theirs?" the man asked.

"Steve and Linda are close friends to Amelia and me," said Ollie, chastising himself for giving the owner her name. The two of them were still near the top of Aissa Messai's Most Wanted List, and any slip of the tongue could give them away. "Bradley here has never met them, but we plan to introduce him as soon as we find them."

Then, using his British accent, he offered a slight fabrication of the truth.

"We have hosted them in England and visited with them in the states, but never in their home here in Springfield, even though we talked about it. I can tell you they are proud to call this place home."

"The nuclear war stuck us in the U.S., so we're looking for acquaintances to help us. Since we can't contact Steve and Linda by telephone, we need someone to show us where they live, or take us to their house, but no one will. This town may not be as friendly as the two of them say it is."

"You aren't far from their house. I will give you the address and write the directions for you. I hope you find them with no trouble. If you don't mind me saying, all three of you look exhausted."

"We appreciate this so much. And trust me, we're worn out. We've had a really long day."

They left and drove straight to Steve and Linda's house, just as the man said. Outside, Ollie and Amelia both recognized the Lincoln Navigator, but did not see any other vehicles the group drove.

"Do you think they went somewhere else?" Amelia asked, with obvious concern in her voice.

"I'll bet the other cars are in that four-car garage," said Bradley. "It should hold all of them." His suggestions had been on target all day, and this one made sense too.

"I'm guessing you're right!" said Ollie. "Let's see if we can peek through a window."

"Ollie!" said Amelia, "you're not doing that! We will walk up and ring the doorbell."

When they did, Steve opened the door and burst into a wide smile. Not wanting to make noise or draw attention, he pulled all three of them inside and embraced the couple.

"Bradley Rodgers," said the other man, reaching for Steve's hand.

"Bradley, it is good to meet you at last. Thank you for all you have done for the Smyrnians."

"It has been an honor, Mr. Phillips. And it is a greater honor to be one of you!"

"Call me Steve, please. We are teammates and brothers, so first names only. Now, let's go into the den and call everyone else. I hate it has to be this way, but when someone comes to the door, the others run and hide while I answer it."

As they walked into the next room, Steve yelled for the rest to join them. A momentary celebration occurred when they saw each other.

"*Ollie!*" Beth squealed as she did when he came to the U.S. to cover the story of Aissa Messai's election as Secretary-General of the United Nations. That was also the time he believed in Jesus.

They all embraced, and Bradley got introduced to his fellow Smyrnians. But Amelia noticed someone was missing.

"Where is Evan?"

Ally broke into tears and they realized who had not survived.

"Oh no, not Evan." Amelia pulled Ally close and cried with her. "Ally, honey, I am so sorry. I know how much you loved Evan. We loved him too."

"We were leaving, and Blake started back inside to get the hard drive with all the information on it. But Evan volunteered to go and ran back in. He made it back up into the cabin and waved at us through the window, holding the hard drive in his hand. Then the bomb hit..." Her voice choked up with so much emotion she could not continue. The room filled with tears again.

"But I have another story to tell that I think you will want to hear," said Anders.

•   •   •   •   •

Trey flew over Iran, knowing there was just as much danger of getting shot down in Iranian airspace as Chinese airspace. Rickie slept in the back, leaving him alone with his thoughts. He prayed, sang, talked to himself, whatever it took to occupy his mind and avoid imagining a missile slamming into the plane any minute.

The passage over Iraq was smooth. But flying right over the middle of Iran, Afghanistan, and Pakistan created some anxiety, even for a seasoned combat veteran. He had flown too many missions in the Middle East during his days in the military to not stay alert to potential danger, especially in Iran. So far, things were smooth and his mind dwelt on rescuing the three Smyrnians.

The valley flashed through his mind. He would circle around Beijing, north near the border of Mongolia, then land heading south where he could take off as soon as the men got on board. His hope continued to focus on the men making it to the valley. They had not communicated with each other. He was acting only on a vivid dream, a gentle breeze, and three simple words: *get them out.* The sound of footsteps roused him from his thoughts. Rickie was awake.

"Looks like we're still in the air. I guess that's a good sign." Rickie yawned, running his hand through his rumpled hair.

"Yes, we are, partner, straight over Iran."

"You sure get a guy excited right after he wakes up from a sound sleep."

"Don't think I haven't thought about it since we crossed the border. Iraq made me nervous, but Iran shakes me up. I wish we had time to fly the southern route and avoid these three countries, but we wouldn't get there till daylight, if we did."

"You're doing fine, man. Just keep this thing moving."

"That's what I intend to do. We're a quarter of the way there, but it sure seems slow."

They flew on talking for about fifteen minutes when a sudden alarming sound sent them scrambling.

"*SAM!*" Rickie yelled.

The aircraft immediately engaged in an anti-missile maneuver as the incoming surface-to-air missile flashed by on their left.

"I didn't think the doggone Iranians would let us pass over without trying to knock us down," said Trey. The missile approach warning sounded again. Another countermeasure, avoiding the device intended to destroy them.

"Climb!" shouted Rickie.

"Going up! We have to get above their range!"

The big plane gained altitude as fast as possible.

"You know what's next."

"I do, and there they come!"

Two Iranian bombers flew toward them, ready for action. The warning screamed again, and the plane entered another evasive maneuver.

"This has gotten old real quick. I wish we were flying our bombers again. We'd school these boys a little, then take them out before they realized what hit them. But I feel like a sitting duck in this thing because we can't fight back! How long can we avoid them?"

"Now there's three of them!"

All three bombers lined up behind them.

"We're locked up!" shouted Trey. "There's nothing I can do if all three fire at us, and that's what they're getting ready to do!"

The MAW screamed at them one more time, then went silent within seconds.

"What the heck just happened?" asked Rickie. "I think we're done for."

It all occurred as if in virtual slow motion. The three bombers sent missiles at the plane, but the system remained silent, with no countermeasure this time. Both men prepared for impact, realizing missiles were coming and knowing it was over. They gave it their best shot.

Trey wondered why Jesus called him to go, then worked out all the details just to allow this to happen. *Some things defy explanation*, he reasoned.

Three missiles zeroed in on them, with impact imminent. Some say pilots never see missiles coming their way, but Trey and Rickie saw these. All three deflected left or right, zooming away from them, leaving behind a trail of white smoke. The two men glanced at each other, wondering how the bombers missed from such close range.

"Do you see that?" asked Rickie.

"I see it, but what is it? It looks like a giant bubble."

They watched as missiles launched one more time, again deflecting and trailing away. This time they saw what happened. The bombs hit the shield, which they now realized was invisible to the invaders, but clear to them. The attackers left them, no doubt frustrated by something they could not comprehend. But the two men flying toward China understood perfectly.

"I prayed for a hedge of protection around us as we flew," said Trey, "but I never envisioned it like this. We're surrounded by an invisible safeguard. Nothing can touch us!"

"Bring on Afghanistan, and even China," said Rickie, the excitement in his voice unmistakable.

Bruno and Magnus explored the valley for hours. At one place, they discovered water flowing from the rocky mountainside. It tasted like the sweetest water either had ever drunk. They enjoyed the soft grass beneath their feet as they walked around the perimeter and ran on the hard surface in the middle. The mountains surrounding them provided perfect protection. If only the team was here. This place must be the safest location on the planet!

"I can't help but think about Malachi and wish he was here," said Magnus.

"Me too," said Bruno, "but I also understand he would want us to escape from this wicked country. So, we need to talk about our next moves."

"I say we stay right here for a few days while we try to figure that out. It will be hard to find us in here. Even if they locate the valley, there are plenty of places to hide."

"I agree. To be honest, I can't think of any way out of the country. The dragon told us he always knows where we are, so does that mean he knows we are here? If he does, no hiding place will stop him from finding us."

"Maybe not, but I can't help but chuckle when I think of him leading Chen and his troops to the cave and not finding us there. I imagine plenty of fire will shoot out of that ugly face."

"Okay, enough of that. Let's talk about a plan."

"We don't have a plan, Bruno, nor can we come up with one. These last few days have taken their toll on us, so I say we take a couple of down days to relax in this valley. We need it."

"Okay, you win. I could lie right here forever."

He stretched out in the green grass that shouldn't even survive in this place and time. There was only one answer, and they both knew it. Jesus prepared this valley just for them.

"Look what time it is," Magnus said, glancing at his watch. "It will get dark soon. We need to hurry back to our *bunking down* place." He smiled as he said, "I'll race you!"

Off they ran like two big kids having fun playing together. They reached the spot, pulled some food from their bags and ate, then sat and talked about the beauty surrounding them. When daylight faded and darkness filled the valley, exhaustion consumed their bodies, and they couldn't stay awake any longer. It had been a tiring, yet wonderful day. Each snuggled down into the soft grass, which was tall enough to provide cover, and within minutes, fell sound asleep.

Trey and Rickie continued their flight with confidence in the safety of their protective shield. The time passed much faster as they talked and planned for what would happen when they landed.

"The valley is massive, Rickie, so finding them may be a tougher task than we imagined."

"But, partner, I promise you they will notice this baby coming over the mountains and touching down. If that doesn't wake them, nothing will. But we have to make sure they realize it's us. How do we do that?"

"We jump out the minute the plane stops and start yelling for them. That will echo up and down that canyon so loud they can't miss us. I'm sure they will recognize these two big mouths. Well, there goes Pakistan. We'll cross the Chinese border soon!"

"Imagine flying right over Beijing with a bubble of protection, knowing they can't get near us. My guess is, they won't even hear us!"

"I think you're right, so let's do this thing!"

The dragon ambled back and forth in his hellish lair, sparks shooting from his mouth, surrounded by demonic beings eager to do his every bidding.

"Someone conceals something from me," he hissed. "The one called Jesus seeks to prevent me from locating the Smyrnians, and achieving my eternal destiny. The two in the cave have moved. I sense it, but I cannot tell where they have gone. Go in search of them, my army, and return to tell me where they hide. I disposed of the spy, but we must not allow the others to escape!"

The screeching, howling creatures flew around him, as one named Belial knelt before him. "We will do as you say, master. We have but a short time to find them, and Michael and his army will surely protect them and fight against us. But he cannot defeat me anymore than the one called Jesus can overcome you!"

His screech filled the air, witnessed only by the evil spirit beings around him. He led the army of demons out, flying toward the mountains.

"Go, my troops, and return victorious!"

He threw his head back and let out a resounding roar as flames shot high into the night. The great battle drew near and he must win. He would never stop trying to destroy Jesus and overthrow the one who cast him out. This was his moment, and the power of darkness would prevail. The roars continued, dispatching his demons on their mission and empowering them to conquer the enemy.

Trey and Rickie now flew over Beijing and continued north toward the border of Mongolia, preparing to approach the valley from that direction. The time was 1:30 a.m., just as they planned. Both were aware flying from south to north was more difficult than flying west to east, the direction they flew coming over. But they encountered an unexpected headwind fighting against them.

"I don't understand what's going on with this wind," said Trey. "It's like we're sitting still a few miles from our destination. This thing is shaking like it's going to fall apart!"

"Me either," said Rickie. "It's like some invisible force fighting against us. Does that make sense?"

"We know who's behind it. Do me a favor and pray while I fly because I'm in a dogfight here."

Rickie prayed aloud, then something changed in him. Trey had witnessed nothing like it, unless it was the time Anders prayed for Rickie on the plane returning from Germany. That simple prayer saved his partner's life, but it bore no resemblance to what Rickie was doing now. He stood, hands outstretched toward the front, his voice growing louder with each sentence. Trey watched in amazement, not understanding what was happening.

Rickie leaned in now as if pushing against a force that pushed back against him. His hair blew like he was outside in the wind, his prayer almost deafening.

"Jesus, his forces are attacking us! He seeks to defeat you and destroy us, but *you* are more powerful than him. This is that time of distress that has never happened from the beginning of nations until now. Let Michael, the Great Prince who protects your people, arise and give us victory this night! Send him to fight against the dragon and his angels who oppose us. Overpower them, Lord, and help us break through this struggle. We must rescue our comrades. Fight for us, Lord, for the battle is not ours; it is yours! Defeat them, Jesus, and give us victory!"

Trey struggled to maintain his focus on flying the plane. A battle raged in the spirit world, and Rickie stood in the gap, calling forth the army of God to come to their aid. That sounded like quotes from the Bible, but Trey had never read them. Rickie was praying scripture! He shook now, arms still extended, muscles bulging, veins popping out. Sweat poured from his face. An unstoppable force met an immovable object as the battle raged. One must give in soon.

Rickie could not stand against the force on his own, so Trey prayed too, hearing his own words growing in intensity like Rickie's. He called out the names of Jesus and Michael. The plane shuddered more now, trying to break through an invisible wall that prevented them from making it to the valley and their teammates. He was certain the trio made it there, and he had to reach them. This was no normal war! Satan sought to kill them and deal a blow to their cause. This battle may determine the course of the remaining three-plus years of the Tribulation.

He felt like a drag racer, accelerator pressed to the floor, holding the clutch, waiting for the flag to drop, releasing him to fire toward the finish line. What did his partner see? Who fought against him? Victory would either come soon, or they would crash into the mountains below.

The dragon roared encouragement to his forces.

"Fight, Belial, fight! Attack, my strong ones, for you are mightier than they! His strength pales compared to your own, Belial! You can defeat him in my power!"

The battle raged as the angelic host led by Michael the Archangel pushed back the forces of Belial, continuing the charge until the weakened demonic horde abandoned the fight. Michael left the battle as his forces chased the horde who fled in retreat.

"No!" the dragon bellowed.

Michael charged after him, reaching him within seconds. The dragon had neither time nor power to resist. The mighty warrior angel stood in triumph watching the dragon retreat with his army.

"This is not the end!" he screeched at Michael.

The dragon would now set his attention on another enemy he must defeat. His pursuit of that mortal enemy would lead to a more brutal clash with the Archangel and his forces. He lost this battle, but it was not the end of the eternal conflict. One more battle lay ahead with the Chief Prince of heaven. He must win that one.

Suddenly, Rickie lurched forward, as if released by the removal of an invisible force. His body crashed into the instrument panel, and his head struck the windshield. When that happened, the plane shot forward at full throttle, sending him backwards to the floor. Trey slammed back against his seat with force severe enough to cause whiplash. The sudden forward propulsion hurt neither, but stunned both. Trey had *popped the clutch* and now raced toward the finish line!

Magnus thought he was dreaming again when he noticed the faint sound of a plane. He opened his eyes and found himself outside in the dark, with the plane getting closer. The night air snapped him to his senses. *The valley!* He was in the valley. To his right, Bruno snored as he slept. He must wake him! They needed to run for their lives or hide in the nearest place they could find. The plane would pop over the mountaintop any second, and those inside must not see them.

Chen! He found them! But how? *The dragon.* The vile beast must have given them away. Bruno says the creature always knows where they are. He ran to his partner, shaking him much harder than he intended.

"What now, Magnus? If you're dreaming again, please wait and tell me in the morning."

"I'm not dreaming! Do you hear that?"

"It's a plane, Magnus. Go back to sleep." He rolled over, before leaping to his feet and yelling, "They found us! Run!"

The big plane appeared over the mountain and descended.

"We can make it back to the pass, if we hurry! Come on!" Bruno ran in the darkness but tripped and fell after only a few feet.

"Look," said Magnus, staring at the valley floor.

Bruno raised his head and saw it too, trying to comprehend what was happening. A light glow hovered above the hard ground, illuminating it. Neither man moved, both captivated by what they saw. Something inside them begged to flee, but their legs refused to move. The plane touched down and rolled along the valley floor until it came to a stop a hundred yards from them. All they could do was stand and watch, fearing the fire of the dragon burning them alive.

In the faint glow, they watched the door raise and two men exit the plane. They waited for the rest of Chen's men to spill out, armed, searching for them, knowing they were powerless to stop them.

"Bruno! Magnus! Malachi!"

The names echoed off the canyon walls, reverberating through the valley. They kept coming.

"Bruno, Magnus, Malachi, where are you?"

Both recognized the voices. It was not Chen or the dragon. Trey and Rickie! They ran toward them, the ground underneath them now bright and visible. Maybe it was a mirage, or a dream, or the dragon leading them into his trap, but they ran anyway. The others sprinted toward them, too.

When they met, Bruno and Magnus each grabbed one of their friends and lifted them from the ground in bone-crushing embraces. All four wept from joy until the big men released them.

"Is this real, or am I dreaming again?" asked Magnus.

"Oh, we are very real," said Trey. "Grab your stuff, and let's go. Where's Malachi?"

He knew the answer from the look in their eyes. So did Rickie.

"He didn't make it, did he?" Rickie asked, tears again filling his eyes.

"The dragon killed him. He burned him to death," said Bruno through clenched teeth, his hatred for the beast pouring out. "We buried him in the cave he scouted out as a place for us to hide."

"We can talk about that as we fly. I will back the plane up and give us space to take off while you get your things." The news about Malachi put a damper on an otherwise victorious night.

The four of them loaded up and prepared to fly from China back to Jordan. From there, they would find a way to Israel and the kibbutz, safe from the dragon, at least for now.

CHAPTER 5

It was 8:00 in Israel, and Hadassah returned from an evening walk with her uncle in the kibbutz. She glimpsed a figure appearing between two houses just down from them.

"I'm going to stay out here for a little while before I go in, Uncle. Don't worry, I won't take long."

As soon as he walked inside, she darted for the place and found him standing there.

"Where have you been, Michael? When you sneak back in at this time of the evening, aren't you afraid someone will see you?"

"Something came up I had to handle. No big deal."

"I know better than that. Come, let's go inside, and you can tell me all about it!"

They shared many times like this, and he always filled her in on the details. This was his purpose for being here. God sent him, and he found the perfect entrance when Ben spoke on the mountain that day in Galilee and confided in her soon after. She had a purpose too but hadn't realized it yet. The final years of Planet Earth required his presence as the action ramped up, leading to the great final battle. Followers of Jesus needed help now more than ever, and watching over the people of God had been his role from the beginning.

"It was the dragon and Belial, up to their old tricks again. I realized when we arranged the plane for Trey and Rickie, they would need our help. So the army was on standby and awaiting the call."

"Ah, you fought a battle tonight! You're in good shape for a guy who just faced off with the devil!"

"Yes, but remember, these skirmishes are only preludes to the great battle. I must fight these, but Jesus will fight that one and win! He promised those who believe in him and follow him he will always be with them. Wow, is he ever coming through with that! You might say this is his time to shine! Although, the last battle looms soon, and it will be real."

"I love how Yahweh and Jesus do things, like arranging the plane for Trey and Rickie. Zaid Hassan struggled with the decision but didn't realize it was already made, and he couldn't stop it! Neither did Omar, Ahmad, and Hala understand Yahweh was using them to set it all up. It's fun to watch!"

"Don't forget Trey's dream, going to the valley and hearing those words whispered in his ear: *get them out.* Even having the coordinates put in his mind so he wouldn't forget them. That was great!"

"If you liked that, you should've seen them show off tonight over Iran. They bubble-wrapped the plane so the Iranian missiles couldn't touch it! I wish you had heard their pilots when they saw the missiles bouncing off and nothing causing it. Such language." He shook his head and covered his ears.

"I wish I could have been there to watch. But my walk with *uncle* was important. He plays a huge role in helping our people for the next three-and-a-half years. Come on, you're stalling. Tell me about the battle!"

"It was awesome, Hadassah! Belial thinks he has such power, but he is so easy," he said and grinned. "No, seriously, the fight was tough. Yahweh's army fought hard, and the horde didn't give up without a fight. They tried to stop the plane right over Beijing and keep it from reaching the valley, and they almost succeeded. The prayers of the men in that plane propelled us to victory. I love most how Yahweh uses people to fight his battles and gives them victory."

"I hope his people realize how important their prayers are. They can change everything when the battle is raging."

"They did that tonight. Rickie fought alongside us when he prayed, pushing the horde back and allowing us to advance against them, even though he didn't realize it. The horde pushed so hard against that plane they brought it to a complete stop in midair, not moving at all."

"One man in that cockpit, Rickie Cruz, pushed back. You should have seen him fighting. He is a powerful man, but he did not win this battle with physical strength. His prayer, his courage, his determination... He refused to quit, and Trey joined him, praying as he flew."

"I love it when that happens! Now, tell me more about the battle," she said, eager for details and hanging on every word. She existed for moments like this, and many more of them would come, growing in intensity with each passing day as time grew shorter.

"The hosts of heaven charged them with swords drawn and broke through their ranks, scattering them and breaking their hold. It was so cool! I have picked up their language too, haven't I?" After a chuckle, he continued.

"I must give Belial credit. He believes his master can give him the strength to overcome us, but he doesn't realize the dragon's limitations. When things got rough tonight, Belial ran away like a little child, and the others followed. I flew to the dragon and caught up to him, then he fled with them!"

"But we both know he's not quitting. He will never surrender until Jesus defeats him once and for all. He will turn up the pressure on our people soon. But the next time I get my hands on him will be different. I'll show him and his demonic horde what I can do!"

"And what about your fellow Archangel? He has been busy and the Smyrnians don't realize it."

"Ah yes, Gabriel. He's not as good as me, you understand that, right?" he asked with a grin. "Trey didn't recognize he was the one who took him to the valley in his dream and spoke to him in that gentle breeze. *Gentle breeze*. Sounds like Gabriel, doesn't it?" Another grin. "But Trey listened to him, as true believers in Jesus always do. Gabriel has such a soft side. That's why he is the messenger angel. I love hearing about his stories, don't you?"

She nodded her head, and he continued.

"Me, on the other hand..."

She rolled her eyes, realizing what was coming next.

"I love to fight. That's why I am the Chief Prince, the warrior angel who leads the mighty hosts of heaven. I love nothing more than a good battle! But I also realize Yahweh is the one who gives the victory." He bowed his head in submission to his God.

"That is enough for tonight. The four Smyrnians should be on their way back to Muwaffaq. I am on standby if they need me."

"But for now, I suppose we should retire for the night. But like I've done since being here, I must also protect this place. I'll never forget the night AMPP invaded, and I made the people invisible to them. How much fun was that?! Watching those guys run around..." She cut him off.

"Yes, that was a blast! But now we must, what did you call it, *retire for the night?* Yes, we must, but then, who needs sleep anyway, right? Good night, Michael."

For the next forty-two months, his work would not cease. But the day of rest was coming soon!

•   •   •   •   •

"Okay, here's our plan. We flew this monster because we needed something to make the trip without refueling. It can handle a 7,000-mile trip empty, but that won't make this round trip. We could stop at a U.S. base in Afghanistan, but we can't make it that far on what we have left either."

"So, we'll head over to the Air Force base in Seoul and fuel up. From there, it's a 5,000-mile flight back to Jordan. I'm taking it to Seoul, and Rickie will take it home from there. The two Jordanians will pick us up at Muwaffaq and drive us back to the border. Mordecai, Michael, and Hadassah will take us to the kibbutz from there. Is everybody okay with that?"

"We just want out of China," said Bruno. "General Chen and his men are searching for us, and the dragon always seems to know where we are. I'm not even sure he can't get to us in the air. But the quicker you get us out of this country, the better we will feel."

"General Chen? Wait, you can tell us about him when we get in the air. It's two hours to Seoul, so we should land, get everything done, and leave there before daylight. Hang on, here we go."

The big plane zoomed across the hard surface and climbed out of the valley, heading south, then banked east toward South Korea. Anything across the border made Bruno and Magnus rest easier, but their anxiety would rise when they passed over Beijing.

"Now you can tell us all about what happened here," said Rickie. "I can't believe the dragon killed Malachi. Someone needs to take that thing out!"

"Someone will Rickie," said Trey. "His name is Jesus, and we will get to watch when he does."

Bruno and Magnus told them the stories of Malachi spying on the first meeting, followed by their encounter with the dragon. Next they talked about Malachi's death and their encounter at the meeting hall and the faint glow. What the dragon, president, and General Chen said came next.

"No! They bombed the Shelter? Our entire team died? Are you positive that's what they said? That can't be true; it just can't."

Trey was heartbroken. He and Rickie were both crying now and wiping their eyes as they flew.

"Blake and Beth, Evan, Ally, Anders, John and Kathie... all of them? What now? How can we keep fighting without them?"

"Listen, you two, my entire family may be dead, all of them," Bruno said. "I have grieved that already, but I can't do anything about it until we get to Missouri and find out for ourselves. Magnus helped me realize that. The best thing we can do is get to Israel, then find a way to the U.S. Until we do, I won't learn anything about my wife and kids. Please get us there as fast as you can.

Trey wiped his eyes. "You're right, Bruno. We all need to fly to Missouri and see what happened for ourselves. I'll make sure they fill this thing quickly and check it over. We'll leave the minute they finish and Rickie will step on it so we can get to Muwaffaq as fast as this plane will fly. We just need to pray for the Iranians to leave us alone this time."

They shared that story with Bruno and Magnus and followed it with the encounter over Beijing, which almost prevented them from getting to the valley. There were plenty miraculous stories to go around, but foremost in their minds was hightailing it to Jordan ASAP.

•   •   •   •   •

Anders shared his story with Ollie, Amelia, and Bradley, blowing their minds. Their hearts broke for Evan and Malachi, but they also rejoiced for Anders, Ally, and the rest of the group. They needed to decide some things and act on them soon.

"So, still no word on Bruno and Magnus, other than Anders not seeing them in heaven?"

"Nothing," said Blake, "and no way to get word."

"What about the Israel group? Have they contacted you at all?"

"Not a word from them either."

"We need to do something," said Bradley. "It's foolish to sit here, holed up, wishing we knew something and doing nothing about it."

They all stared in disbelief at his take charge attitude and boldness, talking to them like that when he just met them.

"You'd better listen to the man," Ollie said. "Ask Amelia. Bradley has been right about everything since we arrived at the Shelter. We wouldn't be here talking to you right now if it wasn't for him."

"He told us whoever lay in the debris wasn't there, so someone either carried them away, or they walked away on their own. That meant some of you survived!"

"Then he noticed all the vehicles were missing, meaning you guys drove them and left. After that, he discovered you had been in the barn and crawled out, probably after the explosion. If he did none of that, we would have stood there and grieved, then left without looking for you. He wouldn't let us do that either. That's why we came to Springfield. We owe all of that to him!"

"It comes from being in the military so long and from dogged determination. I was never one to give up on anything. Once I realized some of you survived, we had to find you!"

"Thank you, Bradley. You have done so much for us and are a valuable part of our team. Let's talk about what we do next. Sitting here is the worst thing possible." Blake said it for all of them.

"We have to leave for Israel right now!"

They all turned and looked at Anders. His demeanor told them those words were not a gut reaction to what was just said; he was serious about them.

"Don't ask me how I know; just start packing!"

"How do you suggest we get to Israel?"

"We fly," said Bradley.

"Fly? How can we do that?"

"Paul Johnson," Ally said without hesitating.

"That's it! We flew into there, and he gave us a vehicle to drive to the farm. I believe he will either fly us himself or provide us with a plane to go on our own."

"But what about you, Bradley? Don't you have to get back to Lakenheath?" asked Ollie.

"I have ten years left until I can retire from the military and three years until Jesus returns. So I'll choose early retirement without pay and serve Jesus instead of the military for the next three years. That will pay better in the long run. Count me in!"

"What about the plane you flew over?" asked Blake.

"It will be England's donation to the cause. Besides, they don't need it. They're finished after the nuclear war. Maybe the commander doesn't need to give us a plane. We may already have one!"

"Problem solved," said Steve. "I hate to leave people without my surgical skills, but you guys need me more. Linda, let's go pack."

Bradley got things started, and within two hours, the entire group was on their way to meet with Commander Paul Johnson.

•　　•　　•　　•　　•

Trey and Rickie stayed true to their word. It still took an hour to fuel the plane and check it over for the flight back, but the minute the mechanics finished, Rickie took off for Jordan.

"I'm supposed to sleep, and my body could use it, but there's no way I can sleep without hearing everything else you have to tell us."

"And we're wide awake," Bruno said. "We slept seven hours before you guys got there."

"These thermoses of espresso should keep me awake. They sent enough for all four of us." Trey already had a cup in hand and was sipping it. "Fly on, Rickie, and you guys talk."

He leaned back to listen as Magnus talked first. One minute after he started they heard light snoring, turned, and found Trey sound asleep, his coffee on the verge of spilling. Bruno eased it from his hand and set it aside. Both smiled and promised to keep Rickie awake.

•　　•　　•　　•　　•

At the base in Missouri, Paul Johnson welcomed the large group of Smyrnians into his headquarters. He was not aware of the bombing, Evan's death, or Anders' experience. That part fascinated him until they told him their request. They wanted him to fly them to Israel.

"Do you realize what you're asking me to do?"

"Commander, if you don't mind, let me tell you my decision. These next three years are far more important than my military career or retirement. So I am walking away and giving everything to Jesus. They may consider me a deserter or believe I perished in an accident, but neither matters. My plane and I are flying to Israel with these people on board. You can fly with *us*, bring another plane, or stay here. That is your decision. Although, we may need a second plane, if you understand what I am saying."

"I understand completely, Bradley. You are laying it all on the line and asking me to do the same."

"Yes sir, that is what I am doing, but I am not telling you what to do, only issuing a challenge."

"Don't stop to consider it, Paul," Anders said. "You need to come *and* bring a plane. Flying will be important for what's coming soon. I'm still not sure what that means, but I understand two things: it's true, and we will need every plane we can get."

Paul sat looking at them, weighing the biggest decision of his life. Should he just leave and turn his back on everything he had worked for his entire career? While he mulled that over, Anders spoke up and did not mince words.

"Whoever wants to be my disciple must deny themselves and take up their cross and follow me."

Paul sprang to his feet. "Give me an hour, and I'll be ready to go. I can't waste these last three years! If I didn't believe in Jesus, you couldn't pay me to do that. But I'm going!"

"Can you fly a C-5M Super Galaxy too? We need to make the trip without refueling, and my gut tells me we will need the space. You can haul many people in that cargo hull."

The group's excitement ran high as they all prepared to fly to Israel. None realized Jesus was bringing his warriors together where he needed them to carry out his plans. It was an exhilarating moment, but also the most dangerous time of their lives. Some of them would lose theirs.

•　　•　　•　　•　　•

The meeting started at 6:00 a.m. in Ben and Miriam's kitchen. Everyone needed to be in sync and have faith that Trey and Rickie would arrive safely with Bruno, Magnus, and Malachi. If that happened, three more of their comrades would join them, but they longed to learn more about the others. They contemplated flying to Missouri, but knew they needed to stay in Israel.

"If things go as planned, Omar and Ahmad need to reach Muwaffaq by 10:00 a.m. The trip should take approximately twenty-four hours. You three must meet them at the border two to three hours after that, so arriving no later than noon is essential."

"Don't worry, Ben, we will get there long before noon. And I will keep an eye on my niece and that Omar fellow. I don't like the way he flirts with her." Mordecai glanced at Hadassah.

"Uncle, we're only friends. Perhaps Omar, Ahmad, and Hala will help us someday."

Her smile and sweet voice captivated him once again, and he responded with a smile of his own.

"How do you plan to get them back across the border in broad daylight?" asked Ben. "You went in the dark last time because of the danger involved."

"There's a place where they can cross unseen, a spot guards will not patrol today. Omar and Ahmad will drive them there while Hala watches to ensure no guards show up. They will communicate with her on the way back, and if something goes wrong, abort the mission and take another approach. Hala will signal us and keep us aware of what's happening. We have it all planned out."

"If you say so," Ben said, not at all convinced their plan would work. But he had to trust them.

"Relax, Rabbi," Michael said with a reassuring smile. "Everything will work out just right."

"Michael, how many times have I told you, to call me Ben, not Rabbi?"

"Yes, Ben, you are correct. Look at all Jesus has done already. Do you think he will not bring them back to us? You must pray and trust *him*, not us. He has proven there is nothing he cannot do."

"Once again, the two of you amaze me. We would do well to heed every word you say. Soon you will need to leave for the border. Are you sure this Hala will arrive on time and do her job?"

"She will," said Hadassah. "Hala is always punctual and trustworthy, and she will not let us down. Her name means *halo around the moon*, so she will show us the way." Her smile following that statement revealed her confidence in this plan succeeding.

They walked out of the meeting four hours before Mordecai, Michael, and Hadassah needed to arrive at the border. This time they could take no chances on being late, and they would not.

In Missouri, the group got things together and prepared to board two military planes for Israel, not knowing if they would ever return, or what awaited them in the Holy Land. Discussion centered on those questions and finding a new safe place should they return to the U.S. One thing of which they were unaware would play a major role in their decision.

The Missouri groups faced a fourteen-hour flight, while Rickie's flight from Seoul was less than eleven hours, and they were already en route. All three planes contained enough fuel to make the trips, although Bradley and Paul would cut things close. They would miss each other by four hours, a task Michael could handle, but neither realized the other was on the way. And to complicate things, the two Missouri planes were flying to Israel, not Jordan.

Omar and Ahmad left for Muwaffaq at 9:30 a.m. They should easily arrive by 11:30, but wanted to allow for any interruptions along the way. They drove a larger vehicle this time to accommodate the additional three men who would make the return trip with them.

"The things we do to help Michael and Hadassah," said Ahmad, shaking his head. "Admit it, you have a thing for her, and that's the real reason we are making this trip."

"I really do like her, if that's what you mean."

"That is exactly what I mean. It is written all over your face every time you see her. Have you stopped to consider that she is Jewish and you are Muslim?"

"Of course, I have. I'm not stupid. But that doesn't change the way I feel about her."

"Well, it will change the way your family feels about her. Have you told her?"

"Well, I was kind of hoping she would figure it out."

"You are a big chicken, Omar, and a big flirt too."

"Is it that obvious?"

"Are you kidding? Hala and I talk about it all the time. *Hadassah, it is so good to see you. Hadassah, I am so glad you came.* And who is always the first one to the fence when she and Michael come? You are. Come on, Omar, tell her how you feel about her and get it over with. Hala and I will be behind you all the way. *Far* behind you," he said and laughed out loud, pointing his finger at his comrade and friend.

"We're only about thirty minutes out," said Omar, seizing the opportunity to change the subject. "Do you really think they will make it back? Man, they were embarking on an impossible mission."

"Somehow, I'm convinced they will. There was something different about this trip, Omar. I'm not sure what it was, but I felt it. Otherwise, I wouldn't have agreed to take them to Muwaffaq."

"You felt something too?"

"You mean, you had the same feeling? What was it like for you?"

"I don't know, man. My heart beat faster and I tingled all over. Then it settled down, and I had this incredible peace."

"Are you serious? Me too!"

The two of them continued in silence, each reflecting on the news they had just shared with one another. A mile away from the base, they saw the big plane making its descent, dropping from the sky toward the runway below.

They looked at each other amazed, neither saying a word. It touched down just as they pulled up to the gate. The timing seemed nothing short of miraculous as the guards stepped from their post and walked toward them.

•   •   •   •   •

"Can we stop by the base on the way to the border, Aluf, sir?" asked Michael.

"We have four hours, Michael, plenty of time, but I won't allow you to make us late for the border. What is so important it cannot wait until we return?"

"I need to speak with Ezra and Shimon about some things we are working on for the next phase of our mission. We may not know what will happen, but we must still prepare and be ready, don't you agree? It will take less than thirty minutes and leave plenty of time to reach the border early."

"We need to leave right now. I need to check on something in the office which will not take long either."

Hadassah saw Michael glance her way and grin. She shook her head and returned his smile with a look that asked, *how do you do that?* The three of them climbed into the Wolf and left for the base. Within twenty-five minutes, they arrived and parked in front of the office building.

"I will return in less than twenty minutes," Michael said over his shoulder, already sprinting around the corner to find his friends.

"He could have saluted instead of running off like that. That boy can be quite impetuous. Come with me into the office."

"But he always seems to get things done, Uncle," she said, following along at his side.

Both saluted the two officers standing inside. What she heard next did not surprise her. Something was up with Michael, and she knew it. This brief hiatus was not accidental. Neither did it involve Ezra and Shimon. This was a Jesus moment that played a major role in the immediate future. She was giddy with excitement to learn what would happen next.

"Major General, sir, we have a Commander Paul Johnson of the United States Military on the radio seeking permission for an emergency landing at one of our bases. This requires your attention, sir, if you can communicate with him. We aren't qualified to make that decision."

Hadassah's body tingled all over; a U.S. Military Commander! Here it came!

"All of you get out, so I can speak with Commander Johnson in private."

Once the men left the room, the conversation began.

"Commander Johnson, this is Major General Mordecai Chaim. What is your request?"

"Major General Chaim, I request permission to land. We have two planes flying groups of displaced American civilians who seek asylum in Israel. If you cannot grant asylum, it is urgent that we land and refuel. We can decide our next steps after that. Please grant permission to land."

"Why would you be flying to Israel with two groups of American civilians, Commander?"

"They were displaced in the nuclear war. The United States Military is committed to taking care of American citizens in urgent situations. Again, please grant emergency permission to land."

Her uncle's next question caught Hadassah by surprise.

"Commander, are you familiar with two American pilots named Trey Butler and Rickie Cruz?"

Momentary silence replaced the conversation on the other end.

"Commander Johnson, are you there?"

"Yes, Major General, and I am very familiar with Majors Butler and Cruz. Why do you ask?"

"I have met them here in Israel and discovered they are a part of a group known as the Smyrnians. Are you familiar with this group, Commander?"

After another brief pause, Paul Johnson spoke in a hesitant, yet firm voice.

"I am also familiar with the Smyrnians. What does that have to do with us, sir?"

"Are you also familiar with their leader, an American Jew named Benjamin Abramson?"

"Yes, sir; most people have heard of Mr. Abramson. I still do not understand..."

Mordecai interrupted him.

"Commander, let's dispense with the small talk. I suspect your reason for flying to Israel has to do with more than transporting two groups of displaced Americans. My instincts tell me you are involved with the Smyrnians. You are required to answer that question before I can grant you permission to land at an IDF base."

"Then sir, man to man, I must tell you we are Smyrnians, and we request permission to land."

"I am pleased to make your acquaintance, Commander, and to inform you I, too, belong to the Smyrnians."

Applause and cheers erupted from the radio after another brief pause.

"I will now give you orders, which you will be wise to accept. You may not have permission to fly into Israel."

"But Major General..." Mordecai interrupted Paul in mid-sentence again.

"You will land at Muwaffaq Salti Air Base in Jordan. Are you familiar with that base?"

"I am, sir, after serving multiple tours in the Middle East."

"Then you realize American troops are stationed there. Majors Butler and Cruz are expected to land there any minute, returning from an emergency recovery mission to China."

The cheers grew louder from the American plane.

"In a few hours, three of us will pick them up at an obscure border location and transport them to rejoin the others. I will begin right now working on plans for you to land at Muwaffaq, then we will arrange transportation from there to the same border crossing. We will drive you from there to the kibbutz."

"I look forward to meeting you, Mordecai. May Jesus help you make the arrangements."

"And I look forward to meeting you, Paul. I will contact you the moment I have an answer. You would do well to ask Jesus to make the arrangements, rather than me. My abilities seem limited in urgent matters such as this."

"We will begin praying at once, Mordecai. Our conversation was not a coincidence, so I am confident Jesus already has everything planned and we will see each other soon."

"I agree, Paul. Await my reply, and we will talk within the next two hours."

When Mordecai and Hadassah stepped outside, they found Michael entertaining the others several feet away, well out of hearing range of the conversation that had taken place inside. He was his true self, causing the exchange to be filled with laughter and smiles. The men snapped to attention as the Aluf approached.

"At ease, men. There is nothing wrong with having a little fun in the middle of the day. I see you met our resident comedian and pilot, Michael. We must leave now and allow you to return to your duties. Have a great day, gentlemen."

He saluted, and the three got into the Wolf and drove away from the base bound for the border.

Aboard both planes, joy continued erupting. Paul communicated with Bradley as soon as his conversation with Mordecai ended. Jesus answered their prayers once again. None of them imagined landing in Jordan when they departed America. But this was all arranged before they left Missouri, setting in motion something far bigger than any of them. They could hardly wait to see their comrades and discover what that mission entailed.

"That must mean Bruno is alive!" said Mila, overjoyed by what she just heard.

"Don't forget Magnus," said Anders with a wide smile. "I didn't see him in heaven either."

"I can't wait to see the others and show them we are alive!"

"Remember, Beth, they don't know what happened at the Shelter. Neither are they aware that Evan and Malachi were both killed. The news will be both bitter and sweet to them," said Blake.

"Just like the scroll," said Anders. "This foreshadows the rest of the Tribulation. Although I must warn you, the bitter will far exceed the sweet. We must prepare to face it as it comes."

That one statement turned the mood from joyful to subdued. They all understood what Anders meant. More of them would die before the next three-and-a-half years ended. None of them wanted to see that happen, yet they realized it was inevitable. The group looked at one another, each understanding what the others were thinking: who would be next?

CHAPTER 6

Omar opened the door and stepped out of the vehicle to greet the guards.

"Stay in your vehicle, and we will bring the passengers to you. They have exited the plane, and troops are escorting them here now. They should arrive within ten minutes. You will leave immediately upon their arrival."

"Is everything okay? Their mission was approved by Commander Hassan, so we thought..."

"It doesn't matter what you thought, Private. Their *secret* mission will remain a secret. No one will ever hear anything about it. Do I make myself clear?"

"So, you're saying, what happens at Muwaffaq stays at Muwaffaq," Omar said. But his attempt at humor did nothing to appease either guard.

"Your lives are at stake here. If anyone discovers what happened in the last two days, the military will arrest both of you and hold you accountable for that error in judgment. Do you understand?"

"Yes, sir," said Ahmad. "We will leave when they arrive and tell no one about this."

Armed guards escorted Trey, Rickie, Bruno, and Magnus to the vehicle and stood until they got in and left.

Mordecai parked a quarter mile from the border while Michael and Hadassah waited in hiding close to the fence separating Israel and Jordan. They decided daylight would provide the greatest element of surprise and prevent them from using lights that might give them away.

Hala lay between some rocks across the fence, covered with dry grass she gathered from the area. Radio in hand, she listened for word from her comrades.

Omar and Ahmad left Muwaffaq with four men lying unseen in seats behind them. Their departure was unhindered, leaving smooth sailing to the border. They informed Hala and instructed her to prepare for their arrival in less than two hours. It appeared all was well.

She signaled her two friends waiting on the other side of the border. Two whistling sounds told them everything was going according to plan, while three would signal trouble. A long single whistle would tell them the men were getting near. The pair waited anxiously and breathed a sigh of relief upon hearing the two sounds coming from among the rocks.

Hadassah pulled a small mirror from the pocket of her military-issued khakis and held it face up in her palm. The sun glinting off the mirror sent a flash toward her uncle sitting in the Wolf, telling him all was well. *Things could not have gone more smoothly to this point*, she thought.

"What happened back there?" Omar asked. "This means we need to be more careful."

"Honestly, I neither know nor care," Trey said from his prone position behind Omar and Ahmad. "Commander Hassan was behind it. We're just happy to be with you guys and on our way back to the border. Thank you for helping us out."

"We only helped you because of our friends," Ahmad said with a serious tone.

"Come on, Ahmad, you remember what we felt back there at the base."

"What are you talking about, Omar? We would love to learn more about that."

"It was nothing. Omar gets these crazy whims once in a while," Ahmad said, glaring at his partner.

"Yes, we did, Ahmad. You forced me to talk about my feelings earlier, and I'm going to talk about this now. Something stood out about this from the time we met you guys and agreed to take you to Muwaffaq. On the trip back, we talked and realized both of us experienced the same thing."

"Tell us about that. I'm pretty sure all four of us back here can identify with you."

Ahmad broke and started talking before Omar got in another word. Words poured from his mouth, and he seemed powerless to stop them.

"It was the strangest thing I have ever experienced. My heart raced, my skin tingled all over, and this strange sensation came over me. The only word I can think of to describe it is *salaam*, complete peace, the most wonderful experience anyone can have. If you guys understand it, tell us."

Because of their Middle Eastern tours, Trey and Rickie recognized the Arabic word for the Jewish term, *shalom*, which means not only peace, but wholeness, health, prosperity, and tranquility. They now realized that kind of life came only from Jesus.

These two young Jordanian soldiers had experienced a small taste of what life is like with Jesus. Trey and Rickie longed to tell them more, but was it possible to do that without the pastor's video to help them understand? Magnus jumped in before they said anything else.

"I can tell you, when I experienced it, my life changed forever!"

He was interrupted by the sound of Hala's voice on the radio, bringing them back to the present.

"How close are you? It's almost noon, and we must stay on time."

Omar was jarred to his senses and saw his turn pass by on the left. Skidding to a near stop, he jerked the wheel to the right, making a U-turn, and slinging his passengers around like rag dolls.

"Sorry about that. You guys distracted me, and I passed up our turn."

"Don't blame us; you're the reckless driver. Do I need to take the wheel?"

"Shut up, Ahmad. You were just as distracted as me, and you know it. Besides, I can drive circles around you any day."

"Since when?"

"As long as I can remember. I got us there and back in one piece, didn't I?"

"Guys!" Trey said from the back. "Please focus on the mission at hand. If we're getting close, you need to text Hala."

Ahmad grabbed his phone and sent a quick text.

Just turned on dirt road. B there in 5.

You could've told me sooner!

Just signal the others.

Hala shoved the phone in her pocket, angry at the men, and cupping her hands to her mouth, let out a long, loud whistle.

"That's it!" Hadassah said, as she pulled out the mirror again.

The mirror flashed its message to Mordecai, who started the Wolf and readied himself to roll. Michael seemed almost too relaxed to Hadassah, but she never knew what to expect from him. Since he remained calm, so should she. But with what was about to go down, that was not possible.

They watched as the vehicle pulled alongside the rocky enclosure. Omar and Ahmad got out and strolled up and down the border, then returned to the vehicle. Trey, Rickie, Bruno, and Magnus exited, going down flat on their stomachs the minute their feet hit the ground.

Hala was now up and joined her two fellow soldiers as they stood around, appearing to be nothing more than three soldiers patrolling the border. The four men belly crawled to the fence, concealed by the tall grass growing on both sides. Omar and Ahmad stood on each side of a gaping hole under and through the bottom wiring.

"This is not a man-sized hole," said Bruno. Magnus quickly agreed.

"No way. I don't see either of us fitting through there."

"Then I guess you prefer to stay with us," Omar said. "Look, we don't have all day. Go!"

Trey slid under first, ripping his shirt on the fence. Rickie followed, their military training kicking into high gear.

"One of you, come on! Give us your hands, and we'll pull you through."

Loud sounds captured their attention. Two Jordanian military vehicles sped through the field behind them while two Chinese helicopters closed in from the front, trapping them in the middle.

"Go!" Omar yelled at Bruno and Magnus.

Bruno dove into the opening and threw out his arms toward Trey and Rickie. They pulled him through, ripping off his shirt and leaving more scratches on his back.

"This is getting old," he said, then yelled to his partner to follow him.

Magnus dove in too, and with Bruno pulling his arms while Omar and Ahmad pushed his feet, emerged on the Israel side with the others.

"Run!" said Trey.

Michael and Hadassah stood from their hiding place and joined them. Mordecai did not wait for them to run to him. He sped up to the fence, bouncing and sliding, and threw the front door open.

"Get in!"

Michael held out his hand and stopped them.

"Wait! Omar, Ahmad, Hala, you're coming with us."

"What do you mean, we're coming with you? We can't!" Omar said, as the soldiers closed in.

Gunfire rang out and bullets pinged off the surrounding rocks, grazing the leg of Ahmad's pants, leaving them no time to think. They slid under the fence, and raced toward the Wolf.

Michael stood facing the approaching vehicles. The front tire of the first slammed into a large rock. It overturned in front of the other, causing the second truck to crash into it, flip over, and land on its top. The impact incapacitated the men and freed the group from the danger behind them.

Now the choppers hovered over them.

"The Chinese!" said Mordecai. "Is everyone in?"

"Where's Michael?" Hadassah screamed and leapt for the door.

Her uncle grabbed her, pulling her back inside the vehicle.

"Hadassah, no!"

The wind from the rotors stirred up dust, blinding them, and concealing their young colleague from sight. Dust filled their eyes, and they dropped their heads to shield them from the billowing cloud.

One more thing met their vision as they did: a bright flash from each chopper. The pain beam. Its glowing rays pierced the thick dust. They watched helplessly, throwing up their hands in a useless attempt to protect themselves from the excruciating pain they were about to experience. The beam would heat the water molecules in their bodies, burning them from the inside out, and creating horrific suffering.

None of them saw Michael. He stood beside the Wolf with nine of his friends inside. His arms extended, he grew in stature and strength, muscles bulging from every part of his body, as his hair grew long and flowed in the powerful wind. The rays of the beam came at him within milliseconds, smashing into his palms and deflecting back toward the choppers.

The searing pain hit the pilots' bodies, causing them to scream and release the controls. Both aircraft spun wildly, sending one smashing into the other. Each lurched to the left, away from the armored vehicle underneath them, and slammed into the ground, exploding in giant balls of fire.

"Michael!" Hadassah's voice could barely be heard above the noise.

"We have to go!" Mordecai jerked the Wolf in gear and shoved the accelerator to the floor.

"Not without Michael!" she said, and grabbed for the steering wheel.

"Not without me? I'm sitting right here!" No one saw him get in.

"How did you...?" Omar was stunned to see his Israeli friend in the seat beside him.

"Get us out of here! Don't wait till more choppers come. I'm sorry, I should have said, Aluf, sir."

Mordecai heeded the charge without acknowledging his apology and took off, bumping across the field, then sliding onto the road and driving away toward the kibbutz.

Paul and Bradley talked as the two planes continued toward Jordan. The closer they got, the more anxious they became to receive word about how to proceed. All they had was the word of Major General Mordecai Chaim that he would arrange landing for them at Muwaffaq Salti Air Base.

"Chaim should call soon, Bradley."

"We had better hear from him soon because we're less than two hours from Muwaffaq. If they don't know we're coming, we can't show up unannounced and expect to land without approval."

"I hope things are okay with Trey and Rickie. That concerns me, since Mordecai hasn't called."

"Don't forget that fuel is an issue, too. We barely have enough to get there, so we'll have to land with or without clearance from them."

"If Chaim doesn't call in the next thirty minutes, I'll try to contact him. Let's keep this between us and let our passengers relax. They've dealt with enough stress the last few days."

"I won't say a word until you contact me with news. Don't wait too long to call Chaim."

"If you guys can keep watch, I'll call Muwaffaq and ask permission for the others to land," Mordecai said, looking around at the nine people riding with him. "Transporting them will be much more difficult. We need a better plan than the one today."

"Wait, Mordecai," said Trey. "You are not the one who needs to call. Rickie and I are good friends with Sergeant Major Robert Clark, the commander of the American troops stationed there. Things were different when we flew back than when we left. Armed guards met us and escorted us out with no explanation why. They were serious about it too. Robert walked by us on the way and slipped a piece of paper into my hand with his phone number. His face showed concern I have not seen in him before."

Trey dialed the number as he spoke, and Robert Clark answered in a low voice. He neither said *hello*, nor waited for Trey to speak.

"Trey, listen to me. I have little time, so let me talk."

The phone went to speaker with a touch of Trey's finger, and the group grew quiet and listened.

"Zaid called me into his office after you guys left and demanded that all of our troops evacuate the base. I assumed he was angry because I insisted he allow you to take a plane, so I tried to appease him, with no success. He ordered me to contact all of my men and leave by tomorrow morning."

"But why..."

"There are two very important reasons. First, Jordan is turning on Israel. One of my men intercepted a call between Zaid, the Chairman of the Joint Chiefs of Staff, and Aissa Messai during the night. Messai plans to form an alliance of Islamic nations surrounding the country to attack it at some point. I don't understand his role in this, but he's definitely the leader of that movement."

"Rickie and I are fully aware of his role, Robert, and would love to talk to you about it."

"We will talk, but you need to hear this next thing. They are onto you guys. Someone in their unit reported on the three soldiers who helped you escape."

Behind Trey, the faces of Omar, Ahmad, and Hala grew pale. They glanced at one another with questioning looks, wondering who may have turned them in.

"I told you," Ahmad said to Omar in a loud whisper. "I cannot believe I let you talk me into this."

"Be quiet and listen. We need to hear this."

"That's why they allowed you to return and leave the base. They tailed you, hoping you would lead them to whoever you're working with. Lay low and keep hidden as much as possible because they have lots of people on the ground in Israel keeping an eye out for you."

"What about you and your unit, Robert? Are you flying back to the states?"

"They confiscated all of our planes and intend to take us into custody. Messai wants us brought to him to stand trial for threatening the peace and prosperity of the world."

"Where are you now?"

"My entire unit escaped before they could arrest us. We're on foot approximately five miles from the base, but there's no place to hide out here in the desert."

"Can you get to the border? We made it safely back into Israel, but they almost got us before we did. We're on our way back to our safe place now, but we can't leave you stranded out there while they hunt you down. If you can make it anywhere along the border, we'll come and get you."

"We're eighty miles from the closest point to the border, so I'm pretty sure we aren't walking there. We'd have to travel at night and avoid being seen. Even at 10 miles a night, it would take us eight days. Do you have any better ideas?"

"I do," Hala said.

"Who is talking?" Robert asked.

"Sir, this is Hala, one of the Jordanian soldiers who helped Trey and Rickie. My brother is also in the military, and each of us has family nearby. If they hear we are in trouble, they will come and help us. Perhaps my brother can bring a military truck and haul all of you to an isolated place where you can cross the border and we can meet you there."

"That's the best suggestion I've heard yet. What do you think, Trey and Rickie?"

"I'm willing to try anything to get your platoon out of there," said Rickie. "There's no way we can sneak back in. But if Hala's brother, or other family members can make it happen, we will do anything we can to help them."

Hala called her brother without waiting to hear any more. When he answered, she did not need to have the phone on speaker for all of them to hear him talking.

"Hala, what have you done? You have disgraced our family. The whole military is looking for you, and they said the three of you may face death by hanging for helping enemy soldiers escape. You have done some dumb things before, but this tops them all!"

It came across even stronger in Arabic, his anger spewing out like venom. But she was undeterred.

"Halil, listen to me! All we did was help some men who needed us and are no threat to us. You would want someone to help you; am I right?"

Halil was quiet for a few seconds before answering. "Yes." He said no more.

"There are more, and they need our help or they will die."

"More American soldiers? Hala, did you know Jordan just joined forces with Messai and other Muslim countries against Israel? America is Israel's ally, so that makes them our enemies!"

"Yes, I knew that! Does that surprise you? You're not the only smart one in the family. These men are not our enemies. Until a few hours ago, they were our friends and comrades. Just tell me; will you help us, or not? If you will not, I will find someone else. And you had better tell me quick, because I do not have time to waste."

"I will help. Tell me what you need from me."

"First, promise me you will do what I say and not turn us in."

"Okay, I promise. Now tell me what to do and how many men to recruit."

"No one goes but you. I can sneak across the border and join you, but they're searching for me, so I don't want them to catch me with you. They have no reason to suspect you right now."

"Other than knowing I'm your brother. They're probably already suspicious of me."

"Find a truck you can take out at night, and I'll get back to you with where to meet them. And Halil, not a word of this to anyone!"

"I almost forgot about calling Paul Johnson!" said Mordecai.

"What will you tell him, Uncle? They should only be an hour away by now and cannot land at Muwaffaq."

"I have an idea, Aluf," said Michael. "Ask them to land at Ben Gurion."

"Ben Gurion! Are you crazy?"

"I never deny being crazy, sir," the boy said with a smile, "but it should work. The airport is closed because of the bombings and the Chinese siege. Why can't we use it?"

"Because it is still a very public place and always watched closely. Besides, the bombs did significant damage to the runways and infrastructure. No pilot should try to land there."

"Sir, I feel certain it will not pose a problem. There are empty hangars since many planes could not fly back in after the attack, but maybe there are runways that will sustain a landing. U.S. military planes have landed there before bringing supplies for the IDF. We can meet them there with trucks of our own and take them to the kibbutz."

"You cannot hide the two huge planes they are flying. Someone will spot them and be there waiting for them the minute they land."

"Excuse me, sir, but I see no other options. You must take the chance and believe everything will turn out as it should."

"I don't know why I trust you with decisions like this, Michael," Mordecai said, shaking his head. "I will call Commander Johnson and let him know. Then I will contact a civilian friend who owns a large box truck big enough to transport the group back to the kibbutz. No one should suspect it."

Hala covered her phone with one hand and spoke to the group.

"Halil has secured a truck. Trey, tell the Sergeant Major to provide us with the location to pick them up, and Halil will meet them at 1:00 a.m. tomorrow. He will bring them to a spot along the border fence north of the Allenby Bridge crossing that we know very well. They should arrive no later than 3:00 a.m. We will also need trucks to bring them to safety."

"Hala is the organizer among us," Omar said as the others stared in disbelief at what they just heard.

"My friend says I can borrow his truck. Paul Johnson has informed the other pilot, and they will land at Ben Gurion in less than an hour. Fortunately, Samuel's house is only a few miles away. Hadassah and Michael can come with me, while the rest of you return to the kibbutz and make plans to rendezvous with Robert Clark and the others tomorrow night."

All in agreement, they parked down the street from Samuel's house, let the three of them out, and drove away. They hoped to see them again in a few hours.

Aboard the plane, Paul Johnson was happy to have a place to land but nervous about landing at Ben Gurion Airport. He had secured permission to land there a few weeks earlier, but this was different. Mordecai Chaim believed it was safe, and he must trust him. In forty-five minutes he and Bradley would set the big planes down on a runway in the dark. In fifteen to twenty minutes, they would begin their descent. There was no turning back now.

"We will land at Ben Gurion in forty-five minutes. Prepare to begin descent in fifteen minutes."

"Ben Gurion?" asked Blake. "Is that safe?"

"Mordecai Chaim says it is. Besides, what choice do we have?"

"I sure hope he knows what he's talking about."

Both planes contained a mixture of faith and fear. Safe or not, in forty-five minutes, they would land at Ben Gurion Airport. Their minds were filled with thoughts about the possibility of being shot down before they could land, or arriving and being arrested when they stepped off the plane. The two aircraft were filled with prayers for safety and protection.

Mordecai rang Samuel's doorbell and heard his friend's footsteps approaching. The door opened and the two friends greeted each other, but Mordecai's demeanor showed he had no time to waste.

"Mordecai, my friend, come in. We have much to catch up on since I last saw you."

"I would love to, Samuel, but I need to pick up my cargo in an hour. Thank you so much for letting me use your truck. I will return it without so much as a scratch."

Samuel handed him the keys and walked him behind the house where he parked the truck.

"Do not worry about this old thing, Mordecai. One more scratch may do it good."

"It is perfect, just as I remember, Samuel. I cannot return it until tomorrow. I hope that is okay."

"Take your time. I seldom drive it these days."

Mordecai thanked the man one more time and pulled into the street. He stopped a short distance away and allowed his niece and her soldier friend to get on board. They sped away to Ben Gurion.

The others arrived at the kibbutz, but there was no time for greeting and talking. Darkness had settled over the land, and that included Ben Gurion Airport, where two American military planes would land soon.

This was a time for prayer, but planning for the rescue of American troops from Jordan was also a priority. They would do both.

"Ahmad, Omar, and Hala, I have a video you must watch, then I want to speak with you about a very important matter. But alas, that must wait until after the rescue mission."

"There is no time to watch a video now, sir. We must talk and plan because lives are at stake."

Mordecai parked the truck as close to the airport as possible, still leaving a lengthy sprint for his young passengers. He would wait to receive word from them, then speed in and allow the groups to jump in the back, before driving away as fast as the truck would go. While he waited, a thought hit him. He found a screwdriver in the glove box and removed the license plate so no one would trace it back to Samuel.

"Slow down, Michael. I need a break to catch my breath."

"We don't have time for a break, Hadassah. Do I need to carry you?"

"No, you don't, wise guy. I can outrun you any day."

His challenge worked as she dashed ahead of him and looked back, laughing. He quickly caught up and ran beside her.

"Wow," he said, as they got close. "The fence is demolished. They'll have no trouble getting out."

"You stay here and stand guard. I will go in, help them, and let you know when we're coming out so you can call your uncle."

"But I want to be in there with you. I always get left out of the action."

"After today, how much more action do you want? We barely escaped the border with our lives. Besides, you'll get a lot more action out here, if AMPP, our military, the police, airport security, or the Chinese figure out something is up and discover you."

She swallowed hard, her eyes wide with fear. The reality of the danger involved with their mission hit her for the first time. To this point, she had run on adrenaline, but now was the time for action.

"You sure know how to make a girl feel safe."

"The girl may stay safe if she hides well enough. There's a huge hole to your right that would seem like the perfect place to hide. Make sure it isn't too deep before you jump in. I won't have time to fish you out when I return. It's go time," he said, sprinting away and leaving her standing alone.

"Michael!" she said in a voice not much louder than a whisper, but she spoke too late. He had already disappeared into the darkness. She knelt on her hands and knees and crawled, feeling for the hole. How did he know it was there, and that the fencing was destroyed? Could he see in the dark? His abilities amazed her.

Paul radioed Bradley and told him the plan. They had decisions to make before landing. He would go first and test the runway. Having no runway lighting would make things more difficult, but they had no choice, with fuel gauges near empty. Bradley would land ten minutes later to allow him time to taxi off the runway. Paul started his descent and knew the airport was approaching fast, but all he saw in the distance was darkness.

Michael stood at the far end of a severely damaged runway. His night vision always helped during times like this. The roar of the planes in the distance told him they were descending. The first should be only ten minutes from touching down. He raised one hand toward both planes and made circular motions. The roar stopped, and the planes became invisible.

He took a step forward and stretched out both hands, waist high, palms facing down. Light emanated from them, illuminating the runway, and rising three feet above it. The light was not visible outside the airport or in the nearby area. Only he and the two pilots could see it.

His hands now dropped to his sides, palms up, and raised slowly back to waist high. A low rumbling started below the surface but affected only the runway from one end to the other. Broken and scattered concrete underneath the pavement began coming back together, piece by piece. Pavement reunited above it and became smooth. He smiled, checking out his handiwork, then looked toward the sky and nodded his head. A brief flash of light told him he did his job well.

Paul Johnson could hardly believe his eyes. The lighted runway appeared out of nowhere, with nothing but total darkness surrounding it. A few lights shone from the city of Tel Aviv, but the translucent glow provided the best lighting he had ever seen for landing a plane.

Bradley saw it too and understood another miracle was happening. *There is never a dull moment in this Jesus journey*, he thought as he waited for his turn to land. Fear of being spotted from the ground tore at his mind as he flew, not realizing the plane was unheard and unseen.

Hadassah lay inside her cavern, listening for Michael's call. She estimated the depth at five to six feet after sliding in. The jagged pavement ripped her military-issued khakis, digging into her leg as it did. All she could do now was wait and allow Michael to do his thing. She wished he would let her join him one time, but it never happened.

Mordecai sat in the truck, hoping no one would see him. Should he entrust such important work to two young soldiers? It was too late for those questions, so he prayed for a phone call to come soon.

Michael stood and watched as the massive plane touched down and sped toward him. He again raised his hands and held them out toward the approaching aircraft, watching it slow down much quicker than normal. *Sure, the commander has things under control, but a little help never hurts,* he mused. As the plane drew near, he pointed to the right, and Paul steered toward an abandoned hangar. Bradley followed suit, and both planes taxied toward separate hangars next to each other.

Hadassah's phone vibrated, catching her by surprise and causing her to drop it. By the time she located it, the buzzing stopped. Before she called back, a text came from Michael.

R u ok?

I'm fine. Dropped my phone.

On the ground. Call the Aluf. Tell him 5 minutes.

Five minutes? She fumbled with the phone again, trying to call. Hands shaking, she finally steadied them enough to touch her uncle's number. He answered before she even heard it ring.

"Hadassah, what's going on in there? I'm getting a little nervous sitting out here."

"They're getting off the plane and need you here in five minutes."

"On my way!"

Michael met the groups as they exited. "Come quickly and follow me."

"What is your name?"

"I am Michael, but we can talk later. The Aluf will be parked and waiting in two minutes."

They were drained after a fourteen-hour flight, but they sprinted after the young man leading them. When they passed the runway, it was broken and buckled, as it was prior to their landing. How did they land on *that?* Then the lighting faded and disappeared. Both Paul and Bradley realized something special had happened, but they could not talk about it now. Maybe they would ask later.

Now walking and stumbling in the dark, they reached Hadassah just as Mordecai arrived. *Perfect timing!* There was no time for talking. Michael raised the door of the box truck and helped them climb inside, then pulled it down and jumped in the front with the other two. Mordecai mashed the accelerator to the floor, slinging his passengers in the back into walls and each other.

Exiting the airport and pulling onto the main road, he glanced through the side mirror and noticed flashing lights behind him. *I don't have time for this.* But he had to stop, regardless of the time. He stopped and put the window down. A young officer strode cautiously toward them, gun in hand.

"Sir, may I see your license and registration. Why would you drive with no tags on the truck?"

Mordecai turned to face him through the open window.

"You are the Aluf..." he stammered. "I mean Major General Chaim. I apologize, sir. You may continue. I'm sure you have good reason for...." He stopped talking and walked away.

"Sometimes it helps to be someone important," said Michael with a grin. "One rescue down; one remaining, so let's get them to the kibbutz, and hustle to the border."

CHAPTER 7

The group's arrival created an obvious issue with space in the kibbutz. They had not planned for further expansion. This would require some extended families moving in together, leading to overcrowding in several homes, but opening up housing for the new arrivals.

There was no time for conversation. Trey and Rickie, along with Omar, Ahmad, and Hala had left for the border. Mordecai arranged two trucks for them from Camp Filon. The moment the others climbed out of the borrowed truck, Mordecai, Hadassah, and Michael drove it away, hoping to arrive in time to help the American soldiers navigate the crossing. Those at the kibbutz would not share any news until they were all together. For tonight, they needed one thing: sleep.

"This is the place," Omar said. "The problem with this spot is nowhere to hide the trucks, but traffic is light here late at night, especially with the siege. Even if someone notices you, no one should suspect two Israeli military vehicles patrolling the border. However, if they see three Jordanian soldiers on this side of the fence, that would cause a serious issue. The three of us need to lay low here or get to the other side."

"We need Mordecai, Michael, and Hadassah," said Rickie. "Israeli soldiers patrolling the border won't arouse suspicion either. I noticed some abandoned bunkers on the hill across the highway."

"Yes! Those are perfect places for you guys to hide and be ready to move when we need you!"

Hala's phone vibrated. She answered and walked down the hill, out of hearing, as she talked.

"Halil, where are you?"

The others lay over the crest of the embankment, waiting for her to return. She appeared, running toward them, speaking as she ran.

"They're almost here! We need to get in position. There is no time for the bunkers now. Everyone move! Where are the Aluf, and Michael and Hadassah? We need them!"

Seconds after the words came out of her mouth, they heard a vehicle coming and raced for cover. The truck stopped and their friends leapt out.

"Omar, Ahmad, Hala, are you here?" Hadassah asked quietly.

They stood and waved as the sound of Halil's truck met their ears. He drove slowly with the lights off. The man knew the area well enough to do that. Mordecai parked the box truck between the other trucks, hoping if anyone passed by, it would appear the military had stopped a suspicious vehicle. He remained in the truck, keeping an eye out for Chinese helicopters.

The five soldiers, three Jordanian and two Israeli, formed an unlikely team as they ran toward the fence to rescue American troops escaping the country. It was an alliance that would happen no other time, but it occurred at the midpoint of the final seven years in the history of Planet Earth. Amazing was the word, but *unbelievable* was a more accurate description, had it not been for Jesus.

Halil stopped long enough to allow the Americans to leave the truck. When Robert Clark signaled they were out, he took off, waving at his sister and wondering what was going on. A car went by and they hit the ground. Ahmad was outside the box truck *arguing* with Mordecai, who was dressed in full military gear. The vehicle continued, suspecting nothing more than a Palestinian driver being harassed by the IDF. When the car left, the others jumped into action.

"Over here," said Omar, pointing to another rare opening in the border fence.

Ahmad spoke much louder than he intended, "Move!"

The Sergeant Major fell on his stomach and crawled through the hole. The others followed, one at a time, until all of them stood on Israeli soil. It took longer than they hoped.

"To the trucks!" Robert said, issuing a command to his 200 troops as each made it through.

They moved fast, scurrying up the embankment, sprinting to the trucks and climbing inside.

Trey and Rickie pulled Robert to the side as his soldiers ran past them to the two military trucks.

"Major General Chaim and the private are taking your men to an IDF base. There is no room for all of you where we are staying."

"The Aluf is with you? I didn't even get a look at him."

"He stayed with the truck. Yes, he's part of our group and will help you with whatever you need."

"I have no idea what you guys are doing here, but I trust you will tell me when the time is right."

"We will, and that time will come soon. Enjoy your accommodations. They will take good care of you, and we will stay in touch. God bless you, Robert. We appreciate you."

The look of shock on his face showed his surprise at Trey's last statement. The two pilots he knew never mentioned God. He didn't know what had happened to them, but he intended to find out.

With no time to waste, all three trucks pulled onto the highway. Mordecai and Michael drove the two bound for Camp Filon. Hadassah joined Omar, Ahmad, and Hala in the back of the box truck as Rickie took off for the kibbutz. Trey sat up front with him. The day and night had been long and harrowing for all of them, but hopefully they were safe now.

Ben let everyone sleep late and announced a meeting of the Smyrnians at noon. He spoke with none of them, but stayed in his house praying for the others on the last rescue mission of the day, until he fell asleep. They convened, coming in at separate times, but all present by noon. Ben stood to address them and discuss plans for their next moves. He looked around and found some missing.

"Where is Evan? Don't tell me he's still asleep. If that is the case, someone wake him up!"

The group was quiet as Ben's question brought back memories of the day the bombs fell. Ally tried not to cry, but the sobs came despite her efforts, and no one could miss them, including Ben.

"No," he said, his voice quivering with emotion.

"They blew up the bunkers Ben, and Evan didn't make it." Blake broke down when he spoke too.

Tears flowed from Ben's eyes. Miriam came to him and held him tightly, weeping with him. No one could contain their sorrow now. They all mourned the death of their friend together for the first time since he died.

"Malachi?" asked Ben, realizing he was not present either. He looked at Bruno and Magnus.

Both big men shook their heads.

"Two of our comrades have fallen since we last met. I realized these moments would come, but it breaks my heart to lose them. Evan is the reason we are all here, but both were valuable to our team and cannot be replaced. However, we must continue on, even with such big shoes to fill."

"Ben, may I speak?" asked Anders.

Ben gave his approval, and Anders walked to the front. Those who left Missouri before the attack on the Shelter had not heard his story.

"I was also killed in the explosion."

"But you are here. How is that possible?"

"Listen to him, daddy," said Ally, addressing Bruno. "He's telling the truth."

Anders continued, giving no one else a chance to speak. "I went to heaven and saw Angie and our three kids. All of our teammates who have died came to me too: Evan, Malachi, Johnathan, Doc Sanderson, and John and Mary. Last of all, I saw Jesus!"

His thoughts wandered off for a few minutes. They watched him relive the experience in his mind and gave him time. A glow surrounded his head once again, as it had that day in Steve's house when he first told his experience.

"None of us wants to die, but if we do, what awaits us there is far better than what we have here."

He told his story in great detail. It seemed his body was with them, but his mind and spirit were elsewhere. They sat and listened for an hour, entranced by every word. Their faith grew more in that hour than it had in the last three years. Jesus increased their faith because he knew they would need it to continue fighting for the next forty-two months, or however long they survived.

The meeting continued with a mixture of joy and heartbreak. They realized once again their feelings this day represented those of every life. Everyone goes through both good and hard times, but believers in Jesus find contentment in every situation. Michael raised his hand, and Ben nodded at him.

"The Chinese will leave soon so Messai can assume control."

"How do you know that, Michael?" asked Mordecai. "Do you have a direct line to Jesus?"

"Something like that," he said with a smile. "Trust me, that day will come."

Ben and Mordecai looked at each other as Michael glanced at Hadassah and winked. She frowned and shook her head as if saying, "Don't give yourself away." He loved playing these little games.

"We shall see if you are right," said Mordecai with a hint of disdain. "I hope you are, for the sake of our people."

"I suspect you will not hope so when Messai takes charge, but as you say, we shall see."

The meeting ended soon, and the next day proved Michael's words true. PLAAF choppers and planes flew out of the country, leaving Aissa Messai again boasting that he had brokered peace by convincing them to go. People celebrated throughout the country. Businesses and restaurants reopened, and life reemerged in the land of Israel. The nation now believed in Messai even more.

Two days later, with power fully restored nationwide, the Secretary-General announced a news conference from the Temple Mount at 4:00 p.m. the following day. He planned the time to coincide with the end of the evening sacrifice, which occurred at 3:00 p.m. All of Israel waited with the rest of the world to hear what Aissa Messai would say. But what they witnessed as they watched would overshadow any words he spoke.

Everyone in the kibbutz shared the same concern for Moshe and Eliyahu, who left to go out and reach their people, despite the danger involved. No one had talked to them since they left and could not contact them. That would change soon, but not as they hoped or expected.

In the meantime, the movement in Israel had dried up. No news came of anyone turning to Jesus and accepting him as their Messiah. Their best calculations placed the number of believers at 140,000, where it had remained since the large gatherings stopped. That continued to be of great concern to Ben. But this day brought renewed hope from an unexpected source.

"Someone is at the gate!"

Ben met Alexander and Blake as all three rushed toward Bruno and Magnus, who stood near the entrance on guard duty while a man banged loudly on the gate. Some armed men of the kibbutz sprinted to meet them.

"Did you get their names?" Ben asked the two big men.

"There are two of them, and they said their names are Reuben and Gad. Sounds suspicious to us."

Ben and Alexander looked at one another, confused by what they had heard.

"Do you suppose this is some kind of trick to get us to open the gate? It could be an ambush."

"I don't think so, Blake. They claim the names of the remaining two tribes of Israel who lived across the river in Jordan. What do you think, Alexander?"

"Please listen to us. We bring news of Moshe and Eliyahu, who sent us here. It is important that we speak to you."

Now all five men stared at one another. What did their two friends have to do with this? Had something happened to them?

"Open the gate and let them in."

"But Ben, shouldn't we know more about them before we do that?"

Others came now, creating a small army of men with guns waiting for the gate to open. Bruno opened it just enough for the two men to walk inside, then closed it right back.

"Where can we sit and share news with you? This cannot wait."

"Follow me to the meeting hall. Blake, bring some of ours, and Yaakov, bring the other leaders of the kibbutz. We will meet at once."

Within minutes, the group assembled, and Ben gave Reuben and Gad the floor. The two men wasted no time getting started.

"I am Reuben, and this is Gad. Our families have lived in the land of our ancestors in Transjordan for many years. My great-grandparents arrived in the early 1800s when many Jews migrated to Israel, and Gad's family came soon after. But instead of living in Israel, they settled in our original tribal lands. I assure you, our tribes are not lost!"

"But we have lived covertly our entire lives," said Gad. "Many annual censuses have reported no Jews living in Jordan. The country is over ninety percent Muslim. Our communities have maintained a good relationship with our neighbors, as they consider us to be a splinter group of Islam. However, we have continued to be practicing Jews who serve Yahweh."

"Recently," Reuben said again, "two of your men came to our villages and began telling people the Messiah has already come. They were met with rejection at first, but their boldness impressed many of us. Gad and I put our faith in Jesus first, then told everyone in our tribes. All of us now follow Messiah Jesus and are 4,000 strong."

Ben and Alexander sobbed with joy at his last words. The Smyrnians did not understand why this was so powerful for them, but the men of the kibbutz recognized it immediately.

"144,000," said Ben through his tears. "12,000 times the twelve tribes equals 144,000. Twelve is one of God's perfect numbers. No more Jews will turn to the Messiah from this point on. Now is the time to unite our people under the banner of Jesus Christ, our true Messiah."

"One more thing: we must leave Jordan," said Gad. "Things changed overnight and Jews are now the enemy of the Hashemite Kingdom. They already suspect us and may wipe us out soon if our groups do not go. We have ways of crossing the border without getting caught, but we need places to stay after arriving. Moshe and Eliyahu sent us to you for that reason."

"This place is not large enough for 4,000 people," Alexander said.

"I have a suggestion, Ben. These men from the kibbutz spent time in their tribal areas and became familiar with the people. The tribes will provide shelter and protection for them."

He looked at Reuben and Gad as he continued. "You can spread out by families through the other ten tribes, or stay together in an area big enough to handle all 4,000 of you. If you can cross the border into Israel, we will find places for you to live."

"But it will not likely be for long," said Ben. "Something is coming that will put all of our lives in danger. When it does, we will face a choice. And I am certain it will come soon."

"Wait, what about Moshe and Eliyahu?" asked Alexander. "Why have they not returned to us?"

"They told us Phase One of their work is now completed, and Phase Two will begin. I don't know what that means, but Moshe said the entire world will *witness* it."

"I wish they would come home, because we need them. But something changed in them that day on the Plain of Megiddo. Our people believe God gave them a special purpose from birth. Now it is time to reveal that purpose, and it sounds like we will witness it along with the rest of the world."

The men left, and Ben rejoiced as he thanked Jesus for what had happened with the final two tribes discovering their Messiah. But something told him the day of decision was closer than any of them realized. What did Michael mean when he said, *I suspect you will not hope so when Messai takes charge?* They would find out soon enough, and he was sure it would not be good for his people.

Two days passed, and the time drew near for Messai's news conference. Everyone in the kibbutz gathered in front of televisions or sat glued to other devices. The Smyrnians met in the meeting hall to watch, joined by Alexander and Elizabeth, Mordecai, Michael, and Hadassah. The latter two beamed with joy as they entered.

"We present to you the newest members of the Smyrnians," Hadassah said, pointing to the door.

Omar, Ahmad, and Hala walked through. The looks on their faces left no doubt they had put their faith in Jesus and committed their lives to him. The walls shook from the raucous applause and shouts that came from everyone in the room. A hug fest ensued until Ben announced it was 3:50 and almost time for the conference to begin. They settled down and got ready to watch.

Messai appeared on the screen, his usual charming self. Rows of reporters sat before him as he prepared to speak. Something unique was about to happen. They all sensed it.

"Thank you for joining me today, ladies and gentlemen. I am thrilled, as I know you are, that the Chinese have left, the war has ceased, and we can now rebuild our lives and country. We will also begin restoring the journey to peace and prosperity that has been impeded by the grievous events of the past few weeks. I am honored to lead this effort and humbled by your trust in me."

"The things we just witnessed make clear the steps we have taken together. Observing the sacrifices in the grand Jewish Temple once again points to the miracle of peace in the Middle East. I will now make Israel my primary place of residence and this temple the place of my worship."

Thundering voices penetrated the air, drowning out his words. The people in the kibbutz recognized them immediately. Their first word set in motion a conflict with the man at the podium.

"LIAR!"

The Temple Mount became silent as that explosive word pierced the air. Messai stopped talking as the people's attention moved from him to the sources of the proclamation.

"This is the house of Yahweh and of his Messiah, Jesus Christ! Aissa Messai's power comes straight from the pit of hell! Do not listen to him or believe his lies. Jesus is truth! He is the Messiah, the King of kings and Lord of lords, and he is Lord over this deceiver who stands before you!"

Every camera operator quickly turned their cameras toward the sound of the voices, showing two men dressed in sackcloth, with scraggly beards and a disheveled appearance. They held staffs in their hands and raised them toward the sky as they spoke. Their companions in the kibbutz were shocked by what they heard and who they saw: Moshe and Eliyahu.

Messai spun around and faced them with a sinister stare, still appearing calm and unfazed to people watching around the world. He motioned to an AMPP patrol, who provided security for the event. Two of them stood and charged the temple steps where the men continued to shout.

"Repent, for the kingdom of heaven is at hand!"

The men reached them, weapons drawn, intending to arrest them and deliver them to their leader for his normal judgment: interfering with the peace and prosperity of the world. When they lunged at the two men still thundering out their message, fire erupted from Eliyahu's mouth, as it had on the Plain of Megiddo. Both AMPP men were incinerated within seconds. Nothing remained where they had stood but a small pile of ashes.

"Get them!" Messai said, his voice weak compared to theirs.

Four AMPP men ran at them now and experienced the same fate. Messai turned and faced the cameras again, still appearing undaunted by what had gone on.

"Ladies and gentlemen, pay no attention to the two lunatics behind me..."

His mouth continued to move, but his words were overpowered by the booming voices that dominated the day.

"Declare with your mouth, 'Jesus is Lord,' and believe in your heart that God raised him from the dead, and you will be saved!" (Romans 10:9)

Messai stepped down and walked away without uttering another word. Moshe and Eliyahu continued booming out their message about the true Messiah. No one left, but everyone listened to what they said.

"The two witnesses," Anders said.

"Excuse me?" asked Blake.

"Revelation Chapter 11. Further proof that the mid-point of the Tribulation has arrived. First, nuclear war began as foretold in Revelation Chapter 8, and culminated with Israel. Then the PLAAF left the country after tormenting the people for 5 months, as Chapter 9 said they would. I was taken to heaven and told to eat the scroll, just like John in Chapter 10."

"Now we see Chapter 11 fulfilled before our very eyes. Jesus told me these things when the scroll entered my stomach. I didn't get specifics, but I know the timeline, and we are halfway through."

"We all know that, Anders," said Ben. "The three-and-a-half year mark has arrived. The Tribulation will last seven years. It doesn't take a mathematician to figure that out."

"You're right, Ben, and we all understand things will get much worse. However, I received three words from the scroll before Jesus sent me back which make that more true than we realize." He paused, longing to keep those words to himself and spare his friends the pain they would bring.

"Tell us partner; we can handle it."

"*Reign of terror.*"

The room fell silent as they contemplated those words until Anders spoke one more time.

"We will soon lose two more of our own."

The silence became deafening as conflicting thoughts ran through their minds. No one said a word, but each understood what the others were thinking: *Is it me?* They realized it could be any of them, so they sat alone with their thoughts for several minutes before Ben broke the silence.

"Jesus brought us all here for a reason, and each in miraculous ways. Bruno and Magnus should not have escaped China alive, but they did. Trey and Rickie, Hassan should not have given you a plane to *get them out*, but he did, not to mention you making it back across the border."

"Blake, none of you should have survived the bombing at the Shelter, but all of you did, except Evan. Ollie and Amelia, your escape from England and Bradley's willingness to fly you to Missouri was orchestrated by Jesus himself, although you are escape artists in your own right."

That brought a brief smile during a serious conversation.

"Paul and Bradley should have run out of fuel and crashed with no place to land. I am still amazed that you landed at Ben Gurion, especially with the runways demolished. We must also include the rescue of the American troops from Jordan, followed by Reuben and Gad coming with news of their tribes turning to Jesus. Yes, these few days have been miraculous. Jesus is up to something."

Trey and Rickie traveled to Camp Filon to meet with Robert Clark, and took Mordecai, Michael, Hadassah with them. Their purpose was twofold: help his unit find a place to stay, and show him the video, hoping he would believe in Jesus.

"Welcome to our home, gentlemen, and lady," Robert said, acknowledging Hadassah.

"That is one reason we came, Sergeant Major Clark."

"Please Aluf, skip the formalities and let's use each other's real names, shall we?"

"As I was saying, one reason we came, *Robert*, is to help find lodging for you and your company."

"That is much better, *Mordecai*. Be thankful the recent withdrawal called most of the troops home from our brigade. We were once 2,000 strong. It is easier to find a place for 200 men and women than 2,000. Any accommodations need to be temporary, because we will all return home soon."

"We can send you to the Negev where our bases house thousands of soldiers, or we can split you up and place you in multiple camps. Flying out of Israel may not be an option for months."

"Oh, we are not stuck here, Aluf. I am grateful for your rescue efforts, but my troops and I will travel to the U.S. at the first opportunity."

"I thought we were on a first-name basis, Sergeant Major. Consider your options and tell me your decision, and I will arrange your transfer to the base, or bases, of your choice."

"If the two of you are finished with all the professional military lingo, I would like to say something," said Trey.

"Robert, we want to show you a video. It appears you don't have a lot going on, so this will occupy your time for an hour. What do you say?"

"I say, you are out of your mind, Trey Butler. I have no time for such things. These days can be used for training and work. So, you may keep your video to yourself."

"Oh, come on, Robert. You owe this to Trey and me for our friendship through the years. And as I recall, we just rescued you and your men. You owe us a favor for that one, too. Consider this video an hour of personal development. Where else can you get that in one hour?"

"You drive a hard bargain, Rickie, but my answer is still no."

"You are a stubborn man, Robert. If you weren't, Zaid would not have let us use a plane to rescue Bruno and Magnus, so we are also thankful for your stubbornness! We'll just leave this with you and hope you'll watch it when you have time. If we didn't believe it is important, we wouldn't ask you to watch it. It changed our lives, and I promise it will change yours too."

Trey pulled a thumb drive from his pocket and handed it to the man.

"We shall see. Now Mordecai, about those accommodations."

•   •   •   •   •

Aissa Messai called another news conference, this time choosing a different location, hoping to avoid the wild men who interrupted his last one. Teddy Stadium, a massive sports facility in Jerusalem with seating for 34,000 people, provided the space for his largest audience ever. He would offer free food and deliver a hope-filled speech that was broadcast worldwide.

He expected people to pack the place after the last one, thinking the two men may show up again. But he would ensure they did not. *Heightened security will keep them out,* he said to himself before taking the stage. If AMPP stationed patrols at every entrance, surrounded the outside, and covered the inside, the men could not possibly get in. *They are easy to spot.*

Cameras rolling, he strode to the middle of the platform, stood at the microphone, and listened to the deafening applause from his adoring public. He took a moment to soak it in. Those in attendance included every Smyrnian and person from the kibbutz, their eyes peeled, looking for Moshe and Eliyahu. They could not imagine the men would miss a gathering of this magnitude.

Messai began with flattering speech for his listeners, droning on about their importance to him and his mission to bring peace and prosperity to the world. His speech espoused his favorite subject.

"I stand here today in this beautiful city, which has become my home, speaking to the entire world. We face the difficult task of rebuilding of our planet, following nuclear holocaust. World leaders asked me to assume leadership over this huge undertaking, and I accept that responsibility. I remind you, we are the gods of this world, and we have the capacity to make that happen. So..."

A sudden buzz arose from the crowd, and they shouted louder than the deafening cheers when the home team scores a goal. *"There they are!"* Phones and cameras flashed all over the stadium, as people tried to get pictures of the two wild men who appeared out of nowhere.

"LIAR!"

Messai spun to his right, then left, seeing Moshe and Eliyahu standing on each side of the stage. How did they get in? *That was impossible!*

Some in the crowd applauded, while others tried in vain to shout the men down.

"Your lies are a stench in the nostrils of Yahweh and his Messiah, Jesus. Because you continue to deny him, he will withhold rain from the world so you may know that he alone is God!"

Eliyahu pointed his staff toward the sky and proclaimed in a booming voice, "As the LORD lives, neither dew nor rain will fall, and the earth will remain parched, until Yahweh commands it again!"

Blazing hot hurricane-force winds suddenly blasted into the stadium, creating havoc, as people ran for any cover that would shelter them from the tempest. Messai could not stand against the wind, and with nowhere to escape, it hurled him off the platform to the ground before his security patrol reached him. The incendiary gale stung his skin and sent him crawling under the stage for protection.

The soft green grass, where football players normally ran, turned to crusty brown chaff instantly. Outside, leaves covered trees, thanks to the rainy season in Israel. But the scorching wind dried them up and blew them away, leaving barren branches projecting from scaly trunks. The parched and broken ground no longer held water for root systems, as all of nature seemed to break down.

News reports interrupted the broadcast to show similar videos from all over the world. The earth dried up within minutes, and no rain would fall. The prophet Eliyahu had spoken. It brought back reminders of year one of the Tribulation as the first half now came to a close.

Messai crawled out from under the stage, stood to his feet, and surveyed the situation. The wind had ceased, replaced by oppressive heat. Debris and garbage littered the stadium. Empty seats from departed attendees met his sight, and an eerie silence greeted his ears. Gone were the cameras and reporters. He found himself alone with his thoughts.

He turned to face the men on the stage, but they had disappeared. On the platform lay four piles of ash where his AMPP men had stood. At least they tried to do their jobs. He walked to the middle of the football field, threw back his head, and unleashed the loudest scream that had ever erupted from inside him. Lightning flashed throughout the stadium as streams of dark vapor poured from his body. Demons screeched and howled, and flew all around him.

His time drew near, and he was ready. He had awaited this moment his entire life. The dragon chose him, but he knew from childhood his destiny was to rule the world. The dragon simply gave him the opportunity to fulfill the purpose for which he was born. Since the day he sold his soul to the beast, he served the monster faithfully, and received the position of Secretary-General because he did. Soon the beast would give him its full power and elevate him to his second in command.

The two men were simply a momentary distraction. This was their moment, and he would allow them to have it. However, he would soon end it himself for all the world to see. Relishing the thought brought an evil smile to his face. He did not need the dragon's help with that. *But it will please the creature and prove my commitment to him*, he said aloud, trembling with anticipation. The beast had one more task to complete, then his day would come.

CHAPTER 8

The group arrived back at the kibbutz and found the gates standing open. Every man jumped from their vehicles, weapons in hand, and cautiously crept inside. Two men in gleaming white stood in the middle of the street before them. The group covered their eyes, unable to look at them. By now, the others joined them.

"Fear not. The Messiah is with you. He will bless you and keep you, make his face shine on you, and be gracious to you. He will turn his face toward you and give you peace."

"Moshe!" his wife said. She ran toward the men, then collapsed like she hit a wall.

"Do not come near, for no one can approach the glory of the Lord. You will soon see things that will shake your faith. The Lord planned them before the creation of the world. Believe in him; trust him; serve him. We will all be together again soon."

A third figure joined them, his appearance so brilliant it radiated out in a ten-foot circle. The entire group of Smyrnians and people of the community fell on their faces before him. The ground shook beneath them. Thunder crashed and lightning flashed as they lay face down.

"This is my son, whom I love; with him I am well pleased. Listen to him!"

Anders stood to his feet and walked toward the three men. The others lifted their heads to watch him, shielding their eyes from the blinding light.

"Jesus," he said in a voice unlike any they had ever heard. The glow they had seen before returned to him, shining more brightly the closer he got.

He continued his approach and knelt close enough it appeared he could reach out and touch the Lord. Jesus spoke, but they could not make out what he said. Anders understood every word. He rose and returned, joining the others, bowing low beside them. A cloud enveloped them, and a hand touched each head. Power charged through their bodies like a jolt of electricity.

"Get up. Don't be afraid. Fight the good fight, finish the race, keep the faith. A crown of righteousness awaits you when you see me again. And I will give you the crown of life."

They stood to their feet and saw nothing but an empty street and the houses where they lived. Anders pulled them together, eager to share with them the things Jesus told him.

• • • • •

Aissa Messai sat alone with his thoughts following the debacle at Teddy Stadium. The memories flashed through his mind. Pride surged when he recalled stepping to the microphone and watching the people stand and greet him with thunderous applause. He could not help but smile, thinking about the power and prestige that came with his position. That would soon become even greater.

Anger filled his mind at being interrupted by the two crazy men. Their opening word came as real as when he first heard it: *"LIAR!"* He lost the audience right before that moment, their attention drawn to the men. How did they get in? Security was so tight no one could have gotten into that stadium. One AMPP member told him they appeared out of nowhere and stood on the stage.

The words came from his mouth, though no one was there to hear them. *The false messiah, the one called Jesus thinks he can defeat me, but the all-powerful one empowers me! I will begin by destroying his so-called prophets.* Thoughts of killing Moshe and Eliyahu consumed his thinking. In that moment, another fascination departed. He would not have considered releasing her, but his thirst for power, and overcoming the other self-proclaimed messiah, seized control of him.

Blake and Beth lay on their bed talking about the incredible events of the day. She experienced a momentary chill, and Blake saw her shudder. He reached out to grab and hold her, protecting her from Messai's presence. The chill disappeared, and she sat up, happiness written all over her face.

"Blake! Something just happened!"

"I saw it, Beth. It was him, but I will not let him have you!"

He was on his feet and prepared to fight, understanding he faced an impossible battle, but ready to do anything necessary to protect his wife.

"You don't understand; it's not like that. Something broke his hold, and he released me. I'm free, Blake, I know it! He will never bother me again!"

There was no question. Her expression and the tone of her voice made that clear. *That is what real freedom looks like*, he reasoned. He had not seen her this happy since the day Messai took her. He knew she was free. Both of them fell on the bed together, rolling and laughing hysterically. Yes, this was how real freedom looked, and it felt amazing!

The chill entered the room, and Messai knew what to expect next. The dragon reassured him and released him from his fascination with Beth Jennings instantly. He fell to his knees and bowed low, paying homage to the beast, as he always did. The putrid odor filled his nostrils, and heat stung his face. He waited for the creature to speak until the low, gravelly voice sent fear into his soul. It happened like this every time. But his excitement always overcame the fear.

"Aissa." The voice sounded more evil and powerful than ever, but it still intoxicated him.

Terror overwhelmed him. The weight of the creature's power hung over him. Could any human being come this close to pure evil and survive? Death seemed imminent as the beast drew near. Would it kill him here and leave his promises unfulfilled?

"Get up."

"But, your majesty..."

"Would you prefer I lift you up?"

Messai felt a sharp claw dig into his back and stood quickly.

"Your day approaches fast, Aissa. I assume you are ready?"

"Yes, your majesty. I have waited for this day and worship only you. Tell me what more you require of me, and I will do anything you ask."

"I require only obedience. Because you have obeyed me and given yourself completely to me, I will grant to you my authority and rule the world with you by my side."

"May it be as you say. I promise to never let you down."

"We must each remove the obstacles first. Handle yours well, Aissa. I will enjoy destroying mine."

"I will do the same, master."

The Great Red Dragon turned to leave in full view of Messai. His gigantic, scaly body seemed to fill half the room. Scratching sounds accompanied sharp claws scraping the floor as he ambled toward the door. Smoke poured from nostrils forming the end of a long pointy nose, as flames shot from an open mouth lined with razor-sharp teeth. The long tail dragged on the floor behind him.

Before reaching the door, the beast vanished with one final roar, leaving Messai standing alone. He had received his marching orders and understood his next move. He relished this one and would carry it out with pleasure. The dragon had long awaited his opportunity and would perform it with gusto. Both must carry out their missions before Messai's big day came. He must proceed and reprove his commitment to the creature. The world needed a word from him again.

The Secretary-General stood at the bottom of the temple steps again to deliver another speech. Members of the press stood before him, with no one else allowed in attendance.

AMPP personnel stood guard around the perimeter of the area, keeping watch should the two men show up again. None would approach them for fear of losing their lives, as had their brothers in arms. Messai himself forbade it out of concern for his forces. When the time came to speak, he began cautiously, listening for Moshe and Eliyahu on the steps behind him.

"Good day, citizens of our planet." He was clearly off his game and not his usual self. Something occupied his mind. He cleared his throat and continued.

"Together we face a crisis caused by the two men who have become a dangerous threat to our peace and prosperity. By using some magical powers, they stopped rain from falling on our planet. But they cannot stop *us!* Your fortitude and determination never cease to amaze me. The great news is this: most of the world's systems which provide drinking water remain full and will meet our needs for a long time. They tried to stop us, but they failed!"

"LIAR!"

Nervous energy, accompanied by thrilling anticipation, arose in him at the sound of that word. They had come! He secretly hoped the men would show up. He instructed his men to not go near them, but to come fully armed. With a nod of his head, the signal went out to the patrols. Every man dropped to his knees and took aim.

Fire exploded from Eliyahu's mouth and raced toward the men like a rushing torrent. It reached its target before any could pull the triggers, melting the powerful weapons in their hands. Screams filled the air as melted aluminum, steel, and hard plastic poured back into their hands, searing them with third-degree burns. Messai spun around to face the two prophets again just as Moshe bellowed out a proclamation, his staff raised and stretched out in front of him.

"So you may know that Yahweh is the only true God, the waters of the earth will turn to blood until Yahweh restores them. Oceans, rivers, ponds, reservoirs, and every source of drinking water will become blood. Creatures that live in them will die."

"Turn and worship Yahweh and believe in his son, the true Messiah. His name is Jesus. Aissa Messai is a fraud who leads you down the path to hell. Do not listen to his lies; instead, follow Jesus! He is the way, the truth, and the life, and no one comes to Yahweh except through him!"

The men vanished, leaving Messai speechless and his men writhing in agony, their hands seared to the bone. Once again, the cameras of newsmen and women captured the events and broadcast them to the world. Medical personnel rushed to assist the injured men, while Messai gathered himself and turned to face the reporters again.

"Pay no attention to the ravings of these madmen. They are lies. The rain will soon fall again, and you will find our water as drinkable and refreshing as ever. No water anywhere will turn to blood."

The reporters gasped and pointed toward the large bronze basin sitting in front of the temple. It held water for the priests to wash their hands and feet before entering the house of the LORD. Messai whirled around and saw the reason for their reaction. Liquid poured over the side of the basin, but it was not water. Blood ran down the side in a continual stream, flowing toward them.

Messai tried to speak again, but both camera operators and reporters fled the scene. He must remove his obstacles soon, while allowing the dragon to work on his own time. Plans formed in his mind before he left the Mount.

News reports from every country showed blood-filled fresh and salt water. Bottled water in homes and on store shelves turned blood-red. Thirsty people dug deep into the ground in search of drinkable water. Desperation fueled depravity. People would do anything to get water.

Dead and rotting seafood lined seashores and river banks. The smell was nauseating, and seafood unavailable. The plague reached epidemic proportions, affecting every person on earth. People directed their anger at two people: the prophets on the Temple Mount. They caused this. The world turned to one man for answers, their savior, Aissa Messai.

Moshe and Eliyahu continued proclaiming their message about Jesus without hesitation, while denouncing Messai as the *anti*-messiah. After previous episodes at the temple and Teddy Stadium, their preaching became more powerful. But they grew less popular every day.

Many died while attacking them, attempting to stop their denouncing of sin and of the man they called the *Antichrist*. Each person experienced the same brutal death, incinerated by the fire that shot from their mouths. No one dared attack them physically now, but the verbal assaults spread worldwide, until hatred for them was at fever pitch around the globe. The media joined the frenzy, attacking them daily, spreading lies, and fueling animosity.

"Those two crazy men are destroying our lives," said the Prime Minister of Australia during a sit-down interview. "Australia shares a close relationship with the nation of Israel. We denounce this plague they have brought upon them, our country, and the rest of the world. Someone must stop them before they destroy the entire planet!"

"Everyone knows we hate Israel and the Jews," said the Supreme Leader of Iran. "We denounce them for allowing these two men to pronounce judgments which affect the rest of the world in the name of their false god. We must destroy Moshe, Eliyahu, and Israel!"

Similar reports came from country leaders around the world. Mobs gathered to hang and burn effigies of the two prophets of Yahweh and shout chants demanding that someone bring them to justice. The protests turned violent, filled with rioting and unnecessary deaths. Every interview, news report, talk show, and protest fanned the flames of hatred for Moshe and Eliyahu.

Messai took advantage of the situation. He combated their harsh words with positive words. People welcomed that, believing him and trusting him even more. While the prophets railed against sin, he promoted the rights of everyone to live as they choose, and disavowed any belief in God or the absolute truth of the Bible. He spoke live from a remote location.

"These men spew hatred and violence, trying to end peace and prosperity in our world. I seek to bring love and hope. Reject their lies and accept the truths of science and knowledge. We have no need of a mythical, vengeful god who sends judgment against good people seeking to live in peace. I came to give you abundant life!"

He no longer visited the temple, but avoided the two men, and allowed the press to give them all the negative attention he needed. The more bad publicity they received, the more the world saw him in a positive light. The men played right into his hands and did not realize it.

"Yahweh will end the plague on water tomorrow," Moshe said. "The blood will disappear and water will become pure and potable again. Oceans, streams, and lakes will once again teem with life. You will drink the water and enjoy the seafood they provide. But if you continue to sin against Yahweh and reject Jesus, another plague will follow!"

Messai followed their announcement with one of his own.

"Their *god* will not stop the bloody waters; *I* will! They use their deity as an excuse for their failure to overcome my power. If they use their magic to bring another plague, I will stop it too! Continue living as you wish and understand there is no such being who commands you to stop enjoying your lives and finding fulfillment in who you are. I only ask that you do nothing to interfere with the peace and prosperity of the world. Apart from that, live as you choose and be happy!"

The next morning, people in every part of the globe awoke to frogs covering the land. From palaces to slums, frogs were everywhere. Once again, the plague ended with the disappearance of the amphibians, and Messai claimed credit.

"These men will fail at their attempts to destroy us and our world! I will end every curse they bring on us. Know that I am affected by them, just as you are. They place curses on us through witchcraft and sorcery, but we defeat them with the power of love and kindness. This too shall pass. Follow me, and we will achieve an even brighter future and better world than we dreamed possible!"

People accepted his words without question and continued living as they pleased, defying the words of the prophets and the God and Messiah they proclaimed.

"Because you refuse to repent and turn to the living God, the next plague will be worse than the last," said Moshe from the Temple steps. "You still reject Jesus as the true Messiah and follow Aissa Messai. Until you denounce him as the false messiah and worship Jesus, the outbreaks will continue. Yahweh continues to await your response. Let the infestation begin!"

The minute he raised the staff in his hand, lice covered the earth. Attempts to remove them from homes, clothing, businesses, and everywhere else were futile. No one could walk outside without being covered with the microscopic parasites. Even Messai wanted to approach the men and ask them to stop the infestation, but he dared not show weakness and cause people to view them as stronger than him.

The lice brought extreme suffering from incessant itching and infections that developed from continual scratching. People begged for relief but found none. Though their animosity toward the men who called forth the infestation grew, they welcomed Moshe's next appearance on the news.

"The lice will leave today, but Yahweh still calls you to repentance. Failure to repent will bring another infestation tomorrow. If you turn to Jesus, Yahweh will spare you, but if your rejection persists, you will once again suffer the consequences."

"Protect yourselves from whatever epidemic these madmen unleash next. Wear coverings, stay inside and lock your doors. Stay safe and healthy, the opposite of what they and their so-called *god* want for you. If we stick together, we will overcome these plagues, defeat this enemy, and emerge victorious. We can achieve no victory without determination, endurance, and unity. Consider all we have accomplished because we stuck together. This will turn into our greatest achievement yet!"

Messai always followed their announcements with proclamations of his own, each giving the people of the world more confidence in him and faith to survive what came next.

The next morning cameras filmed and reporters stood covered in protective gear, anticipating the next proclamation of judgment from Moshe. They watched as he appeared out of nowhere on the temple steps, per his normal M.O., then waited for him to speak. They did not have to wait long.

"What is worse than a world covered in lice? A planet that swarms with flies!"

He said nothing more, simply held out his staff and stood firm while an incessant stream of flies swarmed from it. The loud buzzing drowned out the reporters' words. Cameras inadvertently captured images of their protective facial coverings blackened inside with flies as the newscasters ripped them off their heads and ran, swatting at the pests attacking them.

Moshe's voice thundered above the droning of the flying insects as he spoke one more time before disappearing again. It was the last thing microphones picked up before stations cut them off.

"Yahweh says, 'I distinguish between my people and you.' The plagues are not affecting them because they believe in my son, the Messiah, and follow him."

"It's true," said Ben as he watched the news coverage with the others. "All ten plagues Yahweh sent on Egypt are happening now, but they're not affecting people who believe in Jesus. They only touch those who refuse to believe. We have contacted every tribe, and they are experiencing the same. That must hold true for believers all over the world."

"None of them last long. The flies are plague number four, leaving six more to come. But I fear for Moshe and Eliyahu. Messai's hatred for them is clear, but now the entire world despises them. Jesus gave them a way to protect themselves, but will their supernatural protection end?"

"I fear it will, Blake, but we can't do anything about that, except pray for them. Another question troubles my spirit. It hit me during the night while I lay in bed, unable to sleep. This thought kept coming to my mind: why the plagues, and why Moshe? God sent the plagues on Egypt through Moses to deliver his people from slavery and the hand of a ruthless dictator. Sound familiar?"

"Ben, you may be onto something," said Mordecai. "Messai is definitely a ruthless dictator, and you could say we are in slavery to him. He hates all followers of Jesus, but especially the Jews."

"Yahweh told our ancestors to prepare for a sudden departure. I believe we must do the same, but how do we prepare for that which we don't understand? Jesus hasn't told us how, when, or where."

"Ben, do you remember when we realized we will need lots of pilots for what's coming?" Michael asked. "I formed a team of IDF pilots, and Jesus brought Trey and Rickie here. Now we have Paul and Bradley, and their planes. So, whatever it is, we're ready! What do you say, Bradley?"

"You know I'm ready! How about you, Paul?"

"Bring it on! Those planes are here for a reason, and they're sitting in those hangars at Ben Gurion waiting for the right time. I'm ready whenever that time comes."

"We will meet soon to discuss and plan. All of us need to agree on how we will proceed."

"For now, we pray for our two comrades, who battle an enemy they cannot defeat on their own."

• • • •

One week later, the people of the world cursed Moshe and Eliyahu because of the flies, yet pleaded for relief at the same time. Hatred for them intensified by the day. Networks stationed multiple Live Cams around the Temple Mount, all trained on the temple 24/7. If the two prophets showed up, the world would know. They did, on the seventh day of the plague of flies.

"The flies will die today," Moshe shouted in the booming voice people came to expect. "But your continued refusal to repent and trust in Jesus will bring an even worse outbreak tomorrow!"

No one knew what to expect this time. Moshe's proclamation was vague, so they would wait and see what came. The word *worse* sent fear into their souls, leaving them longing for a word from their self-proclaimed messiah. That word came thirty minutes after Moshe spoke.

"Ladies and gentlemen, we do not know what this madman plans next or how long it will last. Whatever it is, we will get through it together. I advise you to protect yourselves again. Take every precaution to ensure the safety of your family. Stay tuned for news updates and expect daily briefings from me. Do not follow their misguided challenge to accept the false messiah because no invisible god exists. Refuse to believe that which you cannot see."

People living in cities and suburban areas awoke the next morning to no visible signs of another outbreak. They breathed sighs of relief until news videos showed millions of dead livestock in every part of the world. This one devastated farmers and ranchers, except those who followed Jesus. Their livestock flourished.

This plague continued more than one month, though the meat shortage would last much longer. Meat prices soared until the crisis reached its peak when no meat was available anywhere. It forced people into vegan lifestyles without meat or animal products.

"I realize the disastrous effects of this unfortunate catastrophe," said Messai from his remote location. "But we must realize fruits and vegetables remain plentiful and available. The livestock will return since not all died. Stay patient while we survive another crisis together."

With demand for meat, milk, butter, and other products at its peak, Moshe and Eliyahu reappeared at the temple, which was still closed because of the plagues. No sacrifices took place, and no priests performed their work. Jewish worship in the glorious rebuilt structure ceased.

"Yahweh gives you another opportunity to repent of your sins and put your faith in Jesus," Moshe said, as if pleading with them to heed his offer. "Because he is loving and patient, you have three days to obey him." After a moment of silence, his voice rang out again.

"However, if you decline his grace once again, the fourth day will bring physical suffering of the worst kind. Please heed Yahweh's word before that day comes!"

Messai stood in direct defiance of the Living God as he spoke again.

"I defy the ravings and attacks of these madmen and refuse to allow them to stop what we started when we created a unified planet. Ten members of the Peace Patrol will stand atop the steps to the Altar of Burnt Offering the third day at noon. I challenge Moshe and Eliyahu to meet them there. We shall see who has greater power. If my men emerge victorious, the plagues will stop!"

The entire world watched three days later to see this battle of behemoths. They observed the AMPP patrol hesitantly ascending the steps to the Altar of Burnt Offering. But when they stood alone on top, they surrounded it, raised their weapons, and screamed a loud shout of victory.

Moshe and Eliyahu materialized below them and began moving up the steps slowly, their eyes staring straight ahead. The captain of the patrol shouted, "Fire!" Each man shouldered his assault rifle and pulled the trigger. Moshe extended both hands, deflecting every bullet away. The patrol emptied the last of their thirty-round cartridges as the men reached the top step.

Moshe held his arms in a circle surrounding the altar. The men tried to jump, but an invisible barrier prevented them from moving. Eliyahu extended his arms toward the sky, and water fell on the altar, soaking the wood and overflowing the sides. Moshe jerked his arms forward, throwing all ten men on top of the saturated wood.

Eliyahu threw back his head, then brought it forward, unleashing fire and igniting the wood, incinerating both it and the men within seconds. Screams barely escaped their mouths before the blazing inferno extinguished them in death. The world watched in horror and loathed the two prophets even more after viewing such vicious killing of innocent men. The incident brought Messai's face to their screens again.

"Ladies and gentlemen, anger has never defined me. I am a man of love and peace. But today, I stand before you, appalled and livid at the horrific scene I just witnessed. The men of AMPP also love peace and work to maintain it. Their one task continues to be creating peace and prosperity in our world by protecting it from maniacs like the two men who torment us now. I feel certain another assault will come tomorrow. Please protect your family every way you can. I assure you we will soon rid the world of Moshe and Eliyahu!"

Messai awoke at 6:00 a.m. the next morning in excruciating pain. He leapt from his bed, ripped off his nightshirt and stood horrified in front of his full-length mirror, looking at large boils on his chest and stomach. Pain wracked his body, so he knew the sores covered every part of him. He also knew they affected every person in the world.

"People of the world," he said, standing before the camera in his den. "I want to show you I suffer along with you from this scourge, perpetrated by the madmen on the Mount." He wore shorts and a t-shirt, a view of him the world had never seen.

"You can see my arms and legs covered with painful boils." He winced, moving to offer a close-up view. "I feel sure you suffer from the same thing. This cannot continue! The leaders of my security team are adapting plans at this moment to remove Moshe and Eliyahu. I hope that happens before another pestilence occurs. However, I cannot guarantee that. I intend to seek medical help today and encourage you to do the same. My team works diligently to prevent more episodes."

Hatred for Moshe and Eliyahu now reached a breaking point, resulting in expressions of rage. Many wanted to fly to Jerusalem and take the men out themselves, but fear held them back. Jesus protected his followers from the plagues, and they stood by the prophets of God. But they also understood the two men's lives were in imminent danger. They prayed while the world suffered.

Something occurred to Messai as he tried unsuccessfully to treat the boils covering his body. The men said the *Jesus people* did not experience the afflictions with the rest of the world. An evil plan took shape in his wicked mind. It involved only Israel and the Jews.

Many of them still worshiped their false god, Yahweh, but had not joined the Jesus cult. He would take care of them later. But now he must locate Jewish followers of Jesus. His men should discover them with no problem. *They are healthy and unharmed,* he said with a wicked grin. He dispatched every AMPP patrol in Israel to search for and discover this group. Their time would come soon.

The boils healed, but not until people endured horrible suffering. Moshe announced the next two plagues would come back-to-back, eradicating the world's remaining food supply. Golf ball sized hail came first, continuing for a full day, stripping every tree and plant and destroying fruits and vegetables. Crops pummeled by the onslaught lay in ruins across the globe. Many people also died who got caught outside in the barrage of hail. Still, no one dared approach the prophets of Yahweh.

Swarms of locusts followed that, covering the globe and consuming everything left by the hail. They devoured every leaf and plant they could find. The planet was on the verge of a worldwide famine. The scarcity of food led to further desperation, and an increased desire to annihilate the two men who caused it. AMPP searched for and discovered many locations of *Jesus Jews*, as they called them. They would pay the price too, Messai told his men. That day drew near.

People ridiculed Moshe's announcement of plague number nine. *Darkness*. The planet would turn completely dark everywhere, he said. Everyone knew that was impossible with electricity, generators, lamps, flashlights, cell phones, light from vehicles, plus the ability to start fires to provide light. The men had been right to this point, but this was one they could not pull off.

Then it happened. When morning dawned, the darkness did not disappear. People frantically flipped light switches, with no success. Generators failed to start, flashlights refused to shine, and no fires would ignite, leaving the world in darkness. Total darkness felt deep in the soul, brought despair, anxiety, and depression. No one could see, and no light came.

The darkness continued ten days, then twenty and thirty, with no relief in sight. Residents of the kibbutz saw the darkness outside, but inside the days were bright and lights functioned at night. Looking out reminded Blake and Beth of the eclipse and invasion of darkness that came with it. But that darkness only lasted 26 minutes and 51 seconds. This had already lasted over thirty days.

Men and women lost their minds. Some went blind like fish in caves that never experience light. Suicides became commonplace. Businesses closed, meaning people were not only out of light; they were also out of work. Hospitals could not provide care for patients, leaving life-saving surgeries and all other procedures out of the question.

One or two days would have been bad, but 30 days and counting were debilitating. Messai had a plan, if only his AMPP personnel would think to carry it out. He had sent them all over Israel to identify Jews who now followed Jesus. This provided the best opportunity yet to do that. If Moshe was right, they would have light in their homes. Messai hoped his men were taking addresses.

After a couple weeks, the darkness started affecting him. He assumed his power would allow him to see, but it did not. Where was the dragon? The beast could give him sight. But the creature did not come, and neither did the light. If he could get to the two men, he would plead for them to dispel the darkness. The people of the world cried out for help, and it finally came.

On the morning of day forty, the sun rose and light flooded the earth. Human beings across the world celebrated the light. They flooded doctor's offices and hospitals to receive treatment for physical ailments, especially those related to eyesight. Families and first responders discovered suicide victims who surrendered to the darkness. Celebration quickly turned to rage. The targets of their animosity appeared once more in front of the temple.

"Yahweh has given you nine opportunities to repent, but each time you hardened your hearts and rejected his mercy. He will now extend his grace one more day. He wants no one to perish but everyone to come to repentance. If you refuse him this time, he will send one final plague. The others will not compare to what it brings. He awaits your response. You have twenty-four hours."

CHAPTER 9

"Where have you guys been? We thought you forgot about us."

Robert Clark grabbed Trey and Rickie, gave both an enormous bear hug, and smiled at Mordecai. They looked at each other, then kept walking.

"I think the darkness got to him," Trey whispered.

"I heard that!" Robert said, before cutting loose with a big belly laugh.

The three men said nothing now. Their friend, the Sergeant Major, surely lost his mind amid the recent chaos. Maybe they could help him and his troops.

"What's the matter? Aren't you going to welcome the newest member of the... what do you call yourselves... Smyrnians?"

Trey finally wheeled around and said, "Do you mean...?"

"Yes, that's what I mean! We saw the news every day about those madmen at the Temple. The water to blood thing was bad, but those accursed frogs, lice, and flies about drove us insane. We heard about the livestock dying. That didn't affect us. But the doggone boils hit us all, and they were rough. Then came the hail and locusts, and I realized the two men had been right every time. Something was different about them, and it wasn't their choice of attire either." He grinned.

"When they said darkness would come the next day, I laughed out loud. But we checked our flashlights and charged our phones, just in case. I mean, they hadn't missed yet. Then when daylight didn't come the next morning and our stuff didn't work, I realized something wasn't right, but I couldn't wrap my mind around it."

"A week went by, then two, and it was still so dark we couldn't even see each other. You're right, Trey. The darkness did get to me. I was lying down one day after that two-week mark. What else was there to do, right?

Anyway, I started thinking about that flash drive you left me, and I couldn't get the thing off my mind. It's like it was calling my name and saying, 'watch me!' Now, I'm sure you think I lost my mind."

The look on their faces said, *we've been there*. That elicited a big smile and more talking.

"I told myself, *that'll never work*, because it produces light, but I got up and felt around till I found it and my computer. That thing wouldn't turn on till I put the flash drive in. Then it came right on! I was so excited to have something working, and light, that I gladly watched it."

"I'm a history buff and a numbers guy, so I found it quite interesting, even before the preacher got to the good part. He already had me hooked. So, when he got to the part about asking Jesus into my life, I jumped right on it!"

"I couldn't tell the time because clocks and phones didn't work, and it was pitch dark. Turns out it was mid-afternoon. That room lit up the minute I finished praying to Jesus!"

Three amazed men stood listening to him, their mouths wide open, not saying a word.

"Want me to tell you what I did next?"

He didn't wait for them to respond.

"I got the others and made them watch it too! I could see clear as day, but it was still dark for them. It's pretty amazing what Jesus can do."

They just nodded and kept listening. All three realized he wasn't about to stop talking.

"I still don't understand how we did that, but it happened. They watched it and did the same thing as me. Then this entire camp lit up. It was broad daylight! We threw a party to top all parties, running around all over the place and yelling, *thank you, Jesus!*"

Trey got words out at last. "You just made our day, Robert! When you hear why we came today, you will understand that more. We know what the last plague will be, so we only had twenty-four hours to get here and talk to you."

"You know?"

"I lived as a Jew my whole life, Robert, until I believed in Jesus like you just did," said Mordecai. "So, I studied the Old Testament from childhood.

Most other people have heard the story of Moses and the plagues on Egypt too, but they probably didn't cross their minds during all this."

"The plagues! Why didn't I think of that?"

"And Moshe is Moses in Hebrew."

"No..."

"Yes. Do you remember the tenth plague?"

Robert's face said it all, and a tear formed in his eye.

"The death of the firstborn."

"You have children, don't you, Robert?"

"Yes, and grandchildren."

"Call them right now, Robert, and have your troops call their families, too. If they haven't turned to Jesus..." Rickie's voice trailed off.

Robert ran from the room to summon the others, phone in hand, calling his own family as he ran.

• • • • •

At the kibbutz, Michael, Hadassah, and the group of Smyrnians sat with Ahmad. None of them would sleep, nor would they leave his side. They weren't sure how this worked, but he was an only child, making him the oldest in his family. He had accepted Jesus as the Messiah and his Savior, but his parents were still practicing Muslims.

"Will I die?" he asked in his best English.

"I wish I had the answer to that, Ahmad, but I don't. Did you talk to your parents?"

"I called them, but they disowned me as their son. The radicals put me on their hit list, so they may search for me tonight. If I go, I realize I will be with Jesus, but I want to stay here and help you fight Messai."

"I can't imagine Yahweh would take you, Ahmad," said Ben. "But we're all sitting right here with you all night. We will pray all night too and ask Jesus to leave you with us. That's all we can do."

Michael was quieter than normal. It appeared he was having a silent conversation with someone. None of them wanted to interrupt him, so they left him alone.

The twenty-four hours ended at 6:00 p.m., leaving them with sobering thoughts and praying for every family in the world on this solemn night.

Mordecai, Trey, and Rickie stayed with the troops at Camp Filon. They wanted to be present in the event any bad news came. Some of them were the oldest in their families too, so they did not know what to expect, either. The night promised to be long for all of them.

When the clock struck midnight, everyone in the kibbutz, and every soldier at Camp Filon felt it. It wasn't like the chill Messai brought. It was different, like a cool breeze that makes a person want to grab a jacket. They sensed someone, or something, riding the breeze. The feeling was more eerie than any they had experienced during the last three-and-a-half years, and they knew what it was.

The group surrounding Ahmad saw his face turn white as he collapsed to the floor. His eyes rolled back, and his lips and face turned blue. Hala fell beside him, yelling his name, and shaking him. Michael still stood to the side, appearing to continue his silent conversation.

"He's dead!" Hala said as Omar and Hadassah joined her on the floor. They held each other and cried together, while the others grieved with them. Michael walked over and stood by them.

"Are you sure?" he asked. "Maybe anxiety got to him and he passed out. After all, he had plenty to stress about. Let me see," he said, bending over his friend.

Color returned to Ahmad's face, and his body trembled. He opened his eyes and looked around as the others stood in shock at what they were seeing.

"What happened? Why are you people crying? I'm still okay, but the night isn't over yet."

"Ahmad, you died!" Hala said, with a stunned look on her face.

"Don't listen to her, Ahmad; you're just a wimp, that's all. You're fine."

They talked the rest of the night and kept a close eye on their comrade. None of them understood what happened, but they still weren't taking any chances.

Ben sat looking at Michael. Jesus brought the young soldier to them, but for what reason? The boy never ceased to amaze him, but what took place tonight was not normal. *There were other times too*, he thought, remembering accounts the others gave, especially from recent months.

The Chinese choppers and pain beam at the border. When the beam came at them, they were powerless to stop it, but it somehow deflected back at the helicopters and destroyed them. Michael wasn't in the vehicle, and Hadassah tried to stop her uncle from driving away. Then out of nowhere Michael was there with them.

Ben Gurion when Paul and Bradley landed. They had listened to reports of the runways being demolished; the airport closed because no planes could land or take off, and there were no lights. Hadassah said Michael went in by himself and would not allow her to go. Both planes landed safely, with lights and a solid runway. Paul and Bradley confirmed seeing the severe condition of the pavement as they ran for the truck, yet they had smooth landings. *It was miraculous,* they said.

Then there were the times Michael just disappeared and returned a few hours later. That happened while Trey and Rickie fought to get to the valley and rescue Bruno and Magnus. He tried to find him that night, but he was nowhere to be found. The timing matched the same time frame they gave. *Hmm...* Ben whispered. He would keep a close eye on Michael, but he would also rely on him much more.

$$\bullet \quad \bullet \quad \bullet \quad \bullet \quad \bullet$$

Morning arrived after an excruciating and long night for the world. People mourned the loss of firstborn children, from newborns to adults. Millions died in a single night during the tenth plague. As people buried their dead, their hatred for Moshe and Eliyahu turned to murderous rage. They wanted nothing more than to witness the deaths of the two prophets of Yahweh.

"Ladies and gentlemen," Messai said, speaking remotely from an anonymous location. "After last night, my heart breaks for all of you who have lost children. I have no children, but I mourn with you. The two men called Moshe and Eliyahu perpetrated this heinous act, and the blame for millions of deaths lies squarely with them."

"LIAR!"

It was clear to the watching world the scream shook Messai. For a brief moment, people saw fear on his face. The unflappable leader of the world, who was always calm and in control, experienced momentary uncertainty. What would he do now?

The two men stood by the temple, with no microphones and no reporters, only cameras.

That is impossible! Messai thought again. There was no way their voices overrode his own when they were not in the same place.

"You have witnessed the power of Yahweh! Unless you repent, you will all likewise perish!"

Messai regained his composure and screamed into the camera.

"It is *you* who will perish, if I must kill you myself!"

"You may well do so. But know this: Yahweh sees your ignorance and commands you to repent. He has set a day when he will judge the world by the man he has appointed, Jesus, the Messiah. He has proven this to everyone by raising him from the dead! And he will prove himself again when you witness the same from us. Destroy these temples and he will raise them in three days!"

What are they talking about? Messai asked himself, now lost in his thoughts. Then he felt the chill creep throughout his body, as searing heat touched his cheek. Each time it seemed the flesh would melt from his face, but that never happened. The high-pitched voice whispered into his ear.

"Do as they say, Aissa. Destroy them. Your time has come."

"But how, Master?" he asked. "They have such power."

No one else heard it, but the voice thundered inside his head, reverberating through his brain.

"You fool! They have no power over me, and I empower you. *Destroy them!*"

The creature left as fast as it came, leaving Messai alone with his thoughts, while the world waited and yearned for his next words. What did Moshe mean he would witness the same from them? Could they really...? No, if he killed them, they would remain dead. He concocted an insidious plan during that moment of silence.

"I will meet you tomorrow at noon on the Mount. I challenge you to be there, and we shall see who is lord of Shabbat!"

Then, speaking to viewers around the world, he said, "I invite you to tune in tomorrow as we rid the world of these murderous mercenaries forever! Greater peace and prosperity than ever before will come after that! Vengeance is *ours* and *I* will repay them for their abhorrent acts on you!"

All over the world, people seeking revenge celebrated his challenge with eager anticipation of what tomorrow would bring. They wanted nothing more than to see the two prophets die.

"Isn't there something we can do, Ben?" asked Alexander, as Moshe and Eliyahu's wives stood before them pleading for the lives of their husbands. "They fought for us and rescued us many times. Can we not do the same for them now when they need us?"

"We must stand still and see the salvation of Yahweh." It was not Ben who spoke, but Michael.

"Will Yahweh win the battle for them?" Moshe's wife asked in a demanding tone.

"I believe he will, but it may occur in ways we have not considered."

"Michael is right," Ben said as gently as possible. "Jesus has something special planned for them. I don't understand what that will be, but we will witness it. Do any of you remember how Johnathan Baldwin died?"

Even those who had not witnessed Johnathan's execution had heard the story of the peace on his face when the bullets ended his life. Moshe's wife broke into tears.

"But I cannot bear the thought of seeing Messai murder them," she sobbed. "We must go there and fight to free them. Messai is the one who must die!"

"He will, Meira, when Jesus returns," said Alexander. Elizabeth walked over and put her arm around the woman, holding her as she sobbed.

"Jesus had a special plan for them, Meira; we all realize that. The miracles they have performed are things no normal human beings could do. The power of Yahweh indwelt them, beginning on the Plain of Megiddo. Since that time, his spirit has controlled them. We must not interfere with his plans, because whatever they are, they will send a message to the entire world."

"We will watch and trust Jesus, Elizabeth. I also trust Moshe and Eliyahu. Whatever happens, I understand they belong to Yahweh, not Eliana and me."

The group joined hands and prayed for the two men, but realized in their hearts Jesus' plan would not align with theirs.

The Jewish Sabbath arrived without the usual fanfare. No crowds marched to the Mount and filled the temple courts, and the Altar of Burnt Offering contained no fire. No priest was present to offer sacrifices to the Lord. The majestic structure stood in eerie silence until the three people appeared.

Messai ascended the steps from the south which led directly into the Court of the Priests, bypassing the Court of the Gentiles and Court of the Women. That was important to him, as would soon become apparent. He stepped out into the court and saw Moshe and Eliyahu standing beside the Altar of Burnt Offering. Without stopping, he continued until he stood within ten feet of them.

"Now, Eliyahu," whispered Eliana. "Send forth your fire and consume him."

"Raise your staff, Moshe, please," Meira said, standing beside her. "Call forth a plague and devour him."

Fire did not come, nor was the staff raised. Neither man moved.

"They cannot do that," Ben said in the most gentle voice he could summon. "Nobody can destroy him except Jesus when he returns."

Both wives wept as they saw their husbands standing stoically, staring down the Antichrist, neither flinching nor showing emotion. The entire group looked on as Messai walked closer and pulled a weapon from inside the pocket of his suit coat and aimed it at their foreheads. The man threw back his head and laughed, then turned toward the cameras, which continued recording.

"Behold the power of your leader!" he shouted. "These murderers have no power against me!"

Turning back toward the prophets, he aimed the gun again and fired twice. The two men dropped to the ground. A close-up view from one camera showed a hole in the forehead of each, with blood oozing out and flowing to the pavement where they lay.

"No," both women said through tears, seeing their husbands gunned down by the evil Messai.

"Why didn't they do something?" asked Meira, gasping for breath through her sobs.

Messai turned back to the cameras and raised his arms in victory, still brandishing the gun.

"People of the world, our enemy will torture us no more! We need not worry about their divisive rhetoric or destructive plagues. Those who brought death to the world have now died themselves!"

The team gathered in the kibbutz failed to understand why this happened. Unlike Johnathan, Moshe and Eliyahu neither smiled nor revealed any signs of peace. Jesus must have something else planned, or they died in vain. Then Messai announced his evil plan to the world.

"Ladies and gentlemen, these men deserve no burial. After committing such heinous acts, I will leave their bodies to lie and rot in the sun. We will move them to Zion Square in the modern city where they will stay until nothing remains of them. Let their bodies decay and dogs eat their flesh! I will also post a guard around the clock to ensure none of their *friends* come and steal them away."

It was obvious he relished this day of triumph. Then he continued, once again.

"First, I offer you who live in Jerusalem the opportunity to go desecrate their bodies any way you choose. Many of you saw firstborn children die during the tenth plague. Take advantage of your chance to exact revenge on their dead bodies."

"I also invite all of you to come and do the same. We would love for you to visit our fair city, and what better reason to come?" He paused for effect, leaving his listeners hungry for his next words.

"Second," he went on with gusto, "I proclaim the next week an international period of celebration! Feast, give gifts, party with friends and family. Commemorate this special occasion of your freedom from the tortuous actions of these two madmen. Let the entire world rejoice as I and all my associates join the party with you."

The Smyrnians longed to rush to Zion Square and stand guard over the bodies of their friends. They recalled the times Moshe and Eliyahu had saved their lives, and how they protected Ben during his teaching trips.

How could they leave their bodies lying there to rot or for animals to eat? But they could not take such a chance. Their only task was staying in the kibbutz and taking care of the two widows left alone by the vicious murders of their husbands. These would be difficult days.

Anger overwhelmed the American soldiers stationed at Camp Filon after viewing the slaughter of their two comrades. They had not met the men, but had heard much about them and lived through the events of the last several weeks. Listening to them fiercely proclaim the truth of Jesus and seeing their powerful miracles endeared them to their fellow soldiers in the faith.

Mordecai traveled back there immediately after the shootings, knowing the unit would want to find and eliminate Messai, which was an impossible mission. It provided a teaching opportunity and time to prepare them more for their real mission, which would come soon. He did not understand what it would be, but the Americans would play a vital role when it came.

"Why didn't Jesus stop this?" asked Robert Clark. "We did nothing, and he did nothing. I didn't think it was possible for Messai to kill them. They were prophets of God, filled with his power. How did this happen?"

"None of us understand, Robert, but we feel God has a plan. We are waiting for it and hoping he reveals it soon because I can't bear seeing their bodies lying there, mocked and unprotected."

"Neither can I. Give the command anytime, and my unit will go there and provide protection."

"I wish I could, but for now, let's get to work preparing for whatever is coming. We are certain it involves planes and pilots. Beyond that, we don't have a clue what will happen, or when. I can tell you that Camp Filon can stay your permanent base for as long as you need it. All IDF troops have moved elsewhere, so the camp is yours. Let's get to work." He smiled and shook Robert's hand.

•　　•　　•　　•　　•

In the kibbutz, people took turns watching televisions and checking their computers and mobile devices regularly, keeping a close eye on the situation in Zion Square. The task was grueling, but they stayed at their posts, ready to inform the others should something happen.

Day One passed, and the bodies of Moshe and Eliyahu still lay where Messai's men placed them. News abounded with video of people celebrating worldwide. Festive gatherings, drunken soirees, and extreme gift giving characterized the awful observance of this momentous occasion for the population of the world. With each passing day, Messai's popularity skyrocketed even more.

Day Two only made watching more difficult. The bodies were so abused they no longer resembled the men they knew and loved. People came just to gaze at them, then kick and abuse the corpses every way possible. The world partied day and night, making the most of the week-long holiday.

Messai stopped by each day to report on the events, filled with glee and arrogance. Nothing would satisfy him except complete destruction of both bodies. They would lie there until nothing remained of them. Meanwhile, reporters continued to show close-ups of the corpses and interview gleeful folks who came to take part in the *festivities*.

Day Three... still nothing. Little remained of the bodies now, but Messai continued inviting more to come. People flew from everywhere to get in on the *fun*. Hotels sold out anywhere close to the city center. Visitors packed Jerusalem to the point of maximum capacity. The Secretary-General's popularity continued to rise, and the anguish of believers increased along with it.

Day Four arrived. Noon passed, and the afternoon and evening hours gave way to the darkness of night. When midnight came in Israel, 5:00 p.m. in the United States, and various times in other countries, something happened.

"Ben!" yelled Blake and Beth as they charged from their house, passing and activating the sirens, causing them to wail throughout the kibbutz.

Families quickly rose and turned on televisions or other devices. The leaders sprinted toward the meeting hall, Meira and Eliana close on their heels. Blake had the TV on when they arrived.

Radiant light beamed down on the square, appearing to originate from heaven itself. It overpowered street lights and blinded partygoers. Messai's guards stood and shouldered their weapons, then collapsed to the pavement like dead men along with the carousing crowd.

Reporters who had kept vigil for three days awakened from their slumber and hustled toward the square. They quickly joined the others on the ground, overwhelmed by the brilliant light. Cameras continued to operate, capturing the action and sending it around the globe, while people from every nation observed the startling scene. But no one expected what happened next.

A sudden gust of wind rushed downward through the light on a narrow path toward Moshe and Eliyahu. Their ripped and tattered tunics fluttered in the gale. The wind nosedived directly into their mouths, and flesh covered their bodies, starting with their feet and moving to their heads. Sparkling white garments replaced their dirty and disheveled robes.

Both men stirred as if awakening from a long night's sleep, sat up, looked around, then stood to their feet. In a remote location from which he spoke a few days earlier, a deep-throated yell escaped from the mouth of Aissa Messai.

"Noooo!!! This cannot happen! Stand up, men, and gun them down again!"

His body trembled as he saw his men lying on the pavement, unmoving. He erupted in a blood-curdling scream, shaking the walls of his safe place, as demonic creatures swarmed out of the abyss and flew around the room, expressing his rage. This moment changed everything, and he knew it. Hell prepared to unleash its fury on earth, and Aissa Messai was ready.

A mighty roar echoed through the heavens when the creature saw what took place. Sulfuric fire blazed from its nostrils as the Giant Red Dragon planned his next move. The people of Yahweh would pay for this travesty. He would hunt them down and destroy every one of them.

Families worldwide gathered and held one another, fearing another attack like those they had already faced. Many wailed at the sight of the two men they hated so much coming back to life before their eyes. Terror covered the entire 25,000-mile circumference of the earth.

Followers of Jesus sat in awe of the greatest miracle they had seen. Renewed hope sprang up in them as they watched, still not expecting what would happen next.

A deafening sound came from above. Followers of the Antichrist cringed, fearing another invasion was taking place. Only those who had put their faith in Jesus understood the meaning of the sound. A voice... a loud voice from heaven.

"Come up here!"

Moshe and Eliyahu rose from the pavement, greeted by a cloud, and victoriously ascended into heaven. Meira and Eliana wept for joy, unable to contain their jubilation! The others celebrated with them, now recognizing God's plan for their two comrades. This was their most glorious night yet. The future would hold untold hardships and danger, but this event bolstered their faith and gave them courage to face it.

The ground shook, gently at first, then convulsed with more power than the night Beth escaped from Messai's mansion. A worldwide audience looked on as the massive earthquake struck Jerusalem. Fissures opened on Ben Yahuda, Jaffa, and Yoel Solomon Streets, then sped toward Zion Square from three directions. They converged, creating a cavernous opening in the pavement which swallowed the square in one large gulp.

Guards, reporters, cameramen, and revelers got sucked in and disappeared before they had time to move. The quake demolished the beautiful shopping areas and sent hotels crumbling to the ground. It spread throughout West Jerusalem, destroying the entire government precinct, Hebrew University, and the Israel Museum. Left standing alone was the Hadassah Medical Center.

Though massive, this quake did not last long, especially compared to the worldwide convulsion from a couple years earlier. But the damage was no less horrific. News helicopters were already in the air, showing the scenes from overhead. West Jerusalem bore a resemblance to the destruction caused by the nuclear war.

Nukes had somehow spared this section of Jerusalem, making it a symbol of hope for an entire traumatized planet. But tonight, that hope shattered into a million pieces before a global audience. The search began for survivors as the city and world mourned.

"Serves them right," said Eliana.

"It doesn't pay to mess with Almighty God!" said Ben in a booming voice.

"I know where Moshe and Eliyahu are," Meira said confidently. "We have to carry on their work!"

"However, I suspect their prophecy was a final warning for people to turn to Jesus, but they rejected it, despite the plagues. If any put their faith in him after this, it will be rare."

"The scroll..."

"What does the scroll have to do with this, Anders?" Ally asked.

"I saw this when I ate the scroll, but didn't understand it until now. It made no sense to me then, but now I get it, and realize what will come next. Ben, it is time to prepare for it."

"Tell us, and we'll get ready. I have known something is coming, but don't understand what it is."

"I saw it, but I can't explain it. The Jewish believers were under attack and fleeing for their lives. It appeared Jesus gave them wings to fly, but it ended there."

"The planes! We need to contact the pilots. What else could *wings* mean? Look how Jesus brought this all together," Michael said, looking around the room. "I don't understand the logistics, but this must be what we've been planning for."

"Trey, Rickie, Paul, and Bradley, we need every plane possible standing by and ready to fly. I will organize every IDF pilot who has believed in Jesus. Mordecai, talk to Robert Clark and get the American unit *on board*, no pun intended," he said with a slight grin.

"You men who spread word to the tribes must tell them to stay prepared for immediate evacuation at any moment. Let them know we will inform them when the time comes. They will need to move quickly. We will only have room for their families and the clothes they wear that day."

"We need everyone else to help get people into position and ready to move in an orderly fashion. There will be no time to spare. I wish we knew exact timing and locations, but we don't. Let's plan and prepare for the day that information becomes available."

Ben sat amazed by the young man. Michael was wise beyond his years, and he remained convinced there was more to him than met the eye. He trusted him, even with these important decisions.

"You are in charge of this, Michael; I only ask that you keep us informed."

"You can count on that, Ben. We need to meet every day to make sure we're all on the same page."

"Agreed. Ollie, we will need your knowledge of this place. You, Amelia, and Ally can help in ways others can't. Anders, you will serve as coordinator for the entire project because your personal encounter with Jesus gives you more insight than us. You may understand things he revealed to you as time goes along. When that happens, tell us immediately."

"It will be an honor to do that, and I can share one thing already. Michael, you omitted one group. Omar, Ahmad, and Hala, you will play an important role in this too. You are Jordanian, not Israeli, so I don't understand that. But I remember seeing your faces in the scroll and know Jesus brought you to himself for this moment."

Michael smiled, as if having prior knowledge of Anders' realization.

"You're right, Anders. And Jesus used one person to make that happen. Hadassah, he also brought you *for such a time as this.*"

Her smile showed she realized that was true.

"Ben, share this on your daily teachings too, so we leave no one out. It breaks my heart that Beth and I can't let other believers know what is happening. Things will get critical for them soon."

"You are right, Blake. Pardon my expression, but all hell is about to break loose on the earth."

"We have known that for three years, and now the time has arrived. Let's do everything we can to prepare."

None of them knew what was coming, but they would be ready when it did.

CHAPTER 10

A week after searching for survivors, the totals came in from the earthquake. Seven thousand dead, others injured, most not seriously, and enormous devastation of property. It would take years to rebuild, but the Smyrnians knew only three-and-a-half years remained, anyway.

Fear gripped the Jews who escaped alive. They flocked to the temple, offering sacrifices, and crying out to God for protection. But even as they called on Yahweh and prayed for the peace of Jerusalem, they refused to believe in Jesus, his son, and their Messiah. During that time of fear and grief, the man of peace entered the picture once again.

"Citizens of Israel and Jerusalem; this tragic experience was one last attempt by the two so-called *prophets* to frighten you and prevent us from achieving peace and prosperity. But you will never need to worry about them again. They have gone, never to return."

"Their mysterious return to life and subsequent disappearance once again revealed their magical powers, which brought death and destruction to our planet. However, the two of them did not operate alone. They belonged to the Smyrnian rebels. We must either destroy them or face more catastrophic events similar to what we just lived through."

"If you suspect anyone of associating with this group, kill them. We will not hold you responsible for their deaths. That is our only hope of returning to the peace and prosperity we experienced before this period of chaos. I am also thankful for the support of an important man here in Israel."

The Jewish High Priest walked out and joined him in the Court of the Priests. He took Messai's hand and held it aloft as a sign of solidarity, as they waved to the cameras with their free hands.

People around the world heeded his words and turned their anger toward followers of Jesus. They planned to annihilate every one of them and remove their scourge from the earth. However, that did nothing to lessen the joy of believers. Worldwide worship broke out in every country, seeming to originate from the throne room of heaven itself. It was especially joyful in the kibbutz in Israel.

We give thanks to you, Lord God Almighty,
The one who is and who was,
Because you have taken your great power
And have begun to reign.
The nations were angry,
And your wrath has come.
The time has come for judging the dead, and for rewarding your servants the prophets and your people who revere your name, both great and small — and for destroying those who destroy the earth.
–Revelation 11:17-18 NIV

"That was amazing!" Beth said, a smile covering her face. Anders' glow returned too.

It sounded like the antithesis of how things were, but they sang with faith in how things would be! Nature responded with threatening signs, a harbinger of things to come. The *reign of terror* lay on the horizon, more ominous than anything the world had seen during the last three-and-a-half years. This group understood what it was. And they knew the time had come to prepare for the storm.

• • • •

The enormous red dragon paced back and forth, fire blazing from its mouth. Leaders of his demonic horde gathered before him, awaiting instructions for their next move. Belial stood beside him, ready to lead the charge with a full understanding of what was at stake. He had awaited this moment since before the beginning of time. Michael would not defeat him again.

"Your army is ready, master. We will not let you down this time."

"Belial!" roared the beast. "Only weeks ago, you allowed Michael to overpower you and rescue two of the enemy from China. What makes you think things will be different now?"

His words stung the demon, but he expected them.

"Must I remind you of our failures through the years?" the creature asked.

"No, your majesty, that is unnecessary. We remember them all."

"Silence!"

Belial dropped his head, and the others did not utter a word. They knew what was coming; the dragon repeated it every time another failure occurred.

"Egypt... Assyria... Babylon... Persia... Greece... Rome!"

Each word pierced the prince's mind, driving home the reminders of each near miss. He dared not mention the garden. The wily serpent succeeded at that one, but Yahweh told him the day was coming when the offspring of the woman would crush his head.

The Messiah, the promised one, Yahweh's *son*, was the woman's seed who would deal that blow. His master had fought from the beginning to prevent his reign. Only one thing would stop that from happening: destroy the one from whom he would come: Israel.

It nearly occurred in Egypt, but Yahweh set his people free. The dragon had been certain Pharaoh would wipe them out, and he almost succeeded. That was the word every time... *almost.* Assyria drove the Northern Kingdom of Israel into oblivion, causing ten of the twelve tribes to disappear from the historical record.

Then came the time for Judah and Benjamin, the two tribes who made up the Southern Kingdom. They were of particular importance because the Messiah was to come from the tribe of Judah. Babylon came close until Persia wiped them out and took control.

Then, when the King of Persia allowed Haman to issue an edict, Belial was certain they had done it. Haman's order commanded the people of the land to slaughter the Jews until none remained. He and the dragon planned a huge celebration, but Hadassah stopped it from happening. *Hadassah.* He despised that name and dreamed of squashing her like a bug. Her time was coming.

Greece sought to Hellenize the Jews and turn them from worshiping Yahweh. They almost succeeded. There was that word again. It had *almost* happened so many times. But somehow they had survived every attempt, and the Messiah was born.

He was certain of success when they crucified and buried him. But on the third day, the resurrection happened. Oh, how he hated the third day. Before his thoughts turned to the Romans' brutal destruction of Jerusalem in 70 A.D., a thought slammed into his mind like a missile.

The two prophets also came back to life on the third day. Were they walking into Yahweh's trap, or would they finally fulfill their mission? The speculation jarred him, but the booming voice of the dragon snapped him out of his trance.

"This time we will succeed! Our target is no longer the *nation* of Israel, but the Israelites who follow... *him*. By destroying them, we will force *his* hand."

Belial knew the beast could no longer bring himself to say the name *Jesus*.

"But first, I must meet with him once more and make sure he understands his role. We will convene again to organize our attack. You must all be ready to do your part in this battle."

"We will win the war, and I will assume my rightful place on the throne. Then you, my faithful ones, will reign with me!"

The screeching and howling from the leaders brought forth more of the same from blood-thirsty, power hungry demons near and far. Evil would soon rule the universe.

•   •   •   •   •

"I sense it coming," Ben said at the daily briefing. "If any of you feel it too, tell us what it's like."

"It's cold," said Beth. "Not like Messai's chill; more like a cold breeze."

"That's exactly what I feel, baby. We've talked about it. But it seems to me the wind grew stronger and colder not long after Moshe and Eliyahu's resurrection. Did anyone else notice that?"

"I did, Blake," Bruno said. "How about you, Magnus?"

"I never saw the dragon until China, but I sensed his presence many times after Messai had been with him. He breathes fire, but the chill is unmistakable when he is preparing to do something evil. I sense it now, and it is increasing, as you said, Blake. Bad things are coming fast."

"Have all of you spoken with your people? Are they prepared?"

"We've done the best we can, Ben, but they're complacent. Things have calmed down, so it's hard for them to believe something serious is on the way. We will try to light a fire under them."

"The pilots are ready to fly at a moment's notice, but they don't know where they're flying. If we just knew where..." Ben cut Trey off.

"None of us realize where or when. We only have a gut feeling that flying is part of this. We're all guessing. Mordecai, what bases can we use, and how many can handle huge planes?"

"I have bases and many cargo planes that can fly multiple missions moving big groups of people. And a former comrade assured me we can use Ben Gurion, too."

"Mordecai, that's great!" exclaimed Paul. "Does that mean Bradley and I can fly from there?"

"That's right! We can transport thousands of people with your planes."

"Great work, Mordecai! Anyone else?"

"My unit and I are ready to assist any way we can," said Robert Clark who had joined the meeting.

"We need all of you, so stay on standby."

"Just tell us what you need us to do," said Ollie. "The three of us are champing at the bits to get back into action. Send us into battle; we're ready!"

While their meeting continued, another important encounter took place in a domain of demons.

Aissa Messai climbed to the place where he often came to meet the dragon. It began as an abode of evil and remained so until the present day. Breathing in the air of depravity, he stepped onto the altar where the beast always appeared in the large niche that once contained a statue of Pan.

Panias. An apt name for a place dedicated to the Greek god of desolate places, he mused. Since the Ptolemaic kings built it as a cult center in the third century B.C., it had belonged to the dragon.

The creature arrived through the cave on the left, known as the gateway to the underworld, though Messai never witnessed his entrance. He knelt on the stone altar before the niche until the stench of the beast's foul breath entered his nostrils and the familiar burn touched his face.

There it came! A chill shot up his spine, causing him to tremble with anticipation. He stifled a nauseating gag at the sickening odor. Heat replaced the cold as the sparks from the dragon's mouth floated down, followed by fire scorching his cheek. He flinched, but dared not raise his head until the beast commanded him to.

Pain from kneeling bone upon stone wracked his knees, something he now expected at these *meetings*. The wait was longer than normal, but he refused to yield to the pain and anxiety he felt. It seemed like hours before the voice finally came.

"Aissa, thank you for joining me today."

Greater fear than normal surprised him at the evil sound of the creature's hissing tone.

"You are welcome, master. Your wish is my command."

"Raise your head and look around you."

Messai obeyed, gazing into eyes of pure evil before turning his head left, then right. Horror filled his mind when he saw them. It took everything within him to keep from leaping to his feet and racing away down the hillside, past the flowing streams, but his legs lacked strength to stand.

Demons filled every small niche carved into the stone base of the mountain. He had not seen them before. Their hideous faces and yellow eyes tormented his soul as he fought the terror consuming his body. Webbed wings too large for their small bodies protruded from each side, and razor-sharp talons extended from each foot. Fierce angst paralyzed him, but he remained, his fear obvious.

"Aissa, our moment has nearly arrived. You understand what must happen before it can come."

"You must destroy Israel. Tell me how I can help, master. I will do anything." His lips trembled as the shaky words escaped his mouth. He hoped the dragon did not notice, but knew he did.

"It is not the nation we must annihilate. It poses no threat now. The real enemy are the Jews who follow *him*. They shall die! Some will die with them, but those who remain will submit to me."

He wanted to speak, but fright prevented further words from coming. The dragon enjoyed playing these games with him, but his instruction always continued after lengthy pauses.

"I plan to launch the assault in *three days*. Why not use *their* number against them? The day they claim brought them deliverance will now bring their destruction!"

Messai struggled to focus, keeping a wary eye on the demonic creatures whose eyes seemed to burn a hole right through him. The huge beast filling the niche of Pan watched him for a full minute before the hissing voice penetrated his ears once again.

"Do you like my army, Aissa? You needed to see them before we move forward with your *position*. I chose not to bring the *princes* because you cannot handle them yet. You shall meet them soon. Now, let's talk about your responsibility while I unleash my assault on the *Smyrnians*."

*   *   *   *   *

"We will not let our master down this time!" screamed Belial, addressing the other eleven princes of evil standing before him, including the Chief Prince. He always made Belial nervous.

The dragon assigned them to the tribes of Israel, and they collaborated on large-scale assaults aimed at annihilating the Jews. Many had met with success, while others failed. Belial relished the victories. Each one brought a reward from the dragon. His greatest triumph came in Europe during World War II. Six million Jews perished at the hands of the Nazi regime, along with millions of non-Jews, a nice addition to their plan. He had proclaimed the mission a success. Then came May 14, 1948. The dragon unleashed his fury on all of them for that one. He would not fail again.

The massive beasts stood tall before him, some matching his own stature, but none equal to the Chief Prince. They waited to hear their names called, signifying the prominence that came with it.

"*Abaddon!*"

The creature stepped forward, pride covering his face. His name meant *destroyer*, and he had done his job well through the millennia since the *eviction*. The dragon assigned him the correct name.

"Baal!"

Baal had also performed well, flooding the world with sexual immorality and adultery of the worst kinds and shattering Yahweh's seventh commandment. His ego was far more prodigious than his gigantic frame. *A job well done*, the dragon often told him.

"Legion!"

This proud demon commanded many lesser demons who bore responsibility for controlling people's minds and destroying them through a variety of means. His most effective tool, addiction, crushed lives and families so well, the master had awarded him in the presence of his peers. While it made some envious, they still approved of his tactics and success.

"Leviathan!"

Millions of men and women perished at sea because of his vicious attacks. He hid his identity so well most people said he was only a myth. More than a sea creature, the dragon had pronounced him *lord of the waters*. The monster took the title seriously and fulfilled his role with excellence.

"Lilith!"

The only female among the princes took special pride in her position. Thought to be nothing more than a creature of mythology, she worked undercover. The others did the same, but people failed to believe in her existence or her vicious work. Her task was attacking and destroying children, and her methods became more evil as time passed. She permeated the world with child sex trafficking and murdered countless numbers of unborn babies through the horror of abortion. It was no wonder the dragon elevated her to such a place of honor among the twelve.

"Haborym!"

The demon of fire remained the only one endowed with the specific power of the enemy. He wreaked havoc throughout history, destroying lives, and often entire cities, with fires both great and small. He commanded armies in final conquests of nations, as they disappeared in his flames.

"Gog!"

The creature bore the greatest responsibility during the seven years and was ramping up heading into the last three-and-a-half. The demon of collectivism, government control of people, began his work north of Israel in Russia, instituting communism. Now his focal point was China, the nation governed by that ideology. He had moved the pieces into place and set the stage for a one-world government and one-world religion under the control of Aissa Messai. It would happen soon.

"*Mammon!*"

This demon worked to deceive people during the end of days. He led Aissa Messai's campaign of peace and prosperity, poisoning people's minds with avarice and greed and planting in them an insatiable desire for more. His work served as the catalyst for Messai's unprecedented rise to fame.

"*Orias!*"

The demon of astrology turned people toward the stars and planets instead of Yahweh in search of answers for their lives. He prepared them for the false and forced worship that would begin soon, an easy task in a godless world following September 11, 2029.

"*Paimon!*"

The great demon of arts, philosophies, and sciences, who reveals secret things roared like a lion who just killed his prey. He had served as the dragon's ultimate deceiver, poisoning young minds and spreading liberal ideology that stood in contrast to the teachings of Yahweh. Humanity succumbed to his deception, lived the lies, and brought about their own demise.

Only the Chief Prince remained. Belial hated to relinquish the floor to him, but the demon outranked him. He did not despise him; they were fellow warriors in the dragon's army. Yet it seemed Belial spent his time fighting while the Chief Prince stayed behind planning and organizing. The beast rose, forcing him to proceed with his introduction.

"*Beelzebub!*"

The massive demon strutted to the front. Belial detested that. He recognized the jealousy that filled him every time this happened. Beelzebub fired up a group like no other. He took great pleasure in inciting riots and leading rebellions. The one that mattered most had failed when Yahweh defeated him and the dragon in their attempt to seize the throne.

The Chief Prince had fought to make up for the defeat since that day. He loathed the *other* Chief Prince and would never admit that Michael was mightier than he. Their battles were legendary, but Michael prevailed in nearly all of them. However, this was the one that counted, and he had prepared the demonic horde well. They would finally defeat Yahweh and destroy his people. He could hardly wait to rule the universe alongside his eternal friend, the dragon.

"It is time!" he said, then followed that proclamation with the loudest screech Belial had heard.

The others covered their ears, but joined him, the sound piercing the air. They were ready to initiate the battle of the ages, convinced the dragon would lead them to victory! In Banias, the other meeting got serious.

• • • • •

"On your feet, Aissa!"

Messai rose, thankful for the relief it brought to his aching knees, and turned his attention to the giant fire-breathing creature in front of him. The stench of its breath mesmerized him instead of sickening him now. The heat warmed him inside and out. He realized it allowed the beast's words to penetrate his mind so he would not forget a single one.

"I and my leaders will attack and destroy the Jews who turned to *him*. We will only call the rest of our army if we need them. Station your men everywhere and keep them on high alert for anyone who tries to interfere with our plan. If you capture them, detain them. They will be your first public executions after you assume control. I'm sure you are eager to try out your new toy. Stay in the public eye and continue earning their trust. None of this must point back to you, yet."

"Yes, master. I will organize my men the minute I return. They will blanket the country with their presence. And do not worry; I will make sure the people trust me and continue believing in me."

"We are days away, Aissa. After we remove them, you will receive your promotion and power, and we will move forward with our plan to conquer the world and rule the universe! In my kingdom, you will sit at my right hand. Then selling your soul to me will be worth it all!"

The Secretary-General of the United Nations, the Antichrist of the Tribulation, bowed to the dragon, then raised both arms in a show of victory.

"I belong to you, master, and I am ready to enforce your will on this filthy planet!"

"Then it is time!" the dragon shouted, striding away, sparks trailing him. His princes would move into place and attack in three days. This was his hour, and the power of darkness would prevail!

· · · · ·

He assigned Beelzebub responsibility for the kibbutz. The Chief Prince knew the dragon trusted no one else with this one. He stood on a hillside overlooking the place, contemplating his moves. Multiple reasons made this the perfect assignment for him.

Everyone down there followed *him*. Watching the proselyte Jews die would give him great pleasure. He loathed all of Yahweh's people and sought their demise. But they were not the only ones here. The Smyrnians also hid in this dump. The powerful demon despised them, too. Reports told him they were *all* in the place waiting for him like trapped animals. This should be fun!

Despite his disdain for them, both were minor compared to the ultimate prize awaiting him. *Michael* was there. How the Chief Prince of heaven and Yahweh's mighty warrior angel made such a tactical error he could not imagine. It was unlike him. But he had, so the question was irrelevant. Removing Michael would all but ensure victory in the last great battle.

An additional little prize hid in the kibbutz, too. *Hadassah*. He knew how much Belial hated her. Perhaps he should save her for him. No, he would handle it and enjoy watching her die. Beelzebub chuckled, thinking about the envious Belial learning the Chief Prince had fulfilled the task he wanted for himself. Perhaps he would take the body to his lesser comrade. That would not happen either. This moment belonged to him, and he refused to share it with anyone, including Belial.

· · · · ·

March 14, 2033. The sun rose over the kibbutz, a beautiful, clear day signaling the approaching end of the rainy season, with the first day of Spring less than a week away. Discussion centered on the death and resurrection of Moshe and Eliyahu and its timing.

"It cannot be mere coincidence," said Ben. "They rose at midnight, March 11, exactly three-and-a-half years, or 42 months, or 1260 days after the Rapture. Jesus took them to heaven, just like he took the believers home on September 11, 2029. Those events parallel each other to the very day and hour halfway through the Tribulation."

"Jesus does nothing by accident, Ben. The earthquake and Beth's rescue occurred on September 11, 2030 at midnight one year after the Rapture. We can learn a lot if we study his timing in historical events, combined with his teachings in the Bible."

"I agree with you, Anders, so are there things we should figure out now? We know the second half of the Tribulation began 3 days ago. I doubt Messai does things by accident either, but what does that have to do with what will happen next?"

"Not Messai, Blake, the dragon."

"The dragon? That makes no sense, Magnus. Messai and his men are the ones who have tried to kill us for the last three and half years. You worked for him, not the dragon."

"Who do you think controls Messai?"

Now Blake got it, as did the others. They stopped talking and listened to Messai's former captain.

"We can figure this out, then make our move based on what we understand. The dragon is predictable. He loves numbers and almost always operates by them. Messai mentioned how the beast hates the third day because of the resurrection. Although he never used that word, I understood what he meant. Now, it all adds up."

"What adds up? I don't follow you."

"This is the third day after the resurrection of our friends. They rose exactly three-and-a-half days after Messai killed them. It would make sense for the dragon to plan an attack three-and-a-half days after *their* resurrection at noon today. If that is true, we have little time to act."

"I think you're onto something, Magnus," said his partner and fellow big man, Bruno. "The dragon told us he knows our locations. He included the Shelter in Missouri and *a kibbutz in Israel.* We know what happened to the Shelter..." His words faded off when he mentioned that.

"If you're right, we have three-and-a-half hours to do something. Jesus operates by numbers too, so I believe he showed you that! We need to leave this place now!"

Kathie spoke with urgency in her voice, jumping to her feet. John joined her, shouting as he did.

"She's right! He has found us every time! Mordecai, do you have a military base, or somewhere else we can go?"

"It may be too late for that," Michael said, cutting off Mordecai before he spoke.

"Too late or not," said John, "I would rather go somewhere than hang out like sitting ducks. If we hadn't left the Shelter when we did, we would have all died."

"I can order vans, and we will join the Americans at Camp Filon."

Mordecai moved fast, bound for the door, a man on a mission.

"Wait, Aluf," Michael interrupted him again.

"There is no time to wait, Michael. Our lives are in danger and waiting may mean death!"

"Uncle, please listen to him. After he finishes, you may leave if you still think you need to go."

Hadassah always melted his heart, especially when she said *please*. He stopped and listened, but stood near the door, allowing him to leave quickly if Michael's response failed to satisfy him.

"I guarantee you the dragon and Messai already have this place surrounded, waiting to attack, or for us to make our move. If we run, Messai's men will gun us down."

"If we stay, they will gun us down!" said Bruno. "Let's take our chances and make a break for it!"

"The dragon isn't after us," Anders said, just loud enough for them to hear.

"Let him speak."

Ally had sensed Anders' closeness to Jesus since he visited heaven and returned. Her calm voice eased the tension in the room.

"He seeks to destroy the Jews who have believed in Jesus."

Anders pointed around the room at Ben and Miriam and all the Israeli believers.

"How can you be so sure of that?" demanded Mordecai.

"The scroll. What I ate never leaves me, and Jesus reveals each part when the time comes."

"He's right," said Michael. "The dragon intends to annihilate the Jews who believe in Jesus when the second half of the Tribulation begins. He wants to remove them first."

"If he finds us with them, he will take us out too!"

"Ben, do you remember your words when AMPP attacked us on the Plain of Megiddo?"

Power surged in Ben, and he stood and thundered those words again.

"Stand still and see the salvation of the Lord!"

Those who wanted to argue with him stood silent. Some remembered that day well and had watched miraculous things happen, for which there was no explanation. His words rang in their ears again as if they were back in the valley, reliving those events.

"We have only one choice," Michael said. "To run means certain death."

"To stay means trusting Jesus," Anders added.

"Everyone go to your houses and stay put, but be ready to act if we call you."

They obeyed his command, seeing no other option. Mordecai was humbled seeing the young soldier take charge, thinking it should have been him instead. He was also proud of Michael and took some pride because the IDF turned him into a strong leader. He obeyed and joined everyone else sprinting toward their homes. Michael ran toward his house, too.

Beelzebub sat atop the hill, impatiently waiting for the time to attack. A squadron of demons hovered overhead eager to see him give the signal to descend on the unsuspecting kibbutz. One hour remained until they would kick off the entire operation by obliterating the group responsible for starting the movement in Israel and hiding the Smyrnians in their commune.

Even better, Michael and Hadassah would die with them. He threw back his head and let out a deafening howl heard only in the spirit realm. His army did the same. If humans could hear, they would collapse to the ground, screaming in pain and rendered powerless, but they could not.

Michael heard them. He already knew they were there, but their howling told him the attack would come soon. One howl. That meant in one hour the demons would unleash a violent assault on the people inside these walls. Michael recognized the howl and knew who led them. Belial had not received this assignment. The dragon sent Beelzebub, showing how important this mission was.

The Chief Prince's power was unparalleled among the dragon's army. Michael paced back and forth behind the house, seeking answers. He only had one option, so he fell on his face and cried out to Yahweh.

The dragon sent messengers to check on each prince, ensuring they were ready. Only thirty minutes remained now until the sneak attack would bring them to their knees and deal a crushing blow to *him*. Nothing could go wrong this time. 144,000 Jewish Smyrnians would die tonight, as would thousands more who stood in his way.

Michael stood and raised his hands toward heaven. He saw them zooming through the sky, groups flying for every tribe of Israel. The host of heaven, Yahweh's army! They were sent to hold off the demonic attack until the Jews could flee. Sensory perception told him few demons attended each prince of hell. The dragon was too sure of himself today. But Michael realized when the believers ran for their lives, his entire army would pursue them with slaughter on their minds.

Ten minutes left. Beelzebub summoned his regiment and readied them for battle. Wings buzzed, talons rattled, and drool ran as they prepared to attack. It took everything he had to hold them back, but the dragon was specific about the timing: noon. Failure to follow his plan was unacceptable and would bring severe punishment, even for the Chief Prince. He waited.

Five minutes. He saw them. Mighty angels of Yahweh surrounding the kibbutz with flaming swords drawn and crossed in the form of an X. He knew what that meant: no entrance. The Garden of Eden flashed through his mind. His master succeeded at leading Adam and Eve to disobey Yahweh, who banished them from paradise. Then he placed angels, like those he saw now, in front of the garden with flaming swords drawn to guard the entrance, ensuring they would not return.

The mighty demon faced a hard decision. He wanted to charge them and fight, but his instincts said live to fight another day. Noon passed as he weighed his options. The mighty angels standing tall and staring them down dared them to attack, but outnumbered and over matched his troops.

Beelzebub realized he could take some out by himself, but his horde would die, as would he, when the host overwhelmed him. The choice crushed him, but he would not allow the destruction of his loyal troops. Neither could the dragon afford to lose him with such important days lying ahead. He summoned his men and left, flying back to the dragon where he would face his master's ire.

The angelic host stood guard at every location surrounding entire tribal areas to prevent the demons from entering. All twelve demon princes arrived back near the same time and reported the news to the dragon. It enraged the beast, but he was glad they made it back safely.

"You made the right choice, my princes. The great battle looms before us, and I must lose none of you before it comes. We will wait, then hit them with a surprise attack, flush them out, and destroy them. The host will think we abandoned our strategy and let down their guard."

"You will each go alone so you do not alert them. Beelzebub, I will handle the kibbutz myself. Do not consider that punishment, for that was my original plan and I should have stuck with it. We will do our work quietly, and our minions will join us only if it becomes necessary. Should we need them, I will unleash them like a flood upon those who try to escape."

Belial could not contain his anger. "You had Michael, Hadassah, and the Smyrnians trapped!" he screamed at Beelzebub. "How could you leave without killing them? I would have..."

"You would have done what, Belial? Attacked the host with an inferior squad behind you? I think not! If the host had not shown up, I would have taken them out, brought Michael and Hadassah's bodies, and thrown them at your feet!"

"Men! You are both mighty warriors, but you must not fight each other. We are all on the same team and have a much greater prize for which we must fight *together*. That includes all of you. Our day will come soon!"

CHAPTER 11

"Over here," Michael said in a voice not much louder than a whisper.

"What are you doing hiding back here behind the storage bins? It seems like a silly place to meet."

"Listen, Hadassah, I need you to cover for me. I have to leave and don't know how long I will be gone. Everyone here will miss me and wonder what happened. Undercover operations seem to be your specialty." He grinned, but she could tell he was nervous about what was happening.

"What is so important that you have to leave at a time like this? Everything is about to go down here, Michael. You cannot abandon these people now."

"I have no choice, Hadassah. This is the big one and requires my presence. Yahweh depends on me, and I can't let him down. I hope to get back here to help, but there's no guarantee that I will."

"I will not cover for you unless you tell me what is going on. What do you mean, there's no guarantee you will get back here to help? Is that, 'I hope to get back *in time*, or I hope to *get back?*'"

"When you put it like that, it sounds so foreboding and more like hopelessness than hopefulness. Come on, Hadassah, you know I'm going, so just cover for me. I will make it back."

"Michael!"

"Shh... keep your voice down! We must be quiet! Why do you think we're hiding behind storage bins?"

"I'm sorry! You don't sound so sure to me. Tell me where you're going and why!"

"Okay, Hadassah, I have always confided in you. Promise you won't tell?"

"Michael!"

"You know I trust you."

"Sometimes you don't act like you do."

She stood before him, hands on hips, showing neither of them was leaving until he confided in her everything that was about to happen.

"It's the big one. I was told it had to take place in the middle of the Tribulation, but now that it's here, my mind questions whether we are ready."

"You mean...?"

"Yes, the war in heaven. The dragon has tried to prevent it from happening. These seven years of time are his last opportunity to prevent the reign of the Messiah. He longs to destroy the Jews, but they are on his side now and following Messai. So he's going after the Jews who believe in Jesus."

"I suspect his foiled attack yesterday was an attempt to divert our attention away from the war, but the host is not easily distracted. The war is here, Hadassah, and the dragon believes he can overthrow Yahweh and take control. He failed before time began, now he's trying one last time before it ends. We have to stop him."

"You sound concerned about that. He can't defeat you... *can he?*"

"Beelzebub is powerful, and Belial is just as strong. The dragon is a master of deception, but he's also a master of war."

"You're strong too, and you have the heavenly host."

"I have a plan, but I only get one shot. If I fail, we lose this war and Yahweh's plans for the future."

The look of concern on his face said it all. Three-and-a-half years remained in the Tribulation, and every event was important. But this one mattered most.

"I realize you must go, so don't worry, I will cover for you here. Michael, remember *who* you are and *whose* you are, then go win this war and come back safely. These people need you."

He disappeared without another word. She wished he would not do that, but he always did. All she could do now was wait, hope, and pray for his return.

"Men, it is time to make our move! The host is preoccupied with protecting *his* followers and will not expect our attack. We can ambush and annihilate them before they realize what happened!"

The horde of demons surrounding the dragon numbered millions. They had waited for this moment for over six thousand years and were eager to attack. Their clamoring forced him to roar with such force it shook the foundations of their vile abode.

"Winning this war means defeating and destroying Michael and his heavenly host. Then we overthrow Yahweh and assume control of the universe. I will ascend to his throne, and you, my faithful followers will reign with me!"

The buzz started again and continued until the giant red creature again held his hand aloft. It served as a mute button for the horde.

"Gather around and listen as Beelzebub and Belial share our battle plan with you. We have incorporated elements that will catch them off guard and allow you to crush your mortal enemy!"

The Chief Prince stepped to the front and stood beside his master. Belial joined them, standing on the other side. Both threw their hands into the air with fists clenched as a sign of coming victory. The horde before them screeched and howled in agreement. They jerked their hands back down, as if pounding their fists on invisible enemies, and silence filled the place once again.

"Our master himself will lead us into battle!" shouted Beelzebub.

The excitement caused by his declaration was unmatched by any time in their history. The dragon once again quieted them.

"Each of you will join your leader and prepare to follow him into battle. We will divide into six overwhelming units and surround them. Once we are in place and you hear my scream, attack from all sides and overpower them before they have time to react!"

"You will save Michael for me, then get to observe his agonizing death. His armies will watch their leader, the mighty warrior of heaven, beg for mercy before he dies. Then we will charge in and destroy them all! The last to fall will be Yahweh. After I finish him, you will chase and demolish his army. Then we will celebrate our victory!"

They began organizing into units, a powerful force, ready to divide and conquer their greatest enemy. The dragon screamed again.

"This is our hour and the power of darkness will prevail!"

Michael assembled the captains of the heavenly host, a solemn group dedicated to serving Yahweh and ministering to his people. They understood the gravity of this moment.

"The dragon, Beelzebub, and Belial assume we are unaware of their plan. But I understand how they think, and I assure you we cannot afford to wait. We must act now. Are they powerful? Yes. Are they more powerful than Yahweh? No! A good friend reminded me moments ago to remember *who* I am and *whose* I am. I challenge you to do the same and realize we belong to the Creator!"

"But I must also remind you of our enemy. Our struggle is not against flesh and blood, but against the rulers and authorities, the dragon and his evil princes, Beelzebub and Belial. We battle the powers of the dark world and the spiritual forces of evil in the heavenly realms. Today is the time for us to strip them of their power and cast them down!"

Instead of screeching and howling, the mighty angels bowed their heads in humility and worshiped Yahweh. The multitude of the heavenly host, dressed for battle, joined the captains. They raised their gleaming swords, then bowed too. Lifting their heads, they burst into a song of praise to their God, ready to fight for him.

•　•　•　•　•

"Hadassah!"

"Yes, Uncle, I am here."

"What are you doing all the way out here by the bins?"

She realized what was coming, so she tried to deflect the question and change the conversation.

"It's a beautiful time for a walk, don't you agree? Why don't you come and walk with me? We never get to sit and talk anymore, and I miss those times so much. Tell me about Abba and Eema again, what they were like, and why they named me Hadassah. I love hearing your stories."

"I love you my beautiful niece, and miss our time together too, but this is no time for relaxing and talking. An enemy seeks our destruction, and we must organize our people and move at a moment's notice. Where is

Michael? He has been in charge of this operation with the pilots, and we plan to meet in a few hours. Have you seen him?"

Hadassah could never bring herself to lie to her uncle, especially now that she followed Jesus. She would need to choose her answers and words carefully.

"I saw him a little while ago, and we talked for a few minutes. He had something important to do and said he will be gone for a while before he returns."

"What could be more important than what we are doing now? I just started trusting that boy, now he pulls a stunt like this! Do you know where I can find him so I can get him back here?"

"No, Uncle, I don't. I think it has something to do with the planes and making sure they are ready for us. You can trust Michael. He knows what he is doing and is committed to the cause. I promise he will not let you or our people down."

"Well, I need him now, and he isn't answering his phone. Can you get in touch with him?"

"I can try to call him too, but..."

"Well, call him! I'm sorry, Hadassah, I did not intend to raise my voice. Please call him."

She called but got Michael's voicemail, just like Mordecai had done. He tried to be gentle with her, but she could tell by the way he walked away, Michael would face his ire when he returned. If only her uncle understood how vital his mission was, but he did not. *Win the war and get back here, Michael, please. We need you; I need you.*

In the heavenly realm, massive numbers of demonic beings crept stealthily toward the abode of Yahweh, which was always guarded by his heavenly host. Each group followed a Chief Prince, with the dragon himself leading them from the center of their circular army.

When they got close, the dragon held up his hand and pointed toward a group of their enemy gathered in what appeared to be a planning session. Glee covered his face as he saw his primary target seated at the head leading the discussion: *Michael.*

Some members of Yahweh's army stood at their posts, but appeared unconcerned, their swords lying out of reach, while others carried on conversations or relaxed, unaware the horde approached. He motioned his Chief Princes closer.

"Our plan worked to perfection! Look at them going about their daily affairs not realizing destruction is about to strike. Move your teams into place and ensure we have them surrounded with no way of escape. Today will satisfy the horde's thirst for blood. I have awaited this day for many millennia, and now it has arrived. We must move fast."

"When your men are in position, signal me, and I will give the command to attack. My scream will not only initiate the charge but also startle the host and throw them into confusion. Then they will be ours for the taking!"

"The horde will storm them from all sides, striking them down as others arrive too late. We will rush the group before us and take them out quickly. You kill the others, then encircle Michael so he cannot get away."

"I will pounce on him and take him to the ground. First, he shall taste my fire as I blast him in the face and blind him. When he lies in darkness, I will slowly torch every part of his body until he screams in pain and begs for mercy. Then we will watch as he dies a slow, agonizing death."

Beelzebub and Belial could hardly control their enthusiasm and remain silent. They would relish this moment, and it would live on in their memory forever. The beast would make Michael's death far more excruciating than either of them could. Their master brought them back to reality.

"With the head removed, the remaining host will flee, but they will not escape our pursuit. We will chase them down and demolish them. Then we will enter the throne room, remove the two from their thrones, kill them, and assume our rightful positions as rulers of the universe. It is time!"

His leaders moved at once, getting their troops into position surrounding the realm of the heavenly host. They left no chance of them breaking through their ranks and escaping. Once every unit of the eager horde was in place, the princes informed their leader his army was ready.

The dragon's scream pierced the air, so shrill even his princes covered their ears. His demons charged the unsuspecting host with shrieks and howls, a colossal fighting force bent on destruction.

Alone in the meeting hall, Hadassah paced back and forth, Michael on her mind. She had never seen him so concerned. He was always sure of himself, but this time she heard doubt, maybe even fear, in his voice. What if the dragon and his horde defeated Michael and the host? He said everything would be lost. He was right.

"Hadassah, is that you?"

She had not even heard Ben open the door and step inside. How long had he been standing there?

"You're going to wear a hole in the floor if you keep this up. Something on your mind? Or should I say *someone?*"

"Sometimes I just need to walk and pray in a quiet place, and with no one here, this matched that description."

"It's Michael, isn't it? I have sensed something special about that boy, and I have a feeling you may understand more about him than I do."

"Michael *is* special, Ben. He has a big heart and a sharp mind and is a great leader. You have witnessed that yourself. We are blessed to have him on our side."

"Come on, Hadassah, there is more to him than that. You can tell me... you *need* to tell me. We have major decisions to make in the coming days that may mean life or death for our people who believe in Jesus. Michael plays a huge role in those, so if I need to know something that will help me understand him more and release greater responsibility to him, please tell me now."

Her mind ran crazy with a multitude of thoughts. She promised Michael she would not tell and assured him he could trust her. But Ben needed to know, and she trusted him. No, she couldn't break confidentiality, but must remain true to her word. Both missions were so urgent.

Michael, please win the war and come back to us. What if he doesn't? *What if the dragon, or Beelzebub, or Belial kill him?* Fear of that possibility showed all over her face, and she knew it. She fought back tears to keep Ben from realizing he was right. *Stay strong, Hadassah.*

"Hello, is anyone in there?" Ben asked, tapping on her head.

"I'm sorry, Ben. I just have a lot on my mind and need to be alone with my thoughts."

"Is that a hint for me to leave? Hadassah, is Michael in danger? If so, you need to tell us where he is so we can help him."

"Michael can take care of himself, so don't worry about him. He will be here to help take care of us when we need him. I am certain of that."

"Whatever you say. I won't force you to tell me anything, but if you decide to talk, come to our home. Please don't withhold information we need to help our young comrade. You speaking up may be what it takes to save his life."

He started walking away, then stopped and turned toward her again. "Hadassah, you are also important to this team, and we need you, too. Never forget that." He left her alone again.

She longed to tell him everything, to blurt it out and bring them all together to pray for Michael. But they must not know who or where he was. Tears now rolled from her eyes as she considered the possibility of losing a war and a cause... and Michael. Yes, if that happened, everything would be lost forever.

The dragon led the charge, moving rapidly, his feet not touching the floor. His power allowed him to do that when situations required it. Flames shot from his mouth as the deafening roar never ceased. They drew closer but saw no movement from the host sitting and standing before them.

"They are ours!" he screamed, just before slamming on the brakes, as his horde did the same.

All of them saw it at the same time. Michael and the group around him rose, joined by those standing guard, flaming swords drawn and summoning others. A vast multitude of the heavenly host swooped down from above, moving toward them at warp speed.

"Retreat!"

The horde spun, obeying his order, but found themselves caught in their own trap. Millions of Yahweh's mighty angels surrounded them, an impenetrable wall of impending doom.

Beelzebub leapt beside his master.

"No surrender! *Cut off the head!*"

He charged the circle of host who sat before them minutes earlier, with Michael as his target. Belial joined him, as did a few of the horde. The dragon realized they had no option but to fight their way out of this. They must overpower the host and emerge victorious!

"Charge!" he said in a loud voice that sounded far less than confident. But his confidence grew as they drew near, with no response coming from the host. They were close enough now to inflict damage.

"Take them!"

The front lines of demons, led by the princes, surged forward and drew even with him. He threw back his head and roared, a blazing inferno streaming from his mouth toward the motionless group facing them. When the flames reached the host, they crossed their swords, and deflected them, sending the hellish fire back around the entire circle zooming toward the attackers.

Demons screamed in pain as fire scorched their tiny bodies. They extended their oversized wings, trying to shield themselves, but they were no match for the blistering inferno.

Beelzebub, Belial, and the other four princes leading the charge dove face first to the ground, hoping to avoid the flames. Instead, the fire shot across them, searing their legs, backs, and heads. They rolled, extinguishing the blaze, but it left them writhing in pain on the ground.

For the first time, the dragon felt his own flames. They penetrated his scaly armor, and trapped inside it, spread throughout, burning his entire body. Howling in pain, he fell to the ground, sparks flickering from his mouth, his fire extinguished. He lay helplessly incapacitated, rendered powerless, and unable to move.

From his prone position, he saw his army laying down their swords and falling to their knees in surrender. He heard steps and turned his head back toward the host they seemed certain to destroy only a short while ago. Sandaled feet and powerful legs came into view closing in with each step.

He did not have to guess who it was. *Michael.* The captain of the heavenly host had defeated him, and he now lay before him, at his mercy.

"Stand!" the booming voice said.

The dragon tried but could not. His legs were not only seared and tormented by the pain, but they were void of strength to push himself to his feet. Strong hands lifted him into the air until they brought him face-to-face with the warrior angel of heaven.

"You have no place in the heavenly realm," Michael said, his voice firm and decisive.

"Yahweh is God and *Jesus is Lord*!" He knew that name tortured the beast even more than the flames that tormented his body.

The dragon felt himself being held aloft above the head of his captor before the powerful arms shot forward and hurled him through the air. He passed through the boundary of the heavenly realm and fell rapidly toward the earth below. His short limbs would do little to break his fall.

When he approached the land, he braced himself for the ensuing crash, then hit with the impact of a colliding asteroid. The breath knocked from his lungs; he gasped for air as pain continued to ravage his body. He opened his eyes and saw the mighty angel hovering over him.

"You will never again enter the heavenly realm," his foe said. "Your time is short, and your ultimate defeat will come soon. The one you fought so hard to destroy will destroy you!"

Michael left as quickly as he came, leaving the great red dragon lying on the ground. He saw his princes and the remaining horde of demons descending toward him, too. They lost this battle and their place in the heavenly realm. But he would not lose the war! Overcoming his pain, the creature stood and faced his army. He already knew his next move and would perform it quickly.

●   ●   ●   ●   ●

Celebration and worship filled the throne room of heaven. A loud voice praised Yahweh and his Messiah, Jesus, and celebrated this defeat of the enemy of all who serve God and follow Jesus.

But Michael and the heavenly host were not the only ones to win the victory over the dragon. The believers triumphed over him by the blood of Jesus, their bold witness, and refusing to yield, even if it meant dying for their faith. True victory came through surrender.

When the celebration neared its end, the voice called on the inhabitants of heaven to rejoice because their enemy was cast out and hurled to the earth. Their shout of joy flooded the throne room and echoed throughout the heavens. The exultation continued until a proclamation of woe ended it.

Heaven rejoiced, but the earth and sea were doomed because the dragon had gone down to them, filled with fury, and realizing his time was short. The angels stood, heads bowed, lined for miles, forming a walkway to the throne.

Yahweh summoned his Archangel, the Chief Prince and mighty warrior, leader of the heavenly host to come to him. Michael came and knelt before his God in humility and awe.

"Well done, my good and faithful servant. You defeated the enemy and expelled him from our midst. But the war is not over. You know what you must do next; go protect our people."

The mighty angel rose and dipped his head, first toward Yahweh, seated on the throne, high and exalted above all. Next, he stepped to his left and acknowledged the one seated on the throne at Yahweh's right hand... Jesus, the Messiah.

Both held gleaming swords and placed one on each of Michael's shoulders, commissioning him for battle. Yahweh nodded, and Michael turned toward his army, who had followed him to victory once again. He took three steps, then lifted off, soaring over top of them and vanishing from their sight in a flash of light. His work during these last three-and-a-half years had just begun.

Hadassah missed Ben opening the door of the meeting hall earlier, but now the unmistakable sound of footsteps entered her ears. She froze, her mind screaming *run* but her body refusing to move.

"You look silly walking around here all alone talking to yourself. If someone sees you, they'll think you're crazy! What is going on inside that brain of yours?"

She recognized the voice immediately. *Michael!* Was she dreaming, or was it really him?

"Well, aren't you going to answer me, or did you forget about me in such a short time?"

It *was* him! She whirled around and saw him sitting in a chair, legs crossed, smiling at her.

"Michael! You're back!"

"Well, that's obvious. Either that, or my ghost is sitting here talking to you." He grinned at her.

"Michael, stop it! I was worried sick about you. You appear to be okay, so I assume all went well. I honestly feared you wouldn't return this time. Now, tell me all about it, and leave nothing out!"

"I hate to disappoint you, but we have no time for stories. We must prepare for the dragon's next move."

"The dragon? If you defeated him, how can he be planning his next moves?"

"Hadassah, no one will destroy him but Jesus. However, you would have enjoyed watching me grab him, hold him aloft, then hurl him to the earth."

"You did that?! Please, tell me everything!"

"That part doesn't matter for us now. I won't say I didn't enjoy it, but what's coming now will be anything but enjoyable."

"What do you mean?"

"We kicked him out of heaven, so those there rejoice. But now the earth will face his fury, especially the Jews who have followed Jesus. Protecting them is my responsibility. I witnessed his wrath firsthand, and I promise you we have no time to lose. Let's go!"

She realized no more news of the battle was coming, but the realization hit her that the war was just beginning. They must call Ben and the others together without hesitation and begin the things they had worked on. Time could run out for them any minute.

Michael sprinted for Ben's house while she ran to get her uncle. Soon they all gathered in the meeting house with Michael standing to talk about the urgency of deciding what they would do. He must give nothing away about where he had been. Mordecai challenged him.

"It's about time you returned. How could you disappear when we had so many important decisions to make?"

"Let him talk, Mordecai," said Ben. "He may know something we need to hear."

Mordecai appeared miffed, but sat back to listen with a scowl on his face.

"I apologize, Aluf, but I had an important mission that could not wait. I returned as fast as I could."

Did he say too much? Hadassah shot a glance, her eyes saying once again, *be careful!*

"I discovered something while I was away that you need to hear. The enemy will attack all the Jewish believers any moment, so we must decide how we will respond and be ready!"

"Exactly how did you get that information?" Mordecai was still miffed.

"It doesn't matter how I got it, Aluf. What matters is, I know it's true! We either decide now, or the dragon will wipe out the entire movement. We don't have a second to lose."

Magnus looked doubtful when he heard mention of the dragon.

"He will never let you escape. He has an army at his disposal, and it's not a natural army. Messai talked about a powerful spiritual force that no human military can stop. They are evil."

"We can stop them, Magnus," said Michael. "But they can't stop us because Jesus is on our side."

"If we are going to make a move, we cannot wait because the dragon will not wait. He and his *demonic horde* will show up any minute. That's what Messai called them, but I don't think he ever saw them. If they get to us before we get away, we won't have a chance."

"But we don't know what we should do, where we will go, or how we will get there," said Ben. "I have known for a long time this day would come, and we would go on the run for our lives, but Jesus has not shown me where."

"Ben!"

Omar dashed into the meeting hall, with Ahmad and Hala right behind him. Whatever they had to say was clearly worth interrupting the meeting.

"We know where you're supposed to go! All 144,000 of you can live there. It's ready for you, and you can move in now!" He was out of breath after running in and talking so fast.

"Whoa, whoa. Hold on, Omar. What are you talking about?"

"Petra! Jesus told me you have to move to Petra to get away from the dragon!"

"Petra? That's in Jordan. They turned against Israel, remember? They will never allow a bunch of Jews to cross the border and travel to Petra."

"I believe Omar is right. I saw a huge, beautiful valley in the desert, surrounded by rock mountains, with a large group of people living inside. It had red rocks and caves, and a huge building with tall pillars carved into a hillside. That is Petra, isn't it Omar?"

"Yes, Anders!" said Hala. "That's Petra, the Rose Red City, the Treasury! Have you been there?"

"Not in person, but I saw it in the scroll. Ben, you need to get your people ready to go!"

"But how can we get 144,000 people to Petra?"

"Ben," Trey said. "What have we planned this entire time?"

"Planes? You can't land planes at Petra. It's all desert and mountains and rocks, and the closest airport is Amman. They sure won't let us fly into there. It's not possible."

"Let Rickie and me take a trial flight and see what we can find. We will go right now. Start spreading the word and organizing the people while we're gone. Michael, line up the pilots. Paul and Bradley, get to Ben Gurion and make sure your planes are ready. Mordecai, can you arrange transportation to move 144,000 people to different locations where we can fly them out?"

"I'm already on that. We just need to double-check every place we're flying from and get word to the people. Then I'll send every truck we need to haul them. Those close to a base, or to Ben Gurion, can get themselves there. It will be a huge operation, but this has been in the planning stages for a few months, so I think we're ready."

"Just slow down, men. We need to think this through before making such a major decision."

"There's nothing to think through, Ben," said Trey. "We know where everyone lives and people there can inform them today and tomorrow. All the IDF bases and planes are ready. It sounds like Mordecai has trucks lined up, so we can move everybody there right now!"

"I not only have them ready, but we have everything calculated down to the most minute details. We know how many trucks it will take to haul all 144,000 people, how many trips they will need to make, and how many flights we must fly. Israelis will suspect nothing more than the IDF flying training exercises."

"What happens when the Jordanian military spots IDF and American planes flying into restricted space? Our planes shot down and our people killed in the crashes? They will not miss that many planes flying into their country."

"Yes, they will miss them, Ben!" said Michael with absolute certainty. "I mean, if we get the planes in and out quick."

Out of the corner of his eye, he saw Hadassah shaking her head and rolling her eyes.

Ben said nothing, but sat looking at the young soldier in amazement. *How can he know that?* he questioned in his mind. *There is something about him...*

"Rickie and I will test the airways with the first flight. We'll fly to Petra and look for somewhere we can land. But we need to do that now. If Michael and Magnus are both right, and Jesus showed this to Anders, we don't have time to wait."

They didn't wait. Both men were out the door and on their way to the base before Ben could stop them. The flight to Petra would take less than an hour. The mission depended on their ability to find a landing place. That sounded impossible, but they had to try.

"What about after we get there? If he always knows where we are, what can stop him from wiping us out there? He will have us trapped inside a fortress with no escape."

"An impenetrable fortress, Ben," Anders said.

"No fortress is impenetrable from the air."

"Ben, what happened to your faith? If Jesus showed me Petra in the scroll and revealed it to Omar, Ahmad, and Hala, I am certain it's where you are supposed to go. You have taught us he is in control and we should trust him. The time has come for you and your people to live by faith. You have known this was coming for a long time. Now, let's get started."

Ben was quiet for a moment, then spoke like a switch flipped in his mind.

"Thank you, Anders. I needed to hear that."

"You're welcome, Ben. Something tells me you need to get everyone to Petra fast."

"Okay, get everybody in here, and let's start the process. We can have the ball rolling by the time Trey and Rickie get back."

CHAPTER 12

Aissa Messai received a surprise visitor as he sat alone, mulling over his future. The creature to whom he sold his soul and who was about to change his life forever appeared in front of him out of nowhere. He instinctively fell to his knees before his master, as he always did.

Messai could tell the dragon was not his usual self. He walked with a noticeable limp and winced from pain when he did. But any lack of vitality was replaced with full-blown fury.

"On your feet."

He recognized the gravelly voice into which his own often transformed in moments of uncontrolled rage. Fear coursed through his body and mind, causing his body to tremble. His legs felt too weak to stand, but he forced himself up and stared into the face of the dragon.

Neither the repulsive odor of the beast's breath, nor fire seeping from his nostrils, concerned Messai as it usually did. One look into the dragon's eyes made him forget both. Fury, like he had never seen glared back at him with murderous intent.

At first he feared for his life, thinking he had angered the creature and realizing he may face death by fire within seconds. His words slipped out through quivering lips.

"What is it, master? Tell me, and I will obey."

"They must die."

"Who, master? Tell me, and AMPP will find them right now and bring them before you."

"Those abhorrent Jews who believe in the false Messiah. But I need no help from your men. I will handle them myself by turning others against them who will do my bidding. Their attacks will begin tomorrow night.

The Smyrnians have already begun their effort to stop me, but I will stop them instead. I have awaited this day! Our time has come!"

"What do you need from me, master?"

"Convince the people of Israel and the Middle East this scum must go before we can live in real peace and prosperity. Call all Jews and Palestinians who remain faithful to our cause to turn on them and slaughter them tomorrow night. Lead the way, Aissa, for you will soon lead the world!"

"I will do as you say, master. My hatred for them goes as deep as yours. Remove them so we can fulfill our plan without their interference. Our moment *has* come, and..."

The beast disappeared as quickly as he appeared a few minutes earlier, leaving Messai alone with an unfinished sentence and much to consider.

He wasted no time calling a press conference for three hours later. He knew the place and the people to call. It was short notice, but they would come. They always came for *him*.

In three hours, he stood in front of the majestic crowning feature of the Temple Mount facing the Golden Gate, looking toward the Mount of Olives. Before him sat the select group of reporters he had summoned for his announcement. Cameras trained on him prepared to broadcast his words throughout the nation of Israel and the Middle East.

They all want to hear from me, he said, his heart swelling with pride. *This is my hour; I will make the dragon proud. I am the most powerful man in the world, but he will make me the all-powerful god of the world!* This was his last press conference before that occurred. He had to make it good.

"Ladies and gentlemen of Israel, this is an urgent announcement that requires your immediate attention. It concerns many of your fellow citizens, and perhaps some of your own family members and friends. Thus, I do not take this matter lightly."

"A group of Jews united with the rebel Smyrnians and recruited large numbers of others to join their destructive cause. Some moved here from other countries. Their number has grown so large they are now a serious threat to the goals we all hold dear."

"If they continue undermining our efforts, we risk losing the magnificent Jewish Temple behind me and the Muslim mosques which have adorned this Mount for almost one and a half millennia. They will destroy our unity and shatter the peace we have achieved in this part of the world."

"*We* promote peace, but *they* have nothing to do with peace. Their divisive rhetoric and relentless recruiting of additional converts to their radical agenda put peace in peril, here and around the world. But you do not need me to tell you that; you have witnessed it with your own eyes."

"We all lived through the horrific plagues conjured up by Moshe and Eliyahu, the two prophets sent out from this evil cult. The evidence clearly shows they did not come in peace. Their actions reveal the extreme hatred these apostate Jews hold for the world, and for you and me."

"If we do not end this threat now, it may be too late. When we stop it together, our reward will be prosperity like we have never seen! I ask all of you Jews and Palestinians alike to help us remove this scourge and restore peace and prosperity to our country, region, and world! Prepare yourselves to go, because the time is short, and we must not wait!"

"Perhaps you ask, how will we know who they are? I am told their houses emit an evil yellowish glow after dark that you will recognize when you see it, so the attack must take place at night. Thus, we will unite in our effort tomorrow at midnight. Take action against any house where you see this sign. Thank you for stepping out and taking back what these animals have taken from us!"

The conference ended, and he was off to watch his master's rage in action. The dragon would eliminate thousands of Jews during the next few days, and Messai would enjoy the show.

●　　　●　　　●　　　●　　　●

Trey and Rickie crossed into Jordanian airspace, two American fighter pilots flying an IDF helicopter. They would fly over Petra in less than thirty minutes.

"I agree with you, Trey, but how do we land planes at Petra? That whole place is nothing but rocks and mountains."

"I don't understand either, Rickie, but we're supposed to check it out. We'll set this thing down and see what we can find."

"We have both seen the terrain during our tours here. I just don't see it happening."

"Neither do I, but nothing is impossible for *you know who*."

"I agree with that as well. Because I can't see it, doesn't mean Jesus can't handle it."

"Bingo!" Trey said with a wide smile. "Just relax till we get there, and we will find out for ourselves."

"What the...?"

Dust engulfed the chopper out of nowhere, completely obstructing their view. Trey was flying blind, clueless to what lay ahead of them or which direction they were flying.

"Brownout!" said Rickie.

"I can't see anything! I need to go higher if we're getting close to the mountains!"

"Stay the course and don't make any sudden moves! We were on the right track."

The helicopter lurched left, then right, as the rotors fought against the strong wind driving the dust and sand.

"I'm losing control!" Trey shouted, fighting to keep from crashing, using all of his skills. "It's the dragon! We should have known he would try to stop us. That means Petra's the right place, or he wouldn't try to stop us from going there!"

"During our flight back from Germany, when you were so near death from your injuries, I flew the plane and the others in the back prayed for you. Jesus answered them, or you wouldn't be here today! Remember the struggle when you and I flew to rescue Bruno and Magnus? I didn't think we were going to make it, but you prayed, and we did! Here we go again, so start praying. *Now*, Rickie! I can't see *anything*!"

When Rickie started praying, unseen to them, Beelzebub stirred up more dust and sand, while rocking the chopper back and forth with his powerful arms. In his mind, the dragon shouted encouragement.

"They are yours, my prince. Take them to the ground!"

Trey fought the greatest battle of his life. The helicopter was out of his control, and all his efforts were useless. Going against his training and instincts, he released the controls and joined his partner praying. Rickie was so engrossed in prayer he didn't notice.

Three mighty angels of the heavenly host swept from the sky, diving toward the dragon's mightiest angel. While two pilots prayed inside the chopper, a battle for control ensued outside the machine.

Beelzebub dealt a blow to one of Yahweh's host and sent him reeling backward, dazed. The others attacked from each side, but the demon was too powerful for them. The battle was one against three, but the one was winning, while the helicopter spun toward a fiery crash.

"Stop!"

Beelzebub whirled around at the sound of the commanding voice. He had drawn the mightiest of them all, his eternal foe, Michael. He would now avenge their defeat in the heavenly realm the day before and get revenge for the dragon.

"Michael!" the evil angel said. "You are the one I was waiting for. I cannot believe you showed up to protect your friends. Are two men really worth saving?"

"Every human being is worth saving, Beelzebub. You force me to defeat you again!"

"Their mission will fail! My master will not allow it to happen! Neither can you defeat me!"

"My master is more powerful than yours, and he will make sure it happens! Say his name, demon: *Jesus*!" Hearing the name sent Michael's archenemy into a rage. Beelzebub flew at him, his mighty arms extended, and killing on his mind.

Inside the chopper, Trey and Rickie's prayer became one word: *Jesus*. They did not realize why, but they could not stop saying his name. They were oblivious to the aircraft spinning out of control with them inside.

"Jesus! Jesus!"

Michael joined their chant.

"Jesus! Jesus! Messiah! Lord of the universe!"

Beelzebub covered his ears as he neared the leader of the heavenly host, the name driving him insane. He swung a mighty blow aimed at Michael's face. Michael leaned back, evading the blow, then landed a blow of his own. The beast grunted, stunned, then turned to meet another blow that sent him flying, the cloud of dust and sand now enveloping and blinding him.

Trey and Rickie felt the swerving stop as the chopper settled into flight again. Now to get their bearings and determine their location. They looked down and discovered they were flying low over Petra. Each was too stunned to talk and amazed at the beauty greeting their sight.

"I wish we had time to set down in there for a while, but we need to hurry. Let's land outside and look things over, then head back to the kibbutz. We just witnessed another miracle. Jesus answered our prayers again."

"I can't wait to step out of this thing onto solid ground."

When they cleared the mountainous range that surrounded the city, neither believed his eyes.

· · · · ·

The dragon screamed as his fury spilled out at his Chief Prince.

"How could you let them escape! They should be dead in a pile of twisted metal by now, but they reached their destination instead! Do I need to send Belial to do the job next time?"

That stung the mighty demon. He and Belial were rivals, though neither would admit it.

"No, master. Michael caught me by surprise. I was defeating the other three when..."

"Silence! I have no interest in your excuses. We must stop a movement, and time is running out."

"Give me another chance, Your Majesty, and I will not let you down."

"The host is protecting those two, so we will not concern ourselves with them. Let them go so they will believe we backed down. It is time to change course and catch them by surprise. We will move our attack up to tonight. You, Belial, and the princes will go after the twelve tribes beginning at midnight, twenty-four hours earlier than planned. That gives them no time to change plans. Stir up the people against them and put murder on their minds. Follow the plan and do not fail me again!"

· · · · ·

"I can't believe my eyes," said Rickie, as Trey landed the chopper outside the desert enclave.

"It's impossible," whispered his partner.

They stepped out and stared at level hard-packed landing strips lying side-by-side, each long enough to handle the largest planes.

"Did someone create this for us?"

"Someone did partner, and we both know who that was. I don't understand how, but neither can I explain many things that have happened. Let's get back and tell the others Petra is ready!"

After a smooth flight back and drive to the kibbutz, they rushed in to report. The entire team gathered, eager to learn what they discovered, but most doubted the news would be positive.

"Some of the best landing strips you ever saw sit right outside the Siq entrance! I can't explain how they got there, but they're level, smooth, straight, and hard as asphalt. It's like someone brought in heavy equipment and made them!"

"I get it," said Anders.

"What do you mean, you get it?" asked his former partner.

"It's right there in the Bible again, Blake. The Prophet Isaiah wrote it, and a voice quoted it from the scroll. Listen and you will understand."

He retrieved a Bible and read the words of Isaiah Chapter Forty, verses three and four.

A voice of one calling:

"In the wilderness prepare the way for the LORD; make straight in the desert a highway for our God.

Every valley shall be raised up, every mountain and hill made low; the rough ground shall become level, the rugged places a plain..."

"Jesus prepared a way for us in the desert! He raised the valleys and brought down the mountains. The rough ground became level, the rugged places smooth... and voila... runways!"

If any doubt remained that Petra was their city of refuge, it disappeared after that. Plans were finished, and all the Jewish believers in Israel prepared to implement them early the next morning.

Mordecai assigned IDF trucks to haul people to IAF Bases and Ben Gurion. Michael released the duty of organizing pilots to Trey and Rickie. His *missions* were more numerous and closer together now, but none of his teammates were privy to their purposes. Mordecai remained indignant about it, but Ben continued to ponder Michael's status among them.

Trey, Rickie, Paul, Bradley, eight IDF pilots, and four pilots from the American unit were already in position with their planes. They checked everything out and confirmed they were ready to fly. All they needed was passengers.

Every Jewish follower of Jesus understood where they must be and what time to arrive. The trucks would pick up many at their homes. Ben instructed them to bring nothing, remembering Yahweh's promise to take care of them. The excitement was at fever pitch as they tried to sleep so they would be rested for the big day. They would arrive in Petra before the dragon could stop them.

Hadassah dreamed as she slept and found herself alone in a strange place. Shudders covered her body, and fear took hold of her. She longed to cry out for Michael, but something told her she must keep quiet or be discovered. *Who are those people,* she questioned within herself, creeping closer until they came into full view. *Those aren't people! They're not human!*

She saw him, the dragon others talked so much about, and crawled under a rock ledge to hide. Michael told her about him, but she never thought *she* would see him. She heard the dragon call the most gigantic and grotesque looking demon. *Beelzebub!* This was the dragon meeting with his demonic princes! She sensed courage and boldness and eased closer to listen.

"We will go *tonight*, men, and surprise them before they have time to maneuver. You will not lead the attacks, but will stir up the people against those who now worship *him*. When you possess their minds, they will obey. This is not possession by the horde, but possession by *you*, my strong ones. Fill them with hatred and thoughts of slaughter, then release them to attack the *infidels*."

They are attacking the believers tonight! Her mind raced with thoughts of what to do. The others must know! The conversation continued, and she listened, barely breathing, and not moving to prevent them from detecting her presence.

"Each of you take one *tribe* and spread our yellow vapor over the houses so the attackers can easily recognize them. Jews and Palestinians shall come together as one army united against the *infidels* and destroy them before they know what hit them. We will wipe them out tonight! Go now in my power! The time has come!"

I have to tell the others! There was no choice except to wait until the princes left. Then she would have to negotiate the rocky terrain and elude the dragon's line of sight. Jesus told them the time was coming; now the realization hit her. This was it; the purpose for which she was sent. He sent her to the Smyrnians *for such a time as this*. But she also realized Jesus had more for her to do.

Hadassah crept back past the ledge, careful not to move a single piece of shale, until she could stand unnoticed. She stood and turned; her legs numb and wobbly from bending underneath her, and found herself face-to-face with the dragon! Panic consumed her. Sleeping legs refused to move. The smell of his breath nauseated her, and the sparks coming from his mouth made her feel as if she would ignite. She froze, trembling, staring the beast of hell in the eyes.

In the tribes of Israel, twelve demon chiefs moved with precision speed, yellow fog spreading from them, hovering above specific houses. Eerie dark haze trailed behind them, covering the entire land, and seeping into the houses of every non-believer in Jesus. It then entered the brains of the people inside, filling them with rage for every Jew who followed Jesus.

The haze, mingled with the earlier words of Aissa Messai, awakened them, and thoughts of carnage filled their minds. They moved robotically from their houses, fiery eyes glowing red, bound for homes covered with yellow fog and occupied by unsuspecting families.

Hadassah awoke, sweating and shaking. It was only a dream, yet she knew it was real. She called her uncle as she sprinted for Ben and Miriam's house, where they slept soundly. Her trembling hands pounded on the door. Mordecai dashed up just as lights came on inside the Abramson house. She did not stop knocking until Ben opened the door. Both looked at her, hands trembling, hair soaked with sweat, a look of fear covering her face, and realized something was terribly wrong.

"Ben... Uncle... I dreamed. I was in a place with the dragon and the princes of hell. It was a dream, but it came from Jesus. They are attacking our people *tonight*. The dragon's chief demons have already left to stir up Jews and Palestinians who don't believe in Jesus, then sending them to slaughter every Jew who believes. We have to do something!"

"Are you certain of this, Hadassah?" asked the Aluf.

"Yes, Uncle, I know it. I realized tonight Jesus brought me to the Smyrnians *for such a time as this*. He showed me, so I could tell you, and we can save his people and get them to Petra. We don't have time to stand around. You must get the trucks rolling and the pilots ready. Please, this is serious. Our people will die *tonight* if we don't take action!"

Ben's and Mordecai's phones blew up with calls from their twelve leaders stationed in the tribes. They answered the first and motioned for others to return the remaining ten. The stories were the same. A voice screamed into Ben's ear the second he answered.

"We are under attack! Mobs surrounding our houses and chanting *death to the infidels!* Jews, Palestinians, Israelis who do not follow Jesus. They are throwing rocks through windows and torching vehicles. It is only a matter of time until they break into our homes. When that happens, many of our people will die!"

"How do they know where *our people* live?" Ben asked, bewildered by what the man said.

"An eerie yellow light hovers above every one of our houses, leading them straight to us!"

"It is the dragon and his demonic horde. We have to move quick. Call the others and tell them we are going *tonight*. We cannot wait until tomorrow."

"But how will we get past the mobs? They have us surrounded!"

"We will drive vehicles, and they won't. They are on foot, so we can drive right through them, and head for the planes! I don't want to kill anyone, but if they refuse to move, we will have no choice. Watch for the trucks and be ready to jump in fast. You'll have to run through them, sneak out a back door, or avoid them somehow. We'll get the trucks there soon. Tell those who are driving themselves to leave now if they can. Otherwise they must go to a pickup point."

A window shattered as the man yelled at his family, then the call disconnected. None of these were isolated incidents. Reports came from the entire country: Jerusalem, Tel Aviv, Haifa, Beersheba, Tiberias, Eilat, every tribe, town, village, and home where Jesus' followers lived.

Mordecai called the bases, telling the drivers to move out fast. Each already knew where he was going and how many people he would pick up.

Others now joined Ben, Mordecai, and Hadassah outside in the street. They all saw it; a yellow haze floated above the kibbutz.

"Warn the others *now!*" Ben yelled.

They ran from house to house, pounding on doors and screaming at families to get up. As they stumbled out of their houses and saw the eerie yellow glow hanging over them, Ben and Mordecai told them what was happening.

"We are leaving *now!*" said Ben. "Take nothing but your families and the clothes you are wearing. Jesus promised to provide our needs at Petra. We need all the space in the trucks and planes for people. Thousands will fit into the planes' cargo holds. And we can cram hundreds into the back of each truck, but there will be no room for anything extra."

"You will not see this place again. However, we will have an amazing new home for the next three-and-a-half years until Jesus returns! Our truck is on the way. It will arrive by the time we get everybody here. Make sure everyone in your family is present, so we leave no one behind."

Families pulled parents and children together to ensure none were missing. Some rushed back to awaken sleeping children. Each family would huddle with one other and take a final count to be certain everyone was present.

The sound of voices rang from outside. An angry mob pounded on the gate and attempted to scale the walls.

"Death to the infidels!" they chanted over and over.

"We need to protect our people before the truck gets here!" shouted Mordecai. "Do not let them penetrate the gate or get over the walls! Stay on guard for things thrown from outside!"

"Spread out around the walls!" Ben said. "The truck will be here soon, so we only need to protect ourselves a little while longer."

The voices grew louder, and it was clear they were increasing in number. Fire bombs flew over the wall, along with rocks and anything else the crowd had to throw.

"We need every available man and woman to stand guard and keep everyone safe. If everyone in your family is here, stay and help protect the kibbutz. We cannot afford to lose anyone. All 144,000 of us must get to Petra."

The initial flight was already in progress. Trey and Rickie flew 25 American troops to the Rose Red City, where they would line the *runways* with flares and guide the planes in with bright lights.

Michael insisted he fly with them, even though they warned him the others may need his help. They feared an attack by the Jordanian military when they crossed the border, but both the crossing and continued flight went well. Jordan's air defense system did not detect the plane, so they completed the flight and returned to Israel just in time.

"I think a guardian angel flew with us," Trey said to Robert Clark. "Don't you agree, Rickie and Michael?"

"There is no doubt about it!" said Michael. "Now we need one for every flight tonight."

"Jesus can handle that," said Rickie.

"He can indeed, and he will!" Michael said with assurance.

When the truck drove toward the kibbutz, the guards opened the gate and forced it closed again as others fought to keep those outside from coming in. The driver did not slow down. He sped into the kibbutz as fast as the big military truck would go.

The residents piled into the back and crammed in like sardines. Parents held children on each knee and little ones in their arms, while everyone sat shoulder-to-shoulder, some on others' laps.

The gate opened as the robotic individuals outside stood clawing and shoving against it. The man behind the wheel prepared to speed through the crowd, hoping they would move, but prepared to mow down those who did not. None of those riding in the back witnessed what happened, but the driver, and Ben, who rode up front with him, watched in amazement.

The mob blocked their way, chanting, screaming, and trying to push the gate back open. When the truck started through, they moved to each side, not stepping, but sliding, as Ben imagined the Red Sea parting. Yahweh did it again so his people could escape to their safe place in Petra. They passed through untouched by the murderous mob on either side.

The truck then sped away toward the military base where they would join others in the empty cargo hold of a C-5 Super Galaxy Military transport plane. Cramming in like this should allow each plane to transport three to four thousand people to Petra. Uncomfortable? Yes, but necessary.

Trucks traveled throughout the nation of Israel, packed with followers of Jesus, and driving to the closest flight locations. When they left their houses and dashed to the trucks, most feared the worst. But the attackers outside parted, providing a clear path to walk unhurriedly to their escape vehicles. None were harmed. The same was true at every location, causing the people to celebrate another miraculous night for those who believed in Jesus.

•   •   •   •   •

The dragon howled in anger and called for his entire demonic horde to come. He was witnessing this with his own eyes and knew his chiefs were powerless to stop what was happening. His only recourse was to unleash every demon at his disposal to prevent believers from escaping. Millions gathered before him, pulsating, salivating, thirsty for blood.

"Look, my minions," he screeched, pointing to a large, clear sphere which showed the nation of Israel and trucks filled with people speeding down roads. "They are getting away! We must not allow them to escape! The chiefs stirred up the people against them, but *he* interfered. You will stop them, but there is no time to wait. *Go now* and destroy them!" They obeyed without delay.

Yellow eyes glowing, hideous faces revealing hatred for the *Jesus people*, they rushed away like a flood of water aimed at washing 144,000 Jewish believers into the pit.

In the back of the truck, Beth started shivering. At first, a few goose bumps popped up on her arms, but that quickly turned to chilling, then freezing.

"Something isn't right. Blake, I thought Jesus wouldn't let him near me again. What's happening?"

"Whatever's going on is happening to all of us!"

She looked at him and those close enough to see in the darkness and realized they were experiencing the same thing.

"Messai," said Beth through chattering teeth.

"I don't think so, Beth," Hadassah answered. "It's the dragon."

"He's the one who gives Messai his power," said Magnus. "Messai often wondered aloud how such cold came from someone who produced such heat. He's chasing us, or more likely his horde of demons. I can feel his presence."

"What can we do?" asked Hala. "I wish Ben was back here instead of up front with the driver. We need Michael with us too, but he's with Trey and Rickie."

"We can keep driving and hope we get to the base and our plane. You can't fight an unseen enemy."

"Yes, you can, Blake." Their man of faith spoke up again. "We fight an unseen enemy by asking our invisible God to deliver us from him."

Anders prayed loud enough for all to hear, quoting the Psalms and asking Jesus to come and rescue them. As always since his visit to heaven, he sounded like a man speaking to Jesus face-to-face.

"We love you, Lord. You are our refuge and strength, our rock, our fortress, and our deliverer. You are our shield and our stronghold, our strong tower. In our distress we call upon you; to you we cry for help. You are a very present help in trouble. We will not be afraid of anything the enemy throws at us but will trust in you. Deliver us from his assault right now, and lead us to Petra, the rock that is higher than us, the mighty fortress where you called us to go. We trust in you."

The chill left, but the dragon's horde closed in and prepared to unleash a vicious assault. The truck veered left, over the center line, then back right, off the shoulder of the road. They could tell the driver was fighting hard to prevent them from crashing, but it wasn't working.

Men, women, and children clung to one another, as a crash seemed inevitable. Their comrades experienced the same thing in other trucks. They all did what they could: prayed and hung on for dear life.

The dragon watched through his evil crystal ball as his demons nipped the truck tires like yapping dogs. They slid under hoods, pulling on wires, belts, and hoses. Some hung underneath, jerking on suspension, steering, exhaust systems, anything they could grab hold of.

"Go, my minions! You are far too numerous for them. They cannot overpower you!"

From his vantage point, Israel looked covered by a black swarm with yellow flashing from inside it. He howled with glee as drivers fought to maintain control of their trucks and people in the back hung on and uttered useless prayers to their phony *messiah*.

The truck swerved off, then onto the road, bumping so hard its passengers bounced up and down in the back, banging into each other. None could hear the others as what sounded like a million barn owls screeched without stopping. They covered their ears to keep the sound from driving them mad. Thrown around mercilessly, with demonic sounds piercing their ears, doubt began to replace faith that they would reach Petra alive.

"I cannot believe Jesus would bring us this far to let us perish without getting to Petra," Ben said to the driver. Then a soft voice came.

"Do not fear, Ben. You will lead my people to the place prepared for you in the desert."

He relaxed and smiled at the driver who did not see him either. The man's eyes were focused on the road and his mind on steering the vehicle. Ben had told him, "Don't slow down or stop for anything or anyone," and he was determined to obey.

The same was happening to every truck in Israel hauling Messianic Jews, but it would not last long. Unseen to the believers, every demon fell from the trucks, rolling behind and joining the horde continuing in pursuit. Without warning, the earth opened behind the vehicles, and demons poured into the abyss like a herd of buffalos running over a cliff. Those behind them, seeing many of their horde perish, came to screeching halts and flew away in panic back to their master.

The dragon's scream reverberated across the earth, echoing throughout the entire universe. In an instant, his rage turned from 144,000 Jews fleeing the country back to another group who would face Aissa

Messai's *reign of terror* for the next 42 months. They would face hell on earth.

In the backs of trucks traveling in the country of Israel, believers celebrated. None of them understood what caused it, but their rides became smooth, the deafening sound ceased, and light illuminated the trucks where they rode. The spell broken, Jewish and Palestinian residents returned to their homes, confused about what had happened to them. Things calmed down in Israel.

CHAPTER 13

Fifty military trucks made eight trips each, hauling three hundred Jewish believers each time, to locations from which they would fly to Petra, Jordan. Another twenty-four thousand drove or walked because they lived close to IDF bases, or Ben Gurion Airport.

Arrival times varied to allow planes to alternate departures as they flew multiple trips to their destination. Precision scheduling was essential for this mission to work. Michael structured arrival and departure times, along with the number of trips and passengers per plane.

The C-130 was a massive transport aircraft, but men, women, and children would still have to cram in. He insisted three thousand pack into the cavernous cargo hold of each plane. The plan was not popular with Mordecai, but the people applauded it.

"Michael, I will not allow this. I know the weight limit and space available in these planes. They cannot exceed the weight limit by that much and make the flight to Petra."

"Mordecai, I don't disagree with your assessment, but I trust Michael. He has not been wrong yet, so we need to follow his lead this time, too."

"But, Ben, this is crazy! I have spent my career in the IDF, and I am certain this will not work!"

"He has the blessing of every pilot, including Paul Johnson and Bradley Rodgers, not to mention Trey Butler and Rickie Cruz. I give him my blessing as well. You are an IDF Major General, but I'm the leader of this movement, and I choose to fly three thousand people per plane. End of story."

Ben's sternness shocked Mordecai, but he knew the man was right. He believed in Jesus because of Ben's work. He could not fight his leadership or this decision, but his face revealed his disappointment and lack of trust in what was about to happen. Michael reached out to him.

"Aluf, I respect you very much, but I believe this plan is accurate, and I guarantee its success. Please trust me and let the people see your support and willingness to cooperate."

"I don't understand how you can make such a guarantee, but it's clear that I am outnumbered. I will support the plan, despite the danger that would normally accompany it. Let's fly."

"Thank you, Aluf. I give my word that I will not let you, or these people, down. Let's load the first three thousand."

That group paraded up the ramp and into the cargo hold, cramming as tight as they could. There would be no seat belts or seating. Their flight promised to bring more discomfort than their previous ride, but they could not turn back now. The big engines whirred, and they felt the plane move. They were on their way. Next stop: Petra.

Michael would travel on the final flight. Ben needed to get to Petra first, and he needed to arrive last. His work was essential to the success of the night and next day, because he not only organized the flights but also those who would accompany them. The pilots would fly the planes, but they failed to realize they would not control them. If they did, every single aircraft would end up on the ground in a ball of fire somewhere between Israel and Petra.

Michael commanded the host, but also supervised the flights himself. "Host, the time has come!" said the Archangel. "You know your assignments. Go fulfill them!"

The plane carrying the group from the kibbutz and more than 2,700 others lifted off. Ben stood in the back with his family, joined by Alexander and Elizabeth, Mordecai, Hadassah, and other leaders. They would step off first and lead the rest through the Siq into the rock fortress, aptly named Petra, where they would live until the triumphant return of Jesus.

"The takeoff was smooth enough," Mordecai said, his nerves still showing as he talked.

"Michael said the flight will only take an hour," Ben said, still trying to reassure the Major General.

"You would think we'd experience a little turbulence," Mordecai said as the plane reached its cruising altitude and soared effortlessly through the air. "I did not expect this."

"Don't forget Michael's guarantee."

"But how could he make such a promise, Ben? He has been right about a lot of things lately, even though he *has* disappeared often when work needed to be done. What is it about that boy?"

"I haven't spoken to you or anyone else about this, but I sense something unique about him. I can't put my finger on it, but I have watched him closely. Miraculous things happen when he disappears. You don't suppose...?"

Mordecai stared at him with a look of wonder. Ben could tell he was thinking, too.

"We should cross the border any minute. If their military spots us, they will shoot us down. That has concerned me too."

"Trust Jesus, Mordecai. If you can't trust Michael, believe what Jesus can do. He called us to Petra, so I choose to believe he's in control, not the pilots, or even Michael."

"I have seen enough miracles since I started following him to believe that too. Forgive my lack of faith. I can hardly wait to walk with you into Petra!"

Unseen to either of them or anyone else, outside the aircraft flew a multitude of the heavenly host. One group flew underneath, holding the plane in the air, while others held the wings steady to prevent any turbulence and shaking. Another group surrounded the plane, preventing any detection by the enemy. On they flew, unnoticed by Jordanian military forces or the dragon and his forces. They experienced a miraculous flight, as would every other group flying this night.

The angry dragon vented his wrath against all his forces, chiefs and horde alike. His crystal ball, now dark, yielded no information about his former targets.

"Where did they go?!"

"We lost them majesty," said Belial. "They seem to have disappeared. Maybe they plunged into the abyss with our troops."

"It will be my honor to lead a search party, your majesty. I feel certain we can locate them."

"No, Beelzebub! Let them go. They were not worth chasing, anyway. We face a much greater foe who we must annihilate. Our full attention will turn to them!"

A member of the horde flitted around him, his grotesque face bursting into a hideous grin.

"The Smyrnians!" he said, his high-pitched voice crackling with evil.

The dragon's enormous clawed foot swung around instantly, and the little demon's life ended as one small shriek escaped its mouth.

"Never mention that name in my presence again!" roared the beast. "Call them the *infidels* or those who follow *him*, but whatever you call them, *we* will destroy them!"

"Shall we attack them now, sir?"

"Not yet, Belial. First, we have a special coronation to take care of, then we will watch them die by the thousands!"

"You speak of Messai, your majesty?"

"Yes, my prince," the creature said, with sparks shooting from his mouth. "I chose him for this moment, and he will do my bidding. The world's inhabitants will worship him, or die!"

"When they worship him, they will really worship you, won't they, sir?" Beelzebub asked, then bowed before his master with his face to the ground. The others followed, the minions of hell kneeling and worshiping their king.

"*Yesss...*" the ancient serpent hissed. "The entire universe will worship me. And you, my faithful subjects will reign with me and ensure they always do."

The demonic chorus rang out, as ghastly as the songs of the heavenly host were glorious. They were ready for the *reign of terror* to begin.

●　　●　　●　　●　　●

The big cargo plane began its descent into the middle of a barren, rocky desert. Its passengers sensed downward movement, but could not see what was happening. The cargo hold fell silent as they clung to each other and prayed.

Shimon saw lights below dotting the landscape and beaming forth in the darkness. He had prepared for this mission since the day Michael and

Hadassah showed him the truth about the real Messiah. Scripture came more alive for him every day, and he knew this mission could not fail. The plane continued its descent as the lights came closer and closer.

The men from the American unit watched the huge aircraft descending toward them. Their excitement nearly matched that of the Jews huddled together on board. They understood the magnitude of this moment for these seven years. Other planes would follow this one and continue until all forty-eight flights were completed and all 144,000 of God's Messianic believers arrived.

Shimon could hardly believe his eyes as the runways came into view. Trey, Rickie, and Michael tried to describe it for him, but it still blew his mind. Four beautiful landing strips side-by-side and perfectly separated in the middle of the desert! He headed toward them thankful that he was the first to land carrying a load of his people who followed Jesus.

"Hold her steady," said the leader of the heavenly host for this initial flight. "This landing needs to feel like sitting down on a cloud."

"*His* runways are nice, don't you think?"

"Perfect, just like everything he does."

"Okay, here we go! It's almost time for touchdown!"

"We must be close," said Mordecai, his nerves still on edge. "What if we...?"

"Aluf!" Ben said emphatically. "Where's your faith?"

"I'm sorry, Ben. I think my military training kicks in during situations like this."

"Relax, Uncle," said Hadassah. "Soon we will walk into Petra! Enjoy the experience!"

"Okay, let's set her down!" said the leader of the host.

"Here we go!" Shimon whispered to himself.

"This is it!" Alexander said loudly, a wide smile breaking out on his face. "Ben, didn't we talk about living in caves?"

"This is far better than a cave, my friend."

The wheels touched the hard-packed surface, and Shimon threw on the reverse thrust, then slowed and taxied to a stop. Cheers erupted in the cargo department, and the men outside celebrated with them. The first group had arrived at Petra!

The rear cargo door opened and the ramp came down. Ben turned, threw out his arms, and shouted to the mass of humanity filling the hold.

"My friends, welcome to Petra!"

Another cheer went up as people clamored to exit the plane. Ben again turned to his comrades standing near him.

"It appears we must move or get trampled," he said, chuckling.

They descended the ramp, and Ben paused before setting foot on the ground. "Friends, let us pray before we exit the plane and thank Jesus for bringing us home. I ask the first two people to turn to the Messiah in Israel to tell him thank you and pray for the others flying tonight."

Alexander and Elizabeth prayed from their hearts, as they had so many times since turning to Jesus. He ended by incorporating the words of Isaiah, Chapter Forty, which Anders read earlier.

"Jesus, you have prepared a way for us in the wilderness and made us a road in the desert. You have raised up the valleys and brought low the mountains. The rough ground became level, and the rugged places became smooth. Now we know the glory of the Lord will be revealed for all people to see. Come, Lord Jesus!"

"Follow me!" Ben said as he stepped out and marched toward the entrance of the ancient city. Sergeant Major Robert Clark greeted them with a salute. The Americans had placed lanterns leading to the opening, and throughout the Siq, illuminating the way for them. They kept a secret, which the walkers would discover when they entered the Rose Red City.

Three thousand people trailed him. In the distance they heard the engines and saw the lights of three more planes preparing to descend, one after another. Shimon was already circling to runway number four to return for another load. He would make two more trips before his job ended.

Trey, Rickie, Paul, Bradley, Ezra, and ten other pilots shared his experience during twelve amazing hours. They began in darkness and ended in daylight, obscured by the heavenly host. Yahweh escorted his people to their new home, where they would live for the next three-and-a-half years.

Fourteen C-130s and two C-5M Super Galaxies made three flights each, carrying three thousand passengers per trip, transporting 144,000 people to Petra, Jordan. The American pilots doubled up on their last flights, allowing one to bring back an IDF plane, so their pilots could stay with their Jewish comrades in their new home. They executed a well-planned mission, but more so, a miraculous venture only Jesus could carry out. They directed their thanks completely to him.

The steady stream of people hiking into the city would have been a sight to behold, if anyone else had been there to witness it. But no one was present, except these Jews who had discovered their Messiah and now followed only him.

Ben and the others marveled as they walked through the Siq. But nothing could have prepared them for the scene that greeted their sight when they stepped out of the mile-long entryway. Most had seen pictures of the place, but none did it justice.

They stopped and stared at the *Treasury*, the magnificent, awe-inspiring structure carved into the mountainside. The sight so captivated them it took a while to notice the secret the Americans already knew. It finally hit them. Even though darkness dominated the outside, the inside shone with the light of day!

From atop a high peak overlooking Petra, Michael sat smiling as he observed the throng of people below celebrating their arrival to the place Yahweh prepared for them. The heavenly host who had escorted the planes sat rejoicing with him.

"Look at them," he said, beaming with delight. "We did it, thanks to your commitment to Yahweh and his people! You won a great victory today, Host, but greater battles lie ahead. Let us celebrate this win, then prepare for the war that is coming. Those who stay faithful to Jesus will need us, and we will be there. Now, I should get down there and join them. After all, this is my home, too!"

Trey flew back to the base and made the drive to Camp Filon, where the Smyrnians and American troops, along with Omar, Ahmad, and Hala awaited him. His was the last flight of the mission, and it was smooth, just as all the others had been. His arrival started a party that would last awhile.

"Trey, you made it!" Beth said, grabbing her friend and hugging him. "Now every pilot made it back safely. Come and tell us all about it!"

She led him to the mess hall where Paul, Bradley, Rickie, and the American pilots were sharing their stories. Rickie saw Trey and sprinted toward his partner, nearly knocking him to the ground as he threw his arms around him and hoisted him into the air.

"Welcome home, partner!"

"I survived three round trip flights, only to return and have you break my ribs. It's good to see you too, buddy."

They spent hours talking about the logistics of their mission and how it felt like they were not even in control most of the time. Blake ended that and moved toward more important things.

"Okay, everybody, that's enough. We could talk all night, but I suggest we get some rest and work on more plans tomorrow morning. The intensity never lets up during these seven years, and we all know it will get far worse in the coming days. Things have changed now, and we need a new plan."

They would sleep that night, not knowing just how right he was.

Michael walked out of the Siq, a huge smile on his face, and joined Ben and those with him in front of the Treasury. The others had gone off exploring the wonders of their new safe place. As Jews, most had never seen Petra. Joyous sounds of laughter and wonder echoed everywhere.

Younger ones scaled the rock cliffs and looked down from above, shouting and waving at those below. Older people who could not climb remained on the lower level, walking and basking in Petra's natural beauty. They all enjoyed the location they would call home for forty-two months.

"Michael, it is so good to see you. I'm glad you finally joined us," Mordecai said with a hint of disdain in his voice.

"Come on, uncle, you knew he stayed back to oversee the pilots, then came on the last flight with Trey. He did exactly what he told us he would. Michael, I *am* glad you made it!" Hadassah said, as she hugged him and frowned at Mordecai.

The Aluf could not stand to hurt his niece's feelings, so he spoke more gently this time.

"Thank you for all your work to make this mission successful, Michael. I appreciate everything you have done, and I am thankful you are here. You are a true leader among us."

"That means a lot coming from you, Aluf. I learned from the best. Thank you for teaching me and believing in me."

Hadassah nodded at him and smiled with approval.

"I know you had an important task and arrived right on time," said Ben. "We have much to do here now. We must first organize these people into groups based on their tribes. Moshe stationed the tribes around the tabernacle in a specific order and established an alignment for them when they marched. That is one option. What do the rest of you think?"

"Based on my current observations, I suggest we organize them by age, including family and tribe. Many potential dwelling places are up high where older ones cannot climb. But as you can see, the younger ones enjoy that."

"You are wise, Mordecai. I can see why you ascended to the high rank you achieved in the IDF."

"Water will be vital too. It rains very little down here, but with a few repairs the ancient water system will bring an abundant supply when it does. The cisterns appear in good condition, so they should hold it well. When rain falls, everyone can gather in sheltered places and stay dry."

"Good thinking, Michael. Let's gather the tribal leaders and discuss that with them. They can follow up with their groups and move all the people into their new homes. They will only live in them three-and-a-half years, but I suspect they will enjoy them during that time."

"Many of those *houses* are actually tombs, but there is no reason to tell them that. What they don't know won't hurt them," Hadassah said, as she chuckled mischievously.

"Maybe we should inspect them and clear out old bones first," Michael said, laughing out loud.

"I agree. If they don't know, we won't tell them such a thing," Ben said, laughing with them.

The two young soldiers took off to summon tribal leaders to the meeting. Peace ruled the day throughout the Rose Red City.

·　　·　　·　　·　　·

Aissa Messai sat alone, considering what was about to happen. The next day, the dragon would change his life forever. Yes, he sold his soul to the creature, but this was different. The beast would inhabit his entire being and exist through him.

He shuddered with excitement, knowing this would elevate him to the position of sovereign leader of the planet. Fear also gnawed at his mind, realizing he would no longer control his own destiny or make his own decisions. But this was his reason for being, and he was ready.

His life flashed before his eyes, replayed one scene at a time as he watched. The name given to him by his parents: *Mahmud*, meaning *praised*, a proud Muslim name, also prophetic of his future life, although his parents were unaware of that. Yes, people worldwide would soon praise him.

His strict Islamic upbringing. Circumcised at age seven, taking part in daily prayers and the Ramadan fast. Memorizing the Qur'an and gaining status for possessing the word of God. His *Hajj* as an adult, fulfilling one of the five pillars of Islam. His commitment was unwavering.

Ascending the corporate ladder and engineering a billion-dollar empire. Consumed with the desire for more, to rule as the most powerful man in the world! Driven by greed and a lust for power, he used anyone he could, then discarded them, all while maintaining his good reputation.

The business trip to Israel. The Jews! He hated them above all other people on the planet. They stole the Mount and falsely claimed Jerusalem as their capital. Watching them walk about filled him with rage and created within him an inordinate desire to annihilate them all.

A life-altering encounter in his hotel room that night. Waking to a chill unlike any he had ever felt. Incendiary heat penetrating his mind while his body trembled from the frigid temperature filling the bedroom. The experience came rushing back, just as real, and with the chill. The voice, a low growl, one word: *chosen*. What did it mean? A name: *Aissa*... another: *Messai*. Jesus Messiah? *It must have been a strange dream*, he thought, but it was not; it was very real.

He had sensed a compulsion to travel the next day, but where? Handwriting on the wall... a place... *Banias*. The chill disappearing, followed by the heat, as though the heat burned it away, then left with it. He remembered understanding one thing: *he had to go to Banias*. He had made that trip multiple times since, but tomorrow he would travel to another place for his special day.

"With Evan and Ben gone, we must come together and lead the Smyrnians. Anders, we will depend on your guidance as things unfold. We must protect believers from Messai any way we can and fight him with everything we have, even when it means death."

"Blake is right," said Anders. "His *reign of terror* begins right after the Jews arrive in Petra."

"I heard Messai talk about this moment many times. He knew it was coming, and he both dreaded and craved it. The world has every reason to fear." Magnus spoke from firsthand knowledge.

"Where will we live?" asked Beth turning the conversation to practical details which must be settled. "We can't live in the kibbutz, and I doubt the safety of this base. We must decide soon!"

The room grew quiet. They realized she was right, but no one had answers. Blake asked for suggestions, and the group offered a few.

"In geography class, we talked about a desert oasis called Ein Gedi, that has waterfalls, pools, springs, and caves," said Ally. "It looks like a place with everything we need."

"How about Masada?" asked John. "It is a mountaintop fortress of King Herod, where the Jewish revolutionaries hid after the destruction of Jerusalem by the Romans. From what I have read in archaeological findings, it still has places where we could live."

"Maybe another kibbutz..." said Kathie.

"I prefer the Galilee," said Bruno before a telling grin while they rolled their eyes at him. "What? It's beautiful, and if it was good enough for Jesus, it's good enough for me!"

"There are several old military installations across the Golan," John said again.

Blake jumped back in. "Hold on a minute. All those assume we are staying in Israel. Is that our plan, or will we split up and travel to different parts of the world?"

"The entire world needs us, Blake, but there aren't enough of us to go everywhere," said John.

"I understand that, but is staying in Israel the best way we can serve Jesus and our fellow believers during the second half of the Tribulation? We can no longer send them emails since the information is lost. So we need to answer that question first."

"I say we stay here and fight him *mano a mano*!" said Rickie.

"*If* we stay, we need a permanent location and places to escape when Messai finds us," said Anders. "Those are all good suggestions. I agree with Ally that Ein Gedi should be one of them. David and his men hid from King Saul there. And you can't get much better than waterfalls and caves!"

"Sounds like my kind of place!" John said.

"Then we put Ein Gedi on the list," said Blake. "I heard Ben and Alexander joke about living as cave dwellers. We may have to do that, but if we have waterfalls and pools to enjoy, I agree with John. That is my kind of place!"

"We can't spend the next three-and-a-half years hiding and vacationing," said Beth. "We have to fight to protect our people every day."

"Come on, honey, we were only kidding. You know we're all ready to fight."

"Beth is right," said Anders. "His reign will begin soon."

"Tomorrow..." said Magnus, his voice trailing off.

The group grew quiet once again, feeling the weight of what was coming. They needed to decide now. Time was of the essence.

In Petra, Ben, Mordecai, Michael, and Hadassah climbed to a high peak above the *Monastery*, the second largest carved structure after the Treasury. The climb was difficult, even though all four were in good shape, but the view was worth it. However, their reason for such an extreme measure on day number one had little to do with the scenery.

"Unbelievable," whispered Ben.

"Yahweh is a great artist," Michael said, smiling as they looked over the incredible colors.

Mordecai was not one to waste time on things like standing and gazing at the landscape.

"I love this too, but don't forget why we came."

"We are thankful for your leadership, Aluf, but I have my phone in hand and have already placed the call."

Blake's phone rang, interrupting the serious moment at Camp Filon.

"Ben, tell me about Petra! Wait a minute, how are you calling me from Petra?"

"I assumed we would have service if we climbed to a high peak, and it worked! But this isn't a climb I want to make every day."

"Let me put you on speaker so everybody can hear. We're trying to decide whether we should stay in Israel or split up and go to other places to help believers."

"I can't answer that for you, Blake. That's a decision the group must make. I wish you could come here, but we know that isn't Jesus' plan. I feel bad because we will stay safe here while you are out there fighting for your lives."

"You can't worry about that. We both know you guys are right where you're supposed to be. Now to figure out where *we* are supposed to be. At times like this, I wish Evan and Malachi were here. Pray we get this right. These three-and-a-half years are important, and we need to determine where Jesus wants us to be and what he wants us to do."

"We will pray. That is the one thing we can do from here. I want to stay in touch too."

"Call me every three days at 7:00 p.m. I will watch for your call and answer if I can. If I don't, you will know something is wrong."

"It sounds like our roles have reversed and you are giving the orders now," Ben said, chuckling.

"Remember the trip when you ordered us to call every thirty minutes? If paybacks are rough, you are getting paid back now!"

"You've got a deal. I will call every third day at 7:00 p.m., but you had better take my call! Don't make us worry about you as you did during that trip."

"It isn't getting dark there by that time, is it? We can make that earlier if we need to."

"It isn't getting dark here at all, Blake!"

"Come on, Ben," John said. "That's not possible, so cut the jokes."

"Are you saying something is too difficult for Jesus, John? Daylight never ceases here. We sleep inside the caves and tombs for darkness, but light around the clock is wonderful."

"Ben," Anders said quietly.

"Anders, is that you?"

"Yes. Ben, the *reign of terror* begins tomorrow."

"Tomorrow? How can you know that? Oh, I know, the scroll."

"I saw it beginning and knew it would be soon, and Magnus confirmed it."

"Anders saw it beginning right after you escaped, and I heard Messai talk about it many times. We must decide what to do because the time is here."

"Magnus is right again," Michael said, interrupting their conversation. "Now we need to stop talking and allow you to make your decisions. The time is very short, so you can't wait until tomorrow to decide."

Ben looked at the young man again, stunned by his statement. How did he know that? It was a question he should not ask. But something special existed in that boy.

"Goodbye, everyone!" said Hadassah.

Everyone near Blake shouted their goodbyes too, then they ended the call. The four in Petra descended the mountain while those at the military base got serious about the task at hand.

• • • • •

Messai remained alone, contemplating the events of the next day as the sun neared the horizon. Dusk slowly disappeared, giving way to darkness. The chill seized him again, causing him to shake uncontrollably. Heat felt like it would blister his skin, but avoided his flesh and went straight to his mind.

The dragon appeared out of nowhere and stood in front of him. Two others joined him. He had not seen them before, but their size and grotesque appearance drove terror like a spike into his heart.

"Aissa..." the hissing voice said.

He never understood why the dragon sometimes growled, sounded human at other times, and often hissed in moments like this. He dropped to his knees before his master, keeping his head down.

"Yes, Your Majesty, welcome to my home."

"Aissa, before we proceed, I must introduce you to my most powerful servants: Beelzebub and Belial. They will be at your disposal and eager to assist you any time they are needed. You will become as powerful as they are and rise to my second in command."

Fear paralyzed him, and he lowered his face before the two demon chiefs in worship.

"Do not do that!" Beelzebub said. "We worship Our Majesty, just as you do. Honor only him!"

Before he could reply, the dragon spoke again.

"Aissa, the time has come. Are you ready for your big moment?"

"Yes, Your Majesty. I will be there at daybreak tomorrow morning."

"Not daybreak, Aissa, *midnight.* Surely you have noticed midnight is my time. I am the prince of darkness, and at 12:00 tonight the darkness will be especially deep."

Midnight... *tonight?* No time to think, plan, or prepare. Midnight was only three hours away!

"But Majesty, I planned to sleep, then rise early and arrive well before the time. Midnight is..."

"I know, three hours away. You must leave within minutes to be on time for your ceremony. You would not let me down, would you, *Aissa?*"

He hissed the name and drew it out, as he so often did, sending shivers down Messai's spine.

"I will be there, Majesty. You know I would not miss this moment for anything," he stuttered.

"I believe you, Aissa, but Beelzebub and Belial will stay here to escort you, ensuring nothing goes wrong and you are not late."

The two massive and terrifying beasts came closer, and each grabbed an arm, lifting him from the floor. He felt weightless as their powerful arms pulled him up. Their arms felt frigid against him, yet heat emanated from their hideous bodies, warming him. His own body heated, and the chills went away. He stood confidently as they released him, eager to begin his new life.

The dragon vanished, leaving only the three remaining in the house. Beelzebub and Belial saw he needed no encouragement now. Their task was simple, and both were excited to welcome the new world dictator at midnight tonight.

CHAPTER 14

Anders sat up in bed and looked at his phone. 11:45 p.m. Something felt different, out of the ordinary, but he could not determine the cause. He would normally think it was a physical problem, but not this time. This was not physical; it was spiritual.

A portion of the scroll appeared before him with blurred numbers. He looked, but could not make them out until they cleared. *12:00.* That was it! Noon tomorrow would change everything, not just for Aissa Messai, and them, but the entire world. It would kick off the horrendous second half of the Tribulation.

A word appeared, also difficult to see. It came into focus as the mist covering it faded away. *Midnight.* The coming event flooded back into his mind with vivid clarity, just like the day he ate the scroll in heaven. Messai... a dragon... two huge grotesque looking creatures.

This will not happen at noon tomorrow; it is happening in fifteen minutes! He ran to call the others and met Magnus, doing the same.

"It's tonight at midnight, Anders, not tomorrow!"

"Yes! The same thing just occurred to me when I woke up and remembered seeing that in the scroll."

"How did I confuse that? Messai talked about his *hour* coming, but he always referred to the day, not the night. I was sure..."

"That doesn't matter now; we have to tell the others!"

Those in the same building heard the commotion and rushed to see what it was all about. Some called others as they ran, and the place soon filled with Smyrnians.

"What's up?" Blake asked, yawning and rubbing his eyes as Magnus almost ran him over.

"It's happening right now, midnight tonight, not noon tomorrow!"

"What in the world?" asked Beth, looking as sleepy as her husband, before it hit her. "Oh, *that*..."

The last minute of the day faded away. *Midnight*... 12:00 a.m., a new day, one that would change the world, meaning three-and-a-half years of terror for some, but prosperity for most.

The room turned icy. They huddled together trying to create warmth, but still shivered uncontrollably, none of them able to speak or move. Each looked at the others, eyes all around the room begging them to do one thing: *pray.* They did so, not verbally, but their spirits cried out to Jesus for protection and answers.

•   •   •   •   •

Beelzebub and Belial guided Messai to a secluded beach on the Mediterranean Sea, where the dragon stood waiting. He walked to the creature, excitement now replacing his anxiety.

"Immerse yourself in the sea, Aissa, then return to me. You are mine!"

Messai moved to the water's edge and stepped in, covering his feet.

"Deeper!" said the dragon. "Go all the way!"

He waded out farther, to his knees... waist... chest... then plunged under the cold water. It chilled him, then became boiling hot, yet his body did not burn. He sank deeper, the water temperature increasing as he went. He took a deep breath and found air, not water, entering his lungs.

Creatures darted around him, but their identities stayed hidden from his mind and eyes. Multitudes of people bowed before him as he sensed power rising inside him. Others refused to bow, causing his mind to flare with anger. He saw faces of the Smyrnians and realized he must crush them.

Things changed rapidly. His next breath drew in water instead of air and he choked, now trying desperately to hold his breath, even while his lungs rebelled against the water invading them. Something propelled him upward as if fired from an underwater cannon.

Nature reversed, heat ceased, and the water turned cold again as he rose. His head broke through the surface and he stood in knee-deep water, facing the dragon who beckoned him to come. He breathed without problems now and took a step toward the creature.

Exiting the sea, he stood eye-to-eye with the beast of hell, powerless to move. He watched as the creature extended his stubby front legs toward his head, claws now razor-like and barbed. His mind fought to pull away, but his soul welcomed the advancing points.

The dragon threw back his head and released a blood-curdling scream, with fire pouring skyward from his mouth. When the flames ceased, he sprang back down toward the man standing before him. His claws penetrated the man's skull and entered his brain before he could move.

An electrical current surged through Messai with voltage greater than anyone had survived. Sparks flew from his extremities and emanated from his body. His heart turned icy and almost non-human. He shook violently, collapsed with a thud, and appeared to be dead. The dragon removed his claws and stepped back. Beelzebub and Belial moved forward and lifted the fallen man to his feet. Messai took a deep breath, turned, and looked at them through glowing red eyes. He threw back his head and screamed. He had done that many times before, but this time was different.

•　　•　　•　　•　　•

"Blake!" Beth said as she clung to him, refusing to let go.

"Hang on! I've got you, and I won't turn loose!"

The group already shivered from the icy chill in the room. Now the entire base shook violently, and everyone there wrapped their arms around anything nearby and held on for dear life. The shaking continued for five minutes, then stopped.

"I want to believe that was another earthquake, but it wasn't," said John through chattering teeth.

"What is that?" Bruno pointed at a nearby window. Black fog seeped through the window sill and moved toward them.

"Run!" Kathie had already taken two steps before Anders' calm voice stopped her.

"Wait." Get everybody you can into the mess hall. Jesus just gave me a message for all of you, and it cannot wait."

"But what about the fog?" Bruno asked.

"The breath of the Lord," Anders said. He turned to face the nearing black haze, pursed his lips, and gently blew. The evil mist retreated and vanished back through the window where it entered.

They stood stunned, watching an ever-deepening side of this man who had been with Jesus. They expected things like this from him, but this one still shocked them and sent them scurrying for the mess hall.

"Friends," he began, as they sat before him still shivering from the cold, "God said in the Prophet Jeremiah, *his word is like a fire.* Heat from a fire dispels cold."

The cold disappeared, replaced by heat that warmed them and stopped their shaking within seconds. They sat astonished by what they just witnessed. Anders smiled and continued.

"Jesus wants you to know he is with us. I remind you what his Apostle Paul told the Thessalonians. Jesus will not come until the man of lawlessness is revealed. You understand who he spoke about, and the world will realize that soon."

"Aissa Messai."

"Correct, John, so this should not surprise us. Then Paul told us exactly what the Antichrist will do, which tells us what will happen next."

"He will oppose and will exalt himself over everything that is called God or is worshiped, so that he sets himself up in God's temple, proclaiming himself to be God."(2 Thessalonians 2:3 NIV)

They had not read that verse before. But now they would watch it come true right before their eyes.

"Paul said something would hold him back, so he could not be revealed until it was removed."

"What held him back, Anders?" Ally asked, a sense of wonder in her voice.

"I'm glad you asked, Ally. The church stood in his way and prevented him from coming until Jesus removed it."

"The Rapture!" Beth said loudly. They all looked at her, bringing a sheepish smile to her face.

"You're right, Beth! My Angie and our kids believed in Jesus and worshiped God. It broke my heart when they disappeared at midnight on September 11, 2029. But when Blake told me what happened, joy replaced my grief because I realized where they are!"

"Jesus even allowed me to see them when he took me to heaven." He paused, a far off look in his eyes. They had seen that look before, so they gave him time to relive the experience again. Beth's eyes moistened as she recalled her mom and dad. Anders' smile returned, and he spoke again.

"The Rapture began the seven-year Tribulation. After Jesus took his people home, the Antichrist was revealed soon, and we understood who he was. Satan's power will dwell in him and he will display signs and wonders, causing the world to believe his lies. But I have good news!" He picked up his now well-worn Bible to read again.

"*The Lord Jesus will overthrow him with the breath of his mouth and destroy him by the splendor of his coming!* (2 Thessalonians 2:8) You just witnessed the power of Jesus' breath."

Now they understood the simple example Jesus gave them when Anders blew the fog away, but what they saw still shocked them.

"I have one more bit of good news that we need to realize now. It is why we can stand up to Aissa Messai and the dragon who gives him power. Jesus' disciple, John, said, *the one who is in us is greater than the one who is in the world!* (1 John 4:4) Jesus lives in us. He is greater than Messai, so we should not fear. Let us run to the battle and remember in life or death we are the victors!"

They filled the hall with shouts of jubilation that sounded for all the world like a battle cry. Ally ran to Anders and hugged him, and he returned her hug. They were two souls united for battle.

"Do you hear that, Aissa?" asked the dragon, still standing with him on the shore. The beast of hell now indwelt the man the Smyrnians knew was the Antichrist.

"I hear the sound of battle," Messai said with the low growl that reflected his master's voice.

"Yes, the sound of a battle they believe they can win. They will refuse to worship you, so you must eliminate them. It is time to enforce our law by setting up our *capital punishment device.*"

"Yes, master," the man said, throwing back his head and releasing an evil laugh that would strike terror into the hearts of any who opposed him.

"Notice, their words come to you even when they speak in secret. My power gives you supernatural vision and hearing. Learn to use it, and it will serve you well and allow you to prevail!"

Beelzebub and Belial came and knelt before him. "Send us, master, and we will go whenever you need us to. We are yours to command."

"Yes, Aissa, you reign with me over all the forces of hell. We are invincible and will also rule the world! You are now immortal, so they cannot destroy you. They will try, but they will fail. When they think they have succeeded, your return will show the world you are all-powerful and worthy of worship!"

"What do you mean, master? How will they try to destroy me and think they have succeeded?"

"You will understand when the time comes. Do not worry, Aissa, you will live forever!"

The four of them shrieked and howled with glee as the dragon and his two most powerful demons prepared to introduce the real Aissa Messai to the world.

• • •

Ben awoke, stood from his mat, and crept out of the Treasury to keep from waking Miriam.

"Benjamin, where do you think you are going?"

"I didn't mean to wake you, dear, but I need to speak with Michael."

"Michael? At midnight?"

"It is midnight in here, but sunny out there, like noonday. Don't worry, we will walk outside and talk so I do not disturb you anymore."

"You haven't answered my question. Why do you need to talk to Michael at midnight?"

"Something evil happened a few minutes ago, Miriam; I sensed it in my spirit. It does not affect us here, but the believers are in danger out there. We need to warn our friends."

"What does that have to do with Michael?"

"I cannot answer that, Miriam. There is something unique about that boy. Miracles always seem to happen when he disappears. Sometimes he leaves for hours, and no one knows where he goes."

"Are you suggesting...?" she asked, stopping with the unfinished question lingering between them.

"I'm not sure what I am suggesting, Miriam. There is something unique about him, and I need to know what that is, or perhaps what he knows that we do not."

"If you are that sure something happened, I agree with you. You need to speak with Michael."

Ben walked into another room where Michael slept each night and whispered his name. When he got no answer, he moved closer and bent over to shake the young soldier. He hated to awaken him, but this was important. His hand touched the mat; Michael was missing.

"*Not again!* Something important comes up, and he vanishes. Show me, Jesus, what is special about your servant, Michael. I need to understand."

•　•　•　•　•　•

Michael sat atop a cliff overlooking the Mediterranean Sea, watching the four beings below. They were unaware of his presence. He chuckled to himself, *and they think they understand everything.* He had just witnessed the Tribulation's most significant event.

"Three-and-a-half years," he said. "Give it your best shot." He should not have left Petra, but the curiosity was driving him crazy. This was one event he wanted to see for himself. Now, he must return before someone discovered his absence. He flew away toward the Rose Red City.

•　•　•　•　•

The dragon, Aissa Messai, and the two powerful demons arrived at Messai's new headquarters, the Jewish temple in the Old City of Jerusalem. From here, he would rule, the messiah coming to his temple and reigning. The world would receive him; those who did not would pay the price.

The *Smyrnians* would not. His disgust for them turned to thoughts of revenge for all the trouble they had caused him. They could not stop him now, but *he* would stop them. He envisioned which would die first. The order did not matter so long as they died brutal deaths. Waves of joy washed over him as he imagined heads rolling. Tomorrow would be the first day of a *new world order*!

"Do not lose those thoughts, Aissa," said the dragon, a thirst for blood driving his words. "No one will stand in our way, not even *them*. Anyone who rebels will experience the same fate. It is time to unite the world in one religion, worshiping us. Our day has come, and we will prevail!"

Messai climbed the same steps he had walked up many times, his *new eyes* seeing clearly in the darkness. This new life was exciting. He prided himself for selling his soul to the dragon as he sensed the power of the creature rising in him. His next step: convince his associate to join him.

•   •   •   •   •   •

"Ben, you scared me!" Michael said, jumping back as his leader's sudden presence surprised him.

"I came to talk to you, but you were gone. Where did you go at midnight?"

"When I can't sleep, I go for a walk. Daylight at midnight is a perfect time for a hike!"

"Michael, you disappear so often, and every time you do, some miracle happens for the believers."

"That's a good thing, isn't it?"

"Yes, but it seems quite coincidental to me it always happens when you disappear."

"Hey, maybe I am Michael, the Warrior Angel you talked about in the Book of Revelation!" He flexed and feigned a sword fight, ending with his arms raised in a victory pose and his foot elevated like it sat on a fallen enemy.

"Michael, the kid in you brings me joy. But enough of that; I came to ask if you sensed the same thing I felt at midnight. It woke me with a sensation that something evil just happened."

"I felt it too. That's why I left for a while. I didn't want to wake you and Miriam, so I decided to wait until morning. Perhaps the *reign of terror* Anders and Magnus mentioned began at that moment. They were certain it would come today, but I thought they said noon."

"You're right! This is the beginning of the second half of the Tribulation, and the world will change in a single day. Our comrades out there will face a life and death battle every day. We need to pray for them! By the way, Michael, how did you know it was the *reign of terror?*"

"That isn't what I said, Ben. I said, *perhaps* it was the beginning of the *reign of terror.*"

"I will let this slide again, but I want to sit and talk with you about this, and other times similar things have happened. You can't run from me. I know there is more to you than meets the eye."

"Remember Ben, I am Michael, the Warrior Angel!" He went into his swashbuckling act again, then chuckled at Ben, who shook his head and walked away.

•   •   •   •   •

Everyone at Camp Filon gathered around TVs, or pulled up computers, tablets, or phones to watch the news early the next morning. No network had announced any special press conference by Aissa Messai, but they knew he would dominate the news this day. Blake and the Smyrnians were watching in a jam-packed mess hall with a large-screen television set up and ready.

"Here we go!" he said, pointing at the screen.

"I understand Aissa Messai is at the Temple Mount to make a special statement," said the anchor. "Without further ado, we take you there now."

"I knew it!" Magnus said. "You will see a different Messai now."

The scene shifted to the Jewish Temple and Aissa Messai. He stood neither in the Court of the Gentiles, nor the Court of the Women, nor even the Court of the Priests. Instead, he took his stance atop the twelve steps in front of the vestibule that led into the Holy Place.

Gathered before him at the bottom of the steps, reporters stood shoulder-to-shoulder, each seeking to get as close to the man as they could. Their number included Jews, Gentiles, men, and women. That was sure to bring sharp criticism and outright anger from orthodox Jews who understood only priests could enter that sacred area.

When the camera panned in on Messai's face, the Smyrnians gasped. This was not the same man they had witnessed for the last three-and-a-half years. Gone was any hint of the diplomatic and charismatic world leader. *Demonic* was the best word to describe him, although that persona would remain hidden from the world's population who followed this man, instead of Jesus. When he spoke, they heard the same in his voice. It even surprised Magnus.

"People of earth," he said in the low growl that often characterized him. Others heard his normal voice, but Jesus allowed the believers to pick up his real tone. "This is the day we take control of our planet and our future. I will no longer allow a radical minority to prevent us from having the peace and prosperity we all deserve."

"Tomorrow I will introduce a device we will use to remove all who persist in doing that. A plan is also in the works which will allow us to identify these rebels. It has two parts and cannot fail. You will understand why it is necessary when I explain it. Please join me for those important announcements tomorrow morning. Follow me and we will change the world together."

Just like that, the press conference ended, leaving the Smyrnians alone with their thoughts and eager to learn more the next day. Magnus was quiet. They could tell he had something on his mind, but none of them asked what it was. Neither did he share it with them.

"He will hunt us down like dogs and make a great spectacle of our deaths," said Anders. "But we are not his only targets. I saw throngs of people slain, many who were not followers of Jesus. But I couldn't tell how he carried it out. I saw piles of dead bodies, but could not see faces."

"This makes our planning crucial," said Blake. "We will watch again tomorrow to learn more about his plans, but today we must determine how we can stay alive and help protect others. I'm not sure we can stay here and remain safe."

"I agree, Blake," said John. "We may need to move after tomorrow."

"I must have a place to set up a hospital," said Steve. "We will need it." He had stayed quiet since they arrived, trying to find his place in the group. They were glad he finally spoke up.

"We will take that into consideration, Steve. Your purpose on our team has not changed, so we must make that a priority."

"May I suggest something, Blake?" Robert asked. "We found a map of IDF bunkers in an old file cabinet here. They're using some, but most are abandoned and isolated. Those could serve as great hideouts. We can always move from one to another if they find us."

"I like that, Robert!" said Trey. "I knew an old military veteran like you would be valuable to the team. The pilots can play an important role, too. Planes and choppers are available to fly you from place to place, but we need to remain cautious."

"Let's decide our next move after we listen to Messai tomorrow morning. I think we should split up and have groups staying in different locations. Let's spend today packing things and try not to leave anything that will identify us and tell Messai we were here."

"It's probably too late for that, Blake. I'm sure he knows we're here. All the more reason to get out. But where will we go? I saw locations in the scroll, but nothing specific, and also grave danger. Staying alive will require the battle of our lives, but I say we fight to survive until Jesus comes!"

Early the next morning, the group sat waiting for Messai's announcement. The morning show was dedicated to discussing what he would say today. For the first time, Messai was fashionably late for this one, making people crave his appearance even more. The moment finally came.

A select group of reporters filled the Court of the Priests, while the less fortunate stood below listening from the Court of the Israelites. Farther down, the Court of the Women and Court of the Gentiles were packed with spectators. Still more curious onlookers walked around the Temple Mount itself. AMPP patrols and the Israel Police Force provided tight security.

Messai waited until the buzz reached a fever pitch before walking out and ascending the steps to the Altar of Burnt Offering. Instead of the normal raucous applause that greeted his appearances, the crowd grew eerily silent. When he spoke, his words boomed through the large speakers, while jumbotron screens projected his image to the farthest reaches of the Mount.

"Ladies and gentlemen, I have often told you we must take drastic measures to stop those who seek to interfere with the peace and prosperity of the world. The time has come to implement those measures and enforce them with capital punishment. I will appoint a special council to oversee the trials of those accused of treason. Those convicted will face swift and harsh punishment."

"I feel certain you have wondered what lies beneath the covering to my left. Follow me and observe the unveiling of the capital punishment device. We hope it will deter rebellion and encourage working together to achieve our goal of worldwide peace and prosperity."

He slowly descended the steps, again creating anticipation. After reaching the bottom, he walked in front of the altar to ensure cameras never lost him from their view. Then he strode to the device and slowly removed the sheet. Loud gasps came from those in attendance, reporters and audience alike. Gasps were also heard among Jesus' followers at Camp Filon, followed by silence.

Messai relished the sense of shock and horror covering the Mount. The guillotine with its shiny, razor-sharp blade sent terror into the hearts and minds of everyone watching around the world.

"Now, ladies and gentlemen, I realize how brutal this appears, but it only serves to deter rebellion which prevents us from living in unprecedented peace and prosperity."

"You mean terrorize the world and force people to submit to you, or face beheading," said Bruno, anger spilling out of him.

"Following the beheadings," Messai continued, "the priest will offer the bodies as sacrifices on the altar. No removal and disposal will then be necessary. Rebels apprehended in other countries will be brought to Israel to stand trial, and if convicted, executed here. Does everyone understand?"

No answers came from anyone on the Mount, only the simultaneous silence of thousands of terror-stricken people.

"Please join me again tomorrow morning at 9:00 a.m. for special announcements, which will be much more positive. You are about to experience the greatest prosperity you have ever known, as we take control of our own destiny. You will live the high life that comes with obedience and a unified effort. I look forward to sharing that good news with you in twenty-four hours!"

Lively discussion now broke out at the base after the conference ended. This news upped the ante.

"I should have known what was coming," said Magnus. "Something Messai said that night in my dream. In my haste to warn everyone of coming attacks, I forgot that statement. He mentioned me being the first to try out his little *capital punishment device* and how it would feel to have my head severed from my body. There was no doubting what he meant. How did I forget that?"

"It wouldn't have mattered if we understood what was coming, Magnus," said Blake. "What matters now is protecting ourselves and other believers, and encouraging any of them we can to reject Messai's demands and stay true to Jesus. We need to make commitments now that none of us will yield if we get arrested. We will know even more tomorrow when we hear from him."

"Ben will call this evening," said Beth. "We need to tell them what's happening. Their prayers can carry us through, and they may have suggestions for us, too."

"I agree, Beth. Let's divide into groups and decide where we will all go. We need several places so we can stay on the move and evade them. They will never stop pursuing us."

"Ally and I will lead one group. Call it the Smyrnians singles group," Anders said, grinning.

The rest looked surprised, but agreed with his plan. They could tell he and Ally had discussed that and had seen their spiritual depth and strength. They were kindred souls.

"Can we join that group?" asked Omar. "Don't forget Ahmad, Hala, and me."

"See, everybody? Our group has already grown to five!" said Ally.

"Robert, you mentioned earlier that *we* could use the abandoned bunkers for hideouts. Does that mean your unit is staying with us?"

"We're staying for now, Blake. The married men and women want to get home to their families. Most of them have believed in Jesus, so they want to get there and protect them. Some haven't believed, so those want to try their best to convince them. We have pilots who can fly them home."

"We're happy to help if you need us," said Trey. "I'm ready to fly anywhere we're needed."

"Our pilots can handle this job, Trey. You and Rickie stay and help the people here."

One of Robert's men spoke up. "Those of us who are flying home need to go now before things get out of hand with Messai."

"How many are going, and who will stay?"

A show of hands revealed half leaving and half staying. They started making plans to fly out the next day.

7:00 p.m. The Smyrnians awaited Ben's call. It came on time, and Blake answered the first ring.

"Impeccable timing, Ben."

"Did you expect a late call? We said 7:00, so I called at 7:00. I don't call late, like some people I know."

"Stop giving me a hard time about that, Ben. You know there were reasons for that."

"I know, but I enjoy ribbing you about it." The entire group heard Ben's chuckle. "So, what's happening there?"

Blake told him about Messai's announcement and the guillotine, then detailed their plans for hiding out and moving around.

"I wish we were there to help you guys, but we're here to stay until Jesus comes. We will do what we can... pray for all of you."

Michael stood beside Ben, already realizing what Blake would say. Ben and the others were not aware of this, but *he* would go help them. However, he knew he could not prevent all of them from succumbing to Messai's *capital punishment device*. He wanted to, but this was the Tribulation, and they were followers of Jesus. That meant some would face death. He would be there to give them strength when they did.

The call ended, and the group went to lie down, hoping to get some rest. They would rise early the next morning to ensure they missed nothing the Antichrist would say.

•   •   •   •   •

The Temple Mount was much less crowded as the time neared for Aissa Messai to speak. Fear kept most curious onlookers away this morning. Reporters stood nervously awaiting the world's most powerful man. The citizens of earth waited with them.

The moment arrived, and Messai suddenly appeared out of nowhere. No one saw him walk in, but there he stood in all his splendor on the porch atop the twelve steps leading into the Holy Place. A confident smile adorned his face, and his immaculate appearance foreshadowed the important announcement he would soon make. The words flowed from his lips as he began.

"People of earth, I understand your fear after yesterday's briefing. Please understand the device introduced yesterday will not affect our law-abiding citizens who seek peace and prosperity along with me. It is intended only for those who attempt to prevent us from achieving that."

"The rest of you will soon enter the greatest period of peace and prosperity the world has ever known, but we must stop those who stand in our way. I will now institute further plans which will help identify those people and allow us to bring them to justice."

"The first part of these plans involves the very building before which I stand..."

A single loud pop captured the attention of those present and others watching and listening via TV or other devices. No one would have given it a second thought had they not witnessed the man on the porch collapse to his knees, then tumble down the steps.

While others scrambled for cover, a lone cameraman zoomed in and captured the terrifying image that was sure to change the world. Messai lay motionless just past the bottom step, surrounded by a pool of blood with a hole in his temple. A trail of blood touched each step from top to bottom.

AMPP personnel rushed to his side, some kneeling before him, while others stood with their eyes peeled, searching for the assassin, but saw no one. Emergency personnel soon arrived on the scene and removed Messai's body. Everyone watching realized the man was dead. A lot had changed in the past forty-two months, but this would alter everything more than anything else had.

CHAPTER 15

The group of Smyrnians at Camp Filon sat in silence, trying to comprehend with their minds what their eyes had just seen. Their minds struggled to accept that the Antichrist was dead.

"I don't understand what just happened because no one can kill the Antichrist. The pastor has been right about everything until now. He said Messai would live until Jesus returns and destroys him."

"You're right, Blake," said John. "What are we supposed to do now that someone assassinated him? If I had known it could happen, I would have taken him out myself to avenge Johnathan's death. You can bet Kathie would have done it too."

"For Doc," she muttered, "and for what he did to my kids."

"I would have helped you," Brita said through clenched teeth. "But you told me it was impossible."

"Add another to that list," said Bruno. "I wanted to kill him because he murdered so many of our family members and fellow Smyrnians."

"We all wanted to kill him. Now, I don't know whether to celebrate or fear. I'm so confused."

"What now, Blake?" asked Trey. "Where do we go from here, because we're all confused right now. Have we believed the wrong man was the Antichrist all along? Perhaps another will come now and finish what he started. I have read the Bible and watched the pastor's video, but I really don't know what is true now."

"Hold on, everyone. Let's talk about what we *do* know."

Anders got everyone's attention. If they respected one person enough to stop talking and listen, it was him. His Bible knowledge and spiritual growth earned him that right, and his encounter with Jesus, the others, and the scroll in heaven gave them even more reason.

"Here are the things we know for sure. First, Jesus changed every one of our lives when we believed in him. Second, he took his people home in the Rapture on September 11, 2029, and we missed it because we had not put our faith in him. Third, Aissa Messai *is* the Antichrist the pastor said would come."

"Shouldn't you say he *was* the Antichrist? He is dead now."

"No, John, I still say *is*. I don't understand why, but I remember something about him in the scroll that's fuzzy in my mind. Maybe it concerned his assassination, or perhaps something that happens after that. I wish I recalled what I saw, but I don't. I do, however, still believe Jesus is in control. Now, back to my list." The interruption did not deter him, nor break their concentration on him.

"Fourth, we know the second half of the Tribulation has begun, and who knows what it holds? But everything the pastor said has happened so far. I don't expect that to change."

"More about that: Fifth, the dragon showed up as the enemy of everyone who follows Jesus. He plays a major role in The Revelation. There's no doubt he is real, because some of you have seen him with your own eyes."

"Magnus and I can attest to that, and so would Malachi, if he was still with us," said Bruno. "That reminds me again how much I hate Messai! Hadassah saw the dragon, too."

Anders continued after Bruno finished without missing a beat.

"Sixth, Ben and the Jews escaped the dragon and fled to the place in the desert already prepared for them, just like Revelation, Chapter 12 said they would. And seventh, we are certain Jesus will come again in three-and-a-half years and take us to be with him! What else really matters?"

"Anders is right!" said Ally. "Did you notice he gave us seven things we know for sure? That was not coincidental. Seven is God's number. Those things are all we need to remember."

•　　•　　•　　•　　•

Reporters rushed to follow the ambulance carrying Aissa Messai's body to Makassed Hospital on the Mount of Olives. AMPP patrols tried unsuccessfully to keep the media away from the emergency entrance. They broadcast images around the world as people sat anxiously awaiting further news of the Secretary-General's condition.

Images of the assassination showed repeatedly as anchors and reporters speculated about who may have carried out the attack and whether Messai was really dead. Other crews followed security personnel as they gathered clues and interviewed bystanders, searching for the assassin. No other news mattered today. The world's future hung in the balance based on what happened in Jerusalem.

After hours of waiting, the news came that doctors would hold a press conference at 5:00 p.m. to inform the public of Messai's condition. Time seemed to stand still as the world held its collective breath, eyes glued to televisions and mobile devices. They finally saw medical personnel step to the microphones and listened intently as the Chief Medical Officer spoke.

"Good afternoon, everyone. My name is Muhammad Nassar. I am the Chief Medical Officer here at Makassed Hospital. Secretary-General Aissa Messai was brought to our hospital this morning at approximately 10:00 a.m. He was unresponsive, and his condition extremely critical. A team of our best physicians worked to revive him and got a pulse, at which time they immediately took him into surgery."

"However, after a five-hour operation, doing everything possible to save Mr. Messai's life, their efforts were unsuccessful. Thus, it is my sad duty to report that the Secretary-General succumbed to his injuries and was pronounced dead at 3:00 p.m. this afternoon. Now Dr. Amir Samaha, who performed the surgery, will update you further."

Samaha went on and on about the surgical procedure, with few people listening. Two words dominated their understanding and left them stunned and disinterested in anything else said during the conference: *pronounced dead*. Aissa Messai died, leaving their hopes and dreams in limbo and their future uncertain. The world was aghast at this sudden tragic turn of events.

The Smyrnians remained just as dumbfounded as the rest of the world. They understood Jesus was in control of their future, but remained confused about their next steps in the present. Blake longed to speak with Ben, but their next call was two days away.

"I ask again, what should we do, Blake?" said John. "I just became even more confused."

"I'll tell you what we will do," said Anders. "I don't mean to take away from your leadership, Blake, but I must answer John's question for all of us. We will stay here and pray while we wait on Jesus to show us our next steps."

"Isaiah 40:31 tells us if we wait on the Lord, he will renew our strength. Then we will soar on wings like eagles, run and not grow weary, and walk and not faint. This whole thing with Messai has weakened us and attacked our faith. I hear it in our voices. If we wait on Jesus to show us what to do, he will make us strong again and we will fly high like eagles instead of sitting around here worrying about what we're going to do."

They sat, quiet for a moment, both stunned at his boldness and encouraged by his words. He was right, and they knew it. Now to follow his lead, wait, and pray. Most of them were not good at waiting, but this time, that became necessary. *Anders is our spiritual leader, sort of like our pastor*, Blake thought, and he was more than willing to allow his partner to assume that role.

Reporters made an announcement on the late news from the office of Aissa Messai. His body would lie in state for the next three days, so people could travel to Israel and pay respects to this man most of them loved and followed. The intriguing thing was *where* his body would lie... his favorite place.

The Temple Mount was packed the next morning as people arrived to view the Secretary-General's body. The extravagant mahogany casket sat where Messai fell, at the bottom of the steps which led to the temple's Most Holy Place. No one would enter the temple, but people from every nation would walk in the Court of the Priests and near the entrance. They would pass the Altar of Burnt Offering, where only the priest could go when he offered sacrifices.

But another motive affected the decision, too. People would also walk directly past the intimidating *capital punishment device*: the guillotine. No one considered that an important detail, but neither did they understand the major role it played in planning the three-day event.

People began arriving at 5:00 a.m., and a line formed that stretched around the Mount multiple times. Aerial views showed the massive crowd, with others pouring in every minute. Security was tight throughout Jerusalem, but especially around the Old City and Temple Mount. More and more people came. No Smyrnian or other follower of Jesus would join them.

"Look at them. How did that man fool people so easily? They blindly followed him and accepted everything he said as absolute truth."

"Because he's the Antichrist of the Tribulation, Bruno. Jesus told us they would follow him."

"This makes no sense," said John, still struggling with Messai's death. "How did he die, when only Jesus can destroy the Antichrist?"

"Wait on Jesus and pray, John. Jesus will show us the answer to that question when the time comes."

His answer failed to appease John and several others. But they would do what he said and expect answers from Jesus, like they received them many times before. What other choice did they have?

Leaders from every country came through with great fanfare, most often escorted to the front of the line, angering people who had already waited for hours. Many people stayed in Jerusalem all three days, planning to attend the funeral on day four. The days moved quickly.

Ben made his scheduled call at 7:00 p.m. on day two of the great event honoring Aissa Messai.

"Ben, you won't believe what is happening here. Messai was assassinated at the Temple, while making his second announcement about his *good news*. The Antichrist died, Ben, and we believed nobody could destroy him but Jesus."

"Messai is dead?" Ben asked. "How can that be?"

"We have all asked that question many times during the past two days, Ben. This makes no sense at all. None of us understands it, or knows what we should do next."

"Wait on the Lord, Blake, and he will give you the answers you seek," said Michael who stood beside Ben atop the mountain. "Do nothing until you hear from him. He will guide you and restore your faith and understanding. Stay patient, wait, and seek him."

"That is exactly what I told them," said Anders. "We're waiting, although that is difficult for some." He turned and smiled at John.

"I admit this is hard for me," John said. "I was sure my faith was so strong nothing would shake it, but Messai's death shattered everything we believed about him."

"Wait on the Lord, John, and your answer will come soon."

Ben stared at the young soldier once again, realizing he spoke from knowledge none of them had. His words came out with more authority than belonged to them. He intended to question him again, but doubted any additional information would come.

"Tomorrow is the third day, Ben, the day Jesus rose from the grave. Do you think he may do something miraculous tomorrow? I can't help but wonder why they planned a three-day event for the world to come."

"Something feels different about this. I haven't felt anything like it in the last three-and-a-half years. Obviously, we won't attend the funeral on day four, but will watch from here. After that, we have decisions to make. Keep praying for us."

"You can count on that, Blake, and my next call in three days. We need to stay abreast of what happens there and keep you updated on how things are going here. We can't ever lose touch with each other until we meet again when Jesus returns."

"That means a lot. I look forward to your call, and to seeing what this feeling in my gut is all about. Talk to you again in three days... and Ben, thank you."

The call ended with both groups praying and asking Jesus to give them answers. Morning dawned on day three with the largest throng yet jamming the Temple Mount and beyond. By afternoon, the crowd increased to over 100,000 people covering the place and spilling outside the wall and down the street, crossing the Kidron Valley. A special announcement came from Messai's office.

In order to allow as many people as possible to view the body, the event would continue through the night, news celebrated by those who feared they would miss out. The number of visitors did not decrease, but continued to increase as nightfall came.

Special lighting was erected, making the area even brighter than the previous sunny days. The telecast kept going around the clock, allowing those who could not attend to experience it, too. Cameras showed things from various angles, offering a more personal experience.

A special camera now revealed a close-up, gruesome shot of Messai's body. Clearly visible was the gaping hole in his right temple. Those who walked past his casket could not see it because he lay with his left side closest to them. But the wound now stood out to everyone watching via media.

"What a horrible mistake," said Blake, his reporter knowledge kicking in. "Don't you agree, Anders? They should fire the person responsible for that camera angle. You would never do that."

"I don't know, Blake. Something tells me that is intentional."

The group determined they would stay up all night to watch. They did not want to miss anything, and tomorrow brought day four and the funeral. Sleep would come tomorrow night. They fought to stay awake and kept the conversation going, so none of them would fall asleep. They were so engrossed in their discussions they almost missed it.

"Look!" Ally said so loudly it got their attention.

Every head in the room turned toward the television. No one noticed when midnight arrived, but then, they would have expected nothing if they did.

A bolt of lightning streaked from the clear night sky and struck the man lying in the casket. Those near the front turned to run for cover, but the massive crowd made that impossible. They were trapped with nowhere to hide. One might also say they were in the right place at the right time, though they did not realize it then.

Other cameras suddenly shut down, leaving only the close-up of the gaping wound in Messai's head. The hole closed and his temple healed as though no bullet had pierced it. Color returned to his face, and his fingers moved. He sat up, pulled his legs up from under the closed lid in the rear of the coffin, and swung them over the side. Screams sounded across the Mount, as pandemonium broke out and people tried again to flee, but security personnel blocked their path, trapping them.

The Secretary-General pushed himself up and slid to the ground, standing tall and looking healthy and strong as ever. He turned and climbed the steps to the porch where he appeared four days earlier. When he spun around and faced the crowd, his face was covered with an evil grin. Once again, the group at the military base knew the world saw a gentle smile. The realization slowly sank in that the Antichrist had risen from death and lived again.

"Now we know," said Blake. "The pastor was right; no one can destroy Messai. He *is* the Antichrist, mimicking everything Jesus did, including his resurrection."

John prayed aloud as if no one else listened. "I am sorry I doubted you, Jesus. I gave up hope, but you showed us the truth. Thank you. Now I am ready to fight."

Beth recalled praying a similar prayer the night Jesus set her free from Messai's mansion. Jesus had done this so many times, why would they ever doubt him? They listened as Messai spoke.

"Good day, ladies, and gentlemen of the world. A new day has dawned, and here I stand before you alive!" He spoke with the gusto they had heard many times before.

"Do not fear; you are not looking at a ghost. Behold my head. You witnessed with your own eyes the gaping hole in my temple from the bullet that ended my life. Yes, I was dead, but now I live! Join me in eight hours for special announcements that are so important you must not miss them."

The lights and cameras remained on him, showing he would stand larger than life atop the steps until 8:00 a.m. The world had followed him for three years, and now he proved their trust was justified. They would tune in and watch with excited anticipation in eight hours.

Michael stood on top of the temple, peering over the edge at the man below. He looked small from his bird's-eye view. The archangel knew Messai *was* small, despite how large he saw himself. Michael understood the Secretary-General's announcements would drastically change the world for the next three-and-a-half years and have a profound effect on every follower of Jesus.

Ben would search for him when morning came, but not find him. This was one event he refused to miss. It foreshadowed things to come setting up the final battle. He must fight the forces of evil for forty-two months, then turn things over to the King of kings. Jesus would take it from there.

8:00 a.m. Aissa Messai stood before the cameras, with the world watching. Powerful speakers boomed his voice across the Temple Mount, and beyond. Large screens installed during the night projected his image to all who saw them.

The Smyrnians had not left the meeting hall at Camp Filon, but waited and watched for the press conference to begin. A vast majority of the world's population joined them from afar. They wanted to hear what this man who rose from death would say. He deserved their adoration and praise. Aissa Messai's opening words left no doubt he now recognized himself as *all*-powerful.

"Loyal subjects, for the past three years I have sensed something special about my life, but have awaited confirmation. During that time, I have fought tirelessly to bring peace and prosperity to our world, and to each of you. The time has come for that to happen!"

"In rising from death, I realize my purpose is far greater than I considered. The moment I returned to life, my true identity was revealed to me. I am the eternal god of this world. No one can destroy me! But you must recognize by following me, you also become gods who rule alongside me. United as one powerful and invincible force, we shall bring peace and prosperity to all!"

"However, to achieve that, we *must* remove all who oppose that goal. The rebel Smyrnians and those who follow their teachings comprise that group. Today, I implement two systems that will allow us to discover who they are and root them out: a unified government, and a unified religion to bring us together. All of us who seek peace and prosperity will unite as one to make it possible."

"I wish he would stop using those words," said John as they watched in the mess hall. "He has nothing to do with peace or prosperity. His only purposes are death and destruction."

Messai stood silent for a moment, hearing words from another place. *The Smyrnians*, he thought. *I will show them what death and destruction look like when they experience it themselves!* He spoke again. This time, he revealed the initial part of his heinous plan.

"My office will announce another special briefing soon where I will explain the specifics of both systems. In the meantime, follow me as we pursue our goals together. If you discover any of the aforementioned rebels, turn them in, and let those found guilty face the guillotine the same day they are sentenced. Our *New World Order* begins today!"

The multitude erupted in applause combined with shouts of approval. The Smyrnians knew the same thing was happening around the world. It was time to run for their lives. Messai would have his day, but they would also have theirs in three-and-a-half years. They all hoped to survive that long, but it remained certain that some would not.

Ben's next call came and went. It shocked the Jews in Petra to hear about Messai's resurrection, *although it should not surprise them*, Ben said. It explained Blake's gut feeling and confirmed the truth they all knew. Nothing could destroy the Antichrist until Jesus returned.

But Ben made one suggestion that could benefit them. Certain areas evacuated by Jews when they fled for Petra flew under the radar with Messai, especially remote locations where Jewish Bedouins lived. Most people believed all Bedouins in Israel were Arab, and most were, but not all.

Primitive living quarters, typifying the Bedouin lifestyle, would suffice for housing. Since the areas were unfamiliar to Israel's government, even passed over in the decennial census, they came and went without detection. Four areas existed: two in the north and two in the south. They were unlikely to use all four, but would almost certainly use one in each direction.

•   •   •   •   •

Messai spent the week in meetings, but none more essential than the first. He traveled to the ancient center of pagan worship and climbed to the stone altar. This visit represented a transition in how future encounters would happen. He knelt before the large niche and waited. Soon the stench filled his nostrils, and a chill caused his body to tremble. He lifted his eyes and gazed at the lord of hell.

"Stand to your feet, Aissa."

The chill turned to heat. Strength surged inside him, replacing the weakness that typically gripped him during these times with the dragon. He understood what came next, and he was ready. The large red creature stepped down from the alcove carved into the side of the rock mountain.

"Take your place, Aissa, and reign in my power. Your *resurrection* confirmed your authority. You are my visual representation on earth, thus when they see you, they see me. You and I are one!"

When Messai placed his right foot inside the niche, the power of hell surged through his body. He lifted his left foot and stepped up inside the dragon's domain. Fire coursed through his veins, and pure evil consumed him. The creature placed a crown on his head, then moved to one side, allowing Beelzebub and Belial to come and kneel before their newly crowned master.

"We worship you, lord," said the chief prince of demons, "as the world will worship you. Today you become ruler of the evil realm. We are yours to command."

"You understand your role, Aissa," said the dragon. "The earth now belongs to you, my anointed one. Rise and conquer because nothing or no one can stand in your way. We will rule forever!"

The beast and powerful demons disappeared, leaving Messai standing alone in the place of power. Another meeting would take place here tomorrow morning. He would summon the man the moment he returned to Jerusalem.

•　　　•　　　•　　　•　　　•

Moving day came for the followers of Jesus at Camp Filon. The Smyrnians would split up for two reasons. One, they wanted to ensure that Messai could not take all of them out at the same time. Two, new believers needed experienced veterans guiding them in what they were about to face.

The American military unit would divide into six groups, with Bradley, Paul, Rickie, Robert, and Trey leading five of them. One remaining group comprised women from the unit. To everyone's surprise, Brita asked permission to lead them, being a former military brat, whose father spent twelve years in the Marines. Now she was determined to follow his footsteps battling Messai and the forces of evil. The wisdom gained from her dad would serve her well.

Robert's research led to a cluster of abandoned bunkers within a one-mile radius of each other. Every group would have their own housing and live close enough to the others to stay connected, but far enough to stay safe. The shelters were rough, but with a little work and TLC, they should become well-disguised places of refuge, not ideal, but functional for those used to *roughing it.*

The singles group had already made their decision: Ein Gedi it was. Where else would you expect a young, enthusiastic, fun-loving bunch to go? Israel's national parks closed after the nuclear attack, and most were abandoned and seldom visited. This natural oasis provided everything they needed, with its pools and waterfalls, plus caves for lodging.

If AMPP came looking for them, they would move from cave to cave, following the example of David in the Bible when King Saul searched for him. Getting in and out would require some effort. They planned to hike to the Ein Gedi Field School, which had also been closed for almost a year. It was a difficult two-hour hike, but no problem for young legs.

Mordecai left the Wolf off-road armored vehicle he used for the border rescue. A spot awaited them off the narrow road to the field school where they could hide it behind some huge boulders. Omar would drive with Ahmad and Hala riding up front wearing IDF uniforms. Being Middle Eastern, they looked enough like Israeli soldiers.

John and Kathie opted to keep their families together, and the rest would join Blake and Beth. The Bedouin communities should work perfectly for both of them. In a non-professional but fun way of deciding who would stay in the north and who would move south, they flipped a coin. Blake won the toss by calling heads, meaning his group would remain in the Golan, and John and Kathie's families were desert bound. Some good-natured ribbing followed, but both were ready.

Blake wanted to send emails to believers throughout the world. But without wireless internet, and all their information gone, there was nothing he could do. The groups would stay in touch via secure phones, and always be there for each other, and for any other believers who needed them. Should the latter occur, the pilots would fly, despite the danger involved. The American soldiers, along with Omar, Ahmad, and Hala, would go so the original Smyrnians could stay safe. But if the need arose, they would *all* be ready. For now, they needed to get away from Filon.

· · · · ·

This is power, Messai reasoned to himself, standing in the large niche on the ancient altar of pagan worship in Banias. Until now, the beast of hell reserved it only for himself. *Today, I take the first step toward ruling the world.* He watched as the man crossed the footbridge over the flowing water, climbed the stone steps, and approached him. The sun appeared over the horizon behind him.

The Jewish High Priest knelt before him, as Messai himself had often knelt here before the dragon. Face to the ground, the man waited for him to speak. He intentionally delayed and watched anxiety build in the man, remembering the powerlessness which came with that. The priest needed to feel the pain of bone upon stone before he commanded him to stand. That created humility.

"Stand and look at me." Messai saw the chilling effect as the man obeyed, his body trembling. He watched the cold turn to heat, causing the man's eyes to glow yellow and red.

"I belong only to you, Master. Your will be done."

He longed to scream and overpower this weak pawn of the dragon himself, but exercised restraint. The priest had sold his soul to the dragon, just as he had. He accepted Messai as the promised Jewish Messiah and agreed to serve him and do his every bidding. A desire for power and prestige controlled the man, but religious zeal drove his actions. That played directly into Messai's hands.

"Caiaphas, you are privileged to witness what your namesake longed to see many years ago. He took an unpopular stand and killed the messianic imposter. Now I have come and you see the true risen one who brings peace and prosperity. The lion will lie down with the lamb in my kingdom. The world will worship me in the Holy City, and you shall serve as my High Priest forever. We must first destroy the enemy who proclaims the false messiah. You know who they are."

"Yes, Master, the *Smyrnians.*"

"Yes..." he said, drawing that word out, trying to imitate the dragon's hissing snakelike voice. "They will have only two choices: worship me or die. You will create and lead a worldwide system of religious observance, which will separate the chaff from the wheat. All who refuse will be cast into the fire and burned, after they are beheaded. We will kill the snakes by cutting off their heads."

"Let us start soon, Master, because waiting will only delay the goal we seek to achieve."

"You will stand beside me tomorrow at 9:00 a.m. as I announce our plan to the world."

"I will prepare my priests to offer the daily sacrifices. May I make one suggestion?"

"You may, although I cannot guarantee I will accept it."

"What if we offer more prominent rebels as burnt offerings without beheading them first? Would that not deter others from rebelling and cause them to submit and worship you?"

"Genius! This is the reason I selected you to assume this role! We will burn alive Smyrnian leaders, and any others in positions of authority within their demented cult, for all the world to see!"

Messai withheld an evil laugh. The look of pleasure on the man's face gave him enough joy. He walked away, knowing the dragon brought him the right man for this job. Caiaphas would lead the Jews to believe in him, or put his own people to death. He smiled all the way back to Jerusalem.

Early afternoon brought his second urgent meeting. He had no time to waste setting up his worldwide system of government, either. Ten leaders of Arab nations sat around the table in the impressive board room awaiting his arrival when he entered right on time. His smile showed he was impressed with their punctuality.

The president of Iran sat next to Messai, joined around the table by the top men of Afghanistan, Egypt, Gaza, Iraq, Jordan, Lebanon, Saudi Arabia, Syria, and Turkey. This ten-nation coalition had one thing in common: their hatred for Israel, the Jews, and other *infidels* who did not worship Allah. Messai shared that hatred, as did the dragon. They would destroy the Jews and seize control of the land they believed was rightfully theirs. The timing was perfect under Messai's leadership.

Military power was also an essential part of their destructive plan. Messai would address that during the meeting by introducing some special guests. Enemies would soon become friends again.

"Gentlemen, I welcome each of you to the table. We share the same goals and desires, and it excites me to tell you the time has finally come to realize those once and for all! I assume your attendance shows your support for our agenda and your willingness to serve in my kingdom." Affirmative responses came quickly from each man in the room.

"The nations of the world will unite with us, and together we will bring an unprecedented time of worldwide peace and prosperity. However, you understand maintaining peace sometimes requires the use of force. You all saw the capital punishment device." Nods, accompanied by smiles, again filled the room. "I will enact laws immediately requiring people to join our common effort or suffer the consequences. Such drastic action should help weed out the divisive minority."

"You will join me in leading the united world government. Your expertise and experience are perfect for overseeing that task. A worldwide system of buying and selling, supported by one common currency, will drive the economy of the world. Paper money, coins, digital, and any other form of currency will no longer exist. Every person will receive an identification image that allows them to buy and sell. Once again, this will pull the world together."

"What happens to those who refuse to accept this system?" asked the man from Syria.

"Use your imagination, friend," said Messai, smiling. "They will accept it, or starve. This system will serve an important purpose in uniting the planet. Think about it. Everyone can buy and sell on every continent, in any country, with a simple mark of identification." They gave their approval.

"Uniting the world also requires a worldwide system of religion." Bewildered looks showed on their faces, as an icy chill descended on the room. "Human beings have always needed something, or *someone* to worship. The gods of this world are nothing more than figments of imagination for people with weak minds who need something to make them feel good. There is only one who is worthy of worship."

The men sat in horror as the beast appeared before them. The giant red dragon ambled around the room, stopping in front of each man, allowing his heat to touch their faces, driving away the chill. Fear replaced their feeling of power.

"The world will worship me by worshiping my man, Aissa Messai, who proved his power by rising from death. *You* will set the example of bowing to me first. That will show you are ready to fill this role and lead the world." His odor now mesmerized them as they stared through hollow eyes.

"Now!" the creature said, stepping away from the table. The men jumped to their feet, went and bowed at the dragon's feet. "Now, you have proven your readiness to lead." Silence. The men stayed in their positions until one finally lifted his eyes and realized the dragon was gone.

"You may return now and sit with me." They stood and went back to their seats, faces pale from shock and horror. "I wanted you to see the one who called us to change the world and reign with him forever! It was he who brought me back to life and now lives in me."

"Now, people will worship him by worshiping me. Those who refuse will prove their resistance to peace and prosperity by their refusal and pay the price. You will attend the press conference tomorrow morning at 9:00 a.m. when I introduce the man who will lead this effort. Don't miss it!" The looks on their faces said they would not.

CHAPTER 16

In Petra, Ben was eager to hear from his fellow Smyrnians. Michael assured him all was well, but this time the young man's word would not suffice. He needed to talk to Blake. The 144,000 Jewish followers of the true Messiah felt little concern for anything outside their new home. Jesus provided protection and enjoyment, and they intended to make the most of it until he returned. At last, 7:00 came, and he climbed the mountain with Michael, Hadassah, and Mordecai and called Blake. No answer. He tried again... same result. Concern set in that bordered on worry.

"Don't worry, Ben," Michael said. "I'm sure they're okay."

"Blake never fails to answer my calls. Something is not right."

"I agree with Ben. This is not like Blake. Have you ever known him to miss one of our calls?"

"I remember him reminding Ben about one, uncle, when he lost cell service in America. That's probably what happened this time, too."

"I still don't like it. And the problem is, we can't do anything about it."

He called three more times, and still no answer from Blake.

"We have stayed up here far longer than we should. Miriam will worry about us. Let's go back down, and we'll come back and call first thing tomorrow morning."

Ben walked into their room in the Treasury and found his wife sobbing.

"Miriam, what's wrong?"

"Oh, Ben, I just had the most horrible nightmare, except I'm certain it wasn't a dream. It was real. Camp Filon lay in a heap of ashes, burned to the ground."

Ben's face turned ashen. He sat down and put his head in his hands.

"Blake didn't answer my calls. I tried to call him many times, but he never answered. They may all be dead."

Both wept together.

• • • • •

Messai conducted one more meeting that evening with leaders of every major religion in the world. All missed the Rapture and now accepted Aissa Messai as their object of worship and teacher of truth. They would join him for the meeting tomorrow morning, where he would introduce them, along with the High Priest.

Buddhism, Hinduism, Bahai, and all others, including Islam, would unite as one, setting aside former differences to worship him. Another group would join, but he would introduce them later. They would play an important role. One would covertly take part, but adhere to their beliefs, until time came to reveal their true allegiance.

Messai stood at the bottom of the twelve steps leading to the Holy Place, accompanied by the High Priest. He beamed with a secret he could not wait to tell! Time neared for his big moment.

"Are you ready, Caiaphas?"

"Oh yes, my lord, I am more than ready."

Cameras rolled. Messai stepped to the podium and spoke his first word at precisely 9:00 a.m., not a second before or after. He must be prompt with this news today.

"Ladies and gentlemen, I come this morning with two announcements which will change the world as we once knew it and advance us toward the goal of worldwide peace and prosperity. It is time to take those goals seriously and come together as one across the globe. I am abolishing old ideals which divided us and bringing forth a new standard which will unite us."

"The first concerns worship. The former cult called *Christians* worshiped a false messiah who was crucified over two millennia ago, outside this very city. Billions of people bought into the lie of his resurrection. Consider the foolishness of falling for such an unproven falsehood. Who saw him *walk out of the grave?* No one. Who *claimed* to have seen him afterwards? Only a *few* of his radical followers. From those few, a lie spread and controlled weak minds for over two thousand years."

"Today, I stand before you as the true risen one! You witnessed my assassination with your own eyes over national media and listened as doctors pronounced me dead. Three days later, you watched again as I returned to life! This is not propaganda; this is real! I am your true Messiah!"

The throng on the Temple Mount broke out in applause and shouts of praise, followed by a spontaneous reaction that spread to the entire world. They collapsed to their knees in worship, bowing to their new messiah. Aissa Messai raised his hands and gladly accepted their worship.

"Now, friends, I introduce the new leader of our one worldwide religion, who will draw us together instead of pulling us apart, as did the past religious systems. Caiaphas, the High Priest of Judaism, and leader of worship at this temple, has realized the fallacy of his previous beliefs and now follows me. The absurd worship of some unseen god named *Yahweh* ends today."

"If such a *loving* being exists, why would he command the slaughter of entire groups of people as proclaimed by the Jewish *Old Testament*? Why would he allow such evil in the world, if he has power to prevent it? A new day has dawned! A day of love, peace, and prosperity!"

People on their knees across the Mount shouted *amen* as Caiaphas climbed the steps to the Altar of Burnt Offering.

"Blasphemy! Imposter!" shouted many Jews in Israel and the world.

"He spoke the *name*," said one in a gathering of Jewish priests as they watched the conference.

"Caiaphas must die with him!"

They failed to realize *they* would soon become the hunted, who would either submit or die.

Caiaphas' voice blaring over the massive speakers drew attention away from the podium and toward the altar. Cameras zoomed in, and eyes everywhere focused on the High Priest. He placed the already slain sacrificial animal on the altar. No fire burned, signifying an end of obeying the Law of Moses and commandment of Yahweh in Leviticus Chapter 6, verse 13.

The animal lay on the cold, dormant metal as people waited to see what would happen. Caiaphas stretched out his arms and proclaimed, "In the name of Aissa Messai, the risen one!" Fire shot down and consumed the offering within seconds. Simultaneous gasps filled the air like a gust of wind passing over the Temple Mount.

"Together we will worship the risen one! Aissa Messai is the true messiah my people have long believed would come. But he is not only *our* messiah; he is *your* messiah too! Those who refuse to bow to *him* will bow and place their heads in the guillotine, for they will prove themselves enemies of the cause. Those who accept will be rewarded with peace and prosperity as the earth glows with the glory of our lord!"

He descended the stairs and returned to the podium with Messai, then pointed to the Temple entrance atop the steps behind them. A long table sat there covered with a sheet. Four priests removed the sheet, turned, and walked back through the doors into the Temple. A gasp greater than the last escaped the lips of those gathered there and from those watching throughout the world. A gigantic image of Messai lay on the table. The image looked human, an amazing likeness, but without life or breath.

Caiaphas walked up the steps and around the table, facing the crowd and cameras. He leaned over the image and gently breathed into its nostrils, then stepped back.

"Live!" he screamed, his powerful voice nearly deafening his listeners.

The world looked on as the image moved. Close-up camera angles showed its chest beginning to rise and fall with shallow breaths, then expand, breathing deeply. The huge throng of people froze in fear. Silence covered the earth for what felt like an eternity. Eyes opened, extremities moved, a head lifted from the table and peered at those present, then into cameras, causing everyone watching to feel like it stared directly at them. The image sat up, then stood, and spoke.

"Worship me and live, or refuse and die. If we come together, the promise of peace and prosperity will be ours! I will allow no one to interfere with that promise because I do it for *you*."

Fear and awe overcame the worldwide audience. They believed in and followed their all-powerful leader, but now feared him also and would do whatever he commanded. One group would not: those who followed the real Messiah, Jesus Christ, the risen, living, and returning Son of the living

God. They would stand against Aissa Messai, even if it cost them their lives. Caiaphas continued.

"We will kneel before our lord three times a day: morning, noon, and evening. When you hear the trumpet blast, stop what you are doing and bow toward this temple and the one who reigns from it. Report anyone who disobeys this order. It is they who rebel against our messiah and try to prevent the peace and prosperity *you* deserve. Each one eliminated gets us closer to that goal."

Messai climbed the steps as his image stepped aside to allow him entrance into the Temple. He picked up a piece of bread from the table and ate it as he pulled back the curtain and walked to the Holy of Holies. An accompanying cameraman filmed and relayed the images to the world. He came back and stood in the doorway, looking over the crowd.

"My new office!" he said. "This building has always been special to me. Now it will be open to all of you, not just a select few! This house will be a place for all nations. Make plans to come for a tour! For those who cannot, I will offer a virtual tour soon. Here's to our new future!"

He lifted a glass of wine and a piece of bread, then ate and drank. Those who followed Jesus understood the reference. The world was changing fast.

Messai introduced the religious leaders next. Each bowed to him and offered their full support. He followed that with introductions of the ten Arab rulers who would join him in leading his N*ew World Order*, which he proclaimed would further create a unified planet. The day ended with majority support of the world's population. Messai's *reign of terror* would now escalate quickly.

•　　　•　　　•　　　•　　　•

Night came, with the believers hunkered down in their separate locations. Some needed lots of work to become livable, but at least they were in. That would begin the next day. None realized they missed a night raid on Camp Filon, conducted by AMPP and select IDF forces. When no Smyrnians were found, they burned the base to the ground to ensure any hiding would not survive.

Blake's group finished moving into the primitive Bedouin dwellings in remote Northern Israel. He and Beth stared at the crude dwellings without modern conveniences.

"We don't even have electricity, Beth. What are we going to do? I wish we had some way to communicate with other believers in the world, but we can't. We lost our hard drives and all our information when the shelter blew up. Even worse, we lost Evan." Fatigue was leading to despair.

"I can't answer that, but it is too late to worry about it tonight. Maybe we can come up with a solution tomorrow. Tonight, we are exhausted, it's dark, and our bodies need sleep."

"You're right. Wait! Ben was supposed to call tonight! Where is my phone?" They looked and finally found it outside where it fell out of his pocket. A list of missed calls from his former boss.

"He will think something happened to us, but I can't call him back. I'll have to wait until he calls tomorrow evening. That's almost twenty-four hours. I wish I could tell him we're okay."

Every group realized the same thing: they needed electricity. They could use candles and kerosene lanterns for light, but they needed to charge phones, among other necessities that required electrical power. Generators provided the best option. Omar, Ahmad, and Hala volunteered to drive into Palestinian towns and purchase them, plus containers for fuel, and deliver them to each location. It would take two days to accomplish that task. They needed a large amount of fuel to operate them, plus kerosene for lanterns, batteries for flashlights, and all the bottled water they could find.

They considered noise from the generators a dangerous issue because it may give away their location. The two Jordanians showed their experience with solving that problem. They returned with thick rubber mats to go under each machine and materials to construct soundproof boxes which would cover them. That should eliminate noise.

A hard couple of days were rewarded with quiet generators, extension cords, bright flashlights, hot plates for cooking, and light-giving kerosene lanterns. Bathroom facilities included outdoor toilets, or finding another private place to *do their business*. By the end of day two, every group was set up and fully functional, from abandoned military bunkers to primitive

Bedouin huts to caves in Ein Gedi. Now to stay hidden and avoid being discovered by Messai.

Ben's mind was put at ease when he reached Blake the next morning, yet both realized it was only a matter of time before things turned deadly for believers. Even their shelters were temporary. They would run for their lives for the next three-and-a-half years. And they would try to save every follower of Jesus they could from Messai's capital punishment device.

• • • • • •

After a week of meetings with his newly formed government, the self-appointed leader of the world scheduled one more news conference for an announcement that would affect the entire planet. This time, he sat in his new office. His presence in the room and changes he made pushed some priests and many Jews beyond their breaking point.

The Temple's Holy Place was the large room in front of the smaller Holy of Holies. It contained three items: the Altar of Incense; the Table containing the Bread of the Presence, and the Menorah. Messai removed these to create his magnificent office. He replaced the items related to the worship of Yahweh with a stunning mahogany executive desk, conference table, and bookshelves.

The intimidating image of himself stood inside the doors. He required all who entered to bow before coming into his presence. The select group of camera operators and reporters obliged as they walked in. They stood around the perimeter of the now impressive sixty-by-thirty-foot room filming Messai as he announced his plan for a worldwide economy. Implementation would begin the next day. His written statement matched that of his earlier meeting with those who sat around the table with him.

"A worldwide system of buying and selling, supported by one common method of exchange, will drive the economy of the world. Paper money, coins, digital, and all other forms of currency will no longer exist. Every person will receive an identification mark that allows them to buy and sell. Once again, this will help us pull the world together."

"This system will go into effect one month from today, giving everyone ample time to receive the mark. We will offer two options: hand scanning and facial recognition. You may choose a tiny biochip, no larger than a grain of rice, inserted just under the skin on your right hand, or a tattoo stamped on your forehead, visible only to a scanner. This will make buying and selling simple and identify you. When you receive it, you join millions of others who are ready to change the future!"

"The first three numbers of every mark will be 666, representing our common humanity. The remaining numbers serve as your personal code. They identify you and allow you to purchase and sell goods, travel on modes of mass transit, and conduct all other business. This will streamline our world and make our lives much better. You will love our new system!"

"Marking centers will open at 6:00 a.m. local time tomorrow and remain open twenty-four hours a day for the next month. This will make it possible for everyone to receive the mark. You must have it within thirty days. Tune in and watch me take mine at 6:00 a.m. Israel time tomorrow!"

•　　•　　•　　•　　•

Each group of believers watched Messai's announcement from their shelters, still able to connect using their secure phones. He set everything up that would allow him to rule as a brutal dictator for the next three-and-a-half years. But he did not understand his time would run out at that point.

Blake knew he needed to get word to believers everywhere, warning them to not take the mark. That needed to happen immediately, *but how?* He sat mulling over potential meanings of 666 when John called and interrupted his thoughts.

"I just realized something, Blake. Do you know anything about Gematria?"

"I'm afraid I don't, John, except it has something to do with codes, names, and numbers."

"I delved into it years ago and found it interesting, but something hit me the second Messai gave the first three numbers of the identification mark."

"666? We read about that in Revelation, so it didn't surprise me. I just wish we knew what it means."

"It didn't surprise me either. But when I thought about the Gematria numerology calculator I used back then, it all became clear to me."

"What became clear, John? You're not making sense. They actually make calculators for that sort of thing? What does it have to do with Messai?"

"They make lots of them. If you will stop with all the questions, I just might explain that to you."

"I'm sorry, John. All I can think about is warning people to avoid taking the mark, even if it means dying for their faith."

"Perhaps I can give you even more to tell them, if you can figure that out. The calculator used the Latin equivalent for each Hebrew letter and assigned it the numeric value based on Hebrew. When I typed in *Messai*, it totaled 656."

"That's great, but you're ten digits short of 666."

"Not when I added the letter *i* to the front. Then it came to exactly 666. Do you remember the password that got Malachi into Messai's personal computer that day in his office?"

"No, John, I don't. Will *you* stop the questions and tell me what you're talking about?"

"The password was *IamMessiah666*. Blake, just like Malachi realized Jesus led him to type in that password, I am certain Jesus told me to open my Gematria calculator and type in Messai. I thought the same as you, then my finger moved to the letter *i* and pushed it. The total changed to *666*."

"A soft voice popped into my head and told me to read Luke Chapter 24, verses 36-40, and I did, right then. Jesus appeared to his followers after his resurrection, and it scared them half to death."

"Are you sure that's what it says, John?" Blake said with a chuckle.

"Okay, it says they were startled and frightened, but I'm thinking that's about the same. Listen to what Jesus told them: 'Look at my hands and feet. It is *I myself*!' Messai has been going on and on about his *resurrection*. I think he is mimicking Jesus after *his* resurrection and saying, 'Look at me. It is *I myself*! I am the real Messiah!'"

"You're right, John! When Jesus said '*I am*' seven times in the Gospel of John, he was saying, '*I myself am...*' Messai is saying the same thing, and people will have that inserted in their hands or stamped on their foreheads. It will mean they belong to him!"

"Spread the word fast, Blake. I will tell our groups. Sounds like Omar, Ahmad, and Hala have a lot of shopping to do so we can stockpile what we need for three-and-a-half more years."

The three Jordanians did their job. They continued their shopping expeditions, traveling to large cities and small towns to purchase items in bulk, but never visited the same locations twice. They had thirty days to stock up on necessary items. No easy task. Steve added a list of medical supplies to the many other things they sought. They found them all.

Centers opened worldwide the next day. True to his word, Aissa Messai received the injection in his right hand at 6:00 a.m. He proclaimed a month-long holiday for everyone. His government would compensate businesses for loss of income during that time. The world celebrated this new beginning, as people happily lined up to get their marks.

Workers congratulated them and scanned them for the first time as they exited. The names of those scanned were recorded in a database listing everyone who came through. When the month ended, Messai and his men would know the names of every person who bore the mark, *and* those who did not. They would begin hunting the latter group on day thirty-one.

Blake and Beth made a dangerous decision. They would hack into news networks and share warnings for everyone in the world. Evan taught Blake how to do that, if he could remember now. He sure missed that boy's technological genius at times like this.

Their efforts would mean nothing to people who had taken Messai's mark, or those who planned to take it. But they hoped believers would see it and take action to protect themselves. They may only get one opportunity before the networks blocked them, but at least they would get the word out once. Messai would go all out to find them after they did. But they had no other option. Both had been through the same thing three years earlier.

They spent the first day recording a warning message. If they could get internet access long enough to hack into every major news outlet, the world would hear until the networks realized what was going on and figured out how to stop them. Their messages needed to be brief and to the point.

Both would appear together and speak, alternating back-and-forth in conversational style. They were careful not to reveal anything on camera that might give away their location. Using their phones to record, they needed several takes before they felt good about the wording. They watched the last one and decided it was ready to air.

"I am Blake Thompson, with my wife, Beth. You who follow Jesus haven't heard from us recently because we lost our means of communicating with you. We are well and pray you are too."

"Listen carefully," said Beth. "We will keep this message brief. It may be the last time you hear from us until we see you in Jesus' presence. You are aware of the danger we all face. The Antichrist has assumed power, just like you learned he would from the pastor's video we played for you three years ago. The time has come for all of us to stay strong and faithful to Jesus, no matter what."

"Aissa Messai just pronounced himself the Messiah and world ruler and implemented the mark of the beast we knew was coming," said Blake. "Anyone who refuses the mark will face beheading in his guillotine. But those who take it will face eternal separation from Jesus in the Lake of Fire. Your choice will be, obey Jesus and die or yield to Messai and live. Please choose Jesus."

"Find a place where you can hide from Messai's forces," Beth said, taking her turn. "Do everything you can to protect yourself and your family. Since you cannot buy or sell without the mark, stock up on the necessities of life during these thirty days. Starvation may be a greater cause of death for people who refuse the mark than those who die in the capital punishment device."

"But," said Blake, "if they capture you, proclaim Jesus and face death bravely, letting everyone watching see your faith in him. Please stay true to Jesus. I promise we will do the same. Until we see you again, either here or with Jesus, know we love you and are thankful for your strength and perseverance in the faith. May God protect all of you. To him be the glory!"

That was it, less than two minutes. If they could pull off the hack just right, the networks could not stop them sooner than that. Now to get internet access, hack in, and play the video.

Ben looked for Michael again and could not find him. He searched high and low, meaning the tops of Petra's mountains and the gamut of the valley below. No Michael. What was he up to now? Something big was about to go down with the believers, he knew it. *Do your thing, my young protégé, whatever it is. I know Jesus is with you.*

Blake stared in amazement as the internet came to life on his computer. The Wi-Fi signal was strong, and he connected with no problem. *How in the world...?!*

Michael sat in the corner of the Bedouin tent, smiling at Blake's bewildered look. If only the man understood internet access was impossible from this location, and Wi-Fi was out of the question. But nothing was impossible for Jesus who wanted his people worldwide to hear this urgent news.

"Beth, I have it!" said Blake.

His wife came running to his side, disbelief written all over her face.

"Internet?" she asked in a tone that betrayed her inability to believe what she just heard.

"Yes, but I'm not sure how I did it. I just tried what Evan showed me and it worked! Now I need to hack into the networks and play the video. But I have to do it quick before I lose signal."

Michael smiled again while Blake tried to accomplish that task. "*You* cannot do that either, Blake," he whispered. "But the world *will* see your video today, including Messai."

He waved his hand toward the computer.

"I think we're in, Beth!"

"You are? Show the video! I wish the others knew what was happening, but we don't have time to tell them. If you're in, play it now!"

Michael chuckled, watching them. They were like two kids who had been given a new toy. "Check this out," he said, playfully twirling his arm above his head. Both were oblivious to his presence.

Blake had already uploaded the video. He hit play and every news broadcast in the world was interrupted. Michael was having fun with it. It came up on screens in every country as an emergency alert, complete with the loud, annoying buzzing sound. No one who tuned in missed it. But it went to more than major news networks; it played on every station and interrupted every program everywhere on the planet.

Sitting in his new *office*, both Aissa Messai's phone and computer sprang to life with the loud, annoying sounds. He recognized the voices the moment they spoke. Blake and Beth Thompson!

"Stop them!" he said, his anger directed toward every broadcast station in the world. "Turn them off! Kill the power! Shut them up!" But the video continued.

He watched closely while he called the director of AMPP.

"Look for any sign of where they are," he said. "Their plan will backfire if we can locate them. Let them be the first to face the guillotine!"

The video started again. Good! That gave more time to look for clues to their location. Nothing.

"Beelzebub! Belial!" The two demons appeared at once.

"Yes, Majesty?"

He pointed to the screens. "Find them!"

When the second video ended, the screens went black. Within seconds, anchors were trying to explain what just happened. They knew there was no explanation, but the lies still came.

"They must die!" he told the two hideous demons. The search was on.

Thirty days passed quickly. Messai celebrated the conclusion of the marking period and assured the world centers would remain open daily from 6:00-6:00, allowing ongoing opportunities for everyone to take the mark. He also issued another warning for those who refused it. There was no need to reiterate the punishment. The image of the guillotine was still fresh in every mind.

Another celebration ensued in the throne room of heaven. Michael knelt before two magnificent thrones, then stood to give his report.

"Not one believer took the mark, Yahweh," he said proudly. "They all remained faithful and have gone into hiding, thanks to your servants, Blake and Beth Thompson."

"Well done, Michael. We saw you make that possible. Quite impressive!"

"Thank you, Lord. I enjoy those moments of miraculous intervention when they cannot explain what just happened." A smile revealed his joy, but faded before his next words.

"I also know there will be sad moments soon, and I will be there during those times too."

• • • • •

Aissa Messai was giddy when he received a call from his chief security director. Their first capture offered the first opportunity to use the capital punishment device. He would carry out the sentence quickly. The world needed to witness firsthand what happened to those who refuse the mark.

"Get the prisoners here now, and we will see whether they are brave enough to die, or if they will accept the mark."

"Yes, sir. I planned to surprise you, but they are already on the way. Their plane should land soon."

"Excellent! I feel certain the Smyrnians and their weak-minded followers will watch, so let's see if this flushes them out. This may be the beginning of their end!"

He called the press to come, ensuring worldwide coverage of this event. Caiaphas was called in next. The High Priest needed to prepare the altar for the burnt offering he would offer following the decapitation. Honored attendees would include the ten Arab leaders who formed his government, among others.

Now to make it the news story of the day, ensuring no one missed it. He sent word to every major news outlet, television network, and streaming service. The notification was more a demand than a request. Each clearly understood, since they failed to stop Blake and Beth Thompson's video hack, they had better not miss this announcement. None of them would.

To nail that down, he dispatched legions of demons under the command of Beelzebub, Belial, and the other chiefs to every single broadcast network and individual station. Minds of executives and producers were already under the dragon's control after taking Messai's mark. The demon hordes would seize their brains and leave no doubt. It was unnecessary, but they enjoyed themselves.

When the news broke, John saw it first, then frantically started calling the others. Who could it be? Messai said they were Smyrnians. Had AMPP captured one of their entire groups, or only one or two? He and Kathie knew their families were safe because they all stayed in the Bedouin camp together. But Ally was with the singles group in Ein Gedi. Bruno and Mila had to know. Blake finally answered his call after several others went to voicemail. John gave him no time to speak.

"Blake, did you see Messai's announcement on the news? He has captured some Smyrnians and will execute them when they arrive later today."

"Who?" Blake asked, his voice horror-stricken.

"He gave no names, just that they are Smyrnians."

"We're all here, but we need to check with everybody else now!"

Bruno dashed in as he overheard Blake's conversation and gathered something was not right.

"What's going on? Why do we need to check on everybody? Tell me, Blake!"

"Messai announced he has captured some Smyrnians and will execute them later today, his first time to use the *capital punishment device*." He couldn't bring himself to say *guillotine*, especially since some of their own would face it today.

"Ally! Someone has to check on them!"

"We've tried to call them, Bruno," said John, "but none of them are answering their phones either."

"He captured them all! We have to do something! John, your group is closer than any of ours. If it is them, we could never get to them on time. Please go to Ein Gedi and see if they are safe."

"It's too dangerous, Bruno. If AMPP found them, they will stay there and wait for others to come."

"John! We're talking about my daughter, and your former student! She loves you. You're not willing to put your life on the line for her?"

"We'll go," said Julian as he and Jeffrey jumped up and ran toward the vehicle parked outside.

Bruno's phone rang, and he started crying as he answered.

"Ally, honey, are you okay?"

"We're fine, daddy. You must come and see this place. It's amazing!"

"Sweetheart, Messai announced he captured Smyrnians and will execute them today. We were so afraid..."

Beth's phone rang with a call from Trey. His group was safe. They checked on the others in the bunkers, and within minutes confirmed everyone was okay.

"Who could it be?" asked Blake, a bewildered look on his face.

"Maybe he's lying, hoping to lure us out," John said.

"I don't think so, John. All we can do is watch news all day and see what happens."

A conference call between the groups led to solemn silence. They would all watch and wait, realizing the horror they might witness before the day ended. Some of their own may die.

CHAPTER 17

Aissa Messai smiled as he stepped to the microphone atop the temple steps leading into his *office*. This would be the first of many such moments. The camera panned left to show Caiaphas standing at the Altar of Burnt Offering, which blazed with red-hot flames.

Reporters kept quiet, joining others in solemn silence, all dreading what they were about to witness. Flames danced on the altar, fanned by a slight breeze. The air felt heavy. This day would change the world within minutes and lead to an ominous future in a dystopian society of life or death choices for every person on the planet. The *reign of terror* began today.

The believers in Israel quietly sat glued to phones and tablets. The wait seemed eternal, yet they begged time to drag by, or Jesus to come and destroy the larger-than-life man with the evil smile preparing to speak. Hopelessness tore at their minds and attacked their faith. They realized these times would come, but that made this moment no less difficult.

"Ladies and gentlemen, today we shall learn whether the Smyrnians will continue their rebellion and die or join us and live. If they refuse, they will pay the price, and we will remove those who stand in the way of our peace and prosperity. Bring out the prisoners."

The Smyrnians recoiled in horror as two AMPP men led Hans and Heidi Meier before Messai. The American soldiers had not met the couple, but they sat quietly while the others struggled with the imminent, gruesome death of their comrades.

"No!" Mila screamed.

Bruno grabbed her and wrapped her in a firm embrace. Both burst into tears, grieving for their friends, realizing what they were getting ready to experience.

The couple stood at the bottom of the steps below the man they knew was the Antichrist, hands bound behind their backs. They appeared small to the viewing audience, but Jesus gave their fellow believers a different view. He stood beside his faithful followers and pulled them into a group hug. They enjoyed a conversation with him, smiling, laughing, and talking.

The others now watched in wonder, their heartbreak turning to joy. Jesus looked into the camera, and they sensed his presence, knowing no one else could see him. He pointed at Messai, laughed, and shook his head. Then he turned his focus to them, flashed a thumbs up, and spoke to them. They did not need to read his lips; his voice came across loud and clear.

"Even though they walk through the valley of the shadow of death, they fear no evil, for I am with them. A certain group awaits them when they get home." He winked. They realized he spoke about their family members slaughtered by Messai's men more than two years earlier.

They listened as Messai spoke again. The look on Hans' and Heidi's faces clearly angered him.

"Bow before me and take the mark!"

"We bow before no one but Jesus!" said Hans. "He is the true Messiah who rose from the grave and the one who will soon come again to defeat you and destroy you forever! We bear *his* mark! People of the world, listen to what I say..."

"Take them away! Sever their heads from their bodies. We will see whether their so-called *Messiah* rescues them."

"Oh, he will!" Heidi said, "but not the way you expect. He stands here with us now, though you cannot see him. You're sending us to Paradise with him. For that, we say thank you! But the place he'll send you is the opposite of Paradise, and you will experience fire much hotter than that forever!" Her voice rang out as she pointed to the altar.

"To the guillotine... now!" Messai screamed.

Jesus motioned for Hans and Heidi to come with him, walking toward the instrument of death.

The men standing by them dragged the couple away. They forced Hans to his knees, hands still bound, shoved his head through the hole, locked it in place, and looked to Messai for his signal.

"This is what happens to those who defy my orders and interfere with *our* peace and prosperity. Let all of you take notice!"

He motioned to the executioner who stood ready to activate the device. Hans sang praises to Jesus and called on people to turn to him. His voice rang with glory only other believers in Jesus understood. Reporters stared in utter disbelief at the condemned man's joy as he prepared to die. He seemed to be excited about going home.

The executioner pulled a lever, and the shiny, razor-sharp blade dropped, reaching Hans' neck within a second. His head dropped into a waiting tub, and his body tumbled to one side. Fear spread through the world like a mighty gust of wind. Greed balanced it. If this was what it took to bring the expected peace and prosperity, people would adjust to it. But nothing said they *had* to watch future beheadings. They would worship Messai and focus on living in peace and earning wealth.

No one forced Heidi. She hurried toward the device, fell to her knees, and stuck her head through the hole. "Here I come, Jesus!" she said, laughing happily. The blade fell, and her laughter ended. The believers watching knew she continued laughing with her husband, family... and Jesus. They mourned their friends' deaths, but celebrated their journey with Jesus.

AMPP personnel carried the bodies to the altar where Caiaphas burned them as an offering to the *messiah*. Messai accepted the sacrifice, lifting his hands, as those present knelt and paid him homage. His voice sounded different when he spoke again.

"People of the world, what you just witnessed will be the fate of everyone who refuses to receive my mark and worship me. I came to restore this filthy planet to its intended purpose. Doing so requires cleansing it of every person who fails to follow me. The choice is simple: take the mark, worship me, and you will live. Refuse, and you will die."

"You can only buy or sell by scanning the mark, so survival will be impossible without it. We now have a database containing the names of all who are marked. My security forces will begin a search immediately for those who did not receive it. If you are captured, they will bring you to Jerusalem where you will face beheading, then your body burned as a sacrifice. Marking centers remain open daily. If you have not yet done so, I suggest you visit one and take the mark as soon as possible."

"To those of you who proudly received your mark, I congratulate you! Thank you for supporting the *New World Order*. Your reward will be great. Do not fear; I will root out and destroy those who oppose us so peace and prosperity may reign! Now Caiaphas has an announcement before we go."

Caiaphas made his way to the temple entrance, leaving the burning bodies lying on the altar.

"Smaller images of the messiah are under construction and will be available next week. We will provide one free statue to each home. You may get yours at any marking center. Kneel before the statue three times a day when the trumpet sounds."

"This is also required, so failure to put an image in your home and worship it will number you among those who rebel against the *New World Order.* Anyone who neglects this order will face the same sentence as those you witnessed today. But those who bow down before the messiah will receive the peace and prosperity only he can give. Let us worship our king!"

• • • • •

Ben's call came right on time, and Blake filled him in on all that had happened. The Jews in Petra grieved Hans' and Heidi's deaths. Mordecai, Michael, and Hadassah took charge of this conversation, and Ben was more than willing to let them.

"Blake," said Mordecai, "AMPP is good at what they do, so I suspect they will find you soon. And the dragon has given their boss his power. You should decide on your next move now."

"I agree with uncle," Hadassah said. "You need to stay one step ahead of him and make it hard for them to find you."

"We anticipate the need for rescue missions in other countries too," said Blake. "Our pilots are ready to fly anytime and may need to bring some here. I am especially concerned about those in Germany after AMPP's capture of Hans and Heidi."

"Blake, you have to be careful," said Mordecai. "Messai wants you original Smyrnians more than anyone. His security forces will ramp up that search and stop at nothing to find you."

"I agree you must move around to avoid capture," said Michael. "However, I do not believe you should move too soon. Your current locations will suffice for a little while. If I understood you, each is obscure enough to make it difficult to find. Stay where you are and operate from there for now. The time to relocate will come, but not yet."

Ben and Mordecai stood quietly while Hadassah tried to cover a smile. She knew his word was true. Her uncle was not so quick to accept it.

"There you go again, Michael. How can you make a proclamation like that with such certainty? I would normally agree with your advice, but they are fighting no ordinary foe, and we must not give advice that could get them killed."

"I agree with him, Mordecai," said Ben. "You must admit, his insight has been on target every time. Neither you nor I understand that, but we can't deny it. Blake and Anders have been my co-workers for years, and I have known Beth in the news business too. The others have been my teammates for more than three years. I care about them, but I still defer to Michael."

Mordecai huffed in frustration and walked away. "Okay, but if they all die, don't blame me."

"It will be okay, Uncle," said Hadassah. "I love you, and I trust Michael. He has not failed us yet, either with organizing the pilots or his advice. I trust the others too. Blake will make the right decisions when the time comes, and we will pray for them every day."

"Okay, Michael, I will yield to your judgment. But Blake, be ready to evacuate at a moment's notice. Choose your next plan of action so you can implement it quickly when the need arises. We will pray for your protection."

"I believe we are safe for now, too, Michael. Your words confirm what I already believe. We will stay put for now with plans to move anytime. If I ever fail to answer your call, you will have cause for concern, because I will always wait for it at our appointed time."

●　　●　　●　　●　　●

Messai continued his assault on followers of Jesus. Beheadings happened every day. His anger intensified each time as none bowed to him or took the mark. Neither did they fight or struggle. All of them walked to the guillotine without force and died for their faith in the real Messiah.

The groups in Israel contacted believers in other countries through friends and family members who had turned to Jesus. Each locale appointed a point person who sent messages daily updating them on their situations. They mobilized on-site teams to go into action in potential *capture* situations. The pilots in Israel remained on standby for emergencies. The Smyrnians committed to doing whatever it took to protect believers from AMPP and Messai's guillotine.

Michael stood once again before the thrones of Yahweh and Jesus in heaven.

"I can summon the Host and guard your people, Lord. Why stand by and allow Messai to slaughter them like animals? Let me shield them until time for your return, Jesus."

"No, Michael," said the almighty God. "This is Satan's day and the power of darkness must prevail for three-and-a-half more years. We cannot interfere."

"But Lord..."

"Look how many have come home already. Have you noticed how happy they are and watched them walk to their physical death with assurance of eternal life?"

"Yes, Lord, but I can hardly stand to watch them die without intervening."

"You cannot? How do you think I feel? These are my chosen people who believe in my son and have committed their lives to him. The Antichrist is Satan incarnate, and he slaughters them at will. This is his day, but the day of reckoning is coming. Do you understand?"

"I do, but it will not be easy. Can you hasten that day?"

"Three-and-a-half earth years, my warrior. Do not concern yourself with details. It will come right on time."

Michael knew he must go back to Petra. Everything within him longed to take Messai out and cast his body onto the altar. But Yahweh did not permit it. He would wait for the appointed day.

•　　•　　•　　•　　•

"Gentlemen, I have asked Mr. Rossi, our head of security, to update us on their pursuit of the Smyrnians," Aissa Messai said as he sat with his government leaders for a late night meeting in his *office.* "I understand they are making progress. Is that correct, Mr. Rossi?"

"Yes, Mr. Messai. We narrowed their locations down to specific regions in the north and south. It appears they have split up and live in different places. My men believe them to be outside cities and in remote areas, possibly staying in primitive dwellings. They use secure phones which are impossible to trace, and we have seen no evidence of computer use, which also points to outlying areas rather than cities. We will pick up their trails within days."

"The north may mean somewhere along our border," said the Syrian president. "It would please our military to join the effort."

"Excellent! We suspect they hide there and welcome all help to root them out. Discovering and eliminating any or all of them will expedite achieving our goals."

"Do you believe those in the south hide somewhere near our border?" asked the Jordanian.

"Just about anywhere south and habitable is near your border." Rossi smiled. The man from Jordan appeared unoffended and returned his smile. "However, we welcome you to join us. There are many caves in that area where they can hide, so the search will be a major undertaking."

The man from Turkey became agitated and combative. "Does this mean because we do not border Israel, we are outcasts? Our country fully committed to this N*ew World Order*, but our opinions don't seem to count. I demand more respect and input into decisions and actions taken."

"Now my friend," Rossi tried to assuage the man's anger, "your country is a vital part of this group. We always welcome your input."

But the man was quickly joined by the representatives from Afghanistan and Saudi Arabia.

"My Turkish friend is right," said the Saudi with obvious disdain. "Because our countries do not border Israel, I feel left out when you decide our next moves. Right now, I say let's unleash our combined forces, go in together, and find the Smyrnians, no matter the cost."

The man from Afghanistan jumped in to support his two colleagues. "I stand with my colleagues from Saudi Arabia and Turkey. We feel alienated from this body and unwelcomed by *you.*" He pointed his finger at Messai.

"Is this a democratic body where each of us has the right to speak or a monarchy ruled by one man?"

Rossi tried to save the day, and the lives of those opposed to his boss's leadership. "Gentlemen, please. Mr. Messai invited you to serve on this body to help him change the world. We must all follow his orders in everything we do. He is our leader."

The Turkish ambassador became more combative. "You said we would join you in leading this new government, and you chose us because of our expertise and experience. But you are only using us to help you accomplish *your* goals."

"Enough!" said Messai, causing the other seven to bow their heads before him. "If you do not want to fill this role, *get out!*"

The three defectors stormed toward the door. Messai nodded to Rossi who motioned to two AMPP men standing guard. Before they reached the exit, an AMPP patrol burst in, grabbed them, cuffed their hands behind their backs, and dragged them across the office into the former Holy of Holies.

"Join me, gentlemen, and watch what happens to those who dare oppose me. The capital punishment device is too easy for them. They will face the one they really defy!"

The men fought against their captors, struggling to free themselves, still defiant. Once inside the smaller room, Messai pulled back the large curtain, allowing the others to see inside. But though it allowed them to stand outside and watch, it also allowed another to enter.

The massive red creature strode through the door, his long tail scraping the floor behind him. He glided across Messai's office and into the smaller room where the men stood, their handcuffs now wrapped around steel posts behind them, preventing them from moving. Their defiance turned to terror. Each pleaded for his life as the dragon stood before them.

"It is too late to beg now. I thought you were kings. Kings do not beg for their lives. You dared oppose my chosen one and usurp his authority. When you oppose him, you oppose me. Let this serve as a lesson to you who remain."

The beast snorted and fire shot out, scorching the men's faces, searing them red and blinding them. They screamed in pain, turning their heads too late to prevent the flames from hitting their mark. He moved to each one, burning their arms, one at a time, fire from his mouth flaying the skin and exposing the flesh underneath. They stood blinded and trembling in shock from the burns.

"Never defy me or my messiah!" His powerful voice shook the room. He threw back his head and brought it forward with flames pouring from his mouth, igniting their clothes from head to toe. The others watched as the three men perished in the fire, death finally silencing their screams, nothing left except the remains of their charred bodies.

Without another word, the dragon departed, leaving his chosen one, Rossi, and the remaining seven behind. Messai motioned to the AMPP patrol, and they entered the room to clean up the mess. He pulled the curtain, leaving them to their grisly task.

"Gentlemen, please take your seats again." He acted like the event they just witnessed had never happened. "Now, let us get back to business. Mr. Rossi, I believe you had more to say."

"First, congratulations to the men from Iraq and Iran. You are the remaining nations which do not border Israel, yet you stayed faithful to Mr. Messai and his vision for the earth. You proved your worthiness to continue governing his *New World Order*. Now, back to my update concerning the locations of the Smyrnians and their followers. Will the gentlemen from Syria and Lebanon please share your thoughts on possible hiding places in the north?"

The two went back-and-forth until the Syrian spoke a word that got Messai's attention. *Bunkers.*

"That's it! Abandoned military bunkers cover the area near the border all along the Golan Heights. They could serve as perfect places to hole up. Search every one you can find! I also feel certain Mr. Rossi is right about caves in the south. Can any of you be more specific?"

"Well, sir, they need a water source, and that is difficult to find in the desert," said the Jordanian. "But there is one that fits the bill perfectly... Ein Gedi."

"Yes! Make that your first stop, Mr. Rossi. If you fail to find them there, scour the surrounding area and search every cave you find."

They left the meeting with a plan of action and locations to search for believers in Jesus. The search would begin the next day with the two chosen locations.

•   •   •   •   •

"This place is perfect!" said Ally as the singles group lounged by the David waterfall. "We have drinking water flowing from the rocks and separate bathing pools. And the caves are cool at night."

"You're right about that!" Anders stretched out next to her, lying by the shimmering pool which held the falling water. Their relaxation was interrupted by the sudden sound of a chopper overhead.

"Hide!" Omar's voice sent them all scurrying behind vegetation or rocks.

"I don't think they saw us," said Hala, as they emerged from their hiding places.

Omar agreed. "I think we're safe, but man, that was close."

"Yes! But we need to get into the cave for safety."

"Ally is right. Let's go." The concern showed on Anders' face as they ran toward their new home.

"Sir, we have a sighting," the pilot told Rossi, circling back toward Jerusalem.

"Where?"

"Ein Gedi. We saw a group of people by the lower waterfall, and they ran when we came into view. I feel certain it is them."

"Great work, men!" He called the AMPP director immediately and ordered several squadrons to descend on Ein Gedi.

"Blake," said Anders, "I fear we were spotted a short while ago. A chopper flew over us, and we tried to hide, but it may have been too late."

"If you suspect that, leave now. You can't take any chances, because you know what happens if they find you."

"All too well. I sure hate to leave this place, but we have no choice. We will hike to the Wolf and leave before they get here."

"Go, now!"

Ally called her parents, and he called Trey when they left the cave and started hiking to the Ein Gedi Field School. They had just disappeared into the mountains when they heard voices on the path to the waterfall.

"Move!" Anders said, trying to keep his voice down.

They heeded his warning and picked up the pace, walking as quietly as possible.

"They have been here, sir," the patrol captain said to Rossi over the phone. "The evidence is fresh."

"Search the caves! They are hiding somewhere."

The captain dispatched his men to locate every cave they could. They scaled the mountainsides and climbed the paths leading to other waterfalls.

"Sir, we found something that will interest you. I know it will excite Mr. Messai!"

"Bring it to me!" He called the others to return as he waited to see what they discovered. The group arrived and handed him a receipt bearing the name, *Ally Fromm*.

"She is with them!" He pulled out his phone and called Messai.

"Find her, captain! Do not let her escape! This is almost too good to be true! She is not alone; some others are with her. Bring them all to me! These executions will shock the world, but I may have *special plans* for dear sweet Ally before she dies. Perhaps I should finish what I started, first. Then I can use her to lure her parents and others out, too. Get them, captain! Get them *now*!"

The men combed the area, looking for any clues that may show which direction the group fled. They had not searched long until one man yelled, "Over here!" All the groups, led by the captain, reached him within minutes. Fresh footprints led into a gorge where a hiking trail continued into the mountains. A candy bar wrapper hung in the branches of a small shrub nearby.

"Rossi, get choppers here! We found their trail leading through a gorge into the mountains, and it is fresh! The patrol is headed in, but perhaps pilots can spot them from the air."

In less than fifteen minutes, choppers flew toward the mountains surrounding Ein Gedi, and every patrol in the area hurried to join the search. They would surround them from all sides, cutting off every avenue of escape.

The group heard the choppers in the distance and knew they were coming for them. They were also sure a multitude of AMPP personnel would join them. Climbing and walking as fast as they could, Anders and Ally called the others, informing them of their plight.

"We have to do something!" said Bruno. "We can't sit back and let AMPP capture them!"

Blake was wracking his brain for an idea, but this was their greatest dilemma yet. "I'm with you, Bruno, but what can we do? We are too far away to get there on time. The Baldwins and Sandersons are close, but what can they do?"

"I don't care what they do. Anything is better than nothing!"

Blake quickly got John, Trey, and Rickie on a conference call, then added Robert Clark at their suggestion. He filled them in, as all the groups listened.

"We have access to a chopper," said Trey. "But what is one chopper against an entire squadron."

"They have to get to the field school and the Wolf," Robert said. "It's a two-hour hike, but they're young and in great shape, so maybe less than that."

"It's just two-and-a-half hours from here. Let's go! We can get there in time to help them!" Bruno was determined to rescue his daughter and the others. Magnus jumped in.

"I'm ready to go with my partner. Robert, can your men pick us up and drive us down there? We need to get as close as we can and outmaneuver AMPP."

"I can do better than that. A few of my men walked out near an IDF base one day and befriended three Israeli soldiers who have not taken the mark and are not keen on Messai or AMPP. They will become targets themselves when Messai discovers them, especially if he finds out they are helping us. None believe in Jesus, but they promised to help us any way we need. My men will call and ask if they will drive them somewhere."

"Are you sure you can trust them? If they turn us in, we're all dead!"

"The men trust them, Bruno. And I have confidence in my men. That's all I can say."

"We have no choice but to trust them. Call them! We don't have time to sit around here and wait!"

Robert made the call and was right back with the group.

"Two men will be here in fifteen minutes with a truck, pick us up, and head your way. Be ready!"

• • • •

"We're putting some distance between them and us, but we need to pick up the pace. I want to be away from the field school so they don't see us leave and follow us."

"Won't the choppers spot us?"

"I hope not, Ahmad, but if they do, we'll cross that bridge when we come to it."

"There is no bridge out here, Anders."

"I'm sorry, man; that's an American expression. I'll explain later. Just go!"

They ran now, climbing at some points, and stumbling downhill at others. One thing was on their minds: get to the Wolf and leave Ein Gedi. Where they would go then was anyone's guess. They could not lead them to the others. But those decisions could wait. For now, they ran, sweat pouring from their bodies, and their legs getting weak and shaky.

"Yes sir, we are closing in, and the choppers are here," the captain said when Messai called.

"Do not let them escape, captain. To ensure that does not happen, I have sent more help."

"Sir, we have things under control. You don't need to..."

"Just do your job, captain, and let me do mine. Help is on the way."

He ended the call, leaving a frustrated captain continuing the pursuit, now more determined than ever to capture their prey.

"We understand completely, Your Majesty," said Beelzebub. "The horde has left for Ein Gedi. Don't worry, they will apprehend the enemy and ensure those AMPP fools return them to you."

The sky darkened with an unseen demonic horde flying toward their destination. Those who pursued the group would not see them, but the horde would deliver the enemy into their hands. The human targets would not see them either, but they would *feel* them.

Ally fell and slid down a rocky slope. Anders rushed to her side.

"Are you okay? I will carry you if I need to."

He reached down and lifted her to her feet.

"I'm fine; just a little skinned up, that's all. Something tripped me."

"Ouch!" Hala smacked her neck and a red welt showed up. "A bee just stung me."

"Ow! Me too!"

Ahmad started swinging his arms, unseen bees swarming around them. They fought them off as best they could, but the stings kept coming.

"Run!" Anders said in a loud whisper he feared their pursuers would hear.

They sprinted, swinging their arms, the invisible horde chasing them and increasing in number. They swooped in, making it nearly impossible for the group to continue.

"We have to be close! Keep going!"

"I can't see anything!" said Omar.

"Fight through it! There, up ahead. I see the Field School! The Wolf should be just ahead off the left side of the road."

"I see it!" said Ally.

They could barely make out the shape of the vehicle but got there, and fighting off whatever was attacking them, jumped inside. The key was under the seat, as Mordecai promised, and it started right up. Omar turned the headlights on bright and still could hardly see where he was going. But he gunned the motor and sped down the narrow road toward Highway 90.

After a short distance, the darkness of the invisible horde cleared. Their hearts sank at what met their sight. AMPP vehicles blocked the road, with patrol members standing or hunkered down with weapons aimed at them. Omar slammed the brakes, jerked the steering wheel to the right, and headed off road, only to find dozens more black SUVs surrounding them. They now heard the choppers hovering overhead. Bullets peppered the sides of the armored Wolf.

"Keep going," yelled Anders from a back seat.

"There's nowhere to go!" Omar yelled back. "We're surrounded, and more are coming!"

While dust boiled from the chase, AMPP vehicles hemmed them in. The noise of helicopters above drowned out their voices, and things moved in slow motion. Anders grabbed Ally and pulled her close. Ahmad did the same with Hala. AMPP blocked them on every side. They heard a deafening bang. A grenade exploded underneath the Wolf, and it spiraled out of control then skidded to a stop. Outside the windows, they saw dozens of AMPP personnel, guns trained on them.

"Out of the vehicle, *now!*"

All options exhausted, they climbed from the Wolf, hands in the air. Men rushed them, jerked their hands behind their backs, and zip tied them tight, causing Ally to cry out in pain.

"Line them up," said the captain who had now arrived with his men. "I want to get a picture to send to Mr. Messai."

They stood side-by-side as the man snapped the photo and sent it. His phone rang within a minute.

"Captain! You captured them!"

"Yes, sir. It wasn't easy; they are elusive. But we were determined to bring them in."

"Can they hear me?"

"Yes, sir. Go ahead."

"Ally, my dear."

He spoke in the low, gravelly voice she had heard before, but now there was something even more sinister, more *evil* about it. This was a far different Aissa Messai than she remembered.

"I have special plans for you. You and I have a date at the King David Hotel Presidential Suite to take care of some unfinished business. I plan to enjoy that! Following our exciting night, I will parade you before the watching eyes of the world and allow them to see you again."

"Then you will watch your friends die in the capital punishment device before paying for your crimes against the state the same way. Seeing your pretty head severed from your body will sadden me, but it will also give me pleasure after the way you embarrassed me. Come to me, all of you."

"Let's go," said the captain. They loaded them and drove away toward Jerusalem, the Temple Mount, and a date with the Antichrist and his guillotine. The Smyrnians' darkest day had come.

CHAPTER 18

The truck driven by an IDF soldier, with Bruno, Magnus and a handful of American troops hidden in the back, rolled down Highway 90 toward Ein Gedi. The Americans, now dressed in IDF uniforms, shielded the two Smyrnians to prevent them from being recognized.

All were fully armed and ready to use their weapons should force become necessary. Killing members of AMPP, who had all taken the mark, no longer concerned them since they had already sealed their doom. It was not their preference, but if it meant protecting or rescuing their own, they would shoot without a second thought.

The trip took longer than they hoped, but the road to Ein Gedi Field School finally came into view. Once he turned onto the road, the driver moved slowly, staying alert for signs of AMPP. Those in the back sat with weapons ready to fire. The truck stopped suddenly, and the driver yelled for them to exit. They spilled out, Bruno, and Magnus coming last.

Fifty feet to their left sat the badly damaged Wolf. A multitude of tire tracks revealed the pursuit, attack, and capture of those inside. The group sprinted to the vehicle and discovered items left inside that belonged to Anders, Ally, Omar, Ahmad, and Hala.

Bruno pulled Ally's backpack out and hugged it. They feared his wailing would draw the attention of remaining AMPP personnel, but refused to interfere. They stood still and let him grieve. Magnus stepped over and called Blake, who put the phone on speaker, so the others could listen. He lowered his volume so Bruno could not hear Mila screaming. Ollie's yell came through loud and clear.

"Amelia and I are going to Jerusalem! We realize who has them and where he's taking them. I know my way around, but if Robert can get a truck and an IDF guy to drive, he will be less suspicious up front." This time he was not privy to Messai's personal plans for Ally.

"Ollie, you wouldn't have a chance," said Beth. "You will both die with them."

"I don't care what you say, Beth, we're going. Right, Amelia?"

"Yes! I refuse to stand back and let Messai murder them without doing something."

"Wait for me, Ollie; I'm going with you," Magnus said. "If I can give my life to save them, I will. They don't deserve to die, but I do because I slaughtered so many believers."

Ollie called Robert, nodded at what he said, then spoke to Magnus, disregarding his last comment.

"One of the Israelis is still at the base. The other two are with you. Have one of them call and ask if he will drive, and we'll meet you somewhere in-between. If two Americans can return your truck, all three IDF guys can go with us. We can't stop Bruno from going too, and I don't blame him."

Things were rolling fast, yet Blake and Beth realized their comrades were preparing for an impossible mission that would likely end with their capture and death, too. But they also knew trying to stop them was useless. Messai would promote these executions to ensure a large viewing audience. They would not occur until tomorrow.

Ben and Mordecai searched for Michael again and could not find him. Mordecai now recognized what Ben saw. Michael disappeared at crucial times, and when he did, miraculous things happened. Both learned to accept it and leave the young man alone so he could do whatever it was he did.

"But Yahweh," Michael said, standing before his Lord and pleading with him. "If I do not help, Messai will execute them all."

"Michael, my warrior, I admire your zeal. You have served bravely throughout the millennia. But you must understand, during the second half of the Tribulation, we cannot intervene. If they die, they will come home to live with us and escape the torment Messai will inflict on your people."

"I understand that, Lord, but just this one time..."

Yahweh smiled and extended a hand toward Michael, touching his shoulder.

"The final battle will come soon when you fight and conquer alongside my son, but the time is not here yet. Be patient, my warrior." The Almighty God smiled at his prince. "Now get back to Petra and join my people there."

Michael realized debating with the creator would not work, so he bowed before his Lord and flew away toward Petra. Many times before, Yahweh had permitted him to help the believers. Now, he refused to allow it during these remaining years. That saddened him, but he would obey.

The vehicle carrying the five singles group members arrived in Jerusalem. The captain left four at a secure, heavily guarded location, awaiting sentencing and execution the next day. Their picture would show around the clock on every major network and social media platform worldwide, along with an announcement of their executions the next day at 3:00 p.m.

"Not you," the captain said, sneering at Ally as his cohorts dragged the others from the vehicle. "You get to visit your former boss in his new office. Then he will treat you to a night in the most prestigious hotel in Jerusalem. I'm sure you remember how well he treats his special *friends*."

"Leave her alone! She stays with us!"

An AMPP man raised his rifle to slam the butt into Anders' head.

"It's okay, Anders," said Ally, smiling, her calm demeanor surprising him. "Whatever I go through tonight is nothing compared to seeing the face of Jesus tomorrow. Your wife and Evan will be there, along with our other friends. You have already seen them. Now it's my turn."

"Quiet!" the man said. His men dragged the others out but held Ally in her seat. "We will see if you think that way tomorrow when the blade releases."

"Yes, you *will*," she said. "And I can tell you, where I go, you cannot come. I feel sorry for you."

They took her comrades down into their one-night prison, and the AMPP vehicle drove away to the Temple Mount and Messai's *office* with Ally inside.

• • • • • •

The two IDF trucks met on an isolated stretch of Highway 90 north of Jericho. They quickly made the switch. Bruno, Magnus, and the two

Israelis left their truck for the one bound for Jerusalem. Two American troops returned to the bunkers driving an Israel Defense Forces truck.

The captain transferred Ally to a black limousine and sat up front with the driver, while one AMPP man sat on each side of her in the back. She longed to pull off another miraculous escape, but realized that was impossible riding with her hands still zip-tied behind her. She felt helpless but still emboldened by her faith in Jesus. Whatever the next twenty-four hours held, he would see her through and welcome her home. That thought sent tingles of excitement through her entire body.

Every news network showed the photo of the group and announced their planned executions the next day. They said Messai would make a special announcement from his office within the hour. The time arrived, and he appeared sitting behind his exquisite mahogany executive desk.

"Hello everyone, and welcome to my office," he said. This time there was no mistaking the evil in his voice, even though the world still did not notice it. "I have good news to share. Today, the men of AMPP captured two of the most wanted Smyrnians, along with three Jordanians who joined them. You will witness their executions tomorrow at 3:00 p.m."

"One has great significance to me. Ally Fromm was my trusted personal assistant before she defected and joined the rebels. A short while ago, AMPP took the beautiful Miss From into custody, along with Anders Norstrom, former cameraman for Smyrnian leader, Blake Thompson. We will hold the others in maximum security until tomorrow, but Miss Fromm will join me shortly as an honored guest at today's executions. She will arrive soon, and security will escort her here to join me. Do not miss this historic moment in our pursuit of peace and prosperity."

He walked out and stood atop the steps, looking toward the Mount of Olives. The limo ascended the Mount and stopped near the steep street formerly called the Hosanna Road.

"This is our stop," said the captain, opening his door and stepping out.

The AMPP man to her right did the same, then extended his hand to help her.

"Thank you, but I can handle this myself," she said, twisting and turning, struggling to get out of the automobile and stand.

"As you wish," he said, watching her clumsy efforts.

The captain started walking. "Let's move."

He led the way down the mountain where they would pass the Garden of Gethsemane and cross the Kidron Valley before climbing up and entering through the Golden Gate. His men escorted Ally, one again on each side. She walked proudly between them. Camera persons walked in front, careful to keep from falling, showing close-up shots of her face. Choppers provided an aerial view from above. No one could question the significance of this moment.

The four made the walk without saying a word. Ally forced an occasional smile for the cameras and tried to appear undaunted by the entire experience, but that was harder than she had imagined when the walk began. They finally reached the gate and walked to the temple courts, which now belonged to Aissa Messai.

A crowd had gathered after seeing Messai's announcement. Many jeered as Ally passed by. This woman had once been the envy of every woman when she served as his assistant. How she could throw that away to join a notorious band of rebels was beyond their comprehension.

When they entered the Court of the Priests, renamed Court of Messai Almighty, she saw him standing and looking down at her. She allowed herself a moment of humor, realizing the first letters of the name formed the acronym, COMA. The man had surely not considered that.

The men led her to the steps and stopped when Messai held up his hand. He motioned for Ally to come, so she climbed slowly until she reached the porch and stood beside him. Cameras captured his smile as he bowed his head to her, then opened the door and led her into the office. He closed the door behind them, leaving her alone with the monster from whom she once fled. A moment of fear consumed her, but the peace that transcends understanding quickly replaced it.

"Welcome, Ally. I am excited about spending the next twenty-four hours with you before you leave me again tomorrow. Now, first things first. We cannot have you appearing so unkempt during the executions and sacrifices this afternoon. Step into the next room, where you will find a change of clothes. Please get changed and rejoin me here in ten minutes. We must not be late, and the time approaches." He removed the restraints and gently nudged her forward.

He sounded as charming as ever, but his evil voice was unmistakable. The voice was not his. It was the dragon's voice she had heard so much about. The man had always been evil, but now the *evil one* possessed him. She recognized that, but the world was blind to it.

She stood at the entrance to the room, knowing it was the Holy of Holies, signifying the dwelling place of God. How could she enter that place? She hesitated. Messai had already defiled the room by entering where only the Jewish High Priest was previously allowed, and then only once a year.

She pulled the curtain open enough to walk through. Of course. There hung the sharp blue business suit she wore when she worked for him. She should have expected that. The room was dimly lit, making her a little more comfortable changing clothes, fearing Messai would walk in. Ten minutes had almost passed, so she changed quickly, gathered herself, and walked back into the Most Holy Place. *This is God's temple, not Aissa Messai's office*, she reminded herself.

"You look stunning, my dear, despite your disheveled appearance. Please let down your hair and fluff it so you appear more businesslike. The ponytail does not befit one who previously served in such a prestigious position. There is a full-length mirror beside the bookshelf on the right. Please hurry. The ceremony begins soon."

Ally obliged, taking down the ponytail and running her fingers through her hair until it looked quite good, if she said so herself. Her mind turned to Anders, imprisoned for the night. She hoped he was okay. She cared deeply for him. The two had become a support base for each other.

"A penny for your thoughts."

"Excuse me?"

"A penny for your thoughts. Those were my words to you when you first came into my office and I prepared to introduce you to the world. You responded the same that day. I will reintroduce you today. What a shame this must end differently. Let's go, my dear. The ceremony is about to begin."

How could he call beheadings a ceremony? What kind of monster could celebrate the slaughter of fellow human beings? The door opened, and he led her outside onto the porch where he lifted his hands to call for silence. That a mass of people would gather to watch such a gruesome event was unimaginable. Members of AMPP led the prisoners to the guillotine where the executioner awaited them.

First in line were Orthodox Jewish couples. She had not even considered that, thinking all condemned people would be believers. Sudden heartbreak hit her like a tidal wave, realizing those people would die without Jesus. If they had believed in him, they would be in Petra with Ben and the other 144,000 Jewish followers of Jesus. They had refused the mark and must surely despise Messai for violating his covenant with their people and defiling their temple.

Messai made another statement about peace and prosperity, and *blah, blah, blah,* Ally thought, tuning him out, thinking about the believers who would die a martyr's death. They faced the device boldly, almost joyfully. People celebrating this and cheering the executioner revealed the depravity that defined Messai's *New World Order.*

The Jews walked defiantly, fighting against the men who dragged them along. They still sought a conquering messiah who would deliver them from the evil world system that enslaved them. If only they realized Jesus was their deliverer who brought true freedom. Ally had experienced his freedom and wished it for them, but they rejected him. She turned her head as the first knelt, hands bound behind her back and her head secured below the razor-sharp blade.

Messai squeezed her arm, causing her to flinch from the pain. "No, Ally, you must watch. Look and see what you will experience tomorrow." He squeezed harder, forcing her to stare at the gruesome scene about to unfold beneath them, then signaled the executioner.

Ally thought she would throw up when she watched the blade hit its mark. She instinctively jerked her head backwards, and her entire body tensed up. Only she heard Messai's quiet, evil laughter. So sinister... wicked. "That will be you tomorrow, Ally. Think about that." He did not loosen his grip until the executions and sacrifices ended and she had watched every single one.

A call from Blake informed Bruno about what just happened at the temple. His anger flared. It awakened something in Magnus, and he sat straight up.

"Wait! I just realized where Messai is taking her! He told me if he ever caught her, they would return to the King David so he could finish what he started. Why hadn't I thought of that?"

That was all Bruno needed. "Let's go! It's already 4:00! We need to get there early and figure something out!"

"I have a plan!" Ollie spoke so loud he scared them half to death, his voice echoing across the back of the truck. "Tell the driver to stop."

Bruno pounded on the truck's rear window, and the driver slowed. He stopped when he found a safe place and joined them in the back. Ollie talked fast.

"I need a Wolf, or anything indestructible that can haul a few passengers, survive a crash, and drive away."

"We have been on duty in Jerusalem many times," one Israeli said. "I know where they park the vehicles. There is usually a Wolf or two there, but how do you plan to take one?"

"Just get me there and leave that to me."

"And me!" said Magnus. "If Ollie can't start it, I promise you I can!"

"Now, the rest of the plan. I know the route Messai's limo driver will take from the temple to the King David. I have driven it many times. There is no other sensible route. However, in case I am wrong, you will watch for them to leave, then follow behind and keep me informed."

"I will park on a side street and wait for them to drive by. Tell me when they are close, and I will race through the intersection and ram the limo broadside at full speed."

"Let one of us handle that part, Mr. Barton." The words came from an American soldier. "You don't need to kill yourself."

"Or Ally!" said Bruno. "I will not let you kill her by being reckless."

"Do you have a better idea? We either do something now, or Messai has his way with her in a hotel room tonight, then beheads her tomorrow."

That silenced Bruno. He did not want his daughter to suffer, then watch her die in the guillotine.

"Okay, now, I'm glad you military people brought weapons, because I need you next. When the crash happens, four of you, one for each door, get to the limo the second it stops moving. If AMPP's men are inside, take them out, and take the driver out, if he survives the crash. I will hit them broadside right in his door and avoid the rear door to protect Ally. You can't kill Messai, so knock him out cold, then grab Ally, and jump in with me."

"Hopefully, my vehicle will still run and drive. We will speed down a side street one block up and park in an alley. You know the city as well as I do," he said, pointing at the IDF driver, "so you understand where I want you to pick us up. We will abandon our vehicle and get away with you. No one should suspect an IDF truck driving out of Jerusalem."

They looked at Ollie in disbelief until Magnus spoke.

"Wow. Did you just come up with that off the top of your head?"

Amelia chuckled. "It's what he does, Magnus. Trust me, my man is a genius and master of escape."

"Okay, we made plans; now it's time to find your vehicle," said the driver.

"Wait, there's one more thing we have to do: rescue the others too. Ally will know where they are being held. If she can get us back there, we'll also need a plan for that. Any suggestions?"

"Let's focus on Ally for now and decide that later. We need to get my daughter away from Messai first, then we can go after the others."

"I agree, Bruno. Driver, let's go find my automobile."

•　　　•　　　•　　　•　　　•

Michael paced the ground on top of a mountain he and Hadassah enjoyed climbing. The view was amazing. But at this moment, the view was the last thing on his mind.

"He forbids me from interfering, Hadassah. How can I stand by and watch them die?"

"Michael, don't even think about disobeying orders. You have been the chief warrior angel long enough to know better."

"Yeah, like *forever*. But this is hard. Yahweh has always sent me into battle and allowed me to protect his people. Why not now? Such little time remains. It seems a small thing to ask."

She grew quiet and somber. "Do you know something we don't?"

"You won't tell, will you? I must never give away confidential information."

"You don't have to tell me, if you don't want to. But if you do, I'm listening, and you *can* trust me, remember?"

"Messai captured Anders, Ally, Omar, Ahmad and Hala. He will execute them tomorrow."

"No!"

"Believe me, I want to save them, but Yahweh won't let me. It would be so easy. I would swoop in there, slug a few demons, knock Messai out, and set them free. Why won't he let me do that?"

She put her arm around his shoulder, sensing his pain. The mighty warrior angel would never cry, but she understood this was breaking his heart. *How long, Lord?* She knew the answer... three more years. *That will feel like eternity.* She realized how ridiculous that thought was.

• • • • • • •

The group passed two areas where IDF personnel parked when they went into the Old City. They saw Wolfs parked at both, but soldiers stood around talking, preventing them from taking one. The third location hit the jackpot. Two soldiers walked to the armored vehicle, covering for Ollie walking behind them. He quickly hot-wired the Wolf and drove away. The others ran back to the truck and left unseen.

They stopped at a place where they could watch for Messai's limo to leave, but had not yet shut the engine off when Magnus saw it.

"There he goes!"

"Not yet!" shouted Bruno. "Ollie hasn't had time to get there!"

Magnus pulled his phone from his pocket and hit Ollie's number immediately.

"Ollie, they're headed your way!"

"They already left? I'm nowhere near my street!"

"We're following them, so I'll keep you updated. But if you don't hurry, they will pass the intersection before you make it!"

"It takes less than ten minutes to get to the hotel. I don't think I can get there in time!"

Ollie stopped talking and drove like a madman, weaving through side streets and praying no Jerusalem police officers would notice him. He turned onto his street on two wheels and saw it was clear. He took a moment to thank Jesus, then yelled into his phone, "I'm here!"

"They're two lights away and stopped. Traffic is heavy, so this will require precision timing! We just dropped off the soldiers and will circle around to the street beside your alley right after we tell you to go. Everything is ready on our end. One light away. It just turned green. Okay... go!"

Ollie glimpsed the limo to his right and floored the Wolf. He braced himself for impact, sped into the intersection, and slammed into the limo full force. The big car spun sideways, striking other cars around it. Screams and horns filled the air, creating havoc.

The soldiers arrived promptly and found the driver unconscious. One AMPP man rode up front, and one sat with Ally and Messai in the back. Unheard shots amidst the pandemonium killed both instantly. A gunstock knocked Messai out cold. Ally was in shock. One soldier dragged the dead AMPP man from the rear seat and pulled her out. He carried her and raced for the Wolf.

The impact dazed Ollie, but he backed the armored vehicle away from the limo and turned it around, ready to speed back down the one-way street he had just come from. This was no time to worry about driving the wrong way on a one-way street. Ally and the soldiers were in the vehicle, and Ollie was fleeing the scene before anyone realized what had happened.

The entire sequence lasted one minute. Less than two minutes later, they abandoned the Wolf, leapt into the truck and fled the scene. They passed along several small streets before reentering the main drag, nothing more than an ordinary IDF truck driving through Jerusalem, seemingly unaware an accident had occurred nearby.

Ally was alert now, but still shaken. Bruno held her, crying and thanking Jesus. But another important rescue must happen now, and they had no time to lose.

"Ally, can you tell us where they are holding the others?" Ollie asked.

"They're in Messai's basement," she said. Her words were soft, but audible.

Bruno pounded on the rear window again, and the driver pulled over. Ollie ran to his window.

"Messai's house. Do you know where that is?"

"Yes! Get in!"

"How long will it take to get there?"

"Five minutes. I will park in the back where no one will see me. Cross two lots and scale a fence to reach the rear entrance. It will be heavily guarded."

"Get us there, and we will handle the rest."

Ollie jumped back into the truck, and in five minutes he, Bruno, Magnus, and three American soldiers leapt back out and sprinted toward the enormous house.

"Remember, this is my time to shine again," said Bruno as they ran.

"We can't leave witnesses, so everyone there must die," said Magnus.

They reached the property, scaled the fence, and landed on the back lawn where a man stood guard. Bruno took him out with one punch. They burst through the door and saw four more guards gathered in the living room. The soldiers dropped to a knee and fired, killing them all. The sound of shots brought the remaining guard charging through the front door. Bruno seized him when he entered, pulled one arm behind his back and placed him in a choke hold.

"Unless you want to join them right now, give me the key to the basement."

The man resisted, but the arm around his neck cut off his oxygen supply. He took a key from his pocket and held it up. Magnus snatched it out of his hand and rushed toward a door he assumed led below. But those steps led upstairs, not to the basement.

"In here!" said Ollie from the next room.

Magnus hurried to him, shoved the key in the lock and turned it. Bingo! The four captives sprinted up the stairs, and Ollie led them toward the back door. Bruno threw the guard to the floor, where one American finished him, then followed the others on a mad dash to the waiting truck.

When they turned onto Highway 90, heading north toward the Golan Heights, Ollie called Beth's phone to give her the good news. No answer. He tried again and got the same result. Bruno called Mila, and Magnus called Blake. No one answered.

"Something's wrong," said Anders. He called Trey.

"Trey, have you guys talked to Blake or anyone with him?"

"No, but I'm not sure about the others. We haven't spoken to them. Why?"

Anders filled him in, and Trey motioned for someone to call every bunker and make sure.

"No one has talked to them. I'll get a patrol over there right now and check on them. It just got dark, so that will give them cover."

"We'll get there as fast as we can. Call me when you hear something."

Five minutes later Robert and a group of his troops left for the Bedouin camp where Blake and Beth's group stayed. Within fifteen minutes, they parked a half mile away and walked from there. The camp was destroyed when they arrived and everyone was missing. The group retreated fast, in case AMPP was still close by.

Halfway back to their truck, the ground shook from an explosion, and they saw a ball of fire shoot into the sky.

"The truck!"

"Everybody, down!" said Robert.

They sought cover behind rocks and in the high grass. Decades old land mines littered the field, dating back to the 1950s and 60s. Some remained active and posed a deadly threat.

"We can't stay in hiding. Let's move in, locate the enemy and eliminate them."

An AMPP patrol lay in hiding, waiting for them to return. Robert and his men encountered them a hundred meters from the truck. The ensuing firefight wounded two Americans, but they wiped out the entire enemy unit. Robert now felt comfortable calling Trey back to report.

"They're onto us, Trey. They destroyed the Bedouin camp, and we found no one there. I fear they captured all of them. We encountered and eliminated the enemy and will get back there in fifteen minutes. AMPP left us a shiny black SUV to drive. But if they know every one of our locations, we all need to pack up and move first thing tomorrow morning! I doubt they will attack tonight. Messai won't miss this bunch before then."

"But we must find Blake's group! Since you didn't find them there and AMPP didn't have them, they must be alive!"

"I'm afraid I'll give them away if I call. They may not want to use their phones either. I don't know what else to do. Searching for them out here is like looking for a needle in a haystack."

"Come on back. I'll pull everyone together and try to decide what we should do now. We'll pack everything and get ready to leave by daylight. But we don't know where we're going."

"We have to make a lot of decisions fast, and search for Blake and Beth. I don't understand how we can do that, but we must. Pull some men and women together to meet and decide, and let the others pack. We'll arrive at 2200. Call the other groups. They need to move, too."

Ollie and Amelia, Bruno and Magnus, the American troops, the IDF soldiers, and the singles group got back an hour before Robert's group made it. Everyone there celebrated their safe return, but too much work remained to rejoice long. They thanked Jesus for the rescue and asked him to protect the missing group. Then they packed and planned. Praying, packing, and planning would define this night.

At midnight, as twelve of them continued an all-night prayer vigil, they heard footsteps and voices.

"Quick, down the ladder!"

Before they could move, someone stepped through the door, followed by others. They were overwhelmed with joy when they saw Blake and Beth come in first. Anders, Ally, and Bruno embraced them, Mila, and the boys, crying happy tears.

"You guys are okay!" Blake and Anders said at the same time. Both laughed through their tears and hugged again.

"They found us, and we got out just in time," said Blake. "We hid out in the field and left when they drove away. It took us seven hours to make the hike, but here we are and thankful to be alive."

"I'll tell you our story when we have time. It's a miraculous one! But now we have to help the others pack. All our locations are compromised, so we need to move before daylight."

"But where? We have made no concrete decisions about that."

"Then it's time we do. We've talked about that since we got here and listed all the ideas we put on the table. I will call the others right now so we can decide and be ready."

Minutes later Blake's and Anders' groups sat with Trey, Rickie, Robert, Paul, Bradley, and Brita charting their course of action.

"Caves in the desert are our best option," said Anders. "Ein Gedi was perfect."

"But they found you," said Bruno. "I don't think captured equals perfect."

"We stayed together in that one spot and one cave. If we had thought it through, living in different caves made more sense. Splitting up may have meant not getting caught."

"I get what you're saying, Anders," Blake said. "There are thousands of caves in the desert. AMPP would have a tough time searching them all and finding us. Even if they found one group, the rest of us would survive."

"I thought about a place where we can all stay temporarily while we decide where we're going next, and it's right under their noses. We can even go scouting caves from there."

"That sounds dangerous to me, Ollie," said Beth. "We should get as far away as possible."

"Hear me out. Many people visited this abandoned village through the years, but after the recent earthquake, the government closed it and made it illegal to go there. It has everything we need."

"You're talking about Lifta, aren't you?" asked Robert. "I hiked there with some troops once. I like it! Can we get in?"

"I know how to get in. We need to get there before daylight, which means we must leave here by 3:00 a.m. Omar, Ahmad, and Hala, you need to drive. All of us will fit in the backs of the trucks. You three can get through checkpoints, being Palestinian, and having your fake cards to prove your Israeli citizenship."

"What if they search our trucks at the checkpoints? They will see you guys." Omar wanted to have every detail covered to keep them from being discovered.

"We can lie on the floor and pile blankets and clothes over us. Then throw pots, pans, and any light stuff on that, and put large items in the back of the truck. They may find us, but they'll have to work hard if they do."

"Ollie, you have a way of coming up with plans when we need them," said Magnus. "I trust you. Get the trucks and let's load up. Blake, call John and tell him to meet us there. Ollie or Robert can give him directions."

Decision made, they loaded up and cleaned the bunkers so no one could tell they had been there. The Jordanians drove as they left the Golan for their temporary home just outside Jerusalem.

CHAPTER 19

Aissa Messai refused medical care, instead demanding they transport him to his Jerusalem mansion. There he discovered the patrol he posted to guard the prisoners shot dead by the rescuers, then later received word that his troop was gunned down on the Golan. Losing his men, plus Ally and the others escaping, infuriated him. He called his security director and ordered an all-out search for the Smyrnians and their followers, plus ensuring apprehensions and beheadings every day.

Most Jews took the mark, but those who did not were easy targets. Believers around the world were more difficult to apprehend, but AMPP's efforts often proved successful despite the rebels' attempts to elude capture. They searched records containing the names of those who refused to take the mark and worship him. They could only run and hide so long. His men would find them, and he would rid the world of them. Then he would defeat the other messiah and reign forever!

Messai was determined to sit in his office the next day and address the world via live broadcast, despite his injuries. He planned same-day executions of heretics from that point on, but more sinister plans formed in his mind. None would escape after this; he guaranteed that.

Smyrnian leaders topped the list. They moved about, but capturing them was only a matter of time. Their affinity for hiding underground told him where they must begin the search. The southern desert's rock cliffs abounded with caves. He would offer seven-figure rewards for information leading to their capture. Someone would rat them out for that kind of money. He would also present a challenge he hoped the Smyrnians could not ignore.

•   •   •   •   •

The groups reached Lifta before the sun rose and found their way inside. Ollie told the truth; the place was perfect. They unloaded just the necessities because they hoped to only stay a short while. Tomorrow groups would search the desert for caves where they might live, but now, they needed to secure an internet connection to watch for an announcement from Messai. After the events of yesterday, they knew one would come. Blake gathered his group for the big moment.

"Okay, here we go!"

Messai sat behind his desk at 8:00 a.m., his injuries from yesterday's collision clearly visible, yet portraying total control and his voice sounding villainous.

"Ladies and gentlemen, I have three things to say, and I will make them quick. First, you may have heard the Smyrnians rammed my limousine yesterday afternoon, killing my driver and two fine AMPP men, then viciously attacked me. I am thankful to have survived, however they managed to whisk away Ally Fromm who we planned to execute today. Then they helped the others escape and brutally murdered six more AMPP personnel."

"We must remove these rebels, or peace and prosperity can never come. So, second, I am offering a reward of one million-dollars per Smyrnian for tips which lead to their arrest and execution. Use your imagination to understand what that would mean for your family. This doesn't include their followers; only the Smyrnians themselves. We will post pictures worldwide and share them online, so you can easily recognize them."

"Third, for every day those anarchists refuse to turn themselves in, one of every three executions will now occur by burning alive on the altar, instead of beheading. Caiaphas will cast lots to determine which captives face that death. If the Smyrnians are watching right now, understand you bear the responsibility for those executions by failing to surrender. Do you care enough about your devotees to stop that? That seems unlikely because it appears you only care about yourselves."

"That is all for today. I call on everyone to help us bring the rebels to justice so the rest of us can experience peace and prosperity forever! Every execution moves us closer to that goal. Remember, you kill snakes by removing their heads. The Smyrnians are vipers whose poison has spread across the globe. Removing them ensures victory for our cause. Let us begin today!"

"Is he serious?" asked John. "Surely he will not stoop that low."

"He is dead serious," said Magnus. "Remember who you are talking about."

"How can we stand back and allow that to happen? We must stop him!"

"We can't do that, John," said Blake. "Messai is the Antichrist who can't be stopped until Jesus stops him, but we need to ramp up our efforts to save others. How can we do that?"

"I told you, Blake, we pilots are ready to fly! Contact the leaders around the world and ask where our help is most needed, and we will take off." Trey knew he spoke for every pilot.

"How do you plan to do that? You can't fly from any airport or military base, and I am guessing your planes at Ben Gurion are confiscated. Not to mention that we have no way to purchase jet fuel. We may be out of options for missions outside Israel."

"Maybe we should turn ourselves in to protect others," Beth said softly. The others looked at her in shock at her suggestion. But each of them was considering it, too.

"No," said Anders, speaking more boldly than usual for the soft-spoken cameraman. "We stay and fight. The scroll said we are warriors who must battle Messai until Jesus returns. He may kill us, but we will fight him as long as we live."

"Then we will fight. Strap on your sword and prepare for battle!"

"You are right about strapping on our swords, Blake, but swords refer not to literal swords. They refer to the Bible. We must speak the Word of the Lord, the truths of scripture. Hebrews Chapter 4, verse 12 says, *the word of God is alive and active... sharper than any double-edged sword.*"

They stared at Anders, knowing he was right. The man's words seemed to come directly from Jesus. And why not? He spent time with him in heaven and heard his voice, then ate the scroll. They would proclaim God's Word aloud from this moment forward during their remaining time on earth. Those words touched them, but his next words shocked them.

"Now, I have a request. Ally, will you come and stand beside me?"

She walked to his side and took his hand while their friends wondered what was going on. None of them could have guessed what he would say next.

"Ally and I want to become husband and wife. Right before Jesus sent me back to earth, Angie said something to me I couldn't understand. But I knew Jesus would tell me when the time was right. Now I know: *Marry Ally.* Angie told me to marry her and take care of her for the last three-and-a-half years. We are both ready."

"Yes, we are," Ally said with a smile. "I fell spiritually in love with Anders when he talked after he returned from heaven."

They nodded, remembering her look when he spoke, but didn't realize what it meant until now.

"We love each other in Jesus," she continued. "That love has grown, and we want to obey Jesus and do what he says."

"So, we have a wedding to perform! Congratulations, partner! I am happy for both of you!"

Beth ran to hug Ally. "We have the perfect place for a wedding right here by the spring in Lifta. We can gather around the pool or stand above it where everyone can see. It's going to be beautiful!"

"No," Anders said again.

"You're making a habit of saying that, partner. Why not here? I agree with Beth. It's perfect."

"We're going to Banias with a few of us and a dozen American soldiers to protect us."

"Banias?" asked Magnus. "That place is the domain of evil. Messai went there to meet the dragon and returned every time even more wicked and vicious than before. Please don't go to Banias."

"That's where we're supposed to get married. Events of the final three-and-a-half years flew through my mind like a high-speed time-lapse video when the scroll hit my stomach. I couldn't make them out. But now, when the time comes, each scene pops up, and I see it clearly."

"In this one, Ally and I were at Banias with a group of people, including some of you. We stood in a large niche in the mountainside with you in front of us and soldiers around the perimeter while we said our vows. We're invading the dragon's domain by performing a wedding in Banias!"

"It's too dangerous!" Magnus said. "How many of you know about Banias?"

Several raised their hands, but Ollie was the only one who spoke.

"I've been there," he said, more softly and with less enthusiasm than his usual tone. "It was once a center of pagan worship and idolatry, but now it's deserted. No one goes there. My crew and I went to film a documentary, despite being warned not to go. Something was there, something sinister and evil. We couldn't see it, but we recognized it. It was a hot summer day, but the temperature suddenly plummeted and we broke out in goosebumps, shaking all over."

"We have all experienced that," said Beth, "and we understand who it comes from: Messai."

"Our crew ran. We loaded in the van and drove miles before things changed. The only words to explain that encounter are *pure evil.* I agree with Magnus. Please stay here and don't go to Banias."

"Ally and I will go even if none of you want to go. We want you there, but we can do the wedding by ourselves. Both of us will understand your decision, and we will still like you," he said, smiling.

"Beth and I will go with you. I think only a select group should go. It will be dangerous because AMPP is searching for us everywhere and may think we're still somewhere in the Golan."

"I wouldn't intentionally lead you into danger. That's why I give you the freedom to stay here."

"I understand why we're supposed to go there," said Ally as they looked at her, waiting for an answer. "This wedding and location will send a message to Messai and the dragon that we have invaded their territory and are not afraid of them. We will take pictures and show them to the world. Blake, can you hack into the networks again?"

"I can, but that's a crazy idea, Ally. It's asking for trouble."

"She's right," said Anders. "We will leave early tomorrow morning, do the wedding, shoot a video and take pictures, then come back here. We will take an IDF truck, and Omar, Ahmad, or Hala can drive. They look the part more than us, in case we get stopped. Who's in? Please, only go if you are comfortable doing so. Some should stay back so there is no chance of us all being captured."

They set the limit at twenty-five, made up of twelve American soldiers, three Jordanians, Anders and Ally, and eight others. They spent the rest of the day choosing their separate living quarters in Lifta, and would sleep that night, before leaving the next morning for the center of evil on earth.

•   •   •   •   •

In Petra, Michael and Hadassah hiked to the top of another mountain they had not visited before. The view was striking, as it was from every vantage point in the Rose Red city. While they sat admiring the scenery, he shocked her with a question she had never considered a possibility.

"I have an important assignment tomorrow morning. Do you want to go with me?"

"What? You mean…"

"Yes, Yahweh has invited you to join me and the heavenly host on this one. Are you in?"

"Yes! But how can *I* go with *you?*"

"Hadassah, the spirit of your biblical namesake lives inside you. You are the modern-day Esther during the Tribulation. You know the Old Testament well. Have you not wondered why your parents died and your Uncle Mordecai raised you? Or how you brought him to faith in Jesus, and Yahweh used him to save the Jews? Yahweh brought you to himself *for such a time as this.*"

"That has bothered me ever since Ben said it. If I am Esther, why was I raised by my *Uncle* Mordecai instead of a *cousin* named Mordecai? How can I be her? Besides, I don't feel like Esther most of the time."

"Yahweh chose your uncle for a purpose, which you have watched unfold. He played a huge role in saving the 144,000 Jews. Doesn't he have a son who grew up with you?"

She looked more stunned than she was by his earlier question.

"*Mordechai*. He's older and protected me growing up. Why didn't I think of that?"

Michael smiled. "Some things only make sense to Yahweh. It is time to fulfill your purpose."

She broke into tears and fell to her knees. "Tell me what to do."

"Meet me here tomorrow before daylight, and I will show you. Pray and prepare yourself."

They hiked back down the mountain in silence, an abnormal thing for them; she engrossed in thought, and him allowing her to think. Sleep would not come easily this night, if it came at all.

•   •   •   •   •

Meanwhile, a movement that started over three years earlier following Blake and Beth's Primetime specials became vocal about their faith. Young adults across the globe could not contain their excitement about Jesus. The time had ended for others to join them, but their commitment to the true Messiah remained faithful and enduring. They searched scripture and lived by everything it said, rejecting the world's sinful ways. That put them squarely in the crosshairs of Messai's men.

They walked by their faith with no regard for his warnings. Their boldness led to carelessness, making them easy targets for AMPP. Youthful believers faced the capital punishment device weekly as they openly defied Messai's one-world religion, refusing the mark and rebelling against bowing to him. Their expressive joy angered him so much he put bounties on their heads.

They reserved their worship for the ultimate concert before the throne in heaven. There they would join all the saints and all of creation praising God and the Lamb, while the beast of hell waged war against the believers remaining on earth. It seemed they could hardly wait to get there, and Aissa Messai was unknowingly helping them go.

The Smyrnians tuned in for the preliminary activities prior to the 3:00 p.m. executions that afternoon. They would not watch the executions, but wanted to know if Messai followed through on his threat. Each was glued to a phone or tablet when Messai appeared on screen and spoke.

"Thank you for tuning in to celebrate with us again as we rid the world of more rebels who fight against our dreams for peace and prosperity. I understand why many do not watch, because of the gruesome nature of these events. As you know, I now only speak before executions occasionally. But today is a special day when we show the Smyrnians how serious I am about their insurrection."

"If they surrender, the extreme measure you witness today will stop immediately. But each day they refuse, the live cremations will continue. To Smyrnians who are watching, I say again, the fault for the torturous deaths you will see today lies with you. Only you can stop them. Caiaphas, are you prepared to do your job?"

"Yes, Your Majesty. I am ready and excited!" The man beamed toward the camera, enjoying the notoriety that came with his position and power.

"Bring out the prisoners."

All were from the youth movement, appearing to range from eighteen to twenty-five years old. They were divided into two groups, men and women. Caiaphas cast lots to determine one from each group who would die on the altar, instead of the guillotine. Each one refused the attempts of AMPP to drag them away, instead walking boldly, with heads held high and singing. Their combined voices rang out a crescendo of praise to Jesus, declaring his name for all to hear.

"Silence them!" screamed Messai, standing above the unfolding scene. But nothing could stop their glorious voices, their rapturous faces revealing the joy they felt inside.

The two chosen to die by burning broke free from their captors and ran to the altar, sprinted up the steps, and lay side-by-side on the wood.

"I can't watch," Blake said, closing the news app.

"Wait, Blake, you need to see this!"

"I can't do it, partner," Blake said. "Messai has gone too far with this one!"

"Quick, turn it back on!"

Blake obeyed, he and Beth huddled closely looking at his tablet, their eyes filled with tears. Every believer in Lifta, and most around the world, watched in silence, before breaking out in praise and applause at what they saw.

For dramatic effect, the altar no longer burned continuously. Caiaphas splashed flammable liquid on the wood and on the two young believers lying on it. They continued singing, the others standing by the guillotine completing the choir. The cameras left Messai so people would not notice his anger.

Caiaphas lifted his hands, and fire fell from above, igniting the wood. The flames exploded upward, as the singing continued. The High Priest stood staring at the inferno before him, finally turning and running down the steps, his face red from the searing heat.

Cameras zoomed in on the pair lying there, untouched by the fire, singing praises, and proclaiming the name of Jesus. Through the thick flames, a figure appeared. Hands bound, the two young believers sat up, turned, and bowed before him. He touched their heads, removed their bonds, stretched out his hands and brought them down slowly, extinguishing the fire, then disappeared.

A shout of praise echoed throughout Lifta. The entire world seemed to quake as the host of Jesus' followers broke out in exultation. Blake and Beth grabbed each other and embraced. Others joined the celebration that should have been audible miles away, but remained silent outside their temporary home.

The two ran to join their comrades standing in line by the capital punishment device. When they did, the Smyrnians and their fellow believers closed their phones and tablets and prayed for them, also praising their Messiah for what they witnessed.

Messai summoned his government officials and religious leaders to separate meetings the next day where each would discuss speeding up their time frame for world domination. Both groups would play significant roles in very different ways. He would also inform them that the one remaining group who had held out would join them soon. Their presence would change everything.

• • • • •

Hadassah climbed the mountain at 4:00 a.m., filled with a mixture of excitement and apprehension. She was thankful for the continuous daylight that allowed her to see at this time of the morning. Michael would be there waiting for her. She reached the peak and gazed at the beautiful landscape spread out before her. Standing at the cliff's edge, a voice startled her from behind, causing her to jump, fearing she may fall to her death.

"You made it! I thought you might chicken out on me. Don't worry, I would have swooped down and caught you just before you hit the ground."

"Michael, you have a habit of doing that to me. Stop laughing!" she said, as he stood chuckling at her. "Sometimes you act more like a kid than an archangel."

"That shouldn't surprise you. Yahweh allows me to go back-and-forth between the spiritual and physical realms. When I'm here, I feel and think like humans do, but I still know about happenings in the spirit world. It's a pretty cool thing! How's that for sounding human?"

"Well, I am thankful Yahweh sent you and allowed me to be your friend. But I must tell you, I'm anxious about what will happen today."

"Yahweh understands that, and so do I. Now, you don't need to overthink it, and we can't afford to be late. So, I say, let's go!"

She wanted to chide him for such an attempt at outdated human lingo, but he grabbed her by the hand before she could get the words out.

"Wait, Michael, I'm not ready!"

It was too late. Her feet left the ground, and she found herself aloft, soaring higher and higher as they flew. Something changed inside her, but she could not tell what it was. A sensation crept through her body and entered her brain. Her mind floated between time periods.

She saw a man wearing an IDF officer's uniform and recognized him: Uncle Mordecai. A second man stood beside him, clothed in a Persian robe with a turban on his head. They looked identical, twins, maybe? No, she recognized the other as her cousin. What was happening?

Xerxes! He stood ahead, beckoning her toward him, the powerful king of Persia. Her people called him Ahasuerus, but he was Xerxes, her husband. *Where is Michael? I can't lose sight of him!* Ben, Uncle Mordecai, Xerxes, Cousin Mordechai, Blake, Beth. She blinked her eyes and shook her head, trying to clear her mind so things would return to normal.

"Are you coming, or have you changed your mind?"

"No, wait, I'm coming! It's just that, something's happening to me I don't understand."

He slowed and waited for her, grinning with a look that showed he knew.

"Come on, Hadassah, we don't have time to waste. Or should I call you Esther? Hmm..."

"I am her, Michael! Why did Yahweh not show me until now?"

"He is opening your mind to the truth. You will understand more as this day unfolds. Come, we are here."

"What is this place? It feels evil. Why would you bring me here? I was expecting..."

"Heaven? You cannot experience it yet because we have much work left to do on earth before these final years end. Follow me, and I will introduce you to a band you need to meet."

• • • • •

With Omar driving and Ahmad and Hala in the front seat, the truck arrived in Banias. In the back rode Anders and Ally, Blake and Beth, Trey, Rickie, Bruno, Magnus, Ollie, and Amelia, plus a dozen soldiers along for protection. There was no room for more, so it forced some to stay behind.

Cool, dank air greeted them as they stepped from the vehicle. Low-hanging gray clouds hovered over the place, while wind-blown limbs in dead trees clanked together, adding an eerie sound to the already formidable environment. Water flowing from the mountain, once clean and clear, was now dark and foreboding. The place would drive terror into the strongest hearts.

"We should leave," Ollie said quietly. "I understand you want to get married here, but let wisdom prevail, and let's go before something bad happens."

The wind emanated from the cave above them. Magnus pointed to the opening without saying a word. Clearly visible to their eyes, evil spirits floated in and out, moaning and crying as they did.

"There," Anders said, nodding toward the flat area to the right of the cave. "Ally and I will stand inside the large niche carved into the mountainside. Follow me."

"You're out of your mind," said Ollie. "This place is just as I remember, and we need to go, now!"

"You're right, Ollie," Ally said. "Anders is out of *his* mind, but he has the mind of Jesus. 1 am ready, Anders," she said again, joining her groom, facing the haunt of demons head on.

Anders started walking and crying out in a loud voice that took them all by surprise. His words reverberated off the rocky mountainside through the surrounding area.

"How can anyone enter the strong man's house and plunder it unless he first binds the strong man? 1 bind you, dragon and your horde of demons, in the name of Jesus, the true Messiah! You are the strong man of this place, but Jesus is more powerful than you! 1 invade your domain in his name!"

The air became heavy, making it difficult to breathe. Still, Anders pressed on. The group followed, gasping for oxygen and pressing hard against an immovable force.

"We have to turn back! Messai has set a trap for us and will capture us all. Please turn back!"

"No, Ollie," said Beth. "Anders and Ally are certain this is where they are supposed to marry, so we will go with them as one. No man or woman left behind!"

Trey and Rickie agreed with that, so being outnumbered, Ollie had no choice but to follow. Amelia grabbed his arm and made sure he did. They fought more than the wind. A powerful force held them back, making walking impossible.

"Hadassah, allow me to introduce you to the heavenly host!" said Michael with a wave of his hand.

Suddenly, a multitude of angelic beings surrounded them, carrying gleaming swords in their hands. The host bowed their heads toward the girl in unison, then circled the entire perimeter of Banias ready for battle. Hadassah, *or Esther*, stood speechless at what she saw. Then she looked down at the struggling Smyrnians below.

"Michael, they need our help!"

"Yes, it seems they do. Are you ready, host?"

The multitude lifted their swords and stood shoulder-to-shoulder, leaving no room for intruders.

"Michael!" Hadassah screamed.

Two massive, grotesque beasts appeared over the mountain, followed by a horde of hideous demonic beings.

"Beelzebub and Belial! To the battle, host! Hadassah, go to Anders and Ally and urge them on. They must not stop or we will lose the battle. You did not realize we fought for you in Persia, and the Jews were saved. Because of that, Yahweh's mission of sending Jesus did not fail. Now it is your turn to fight for the Smyrnians. Go!"

This time, she did not hesitate. Swooping down, she landed in front of the couple, who pushed forward, trying to walk.

"Anders! Ally! It's me, Hadassah! Come on, you must not stop! I will help you get there!"

They continued the struggle, not replying or acknowledging her presence. Of course, they could not see her! She was now the invisible force fighting on their behalf. She faced them, screaming encouragement and making slow progress, when it suddenly felt like her back slammed into a wall. Their movement stopped. Hadassah knew the host fought above them, but would they be too late?

The wind increased, carrying a sickening sulfuric odor. She gagged and could tell she was growing weak, hearing the battle raging overhead. The host would not quit. Neither would she give up the fight below. Suddenly, she stumbled backward and fell. A halo formed overhead, with brilliant sunshine pouring through. The temperature warmed, the gray clouds disappeared, and the water turned crystal clear, with whitecaps gushing over the rocks. Leaves covered the tree branches, and flowers sprang up along the slopes. She knew Michael and the host had prevailed.

"I told you!" said Anders. "Now, who's with me? Let's get up there and have a wedding!"

They climbed the hill and gathered on the stone floor where a pagan temple once stood and a pagan god was once worshiped. Twelve American soldiers stood guard around the perimeter, but their help was not needed. The happy couple stepped into the niche, as the others stood in front of them. They said their vows, and Blake pronounced them husband and wife as Beth videoed the ceremony and Amelia took pictures. Those were sure to go viral the minute the world saw them.

When they kissed, far above them, Evan and Angie celebrated. They understood Anders and Ally would need each other for the next three years. The couple shared something far greater than physical love. Theirs was a spiritual bond that bound them together in Jesus. The group spent the entire day enjoying a brief respite in the safety of divine protection.

Michael and Hadassah sat on ruins of the former temple that surrounded the site, enjoying the event. When it ended, both clapped, understanding their applause was silent to the others.

"What do you think of your first battle, Hadassah?"

"I never want to miss another one. I now realize what you have gone through for us."

"Now, back to Petra and let these people relax and have a little fun. They won't get this opportunity again. Besides, we can't have Ben and your uncle missing us, now can we," he said with a grin.

Away they flew back to the desert, to 144,000 true Messianic Jews who claimed Jesus as their Messiah and lived there protected by him until his second coming.

•   •   •   •   •

Aissa Messai sat at the large conference table in his office, joined by the leaders of his *New World Order*. The remaining seven government leaders were joined by the presidents of China, Russia, and North Korea. This was a new day, the beginning of the end for all who refused to join them.

"Thank you, gentlemen, for your commitment to our cause. The time has come to seize complete control of the world. The powers who have joined us today bring the firepower to accomplish that. Combined with our current efforts, we should achieve that goal quickly and decisively."

"The *New World Order* has already helped us make great strides toward worldwide unity. We are unified around common goals and ideals we seek to achieve. The masses now believe ultimate peace and prosperity are possible. And they will do whatever it takes to make them happen."

"But we cannot achieve such a lofty goal without enforcement. AMPP does a wonderful job enforcing our new laws, namely the mark and worship decree. The capital punishment device serves as a constant reminder against continuing in rebellion. However, our people here can no longer handle the vast number of executions that AMPP brings to us. Please share your suggestions for how we can better expedite the process."

"Well, sir," said the President of Syria, "perhaps you should place a device in each country."

"I agree," said the man from Egypt. "Locate the device in each capital city."

The Iranian recognized his position of influence among the others. He was a member of the original coalition and considered himself a personal friend of Aissa Messai who promised to reward him for his superior efforts organizing this group.

"Mr. Messai, if I may..."

"Of course, you may, my friend. Your suggestions always have great value."

Pride was obvious in the man's smile and his words as he spoke. "You possess records listing the names of every person who has taken the mark, and those who have not. I suggest you place devices in each country based on the number of people who have refused the mark. Your men can still bring more high-profile captives here for execution."

"Excellent plan!" Messai turned to his assistant with orders to set the plan in motion immediately. "Check records, then contact the leaders of every country. We must implement this within a week."

"Mr. Messai, your men from east and north of this country have discussed ways we may help the cause. Our greatest strength is our military might. There is no doubt the capital punishment device has served well to destroy insurgents and deter others from following them. While eliminating individual rebels, families, and small pockets of the resistance, has proven effective, it seems removing large pockets in mass casualties will advance the process more rapidly. We offer our surveillance to locate these groups, then our air power and ground troops to extinguish them."

"Thank you China, North Korea, and Russia for your pledge. We welcome your offer. We must use all means necessary to rid the world of these people as quickly as we can."

"To you men from the nations surrounding Israel, including our friend from Iraq, I remind you we share a common bond, a hatred for the Jews. While that holds true for all of us, it especially applies to the Middle Eastern countries. Our task is to plan one great last battle where we will annihilate those people who mistakenly believe this land belongs to them.

We know it was given to Abraham, father of Ishmael, who is our forefather."

The others frowned at his statement. Though China and Russia recognized certain religions, these leaders clung to Marxism, referring to religion as *the opium of the people*. North Korea was officially an atheist state, viewing religion as an existential threat to the nation. The mention of Islamic doctrine gave them pause about this group. Messai noticed their concern and addressed it.

"We now recognize that this land, and the entire world, belongs to all of us who have united to form a new one-world religion. Together we will conquer the world and rule as one!"

That satisfied the men who responded by leading a cheer of approval. The meeting continued with plans made to wipe out the resistance and a timeline for setting them in motion. It concluded with excitement from leaders of the *New World Order* who would soon rule the world. For Messai, it was straight from one meeting to another. The next one was just as important. But first, he took a break for the afternoon executions and a quick snack. Then he was back at work by 3:30.

CHAPTER 20

In Lifta, those who stayed behind busied themselves working to create space for temporary housing in the ancient stone structures. They tried to keep from thinking about their friends in Banias by occupying their minds. That did not work, so they stopped and prayed for them, asking Jesus to protect their teammates and bless Anders and Ally with a beautiful wedding.

Each passing hour their friends did not return, they became more anxious. They received no word from them and feared the worst. John and Kathie called them all back together and stood side-by-side to encourage them and strengthen their faith.

"We are all concerned about our teammates," John said. "But let's focus on the facts, instead of our fears. The most important fact is this: Anders and Ally were convinced Banias is where they were supposed to get married. He saw it in the scroll, and she agreed with him. Anders has been right about everything since he came back from heaven."

"Fact number two," said Kathie. "Jesus has protected us through some impossible situations since we followed him and formed the Smyrnians. How can we stop trusting him now? I feel sure he is protecting our friends and keeping them safe today, too. But we need to *act* like we believe that!"

"Fact number three," said John. "They have twelve fully armed soldiers with them who are ready for whatever they face. It would take a huge AMPP patrol to defeat them. I trust Jesus, and I also trust the United States Military!"

"Fact number four," Kathie said, taking her turn and changing the mood from serious to not-so-serious. "Ollie and Amelia are with them, and they can wiggle their way out of anything!"

"Okay, we get the idea," said Steve. "Fact number five: Bruno is a beast! He has taken on entire AMPP squads and security patrols all by himself!"

Mila jumped in, getting in on the fun and momentary diversion.

"Fact number six: Magnus and Bruno are partners, and they are both beasts! If AMPP attacks them, it will be both big men's time to shine!" They all chuckled. None of them had witnessed the two gargantuan men in action, but they had listened to stories of their escapades.

The group grew quiet for a moment until Linda broke the silence.

"It wouldn't be right to end this little speech with six things. Jesus loves the number seven. So, here you go. Fact number seven: We will all soon become cave dwellers! Jesus will have to protect us from bats and rats as we lie on our mats wishing we owned cats!"

She got up and walked around like a neanderthal. The others caught on and joined the fun. Soon they were laughing and rolling on the dirt floor, their minds receiving a momentary break from the stress of the day. But it returned within minutes, and they once again joined in prayer.

•   •   •   •   •

Ben and Mordecai walked down the street of Petra and talked about something that had become a common occurrence.

"He left again, Ben, and this time he took Hadassah with him."

"Mordecai, stop worrying about Michael. We both agree there is something special about the boy and said we will stop questioning his reasons for leaving."

"Yes, but now he may put my niece in danger, and I will not allow that."

"Your niece is perfectly capable of taking care of herself. And she has more wisdom and ability than you give her credit for. Lighten up on both of them."

"I can't stand to think of something happening to her. We have taken care of her since her parents were killed. If I am right about our protection, we have it in here, but not out there, correct?"

"That is correct. But what makes you so sure they have put themselves in danger *out there?*"

"Where do you think they are, and what are they doing? I doubt they are out taking a walk in the desert, but wherever they are, the world is evil, and they can't go out and take unnecessary risks."

"How do you know they are out taking unnecessary risks? Mordecai, have you thought about your niece's name?"

"Hadassah? There is nothing unusual about her name. It is a good biblical name, and her namesake was a Jewish hero. Had it not been for her, the Persians would have destroyed our people, and we would not exist today."

"Neither would Jesus have been born, if that had not happened, nor would we celebrate Purim. Everything is about him, Mordecai, don't forget that. Have you noticed anything about her that is uncommon for typical Jewish girls?"

"She received three individual awards for performing heroic feats and made me very proud. I once credited her with saving our country by alerting me to an approaching enemy. Hadassah is a special girl," Mordecai said, his face beaming with pride.

"What if she and Michael are performing a heroic feat today, instead of taking an unnecessary risk?"

The question clearly hit home and left Mordecai in deep reflection. Was there more to his niece than met the eye? No, she was a normal girl, who had lived a good life in his home, then made him proud by her service in the IDF. When Michael brought her home, he would demand answers.

·   ·   ·   ·   ·

Messai entered his office again. Leaders of former world religions now sat around the table, with Caiaphas at the head, clearly priding himself on being in charge of Messai's new one-world religion. The world ruler sat in his plush chair, hiding a secret that brought a twinkle to his eyes.

"Good afternoon, ladies and gentlemen. I am thrilled that all of you have led the adherents of your former religions to join this new worldwide religion that binds us with an unbreakable bond. Prior to today, the entire world had become part of our new worldwide system of worship, with one notable exception." He turned and motioned toward the door.

When the man walked in, flanked on each side by two others dressed in ceremonial robes, the group stared in disbelief. The Catholic Pope and two Cardinals took the seats left vacant for them.

"That's right, the Supreme Pontiff of Roman Catholicism and his hierarchy have recognized the truth and abandoned their former practices to join our movement. Let us welcome them."

Half-hearted applause came from the other attendees, the doubt on their faces evident. Messai continued, seeming not to notice.

"Many followers of this religion vanished in the September 11, 2029 alien invasion of our planet. Most of those who remain will follow their leader and unite with us. Those who refuse will face the same punishment as other rebels if they are captured. All those who live in Vatican City will receive the mark in a televised event from the Apostolic Palace this Friday at 8:00 a.m."

"Before the Pontiff comes to make remarks, I have one more important announcement. During the next thirty days, I will relocate my headquarters to The Vatican and move into the Papal residence inside the Palace. The Pontiff will live in an apartment there, which will be furnished specifically to meet his needs. We will make no changes to other housing arrangements. Smaller gatherings will take place in my meeting room and all administrative work in the Pope's former office."

"However, despite this move, I will continue to maintain this office here in my temple and spend most of my time in Jerusalem. This place has become my home, and I expect to live here forever. You may ask questions or make remarks later, but first, let's hear from our newest member."

The pontiff thanked Messai and made a few general comments. Everyone in the room could tell he meant nothing he said. The world's wealthiest religion could no longer exist or conduct business apart from taking the mark. Their financial support had dwindled, putting the church in crisis mode. After doing everything possible to correct the problem, they finally surrendered to the inevitable and joined Messai's one-world religion and the *New World Order*.

The control exercised by the Vatican and the Holy See had brought kings to their knees before them, but also made those kings and their countries wealthy. Merchants had flourished from selling the church's icons and other popular items. All must now conduct business with Aissa

Messai. Nothing occurred outside his regulations, and the promised prosperity seemed an eternity away.

The hierarchy of the Roman Catholic Church had long perpetrated falsehoods that served their own selfish desires and bore the blood of many saints on their hands. Now the once proud religion became another victim of the Antichrist's evil regime. Payday had come for them.

Caiaphas spoke last. Some around the table dozed as he droned on about Messai choosing him as his prophet and his many accomplishments since assuming the position. His boss sat, wishing his religious leader would stop talking so they could wrap up and dismiss. He finally ended his remarks, and Messai closed the meeting and left for his mansion at 5:15. That meant getting home by 6:00 for the evening news. It also meant watching himself and viewing a few executions.

$$\cdot \qquad \cdot \qquad \cdot \qquad \cdot \qquad \cdot$$

Halfway back to Petra, Michael pulled up and sat on air, with a serious look on his face.

"What are you doing, Michael? We have to get home. If we're late, Ben and my uncle will think something is wrong and send a search party to look for us. This time *I* am with you. They're used to you disappearing like this, but when I'm included, you may have to explain yourself."

He disregarded her statements, as if she had not said them. "Something bad is getting ready to happen, and Yahweh hasn't shown me. Neither will he allow me to interfere."

"But you're his warrior angel. Why would he keep that from you? He let us help them at Banias."

"During these last three-and-a-half years, things are different. We are only allowed to interfere in specific situations. This time even I must wait until after it is over to find out what happened."

"Can't we do something?"

He had already flown on, and she had to follow. She had never seen him this sad before.

$$\cdot \qquad \cdot \qquad \cdot \qquad \cdot \qquad \cdot$$

"We need to show these on the evening news!" Anders said as the group looked at photos and the video from the wedding.

"I agree, but right now, we need to get back to Lifta," said Magnus. "We've been here all day, and it will be dark in a few hours. They're probably wondering what's happened to us. However, I don't trust Messai, either, so the longer we stay, the greater the danger. Besides, we can't hack into the networks from out here."

"We may not have to," Blake said. "No network will turn these down when they see them. Think about it: The Smyrnians posting a video and photos, daring Messai to come after us? That's a juicy story! I can send these from my phone directly to the networks."

"You're right, Blake!" Ollie said. "If we get these to the major networks, they will air everywhere! But we need to send them to every station in Israel, too."

"I'm telling you, Messai's power comes from the dragon, and I'm not comfortable standing out here smack in the middle of *his* domain."

"Look around you, Magnus. This is not his domain today. It is Jesus' domain, and we're standing smack in the middle of *his* protection! It won't take long to send these, then we'll head back."

He and Ollie shared the duties, using their secure phones and miraculous ability to connect to the internet. The video took more time to send, but in thirty minutes all were gone and in the hands of news networks and stations worldwide. Oh, to be flies on the wall when Messai watched them.

The man arrived home to find the chef had filled his dinner plate and set it out for him. He carried it into the den and turned on the television to watch the news while he ate. Hopefully, they gave accurate reports from the day's meetings, *and got my good side*, he reasoned, chuckling. The 5:00 crew was wrapping up before turning things over to the 6:00 group.

"At the top of the hour, we will show you *must see* videos and photos we just received."

That must mean they will show at least one execution, he said to himself as he took a bite of food. *I wonder how the world will accept the Pope and his hierarchy joining us?*

"Good evening, ladies and gentlemen, and welcome to your news at 6:00. As promised, we have photos and a video to show you that are sure to shock the world."

Messai sat up and turned his attention to the screen. It did not sound like they were talking about *his* meetings. *Of course, the Pope*, he thought and smiled. *That will indeed shock the world!*

"It appears the Smyrnians are calling out Aissa Messai."

He jumped up, and his plate hit the floor with a clang.

"Are you okay, Mr. Messai? I heard a noise, and..."

"Get out!" he yelled, and his chef turned and hurried from the room.

"The rebels celebrated a wedding in Banias, the deserted location at Mount Hermon. The date on the video confirms the wedding took place today. We received the email thirty minutes ago. It came from a fictitious account, but listed the names of Blake Thompson and the other Smyrnians present. Those include Beth Jennings Thompson, Anders and Ally Norstrom, (the bride and groom), Trey Butler, Rickie Cruz, Bruno Fromm, Magnus Larsen, and Oliver and Amelia Barton."

Hearing the names read, then seeing them, sent Messai into a rage. His servants had learned to leave him alone when that happened. Fire darted around the room, lightning flew from his fingertips, and the room trembled, causing his attendants to flee the house for the back yard.

"We will show you the photos first. This reporter has traveled to Banias and found it nothing like what these pictures show. We encountered a dark, dreary, overgrown wasteland that seemed, for lack of a better word, *haunted*. It was like nothing I have ever experienced before. I'm not ashamed to tell you our crew got out of there fast. I once watched a documentary by the renowned British journalist, Oliver Barton, one of the people in the photographs, who witnessed the same things we did. So, I must tell you, what I saw today astounds me."

The pictures popped up. Messai stared at the sunshine, flowers, clear water, and happy faces. He recognized them all, except Rickie. The mere sight of them, especially Blake and Beth, Ally, and Magnus, his former captain, made his blood boil. He would not let them get away with this.

"The pictures tell a beautiful story, but you will enjoy watching the video of two young people in love uniting in marriage. However, remember these are all Smyrnians, the most sought after revolutionists on the planet. Their whereabouts are unknown, yet we see them in broad daylight performing a wedding. Are they living in Banias? I cannot imagine that being true. Do not go away. When the video ends, I will read the email, which is addressed to *every person in the world*."

When the video began, Messai sensed someone in the room with him. The burning heat, sickening breath, and putrid stench no longer bothered him. Instead, he welcomed his master's presence.

"Aissa, they invaded our location and trespassed where they do not belong, then left to return to their hiding place. They must pay."

"They *will* pay, when I find them, Master. Tell me where they are hiding and allow me to see it."

"I will do as you wish, Aissa. Make... them... pay..."

He was alone again as the video ended and the man read the email.

"Aissa Messai is the Antichrist, the evil leader of the *reign of terror*. Do not believe his lies or take his mark; and please, do not worship him. Jesus is the true Messiah..."

A half-empty glass flew across the room, spraying liquid and shattering the screen. It was too late to stop the world from watching, but he did not have to listen to their lies. A whisper came.

Lifta...

"What?"

Lifta... the word came again. He heard it clearly this time and reached for his phone.

•   •   •   •   •

The team left Banias at 6:00, later than planned, but allowing them more cover by driving the last miles after dark. Looking back, they watched the brightness fade and the gloom return. They had witnessed Jesus turning darkness to light. And why not? In the Gospel of John, he called himself the light of the world. Their experience confirmed that! But each also knew Jesus brought light into their darkness, too. They planned to praise him during the next three years, then worship him forever after that! This day gave them a glimpse into what that would be like.

Omar insisted they take the longer route back, traveling Highway 65 and 90 to avoid the larger cities. Not taking the mark prevented them from purchasing fuel, so they depended on tanks they stored in the back of one truck. That meant conserving fuel and limiting travel as much as possible. But for this trip, they agreed on safety first, even if it meant using more fuel and taking extra time.

Omar could have made the trip in two-and-a-half hours if he took the shorter route through Haifa and down the coast, going around Jerusalem to their destination south of the city. But he was much more comfortable with this three-hour drive. If the trip went well, they should be in Lifta by 9:00. They would breathe a lot easier when they arrived. The drive was tense, but going smoothly so far.

Michael and Hadassah arrived in Petra later than expected. They had been gone all day and were sure the others had noticed. Instead of coming down the mountain, they opted to walk through the Siq. When they stepped into the city, Ben and Mordecai stood there to greet them.

"Just where have you two been?" Mordecai asked. "It is almost dark out there, and you have been gone all day." He folded his arms and stared at them.

"Uncle! You should not use such a harsh tone or treat me like a little child. I am a grown woman."

"You are still my niece, and I worry about you wandering outside our safe place. I understand we are safe only in here. Isn't that what you said, Ben?"

"That is my understanding. Now, you need to tell us where you have been."

"We went on an adventure," Michael said. "Neither of us intended to get back this late, but we had a good day. Don't you agree, Hadassah?" He tried, but his words sounded hollow.

"Yes, adventure is the right word! It's hard for me to grasp what happened. Michael was amazing, and I was pretty good too!" Michael nodded in agreement, but he couldn't hide his concern.

"Is something going on between the two of you? Michael, you must ask before you date my niece."

"Uncle!" she said again. "I can't believe you said that. Michael and I are good friends and like to hang out together. That's what friends do, you know."

"It just looks suspicious when you leave all day, then come back this late. You should..."

Ben cut him off, seeing Michael standing by himself, not engaging the conversation.

"Michael, are you okay? You don't seem like your normal cheerful self. What's wrong?"

"I'm not sure, Ben, but thanks for noticing," he said, frowning at Mordecai. "I have this feeling that something bad is going to happen tonight, and I can't shake it. Have you talked to Blake today? No, you don't call him till tomorrow, do you? I wish these thoughts would go away, but they won't, no matter how hard I try. Something's coming, and we can't do anything about it."

"Maybe you're just tired from *walking all day*." Mordecai's tone showed he still didn't buy their adventure story.

"I haven't sensed anything either," said Hadassah, "but it hit Michael hard. I've never seen him so down. We can't check on them, but we can pray. If Michael's intuition is correct, they need that."

"I agree," said Ben. "We need to take this seriously if Michael feels so strongly about it."

Michael suddenly dropped to his knees, as if someone punched him. His face turned white and tears started falling from his eyes. Then his angst seized the other three, and they collapsed beside him, tears streaming. They knew he was right. Something horrible was coming, and it involved their fellow believers. Their hearts broke as they started crying out to Jesus. Petra was supposed to be a place of joy for the 144,000 Jews, but right now they only felt sadness.

Messai wasted no time making the call. "General Chen, are your crew and bombers still in Israel?"

"Yes, sir, Mr. Messai, and they remain at your disposal. Whatever you need, say the word. I will contact them right away, and they will do it."

"I just received word the Smyrnians are holed up in Lifta. They fled the Golan and now think they can make us look foolish by hiding right under our noses. I assume you saw the news?"

"Yes, sir. The rebels took things a step too far this time. But they also played right into our hands by showing themselves."

"The important thing is, we now know where they are. I want you to send two bombers to strike Lifta an hour after dark. The reporter said they received the pictures and video at 5:30, so I assume the group left right after sending them. They will travel back down the coast for the fastest route, which should take about two-and-a-half hours, meaning they will arrive around 8:00, right at dark. So, a 9:00 strike should catch them by complete surprise. Can your men handle that?"

"With no problem, sir. I will arrange that and make sure the strike happens right on time."

"Thank you, General. I knew I could count on you. Let me know when the mission is completed."

"I will do that. It will make me happy to destroy your primary target with one blow."

"*Our* primary target, General. The Smyrnians stand in the way of what we all seek to accomplish. I would prefer they face the capital punishment device, but the opportunity to remove all of them at once is too tempting to pass up. If you pull this off, I will reward you greatly. Your family will not wait for their prosperity to come. One million dollars per person killed tonight, General. I assume you are smart enough to grasp the magnitude of that sum for your family's future."

"I am indeed, Mr. Messai, and I am humbled that you would do such a thing for us. My men will carry out the mission with precision accuracy and timing. Consider it done."

After ending the call, the beast of the Tribulation let out a victory cry that shook the room more violently than his earlier scream of rage. If the Chinese annihilated the Smyrnians tonight, victory was almost certainly ensured. Nothing else mattered. He would await a call from General Chen.

Omar drove the speed limit to keep from attracting attention from police officers or AMPP. But something made him anxious tonight. Maybe it was nothing more than the desire to reach Lifta, but it felt like more. He talked non-stop to Ahmad and Hala as they rode, all three dressed in IDF military gear. They would pass through one checkpoint and need to remain calm when Israeli soldiers came to the window. He hoped their comrades behind them could stay quiet, too.

In the back, the Smyrnians lay under piles of blankets and clothes, and the American soldiers sat between them and the exit. Each carried an M27 IAR with enough ammunition for an extended firefight. They hoped nothing would happen that made using them necessary. It had now been nearly two-and-a-half hours since they left Banias, so they must be nearing their destination.

The truck slowed, then stopped. They had reached the checkpoint. Excited voices speaking in Hebrew increased in volume and intensity. The soldiers questioned the three sitting up front about their citizenship and their service in the IDF. They clearly did not believe their stories.

Lying under the clothing and blankets, Blake could tell the guards included a combination of military and AMPP personnel. The conversation was becoming increasingly confrontational. He knew they would search the back of the truck any moment. That realization became reality when he heard the men walking their way, while Omar, Ahmad, and Hala argued vehemently with them.

One of the Americans peered out the truck's rear covering just as an Israeli soldier pulled it open and spotted them. He raised his weapon and yelled to the others. When the American raised his gun, the Israeli fired. Ahmad yelled and dove toward the man, pushing the weapon upward just as the shot rang out, then crashed to the ground with blood soaking through his shirt.

"Ahmad!"

Omar and Hala slid beside their friend and dragged his body underneath the truck. The other IDF troops rushed around the truck just in time to see their comrade succumb to a bullet from an American rifle. They sprinted behind vehicles, and anything else they could find, determined to take down whoever rode in this truck and tried to infiltrate the area tonight.

The AMPP men opened fire as they ran to join them, striking two Americans. Their fellow troops ripped holes in the canvas covering and returned fire, killing every one of Messai's men before they reached shelter. Two Americans were down now, and two moved to help them. The other eight lay on their stomachs behind the metal tailgate that barely shielded them at only two feet tall.

"Stay down!" a soldier yelled to the Smyrnians.

Bullets riddled the tailgate from the Israeli guns. The Americans rose above it and fired back, knowing the group may call for backup any minute. Those who lay on the floor covered with blankets and clothes could only pray for protection as the firefight raged around them. An American soldier grabbed something from his belt and yelled.

"Frag out!"

He hurled the grenade toward the row of vehicles, which protected the IDF crew. Under the truck, Omar and Hala inched their way toward the front, slowly dragging their fallen brother in arms. They crawled out from under the front bumper and stood, holding Ahmad in their arms just as the grenade detonated.

The gas tank on one vehicle ignited and blew up, followed by each of the others in succession. The Israelis, kneeling behind them, died instantly. Shrapnel from the blast tore through the truck, shredding the canvas and shattering windows. The Americans fell flat and shielded their bodies any way they could.

Omar and Hala pulled Ahmad through the opening created by a missing door. He took the wheel, and she held their friend's head in her lap.

"Hold on, Ahmad. We'll get help, but you have to hang in there." Tears rolled down her cheeks.

"Go!" another soldier yelled at Omar.

He took off, soon reaching the truck's 55 miles per hour limit. They needed to go faster, but that was all the big truck would do. It was now three-and-a-half hours since they left Banias. The entire back of the truck was uncovered, leaving its riders exposed. When they got closer, a yellow glow appeared up ahead. Omar pulled onto a side road, stopped, and yelled to those behind him.

"It looks like fire in Jerusalem!" Short of breath from the excitement, he could barely get the words out. "The city is under attack! What should we do?"

"No, it looks like it's coming from Lifta!" yelled Ollie. "Drive, Omar! We have to get there!"

When they got near enough to see, no doubt remained. Omar drove as close as possible and stopped again. They moved quickly to get everyone out of the truck. Omar carried Ahmad, and the soldiers carried their wounded. Fiery skies illuminated a devastating scene, which offered little hope of survivors. They gazed at what was once Lifta, now a scattered pile of rubble.

Bruno screamed, "Let's go!" They ran as fast as they could, not knowing what would greet their sight when they arrived, or whether they would find anyone alive. The latter seemed impossible. They abandoned caution and sprinted ahead. How could this have happened? Yet it did.

CONCLUSION

The group reached the perimeter of the city. The flashlights on their phones provided little visibility as they dashed forward, arms swinging. Bruno screamed for Mila and the boys, Ally close behind him. Blake yelled for John and Kathie, his voice piercing the night, but no answers came.

Magnus ran ahead but soon tripped over large chunks of stone and fell headlong, his head smashing into a pile of rubble. Bruno reached him and knelt beside him. Pockets of flames now gave more clarity to the damage surrounding them. Blood poured from a deep gash on Magnus' brow. Bruno grabbed his comrade's hand and attempted to lift him to his feet.

"No! Go find your family. I will be okay."

He obeyed, running again, calling his family's names with no response, as fear gripped his mind. He should have insisted they go with him for Ally's wedding. Instead, he demanded they stay behind for their protection. Now this happened. How could he live with himself if they lost their lives here? His desperation pushed him, his heart pounding harder with each step.

Trey stumbled too and fell on something soft. He rolled over and looked into the face of his friend, Robert Clark. The Sergeant Major was dead. Rickie came up behind him and saw their fellow military man. Lying nearby, others came into view. These brave soldiers fought for their country and emerged unscathed; now they had given everything for the cause of Christ.

"Over here!" Trey yelled. When they witnessed the scene, it only increased their fear of what they would find when they moved further. Their frantic search continued.

An enormous explosion rocked the ground, hurling them all backwards and showering them with dirt and debris. The flames had reached the truck containing tanks of fuel. Cut, battered, and bleeding, they moved on. There was no time to think about the loss of their ability to travel without fuel and no way to buy it. They only thought about their friends and families.

"Trey!" Ollie screamed, pointing to a large chunk of stone, from which only a face stuck out. The man's body lay trapped underneath: Bradley Rodgers. They could barely hear each other as the fire raged around them, but they kept digging through rubble, trying to find survivors.

The search went on for an hour, uncovering more bodies, many still missing. They expected emergency personnel or AMPP men to rush in any minute, but to their surprise, none came. They were left to search alone, but refused to give up. Phones lost power and fires died down, making the search nearly impossible, as silence gradually permeated the dark night.

They gathered in a circle of grief, holding each other, Bruno and Ally sobbing uncontrollably. Magnus, still bleeding, comforted his partner, while Anders held Ally close and mourned with her. The depth of their anguish was incomprehensible. How could they continue for three more years until Jesus returned? All twenty-five of them sat among the ruins, devastated by the death and destruction around them. That those who died now lived with Jesus provided little consolation. Maybe it would tomorrow, but not now.

Aissa Messai's call came, and the news from General Chen overwhelmed him with evil joy.

"Mission accomplished, sir. I will send a video of the strikes from the jets. Both Lifta and the targets have been eliminated."

"Well done, general. I cannot wait to shake your hand and reward you myself."

Celebration ensued that called forth the demons of hell. The *reign of terror* had intensified in one night. But what was coming next would crush the inhabitants of the world and answer two fearsome questions: *"Who is like the beast? Who can wage war against it?"*

COMING NEXT
EPISODE 5

DAWN OF DELIVERANCE

In this epic conclusion of *The Apocalypse* series, the second half of the Tribulation brings unparalleled devastation and destruction as the world spirals toward its end. The battle between good and evil climaxes as the world's armies join the Antichrist to form an invincible fighting force. His One World Government and One World Religion command the entire earth, and he destroys everyone who stands in their way. That includes his most recent convert in a vicious attack that shocks the world. When the armies march on Jerusalem and stand on the verge of victory, the King rides from heaven and annihilates them. Judgment follows for all who have rejected him and followed Messai. Descriptions of earth during the Millennium and the new earth in eternity will amaze you. Believers in Jesus will get a foretaste of glory as they finish the story!

OTHER BOOKS
BY DAVID O. BULLOCK

When a supposed alien invasion suddenly takes billions of people from the earth, a band of warriors rises up to battle an insurmountable foe in Episode One of *The Apocalypse* series. Join them as they face the fight of their lives that becomes a fight *for* their lives. As you enter the battle with them, your own faith will be challenged and your life changed. Up and coming author David O. Bullock dares you to take the heart-pounding journey with him as he brings The Revelation to life in this 5-novel series.

Episode Two in *The Apocalypse* series brings another major worldwide disaster. An eerie lunar eclipse opens the door to the pit of hell and engulfs the planet in evil darkness for a world-altering 26 minutes and 51 seconds. Aissa Messai's popularity grows as he seeks to bring peace in the Middle East. As the Smyrnians work to combat his corrupt intentions, they become enemies of the state. Death and destruction rule the first half of the Tribulation, and the earth is shaken like it has never been shaken before.

In Episode Three of *The Apocalypse* series, as the Tribulation enters its second year, the lethal epidemic extends its reach and claims a massive number of victims. Then as if the earth has not reached the limit of what it can endure, a natural disaster strikes, killing millions more. Aissa Messai's power increases as he solidifies his grip on the world, while the Smyrnians fight for truth and justice. Still another another long-feared global crisis looms on the horizon, and the question becomes can *anyone* survive?

Don't live the chicken pen existence, picking corn off the ground with all the other chickens. Rise up and soar like an eagle! In this motivational novel, you will find inspiration to get from where life has taken you to where you want to be.

When things look hopeless, there is always hope on the horizon. Discover the connection and watch as your despair and discouragement give way to hope and excitement for your future!

ABOUT THE AUTHOR

David O. Bullock was raised on a farm, but never liked farming. From an early age, his passion was reading and writing. His parents taught him to love Jesus and God's Word. A pastor since age 20, David has long been a student of scripture. However, he had little interest in prophecy until a 2013 year-long search for truth in The Revelation led him to some shocking discoveries. *The Apocalypse* series came about as a result of that intense time of study. His hope is that these five books will help you discover those same truths for yourself.

Email: davidobullockwriting@gmail.com
Facebook: facebook.com/david.bullock.376
Twitter: twitter.com/bullockwriting
LinkedIn: linkedin.com/in/david-o-bullock

NOTE FROM THE AUTHOR

Word-of-mouth is crucial for any author to succeed. If you enjoyed *Reign of Terror*, please leave a review online—anywhere you are able. Even if it's just a sentence or two. It would make all the difference and would be very much appreciated.

Thanks!
David O. Bullock

We hope you enjoyed reading this title from:

www.blackrosewriting.com

Subscribe to our mailing list – *The Rosevine* – and receive **FREE** books, daily deals, and stay current with news about upcoming releases and our hottest authors.
Scan the QR code below to sign up.

Already a subscriber? Please accept a sincere thank you for being a fan of Black Rose Writing authors.

View other Black Rose Writing titles at www.blackrosewriting.com/books and use promo code **PRINT** to receive a **20% discount** when purchasing.